FATELESS

Julie Kagawa is the *New York Times, USA TODAY* and internationally bestselling author of The Iron Fey, Blood of Eden, and Shadow of the Fox series as well as The Talon Saga. Born in Sacramento, she has been a bookseller and an animal trainer and enjoys reading, painting, playing in her garden, and training in martial arts. She lives in North Carolina with her husband and a plethora of pets.

Visit her at www.juliekagawa.com

Also by Julie Kagawa:

The Iron Fey series
The Iron King
The Iron Daughter
The Iron Queen
The Iron Knight
The Iron Prince*
The Iron Traitor
The Iron Warrior

The Iron Fey: Evenfall series
The Iron Raven
The Iron Sword
The Iron Vow

Shadow of the Fox series
Shadow of the Fox
Soul of the Sword
Night of the Dragon

The Talon Saga
Talon
Rogue
Soldier
Legion
Inferno

Blood of Eden series
The Immortal Rules
The Eternity Cure
The Forever Song

*Also published as *The Lost Prince*

FATELESS

JULIE KAGAWA

HQ

ONE PLACE. MANY STORIES

HQ
An imprint of HarperCollins*Publishers* Ltd
1 London Bridge Street
London SE1 9GF

www.harpercollins.co.uk

HarperCollins*Publishers*
Macken House, 39/40 Mayor Street Upper,
Dublin 1, D01 C9W8, Ireland

This edition 2025

1
First published in Great Britain by HQ,
an imprint of HarperCollins*Publishers* Ltd 2025

Copyright © Julie Kagawa 2025

Julie Kagawa asserts the moral right to be identified as the author of this work.
A catalogue record for this book is available from the British Library.

HB ISBN: 9780008737375
TPB ISBN: 9780008737467

This novel is entirely a work of fiction. The names, characters and incidents portrayed in it are the work of the author's imagination. Any resemblance to actual persons, living or dead, events or localities is entirely coincidental.

All rights reserved. No part of this publication may be reproduced, stored in a retrieval system, or transmitted, in any form or by any means, electronic, mechanical, photocopying, recording or otherwise, without the prior permission of the publishers.

Without limiting the author's and publisher's exclusive rights, any unauthorised use of this publication to train generative artificial intelligence (AI) technologies is expressly prohibited. HarperCollins also exercise their rights under Article 4(3) of the Digital Single Market Directive 2019/790 and expressly reserve this publication from the text and data mining exception.

Printed and bound in the UK using 100% Renewable
Electricity by CPI Group (UK) Ltd

FSC
www.fsc.org
MIX
Paper
FSC™ C007454

For more information visit: www.harpercollins.co.uk/green

To Ezio and Altair, who inspired this world. And to Tashya, who made it come alive.

The Hourglass of Time waits for no one. Seasons pass, the suns rise and set, and no one, not even the Deathless Kings, can turn back the sands once they have fallen.

—FIRST KINGDOM PROVERB

PART ONE

ONE

Demon Hour was approaching.

I stood in the shade beneath a rooftop balcony, watching the citizens of Kovass scurry through the streets like ants whose nest had been poked with a stick. High overhead, Solasti, the first of the twin suns, blazed white against the cloudless blue sky. Her identical sister, Namaia, had climbed over the horizon and was closing fast. Demon Hour, when both suns stood directly overhead, twin gazes burning down like the glare of an angry goddess, happened every day. For one hour, every single afternoon in the land of Arkyennah, the air singed throats when breathed in, the sands became molten, and every hard surface was turned into a stovetop under the relentless glare of the suns. Animals fled to find shade or huddled beneath crude shelters. Merchants closed their doors and covered their stalls. Commoners went inside to nap while the wealthiest nobles lounged in private pools as servants fanned them with palm leaves. For one hour, Kovass turned into a dead city as every living creature, big and small, young and old, poor and rich, found whatever shelter or shade or dark crack they could to wait out the hellish heat of the twins.

Stepping back from the balcony, I took a deep breath, feeling the hot air fill my lungs, then let it out slowly. Across the maze of flat white stone and gray tile rooftops, Namaia crept ever higher into the sky. True Demon Hour wasn't quite here, but the half hour that led up to it, with temperatures rising alongside panic and tension as everyone scurried to get things done, was probably the most hectic and chaotic time in Kovass.

It was also the perfect—and most awful—time to do anything you didn't want people to see, which was why I was here, on this balcony, instead of back home in familiar territory. This safehouse was closer to my destination, and the less time I spent beneath the suns, the better.

"Is it time?"

I turned as a soft, raspy voice drifted into the room attached to the balcony. A hunched, robed figure shuffled up the stairs, leaning heavily on a cane. Shadyr raised her cowled head, and her milky, nearly pure white eyes stared right through me.

"Not yet," I said, equally softly. "Soon, though."

"Hmm." She walked across the room and paused just shy of where the rays of the sun drew a line across the balcony opening. One withered hand reached out until the fingertips hit the edge of the sunlight. "Very soon, if you want to reach the Garden District just before peak Demon Hour. I hope you are dressed appropriately."

I glanced past her head to the wall, where a cracked mirror hung above a dresser by the bed. The girl staring back at me was thin and unremarkable. Brown hair, brown eyes, and a face that was completely forgettable. Not that anyone ever saw it. My hood always stayed up, and my clothes were in light, neutral tones that the eye could easily pass over. In a city of limestone walls, bleached rooftops, and dusty, sun-scoured roads, dark clothes would be miserable and bright colors would stand out. Which, in my line of work, was the opposite of what you wanted. I was good at what I did because I blended in and became invisible.

"Of course, Shadyr," I told her. "When am I not prepared?"

She withdrew her arm, the hand vanishing into her robes again. "Odd that you're working alone," she mused. "Where is Jeran? I thought the two of you were inseparable when it came to jobs."

"Not today." I shrugged, though she couldn't see the motion. "Vahn was insistent that I do this one alone. It's fine, though." I gazed across the rooftops again, squinting in the gleaming brightness. "I don't need Jeran. I work better solo, anyway."

Though *he* wouldn't be pleased to hear me say that. Jeran was a year older than me; tall, lanky, with dark hair and a halfway charming smile. He was good at what he did, just not as good as me, and we both knew it.

"Well, don't get too cocky." Shadyr patted my arm. "I remember my days with the guild, before my eyes started failing me. It was always better to have someone guarding your back to keep a watch for the patrols. Especially in the Garden District. Twice as many guards there as here."

I snorted. "Yes, and they'll all be under their little guard cupolas throwing dice," I said. "Even if they do see something, I doubt they'll go rushing out in the middle of Demon Hour to chase it down. But don't worry." I smiled at the old woman, knowing she would hear it in my voice. "They won't see me. They never do."

"You tempt Fate, little Sparrow," Shadyr warned. "You think you can do everything alone, but that is not the way of things. I know." She patted my arm again. "I know what the guild wants you to believe. But sometimes, you have to put your trust in something other than yourself. What do the teachings say? Our threads are all woven in the Tapestry of the World. Together, nothing can break them, but a single strand is weak and easily severed."

I felt a chill in the small, warm room. Shadyr couldn't know what I was doing, could she? No, of course not. I hadn't told anyone about this job. It was just a coincidence that she had brought up the Tapestry of the World.

I stepped back and grinned. "Well, a single strand may be weak," I said, "but it's a lot more flexible with no other threads tangling it up and holding it back."

She huffed at me, as if I had missed the point, and shook her head. "Namaia continues to rise," she went on. "Are you ready?"

Quickly, I ran through a mental checklist, making sure I had everything I needed. Supple but tough leather boots for running over rooftops. Leather gloves for grasping superheated stones and metal railings. The tools of my trade, tucked safely away in hidden pockets. A pair of daggers on my hips and a concealed knife in my boot. And a waterskin to combat the fiery glare of the twins. I hadn't forgotten anything. It was time to get on with it and see what Fate had in store for me this day.

I pulled up my white hood, hiding my features from view, then turned to Shadyr. "I'm ready."

She nodded once. "Will you be returning here when the job is done?"

I shook my head. "No, I'll go straight back to the guild. Vahn is expecting me."

"Very well. Tell the old desert weasel I said hello." Shadyr smiled and shuffled back a few steps, milky eyes gazing through me into the sky. "May Fate smile upon you, little Sparrow."

"And on you, Shadyr."

I stepped back onto the balcony and paused just beneath the overhang, gazing out at the city. My task was difficult, but if I timed this correctly, I would reach my destination just as peak Demon Hour was upon the world. If I got it wrong . . . well, it was going to be unpleasant either way.

The air above the rooftops was already shimmering. At the balcony's edge, I took a last breath of marginally cooler air, then hopped onto the railing and launched myself into open sky.

The heat of the twins, searing and relentless, hit me as I soared over the street, catching fleeting glimpses of the people below. No one looked up. Looking up invited the full glare of the twins upon your face. Gazes remained down, cowls, hoods, and shawls pulled low as the citizens of Kovass scurried to hide from the suns. No one saw a figure in white soar above the narrow space between the rooftops and land on the other side.

As soon as my boots hit the stones, I started to sprint. The "thieves highway" spread out before me, an endless collection of flat stone walls, tile rooftops, domed ceilings, and the occasional temple spire jutting upward toward the suns.

I paused beneath the shade of a small, covered rooftop garden to catch my breath. It was now so close to Demon Hour that the heat radiating from the stones and rooftops was almost as bad as the rays of the suns. In my tunic, I found the waterskin tucked close to my body and pulled it out. It was small, holding just a few swallows, but that would be enough to keep me going. I could probably make it to my destination and back without drinking, but in Demon Hour, I wasn't taking chances. As Vahn always said, *Almost everything can be challenged, almost every rule has a way around it. Except the twins. Do not fight them—they will win every time.*

The water was lukewarm, but it still cooled my throat and moistened my lips, which had gone dry from breathing the scalding desert air. Leaning against a wooden post, I contemplated the journey still to come. The rooftop garden, with its latticed roof and sheer white curtains, provided just enough shelter for me to escape the pounding rays of the suns, but it was still unbearably hot. Sweat ran down my neck and trickled into my eyes, the burn of salt making me blink and rub a sleeve across my face.

And then, across the shimmering rooftops, I saw a figure. Dressed in light colors and a hood like me, they crouched atop a distant tower, watching the crowds below. They were so still that aside from the clothes and familiar hood, they might've been a statue. One of the protector beasts that adorned the walls and roofs of the temples. I stared in shock, wondering who *else* would be crazy enough to be out in Demon Hour. No one from the guild would risk it; I knew that for a fact. So who was this?

Another bead of sweat ran into my eye, making me squint and swipe at my face again. When I looked up, the figure was gone.

Okay. Maybe I'm seeing things. Crazy heat mirages. I guess I am the only one foolish enough to be outside right now.

Regardless, I had work to do. Peak Demon Hour was just a few minutes away, and I still had to get to my target. Tucking my waterskin beneath my clothes, I set my jaw and then slipped into the sunlight once more.

After jogging across several more rooftops, leaping the gaps between buildings, and vaulting over a few walls, I finally reached the edge of the Garden District, one of the wealthiest areas in Kovass, second only to the Palace District. It was easy to tell when you entered the neighborhood of the merchant princes. For one, the dusty, uniform colors of the streets gave way to brilliant splashes of greenery, as bushes, vines, and even flowering plants grew from carefully cultivated plots and gardens. Many of these plants were in the shade or beneath some kind of shelter that protected them from direct sunlight, but it was a staggering amount of wealth on display. The growing and caretaking of plants simply for aesthetic purposes was seen as a frivolous waste by most, but the heads of the merchant guilds had more money than they knew what to do with and flaunted their wealth every chance they had. What better way to show up your neighbor than to plant exotic bushes alongside your house and pay a king's ransom in special soil, fertilizer, and gardeners to keep them alive? Not to mention all the water they wasted on beautiful but useless greenery.

Sometimes, the mindset of the very wealthy made no sense to me. But the suddenly lush landscape wasn't the only sign that I had entered the Garden District.

In the very center, the enormous Temple of Fate dominated the district in all its white-stone-and-marble glory, gold-tipped spires rising into the air and catching the light of the suns. Within, the priestesses and the Ahsani—the High Priestess of Fate—counseled all the souls bound in the Weave, helping them understand their destiny and their role in the story of the world. We all had one, and whether it was big or small, earth-shattering or insignificant, our destiny, our fate, was as inevitable as time itself. When you were born, Fate determined your place in the world. King or peasant, merchant or craftsman, noble or outcast, once Fate chose your place, the only release from it was death. What you did in between, how you lived your life, would define your fate when you were reborn into your next existence.

At least, according to the teachings.

Keeping my gaze on the huge temple, I continued across the rooftops. Fate wasn't something I gave a lot of thought to. I wasn't a scholar or especially book-learned, and though I knew the best escape routes in the city and could pick my way through nearly any lock, the teachings could twist my brain into a jumbled mess if I thought too hard about them. There was a saying among the lower classes: *If it is your fate to be a pig farmer, be the best pig farmer in the kingdom.* I knew what I was good at. And I was *very* good at what Fate had decided for me.

Dropping into a tiny private courtyard covered with a lattice, I took a few deep breaths of shaded air. My timing was pretty much perfect. Not a soul was in the streets. No animals roamed the alleyways, the merchant princes napped in beds of cotton and silk, and the guards huddled in their domed cupolas, waiting for Solasti to move on. For the next hour, the city was essentially dead.

Which made my job only slightly easier.

From the top of one of the tallest buildings, I surveyed my target with a growing sense of dread. Not a home, not the abode of a fat merchant prince, surrounded by luxury and wealth. My target loomed before me, glimmering spires nearly scraping the clouds, almost daring the foolish to attempt the unthinkable.

The Temple of Fate itself.

My heart beat faster, even as I tried not to think about what I was doing. No one could cheat Fate. Fate knew all. There was no sneaking up on it, no pulling the wool over its eyes. It knew you were coming, and what you were going to do, before you even considered it. I was good at what I did, probably the best in the guild, but even I had my limitations. This task bordered on blasphemous. I wouldn't even be here if not for Vahn and our strange conversation the night before.

"Hood down, Sparrow." Vahn gestured to my head as I stepped through the door of his office. The Guildmaster stood behind his desk, lamplight throwing shadows over his weathered face. He had thick dark hair and even darker eyes. He wasn't young, he wasn't old, handsome, ugly, or anything. He was just Vahn. His most distinguishing features were the tiny scar on his lip and the missing third finger of his left hand.

"You know the rules," Vahn continued. "Hoods down in my office. I want to see your eyes when I'm talking to you. Take it off."

"Yes, sir," I muttered, pushing my hood back. Instantly, I felt exposed, as if every eye in the room was turned on me, though it was just me and Vahn. I didn't like taking it off, because then everyone could see me—the real me. I couldn't hide anything. I expected that was the very reason for Vahn's "no hood" rule when he was talking to any of us.

"Good." The Guildmaster nodded, and a rare, faint smile quirked his scarred lip. "It's nice to glimpse your face every once in a while. Every time I see it, it's like you've gotten older."

I grinned. "Is that why you called me in here?" I asked. "To make sure there's not a withered old crone beneath my hood? I bet you don't even know how old I am now."

"Seventeen years, four months, thirteen days," Vahn said automatically, as I'd known he would. "Not counting the weeks you weren't with the guild, of course." Vahn had found me as an infant in a gutted, abandoned house, with the shriveled corpse of a woman, presumably my mother, lying motionless nearby. He had taken me into the guild and trained me himself, and the guild members had adopted me as their own. From before I could remember, I had been raised among thieves, learning their ways and their secrets, until I joined the ranks as one of their best.

"I have a job for you," Vahn continued. "A solo mission, this time. No teams—you'll be working by yourself. I trust you're up to the task."

"Of course." I perked up. In the guild, what you did—or stole—on your own time was your business. As long as you paid your dues and didn't draw attention to yourself or the guild, you could pretty much do what you wanted. Actual jobs from the Guildmaster were a different story, and solo missions were uncommon. Depending on the size and complexity of the job, guild members normally worked in teams of two to five. Which was why I was often sent on assignments with Jeran, who had also grown up in the guild. His father had been a guild member but was caught while on a job and dragged away to prison. Jeran hadn't seen him in years. We worked well together, though lately our missions had turned into friendly competitions to see who was better at whatever we were attempting. There had been a couple of close calls, which had resulted in a warning from Vahn to start taking our jobs seriously. I wondered if that was why I would be going solo this time.

My stomach felt sour. Vahn had never shown me any direct favoritism within the guild, treating me as a highly competent thief and never making excuses for my mistakes, but I had always been more than a simple soldier or a guild asset. I remembered his smiles, his patience when explaining how to pick a lock or move without making any noise, the nods of approval when I completed a challenging task. He had never been overly affectionate, but I knew I made him proud. Especially when I started to complete jobs even the most experienced guild members balked at.

In the past couple of years, though, he had become colder. Distant. To the point where he barely said a word to me that wasn't mission-oriented. I didn't understand it. Was I not performing well enough? Was he disappointed in me? Maybe I had to step up my game. I'd tried. Over the past several months, my ventures had gotten more risky, my targets more and more dangerous, as I'd attempted to show Vahn I was the best. Several times, I should have been caught, and it was a miracle that I'd made it out unnoticed, but nothing seemed to impress him. Even the other guild members had begun to whisper. I was unnaturally lucky, they said; no one could tempt Fate that often and get away with it. But Vahn only drew further and further away.

This was the first time in months that he had called me into his office alone. Whatever this job entailed, I had to do it well.

"Sparrow." His voice sent a small shiver up my back. His eyes pierced a hole through me, as if peeling back invisible layers to find what lay beneath. "You've been with the guild a long time now," Vahn continued. "I've raised you, taught you our ways, and over the years, I've watched you and your talents grow. You've become quite the profitable asset, and the guild is pleased."

My heart pounded, warmth spreading through my stomach, but I couldn't reveal how much that meant to me. So, I fell back on what I was good at. "Thanks," I said dryly. "Being a profitable asset to the guild is all I live for."

His lips tightened. "The sarcasm could use some paring down," he said.

"I'll work on that."

He sighed. "In any case," he went on, "there has been a request to fully appraise your skills and see exactly what you can do. This job comes directly from the Circle. As such, I don't need to tell you how important it is."

I straightened. The Circle referred to the ring of powerful people who essentially owned and ran the Thieves Guild. The Guildmaster reported to them, but as far as I knew, no one knew their names or had ever seen their faces. They pulled strings and gave orders from the shadows, never appearing in the open or within the guild itself. But there was no doubt that they conducted their affairs with an iron fist, and those who crossed them either fell into great misfortune, or disappeared from the city entirely.

A request from the Circle meant they had taken notice of me, which was both a good thing and a bad thing. Good in that they considered me an asset; talent had value in the guild, and those who were skilled were not so easily discarded. Bad because if I screwed this up, who knew what the Circle would do to me?

But the fact that this had come from the Circle, from the leaders of the guild, meant Vahn would *have* to see me now. I couldn't fail this task. This was my chance to impress him once and for all, no matter how dangerous the request.

Meeting his gaze, I nodded with what I hoped was a confident grin. "Whatever the Circle needs me to do, I can do it."

Vahn regarded me a moment more, then reached down and picked up a roll of parchment from among the various papers and coins scattered over his desk. The parchment had been sealed with red wax, though I couldn't see the image branded into the wax from where I stood. For a few heartbeats, Vahn hesitated, staring down at the scroll, almost as if debating whether to give it to me. Finally, his jaw tightened, and he held out the parchment across the desk.

"Don't open it here," he said, pulling back slightly as I reached for it. "These orders are for your eyes alone. When you are finished with the letter, destroy it and speak of it to no one else. You are not to divulge or discuss its contents with anyone, not even me. Is that understood?"

I swallowed. "What are they going to ask me to do, steal the High Chancellor's ring? From his finger?"

Vahn's eyes narrowed and his lips thinned, causing his scar to go white. "Is that understood?" he repeated tightly.

"Yes," I replied, and reached for the parchment. "Understood."

"This is not a game, Sparrow," he said, still not relinquishing the scroll as my fingers closed on it. "Recognition from the Circle is an honor, but they do not tolerate failure. If you fail them, both our lives could be forfeit. Because I am the one who vouched for you in the first place." His gaze sharpened, his voice turning cold. "So be absolutely certain you understand what is at stake."

My stomach dropped. "I'm sorry," I said, as ice coiled around my insides. "You're right. I'll take this seriously."

He finally let me take the parchment, holding my gaze as I drew it back. Glancing at the scroll, I saw the wax seal had been stamped with the emblem of a skull wearing a crown. The image was not one I had ever seen before.

A chill slid up my back.

"Go on, then," Vahn said, jerking his chin at the door behind me. "I imagine you'll want to read that and get started right away. Remember, not a word of this to anyone, Sparrow. The Circle are not to be trifled with."

Clutching the scroll, I hesitated, wondering if I could still talk to him. There had been days that I had spent hours in his office, sitting on a chair while he worked, sometimes practicing my skills on different locks or containers, sometimes listening as he spoke to clients about jobs that only the guild could do. I had been immersed in guild politics and hijinks from the time I could walk, but lately, it seemed Vahn's door was always closed to me. I wished I knew how to open it again.

Vahn studied me in silence, obviously waiting for me to leave, his eyes stony and flat. Biting my lip, I nodded, then slipped into the dimly lit halls and narrow corridors of the guild.

In the privacy of my room, I broke the wax seal and unrolled the parchment. Holding the scroll in the flickering light of a candle, I started to read.

Guildmember Sparrow,

It has been brought to our attention that you are a person of considerable talents and skill. We of the Circle wish to acquire an item, and we wish for you to procure it for us.

I rolled my eyes. *Acquire. Procure.* Terms of the guild. It was amusing how much effort went into dancing around the actual word, as if we were fooling anyone. We were a guild of thieves. We stole things. Simple as that.

The note went on:

The item we wish you to obtain lies at the heart of the Garden District. Guildmember Sparrow, you are to acquire, by whatever means necessary, the Tapestry of the World from the Temple of Fate. You are to present it to Guildmaster Vahn by the end of the week. If you cannot achieve this, we will consider you to have failed.

You are to speak of this to no one. You are to take no one with you. Retrieve the tapestry from the Temple of Fate, or the Guildmaster will suffer the consequences of your failure. We hope you will not disappoint us.

You have three days.

I burned the letter in a daze, my mind reeling as I watched the parchment shrivel into ashes. Steal the Tapestry of the World from the Temple of Fate? Were the members of the Circle mad? *Don't tempt Fate* was a common saying throughout all the districts, from the lowest of thieves and beggars to the highest nobles. If I did this, I wasn't going to be merely tempting Fate—I'd be spitting in her face.

But . . . if I didn't, Vahn would be blamed for my failure. Which meant I *had* to succeed. I didn't *think* the Circle would outright kill him; Vahn was the leader of a very tightly run guild of thieves, the only one in Kovass. It would be bad business to remove the person holding it all together. But I'd heard the stories. I knew they had killed people for less. I could not fail, which meant I had to succeed.

Besides, I mused as the last of the parchment dissolved into specks of ash, the wax dripping onto the stones like blood, *this has to be some sort of test*. The Circle had chosen me to attempt a heist no sane person would even think about. They were either trying to get rid of me—which made little sense, since I was one of their "most profitable" assets—or they were gauging my skills because they truly believed I was the only thief who could pull this off.

Well, if that was true, I had better prove them right.

TWO

According to the teachings, every life—every soul—was a thread bound in the Tapestry of the World. You could not change your placement in the Weave; once your thread was set by Maederyss, the Weaver of Fate, you had to accept your place in the story. A pig farmer could never become a king, a merchant could never become a noble. If it was your destiny to be a beggar, the lowest of the low, that was your place in the story, and it was a blasphemy against Fate to wish for more. The only thing you could do was to strive to be the best at your given path, to accomplish as much as you could with what you had, and pray that in the next life, Maederyss would recognize your great deeds and give you a better place in the Tapestry.

It worked the opposite way as well. If you were particularly evil, corrupt, selfish, or cruel, you might find your next existence even worse than your present one. A greedy prince might find himself cursed to be a beggar in his next life, or a heartless noble might return as a butcher or gravedigger. Some scholars even argued that in the worst cases, you might not come back as a higher creature at all. You might find yourself crawling around piles of waste as a dung beetle or sand fly. But since no one remembered their previous lives, and since dung beetles never wrote down their memoirs, this aspect was hotly debated among the philosophers and scholars of Fate. For the rest of the people, commoners especially, the belief was that you must do the best you could, and your fate would work itself out in the end.

Of course, there were those among the rich and noble class who thought they could buy their way into a comfortable next life. Which was why, in the Garden District, the Temple of Fate rivaled the majesty and elegance of the king's palace on the hill. Standing beneath the overhang of some noble's balcony, I gazed at the imposing structure before me and briefly wondered why, of all the things they could ask me to "procure," the Circle wanted me to steal a tapestry and not, for instance, the ruby gemstone eyes from the carved statues on the rooftops. Or the solid gold candlesticks rumored to grace every corner within.

But I knew the answer. Even if it terrified me. Gold and gemstones were expensive, but physical expressions of wealth meant nothing to Maederyss. The Tapestry of the World, though it was only a weak mortal impression of the real Weave, was far more significant.

And I would be taking it. From the Temple of Fate itself. Literally from right under the goddess's nose.

I took a deep breath, calming my heart and my mind as I continued to survey the street around the temple. There were no crowds walking the sidewalks, no throngs of humanity to blend into and become invisible. The streets were dead, and the heat radiating from the stones was an almost physical thing, pressing down on me. Peak Demon Hour had arrived.

A block down, one of the guard cupolas stood on a corner, its blue-domed roof shimmering in the heat. I spotted movement through the tiny open windows and knew that most of the patrolling guards would be sheltering in those small havens, drinking or throwing dice while they waited for Demon Hour to end. This had been a large part of my plan; normally you couldn't walk ten paces in the Garden District without running into a guard or a patrol who did not look kindly on common street rats and would either run you out of the district or drag you off to jail on principle alone. But now the streets were vacant, and no guard I knew of would leave his shelter during Demon Hour to chase down anyone suspicious. As long as I wasn't directly spotted, no one would come after me.

Across the wide stone road, the doors of the Temple of Fate stood open, ostensibly inviting everyone in off the streets. But I knew better. To put it bluntly, poor people were not welcome in the Garden District, and while that was not an official decree, the merchant princes were ruthless when it came to protecting their wealth. If a guard beat a thief to death in an alley or dragged a beggar through the streets to throw him out of the district, everyone looked the other way.

A pair of guards stood at the front entrance to the temple, though they looked half asleep. Certainly, they weren't expecting anyone to come creeping across the rooftops and around the side of the temple, and then leap onto the sill of one of the open arched windows along the wall. I slithered through the window frame and dropped to the floor, darted behind a pillar, and took a deep breath. I was in, and I hadn't attracted the attention of the guards. Of course, the question of the goddess herself taking notice of me was one I could do nothing about. The only uncertainty there was, would *she* do something about it?

Stepping out from behind the pillar, I hesitated, involuntarily holding my breath. Waiting to see if I would be struck down by lightning, or if the ground would open up to swallow me whole. When nothing happened, I relaxed and began a careful but steady walk toward the far wall, my eyes wide as I gazed around the chamber. I had never been inside the main Temple of Fate. I'd heard stories of its grandeur, but nothing could have prepared me for the reality.

It was noticeably cooler inside, shaded from the relentless glare of the twins. The main chamber was cavernous, soaring to an impressive height, with gold-veined marble columns and a painted ceiling that showed off the ridiculous amount of wealth that had gone into building the temple. The tallest of the huge windows lining the walls were tinted with painted glass that displayed beautiful patterns and blocked the sunlight. The floor was polished white stone carved with narrow rivulets that allowed water to flow across the floor from a central fountain and empty into shallow pools on either side. Bushes, flowers, and exotic plants surrounded the pools, which were filled with actual live fish. My mouth dropped open in amazement. Fish, the most expensive meat you could buy in Kovass, was worth twice its weight in gold, and was considered a delicacy only the merchant princes and the king could afford. But here in the Temple of Fate, the fish were actually swimming around. They were tiny, colorful creatures, most barely larger than my thumb, but they represented a king's fortune darting around the bottoms of the pools.

For the briefest of moments, I was tempted to grab one. It would be easy enough to dart my hand into the pool and snatch a tiny, jewel-bright fish. But I didn't want to kill the poor creature, and besides, finding a buyer would be extremely problematic. Our fence, Nazzir, would probably have a heart attack if I plunked an exotic fish on his desk.

Swallowing my amazement, I forced my gaze away from the obscene display of wealth and continued across the chamber.

At the far wall, past several aisles of smooth stone pews lined with plush red cushions, the enormous statue of Maederyss the Weaver, Goddess of Fate, loomed over the chamber.

Some images pictured Maederyss as a giant spider, methodically weaving the tapestry with her long, jointed legs. That was why it was considered bad luck to kill a spider, and having one in your home was considered a blessing from the Weaver. Maederyss was also pictured as a beautiful woman hunched over a loom, eyes focused on her eternal task. Never sleeping, seeing all.

But some artists and sculptors took a bit of creative liberty with the goddess of Fate. This statue of Maederyss showed her kneeling behind the altar with her arms outstretched and palms up. An enormous length of cloth dangled from her fingers, gold threads glittering in the light.

The Tapestry of the World.

Or an interpretation of it. Obviously, no mortal could re-create the real Tapestry of the World. It was said this cloth had been woven by the most skilled rugmakers in Kovass, using the finest dyed silk from across the Dust Sea. Intricate patterns were designed through the weave, with gold, silver, and turquoise threads laced throughout the cloth. It was made to impress, and it did its job well, but I doubted it looked anything like the real Tapestry of the World.

Staring up at the huge statue, I felt my stomach tighten. The Circle said to steal the tapestry, but the actual weave was enormous. Two people would probably be needed to move it. There was no way I could fit the entire tapestry into my satchel.

But I couldn't fail this task, the Circle, or Vahn. The Circle had to know how big the target was, and they'd specifically asked me to get the tapestry. They wouldn't have sent me if they didn't think I could do it. I had to complete this task alone, but the cloth was far too big for one person to carry.

So . . . what if I took just a piece of it?

Horror filled my stomach. I ducked behind one of the gold-veined marble pillars in a dim corner to catch my breath. *It's not the real Tapestry of the World*, I told myself, leaning against the slightly cool rock. *You're not going to be cutting the threads of millions of lives. This is just silk and cotton and normal cloth.*

In the city's biggest Temple of Fate. With the stone eyes of the Weaver herself staring right at me.

My heart was racing, and I felt slightly sick. For a second, I considered offering a prayer of forgiveness to Maederyss, but I didn't want to draw attention to myself. Of course, if Fate already knew what I was attempting, nothing I was about to do would matter.

I shook all thoughts of Fate, destiny, and repercussions out of my head. I couldn't think like that. I was there, and I had a job to do. My life—and Vahn's—depended on it. Besides, what would

Vahn say when I came back with a piece of the Tapestry of the World? Surely this would show him, beyond all doubt, that I was the best.

I'm a thief, I told myself. *The teachings say to be the best at what Fate has chosen for you. Well, if Fate wanted me to be a thief, then I'll be the best thief anyone has seen and rob Maederyss herself.*

I peered from behind the pillar, gazing around the room. As expected during Demon Hour, the temple was empty. No worshippers were praying to Fate, asking for a better existence in their next life, no priestesses roamed the aisles in their white hoods and robes, offering comfort and guidance for those discontented with their place. The lack of people would make my job easier, if only a little bit.

The Tapestry of the World hung a good fifteen feet from the floor, the edges too high for me to reach from the ground. There was only one way to get to the cloth, and that was to climb atop the statue. Of Maederyss. The goddess of Fate.

I was committing blasphemy after blasphemy today. In my next life I would probably come back as a sand beetle.

Crouching behind another pillar, I observed the statue, searching for the best way to scale it. The stone robes had several folds and creases that would make for easy handholds, so it wouldn't be difficult. I had climbed walls that were smoother.

I took a final glance around the room, making sure I was still alone, then sprinted across the floor to the statue and leaped onto its robes. Without pausing, I scrambled up the carved stone hand over hand, deliberately not thinking about anything to do with Fate. I reached the goddess's knees, then carefully made my way over to the cloth draped over her fingers.

Up close, the weave was even more beautiful, the golden and silver threads glimmering as I reached for one of the edges. Because I wore gloves, I couldn't feel the texture of the weave, but the fabric was surprisingly light. Reaching into my belt, I pulled free one of my daggers and raised it toward the shimmering cloth.

My gut prickled. I froze, the tip of my blade hovering over the tapestry, as a shiver went through me and the hair on my arms stood up. It was the same feeling I got when I was on a job and I could sense a guard's footsteps approaching. I didn't know how I knew, but I never questioned the instinct. Something, or someone, was coming.

Reflexively, I ducked behind the only cover I could see—the dangling edge of the Tapestry of the World. Pressing myself into Maederyss's wrist, I peered through the folds of cloth and gazed across the chamber.

A hooded figure dressed in a loose white tunic and cowl appeared in the temple doorway and walked down the center aisle toward the statue. The guards paid them no mind; I wasn't even sure they'd seen the stranger come in. Their footfalls made no sound against the stones, and they moved with an easy, almost predatory grace. My heart pounded, and I went motionless against the statue, hoping to blend into the stone like a desert chameleon. If I had hesitated a moment longer beside the tapestry, I would've been seen.

Below me, I heard the squeak of a door opening, and then

light footfalls padded across the room toward the stranger. "Is that you, kahjai?" came the quiet voice of what had to be one of the priestesses.

Moving as slowly as a rock tortoise, I peered down and saw that the stranger had stopped in front of the statue. They were tall, though from this angle I couldn't see any of their features. A curved sword hung at their waist, its copper hilt glittering in the dim light.

"It is, High Priestess." The stranger's voice was low and deep. "Apologies for coming out during . . . Demon Hour is what your people call it, correct?"

"Yes, but do not apologize. It is an honor to have one of the kahjai visit us today."

I couldn't see the priestess, but her voice was stiff, as if she were reciting something she didn't really believe. Her footsteps stopped below the statue, but I couldn't see her over the stone edge of Maederyss's knee. The stranger took a step forward, facing the priestess in front of the statue, though their hood was still drawn up, their face hidden by the fabric.

"Are we alone here?" the stranger asked. "We are not in danger of being overheard?"

"The rest of the sisters are asleep or in meditation," the Ahsani, the high priestess of the temple, replied, and I imagined her waving a billowy sleeve toward the back of the chamber. "No one will venture out until after Demon Hour, so our privacy is ensured."

"As you say." The figure raised a hand and brushed back his hood, and I bit my lip to stifle a gasp of surprise.

I had never left Kovass. My entire life had been spent within its limestone walls, and for most people, the city was more than large enough that they never dreamed of seeing the world outside its borders. Especially since everyone *knew* what lay beyond. The wastelands, rocky, barren, and scorching, stretched away to the south until they hit the horizon. To the north was the great Dust Sea, the endless expanse of roiling, shifting sands that swallowed anything heavier than a scroll. Great sand ships or huge mechanical walkers known as striders were needed to cross Dust Sea, and they returned with exotic goods and wild tales of the lands beyond. Stories of people who traveled the desert on the backs of giant beetles, who used the monstrous insects like we used donkeys and oxen. Of clans whose warriors were half feline, with sharp claws and teeth and eyes that could see in the dark.

And then there were stories of the iylvahn.

A mysterious, reclusive people, the iylvahn were said to live in a magnificent city across the Dust Sea that no other race had seen the inside of. They were secretive and long-lived, and they hoarded knowledge like dust mice hoarded seeds. According to common consensus, the iylvahn were universally graceful, elegant, and beautiful, man and woman alike. They had charcoal or blue-gray complexions, strange-colored eyes, and pale hair. But their most distinguishing feature was their ears, which were slender and pointed like a Cyrian dagger.

Below me, the stranger lowered his arms, revealing high cheekbones, twilight colored skin, and slender ears shaped like the curved dagger in my boot. His short hair was white, almost silver, but the face below was young and shockingly beautiful, just like the stories said. His eyes were a pale, pale blue and glowed softly, like the nimbus of light around the moon.

"The queen of Irrikah sends her regards," the iylvahn said, his deep voice sending shivers up and down my spine. "Out of respect for you and your position, I ask permission to be within the city."

"It is granted," said the high priestess, sounding very formal, "as long as your blade does not sever the threads still being woven."

I bit my bottom lip, thinking of my mission, and how I still had to "sever the threads" in the very tapestry providing my hiding spot. I hoped this was simply coincidence and not some sort of omen.

"It is not my place," said the iylvahn, sounding equally formal. "I am the blade that cuts the blight from the tree and the weak threads from the Weave. Nothing more or less."

"Good." The high priestess's voice was tight, her facade of politeness fading. "I know the queen believes your work is necessary, and I will not ask the details of your mission, but I have not seen anything of this darkness she speaks of. The empire that lies beneath us is naught but dust and bones and sand. The Deathless Kings are long forgotten."

A chill slid up my back. *The Deathless Kings?* What did a children's faery tale have to do with the iylvahn? I remembered hearing a story of the Deathless Kings once, long ago, when I was very small. It had been frightening, so frightening that it had kept me from going to sleep for two nights straight, thinking a Deathless King might slither out from under my bed and drag me down to his dark kingdom. Vahn had finally explained that the Deathless Kings had once ruled the world, but they had vanished thousands of years ago, and the stories left behind were mostly used to scare naughty children.

I was a child then, so it might've been my imagination, but that night Vahn had seemed almost . . . angry. Not at me, but at the man who had told the story of the Deathless Kings. My childish fears had faded, though I couldn't remember seeing that thief in the guild ever again.

"I do not question the queen's orders," the iylvahn said in a voice dead of emotion. "She said a darkness sleeps under Kovass, and it will rise unless certain threads are cut from the Weave. I am here to make certain it is done."

The high priestess sighed. "Go, then," she said. "Do your job quickly and return to your people. A kahjai in Kovass only invites death."

Kahjai. I didn't know what that was, but it was clear the high priestess did not approve of them. Though her tone quickly switched back to formal. "May your time with us be brief, may your blade cut true, and may you return to the shadows before any realize you exist."

The iylvahn bowed. Without answering, he pulled up his hood, then turned as if to walk away.

He paused. Standing with his back to me, he turned his cowled head very slightly, as if listening to something behind him. I held my breath, wondering if he could hear my heart thudding beneath my tunic, and pressed myself even farther into the statue.

"Kahjai?" The high priestess sounded concerned. "Is something wrong?"

The hood turned toward the door again. "No," the iylvahn said. "It is nothing." Ducking his head, he started walking away. "May Fate smile upon you, Ahsani," he said. Then he slipped out the door . . . and was gone.

I waited until the priestess's footsteps shuffled across the floor and a door clicked shut behind her before springing to my feet. That had been entirely too close. If the iylvahn had seen me up there, I didn't know what he would have done, but one thing was certain: I did not want to find out. In my seventeen years in the guild, I had seen many dangerous men. Thieves, predators, brawlers, and toughs. Men who would cut your throat as well as your purse, who stalked citizens though the streets and back alleys like sand wolves, who felt no remorse about breaking someone's kneecaps, should the guild give the order. I knew which guild members I could trust and which to avoid, because regardless of guild law forbidding members to prey on each other, we were all thieves. Breaking the law was what we did every day. And we were good at it.

But the iylvahn, with his cold, pale eyes and beautiful, almost alien face, was by far the most dangerous creature I had seen. I knew my fair share of cutthroats and criminals. But there was no doubt in my mind—the iylvahn was a killer.

There was no formal Assassins Guild in Kovass. Mainly because the Circle existed. Its members controlled the organized crime in the city, and they didn't tolerate competition. But there were rumors of shadowy figures from other lands who sometimes appeared in Kovass. I wondered if the iylvahn were the "shadowy figures" those rumors were talking about.

Unease flickered. First that bizarre request from the Circle, and now a mysterious stranger from across the Dust Sea walking into the Temple of Fate. I wondered if the two things were somehow connected, though I didn't like what that implied. The iylvahn was dangerous. His visit to the temple didn't feel like a coincidence. Something was going on, and I might be right in the center of it.

Focus, Sparrow. That's not what you're here for, and you still have a job to do.

Grasping my dagger, I placed the blade against the silken edge of the tapestry. For just a moment, I held my breath, wondering if *this* was when I would be struck down by Fate. If one of the chains that suspended the chandeliers from the ceiling would snap, and I would be crushed under candle wax and iron, a freak accident in the Temple of Fate.

But nothing happened, and I drew the blade down the tapestry, easily parting the cloth. I winced at the noise; it wasn't loud, but the sound of my dagger cutting through the expensive silk made my hair stand on end. I cut a sizable chunk from the whole, large enough that the cloth would be easily recognizable, then stuffed the fabric into my leather satchel.

I have it! I have the Tapestry of the World. How many other thieves will ever say that?

Heart racing, I slid down the statue, hit the floor of the temple, and sprinted outside. The blazing heat of the twins struck me, but I put my head down and kept moving until I had slipped between the buildings across the road and ducked into a narrow alley. Only then did I pause to evaluate what had just happened.

Just to be sure, I reached a hand into my satchel and touched the fabric. It was still there. I had taken a piece of the Tapestry of the World.

I hoped it would be enough to satisfy the Circle. And Vahn.

There were several minutes left in Demon Hour, though Solasti was starting to abandon her sister and make her way across the horizon alone. It would be scorching for another hour, and the rooftops would be thoroughly cooked, a miserable way to travel. I could probably make my way through the streets without too much notice, as the walkways and sidewalks were still completely dead. But guard cupolas sat on nearly every corner in the Garden District, and I was carrying a scrap of the Tapestry of the World in my satchel. Tempting Fate even further, when I had gotten luckier than any soul had a right to, didn't seem prudent.

I took to the rooftops and started the uncomfortable journey home.

THREE

The Thieves Guild of Kovass operated out of the Docks District, one of the poorer and rougher sections of the city, but also one of the most colorful in terms of people. Here, on the edge of the Dust Sea, sand ships and the great mechanical striders would dock and offload cargo from the lands and cities beyond. Exotic goods, plants, creatures, and more passed through the docks on their way to markets or homes or private vendors. But the most interesting cargo was the passengers who came off the striders—Kovass citizens with stories to tell about what lay across the Dust Sea, or, very infrequently, a person who lived in the lands beyond. A wandering Fatechaser would sometimes come to Kovass on their journey to wherever the winds and Fate took them. Once, the entire Docks District was in a frenzy because a merchant had somehow acquired a juvenile rock beetle, the chosen mount of the insect-riding Scarab Clan. Even as a baby, the shiny black beetle was the size of a small donkey, with mandibles that could grind though solid stone. Unfortunately, rumors were that the merchant did not have permission to take one of the prized animals of the Scarab Clan. He was found in a dark alley one night, both arms and legs cut from his torso, and the beetle was never seen again.

But whatever a person's reason for coming to Kovass, whether profit or curiosity or needing a place to disappear into, they all passed through the Docks District. Where, unbeknownst to all, the watchful eyes of the Thieves Guild took note of everything that passed through the sector. And, if it was profitable, acted on it.

Demon Hour had finally passed by the time I reached the district, and activity was returning to normal. The city was waking up as Solasti moved on and the temperature dropped; merchants returned to their stalls, beggars appeared on corners and sidewalks once more, and housewives cautiously poked their heads out of their doorways to gauge the location of the suns.

I dropped from the rooftops and landed in a shaded alley with a sigh of relief. The rooftops were more open, and probably the fastest way to get around the city, but that path required a lot of jumping, sprinting, and balancing, and frankly, I was tired, hot, slightly cranky, and didn't want to expend more energy than I had to. The rough crowds and narrow streets of the Docks District were familiar and comforting. This was my territory; I was more at home here than anywhere else in the city.

"Sparrow."

A figure melted out of a nearby alley, smoothly avoided a body lurching down the sidewalk, and came toward me with a smile and an arm raised. He was dressed like me and many others in the district, in loose clothes with his hood drawn up for protection from the sun. When he raised his head, laughing almond eyes glinted under the cowl. A few scraggly beard hairs were trying valiantly to grow on his relatively young, smooth face.

My stomach gave a weird little flutter, which I ignored. I had known Jeran a long time; he was a childhood friend who had faced tragedy when his father was taken away. We'd always been friendly rivals, always trying to outdo each other, but recently, it seemed as if he had grown up a lot. His interest in me had changed, too, his glances becoming longer and more pointed. I wasn't blind. I knew what was happening. But I had avoided acting on it, making excuses when I could, or leaving the room before things went too far. It wasn't that Jeran was undesirable, or that I hadn't thought about him . . . in that way. I just didn't know if I wanted to go down that particular road. It was easier—and safer—not to deal with those emotions.

"Jeran." I smiled as he fell into step beside me. "What are you doing here?"

"Looking for you," he replied easily. "I couldn't find you anywhere in the base, so I figured you were holed up somewhere else." A grin split his face as he glanced at me. "What's the matter, did you get caught out in Demon Hour and couldn't get back in time?"

I winced. "Something like that." If he only knew. I had just stolen the Tapestry of the World from the Temple of Fate during the hottest part of Demon Hour. That was a lot of capitalized names, and I couldn't even tell anyone about it.

Jeran snickered. "Sometimes, I don't understand why everyone says you're one of the best." He sighed. "I just see you getting lucky, over and over and over again."

I smirked. "You know, I heard that jealousy can stunt beard growth." I casually scratched my own chin. "Besides, according to the teachings, there's no such thing as luck. So that must mean I *am* the best."

Jeran frowned and ran a hand down his jaw. "Certainly the most humble," he muttered, rolling his eyes. I grinned. "Anyway, where are you heading now? Back to base?"

I nodded. "I have to report to Vahn."

"Doing anything afterward?"

"Probably not." Not unless the Circle wanted me to go on another solo heist. I hoped not. After stealing the tapestry, I dreaded what they might ask me to do next. Sneak into the king's palace to "procure" the nose ring from his favorite concubine? "Why?" I asked Jeran.

He shrugged. "There's a firedancer circus set to perform in Highmarket this evening," he replied. "Dahveen and I were planning to attend. You're welcome to join us."

I cocked my head. "And how will we be attending this performance?" I asked in an innocent voice. Performances like that meant large distractions and a lot of people packed into one place, paying little attention to their surroundings or their belongings. Easy pickings if you went for that reason, but it also meant you couldn't really enjoy the show. "Are we going as civilians or workers?"

"Purely civilians," Jeran assured me, and smiled. "Unless an opportunity too good to pass up presents itself."

"Obviously." I thought about it, then shrugged. "Sure, it sounds fun. If Vahn doesn't want me to do anything tonight, count me in."

He nodded, and we continued through the district, weaving

around beggars, sailors, workmen, and everyone else who had returned to life now that Demon Hour was over. Leaving the main street, we entered Warehouse Row, where blocky structures of stone and wood lined the roads, towering over us. The air changed, turning musty, dry, and somehow old. A haze hung in the air, not white or smoky, but amber colored, like the sky before a sandstorm. A fine powder coated every surface and clung to everything, including the people moving through the streets. Men and women passed us, their faces wrapped in cloth to filter out the dust, only their eyes visible through the fabric. I pulled my scarf over my nose, tugged my hood lower over my face, and took shallow breaths as dust began accumulating on my clothes and seeping into every seam

"I hate this part of town," Jeran muttered, his voice muffled by the cloth over his nose and jaw. "The dust is really bad after Demon Hour. I wish Vahn would move the base somewhere else."

"Stop complaining," I said. "You know he keeps it here on purpose. No one likes venturing into this part of the district unless they have to."

"Including me," Jeran mumbled, as the road we were on ended abruptly at a series of piers, wharves, and stone docks.

I shivered in the hot, dry air. Beyond the pier, the Dust Sea stretched out before us, an endless expanse of roiling waves and shifting sands, rising, falling, continuing on to the horizon. Sand eddies danced across the surface; miniature tornados stirred by the wind. Waves crashed against the pier, sending sprays of golden dust into the air to disperse on the breeze. According to legend, eons ago this had been a vast ocean of water filled with life and plants and fish so large they could swallow you whole. I couldn't even imagine such a thing.

A pair of rough-looking sailors, their heads wrapped in cloth, stalked down the road with a barrel over each shoulder, causing me and Jeran to scuttle aside. Per normal, the docks were bustling even this soon after Demon Hour. Sand skiffs bobbed in the waves close to the piers, sails fluttering in the wind. A sand strider crouched near the wharf like an enormous beetle, its four jointed legs hissing steam into the air.

The sand striders fascinated me. The wood-and-sail skiffs peppering the docks were fast and agile, but they never ventured more than a day's journey from the city. Out on the Dust Sea, the winds were fierce and unpredictable, with deadly sandstorms cropping up out of nowhere. Regular wooden ships could get blown around like leaves in the wind and smash on the rocks, or have their sails torn to shreds. Driving sand could scour paint from hulls and flesh from bones, and the twin suns were relentless on the open sea. It was dangerous to sail far from shore.

But the massive sand striders didn't have to worry about wind. They didn't sail across the ocean—they walked. Their jointed legs were long enough to reach the bottom of the dust bowl, which, on the most common routes across the Dust Sea, was only twenty or thirty feet deep. Enough to drown and suffocate a person, but shallow enough for the striders to find solid footing. There were, according to most sailors, places in the Dust Sea that were far deeper, but the striders stuck to the well-traveled routes and didn't venture into the unknown. Few who did ever came back.

I paused, shielding my eyes as I gazed at the inert sand strider, wondering what it was like on the inside. The strider's oval body was made mostly of wood, as I imagined that if it were metal, the twin suns would turn it into an oven, especially during Demon Hour. But its legs were made of copper and iron, with huge pistons that moved them up and down, forward and back. The steam that powered them came from massive boilers tucked into the belly of the strider and a complex tangle of pipes that pumped water where it needed to go.

I didn't pretend to understand any of it, but deep down—so deep I couldn't even voice it out loud—my secret dream was to someday take a strider all the way across the Dust Sea, to visit whatever lands lay beyond. It was a dangerous fantasy; if you were a guild member, you were in for life. Vahn, the guild, and the Circle would never let me go—unless I scraped together enough of a fortune to buy my way out. To offer the guild and the Circle enough money that they couldn't refuse the offer. Obviously, that dream was a long ways away, but under my floorboards, I kept a secret chest filled with the most interesting items I had stolen, in the hopes that someday, it would be enough.

"Sparrow." Jeran stepped up beside me, a slight frown on his face as he glanced at the strider, then back to me. "Come on, the sailors are starting to look at us funny."

I shook myself. "Yeah. Sorry," I muttered. Jeran was aware of my fascination with the striders, but he didn't understand it. For him, Kovass was home and the only place he ever wanted to be. He had no aspirations to see anything beyond the city walls, and he didn't get why I would want to go to unfamiliar places just to see unfamiliar things. In fact, the very idea of it terrified him.

Turning from the docks, we continued farther into the district, the persistent haze of the Dust Sea clinging to us as we went.

On the very end of Warehouse Row, flanked by the Dust Sea on one side and a skiff repair shop on the other, sat a final warehouse. For all intents and purposes, it looked abandoned. The large front doors had been chained shut, the windows were boarded, and a debris field of broken crates, barrels, and boxes lay scattered throughout the yard. A wooden fence, gray and weathered, surrounded the plot, half its boards missing or lying in the sand. Dust coated every surface inside the fence and out.

Jeran and I slipped through a gap in the fence, crossed the yard, and walked around to the back of the warehouse. Our passing left footsteps in the coating of dust across the ground, but the prints would remain for only a few minutes before the wind and haze scoured them clean once more.

We came to a heavy door set into the stone wall at the back of the building. Stepping beneath the arched doorframe, Jeran knocked twice on the wood, paused, knocked twice again, and then once more. There was a click, and then the door swung back, revealing a heavily muscled brute of a man on the other side. He was bald, with a neck like a bull ox and numerous scars across his arms and chest. How he'd gotten so many was a mystery within the guild and an ongoing bet among younger members, including me. Jeran said he must have battled a great sand cat and won. I maintained that with as many fights as he had probably been in, his winning strategy was blocking knife strikes with his arms.

"Bassig," Jeran greeted him as we ducked through the opening. The scarred man grunted at us, closing the door as soon as we were through. Bassig rarely spoke, preferring to loom or glower imposingly from a corner. He knew his job, and he was good at it. Whenever the guild needed someone to help "persuade" a stubborn client or informant, Bassig was the one they called on.

Inside, the warehouse belied its abandoned facade; it was open and well maintained, a haven in which guild members could congregate, relax, and plan their next heist. It was fairly empty now, with most members returning to "work" once Demon Hour was over.

"Sparrow," Bassig said as I followed Jeran across the floor. Surprised, I glanced over my shoulder. "Vahn wants you," he said shortly. "Told me to let you know as soon as you came in. He's waiting in his office."

I nodded. "I'm going there now," I told Bassig, who shrugged and returned to his usual pose, leaning against the wall with his arms crossed.

I wondered what Vahn would say when I showed him the item the Circle had had me "procure." Would he be relieved? Shocked? Or would he smile and nod like he used to, his eyes showing the pride he rarely spoke out loud?

I turned to Jeran, who smirked and held up his arms, taking a step back. "I know," he said. "I can't come with you. Common, petty thieves aren't allowed to step into the Guildmaster's office. You have to be his special favorite to be allowed past the doorframe."

"Don't be a sand ass," I said.

He grinned. "Dahveen and I are heading to Highmarket at sundown," he said. "Come find us when you're finished with the boss. If he can stomach his special little bird slumming it with the no-talent commoners, that is."

I aimed a kick at him. He dodged smoothly and trotted away, laughing. Rolling my eyes, I headed to Vahn's office and tapped on the door.

"Come in," said Vahn's calm voice. The Guildmaster stood in front of his bookshelf, reading from one of the many ledgers stored on the shelves. I always wondered why his office was so plainly decorated; no elegant pictures hung on the walls, no gold or onyx figurines littered his desk. He kept no gems, jewelry, or trophies of any kind, though I knew he had the means to acquire whatever he wanted. Perhaps he knew that as the Guildmaster in a den of thieves, having such glittery items lying around would just be asking for headaches. No one I knew of would dare steal from the Guildmaster—probably—but it was a good idea not to tempt that loyalty.

"You're back." Vahn placed the ledger back on the shelf with the others and came around to his desk. His dark eyes stared at me over the surface. "Were you able to acquire the item addressed in the letter?" he asked.

I nodded. Wordlessly, I removed my satchel and placed it on the desk between us. "It's in there," I told Vahn. "As much as I could get. It was too big to take the whole thing."

His eyes narrowed. Leaning across the desk, he took the satchel and pulled it toward him. For a moment, he fumbled with the leather cords tying it shut, then flipped it open to peer inside.

The blood drained from his face. One trembling hand reached down and drew the strip of silken, shimmering cloth from inside the satchel. The piece of tapestry hissed as it came free, gold and silver strands winking in the gloom and throwing threads of light over the walls and floor.

"The Tapestry of the World," he murmured, holding it up to the light. "You actually did it."

I swallowed a flash of pride and nodded. "From the Temple of Fate itself," I said, trying to keep the smugness from my voice. "Right under the high priestess's nose."

"Then, it is time." Vahn's voice was a whisper. His suddenly wild gaze rose to mine. "And no one saw you?" he demanded. "No one was aware of your presence? No one spotted you entering or leaving the temple?"

I remembered the iylvahn, the slight hesitation, the sudden panic in my gut when I thought he had sensed me. But he had moved on, and nothing had come of it. "No," I told Vahn, shaking my head. "No one saw me."

"You are certain?"

"Yes."

He blew out a slow breath, then quickly stuffed the tapestry piece back into the satchel and flipped it shut. For a moment, he stood there, both hands on the satchel, holding it upright. His eyes were closed, and I saw that he was shaking.

"Sparrow," he murmured, and I held my breath. "I . . ."

Abruptly, he straightened and opened his eyes, that blank mask falling over his expression once more. "You've done well," he said almost absently, tucking the satchel under one arm. "The

Circle will be pleased. You are free to go until I call for you again."

Disappointed, I watched him turn to leave, only the half-hearted acknowledgment of a supremely risky task hanging in the air between us. "That's it?" I asked, frowning. "No reward for stealing the Tapestry of the World from the Temple of Fate? For basically thumbing my nose at Maederyss herself?"

For saving you from the wrath of the Circle? Both our hides were on the line, you know.

He paused, then turned to me. The lantern light reflected in his eyes, washing over his expression, which was suddenly weary and angry and resolved all at once. "You have no idea what you have set into motion," he said in a quiet, almost sorrowful voice. "Soon, everything you know—your entire world—is going to change. I wish to the goddess that it wasn't you, but we are far too close to turn back now. For what it's worth, I'm sorry."

Stunned, I watched him stride out, satchel tucked firmly under his arm, and shut the door behind him. For a moment, I could only stand there staring at the closed door, trying to understand.

What did he mean? What was the Circle planning?

And where did I fit into it?

FOUR

I spent the rest of the afternoon in my room, lying on my small bed with an arm across my face, my single window boarded and curtained against the sun. Thin rays of sunlight still filtered through the wood and cloth, glinting off an assortment of what most in the guild considered useless trinkets. Small mementoes I had taken from previous jobs—clunky old keys, shiny stones that were pretty but worthless, figurines of animals and mythical creatures, or anything else that caught my fancy. Vahn had once joked that he should have named me Sandmouse for all the shiny junk I hoarded. But I liked it. My room was my nest, my own little haven. And, more important, it kept prying eyes away from the real valuables beneath my floorboard; the things I'd collected that were *not* worthless. True, I *was* a sandmouse; I was attracted to shiny objects. But I also knew the difference between a blue stone made of glass and a real sapphire.

The afternoon dragged on. I alternated between dozing—the heist in the middle of Demon Hour had robbed me of my normal nap time—and pondering everything that had happened, from the Circle's mysterious orders to Vahn's words when I'd returned with the tapestry.

You have no idea what you have set into motion. Soon, everything you know—your entire world—is going to change.

That wasn't like Vahn at all. I'd never seen him react so intensely. I tried to ignore it, but the looming sense of unease, and the memory of everything that had happened in the Temple of Fate, continued to plague me as I drifted in and out of a restless sleep.

An hour before sundown, I emerged from my room and wandered down to the makeshift tavern on the ground floor of the warehouse. The tavern wasn't anything fancy; just a scattering of barrels that served as tables and a long slab of limestone that acted as the bar. But Rala, the bartender, had a knack for acquiring rare, exotic, and sometimes illegal bottles from across the Dust Sea and beyond. They were, of course, for guild members only. I didn't drink very often, but there was always an interesting selection to choose from when I did.

"Little dust sparrow, welcome." Rala smiled at me as I ducked through the curtains that hung across the doorframe. Her dark eyes sparkled as I smiled back. She had a fondness for my namesake, the tiny brown-and-white birds that could be found throughout the city, flitting from perch to perch. She left scatterings of seeds and breadcrumbs on fence posts, and a shallow ceramic bowl filled with cool water for them to bathe in. "Sparrows are survivors," she had told me once when I was curious enough to ask about it. "They're on every rooftop, in every windowsill, on every branch, but no one pays them any attention. They're preyed on by the bigger, stronger birds, like hawks and cliff raptors, but they always return. They're small, but they thrive in the harshest environments." She had placed a gentle, ring-encrusted hand atop my head; I had been around six years old at the time. "Much like you, my dear. Vahn did not choose your name by accident. You are small, clever, and very good at getting into places you are not supposed to be. Like my tavern. Now, shoo." She'd removed her hand and made a fluttering motion with it, smiling to soften her words. "This is not a place for children, and Vahn will scold me if he finds you here again. Go on, now. Out."

I had grinned and scuttled out beneath the curtain, only to return time and time again. Eventually, no one took any notice of me when I walked into the tavern. Just like Rala had said.

"Feeling adventurous today?" Rala questioned as I paused at the bar. Her eyes glittered with mischief as she put a hand under the smooth stone surface. "I just got in a bottle of fire beetle wine from the lands of the magma walkers. Up for a taste?"

"Um, no thanks, Rala." I half smiled, half grimaced at her. "You might've had me, until you told me how fire beetle wine is made."

She chuckled. "If you're looking for Jeran," she went on, withdrawing her hand, "he's in his usual corner, losing at dice to Dahveen. I expect he'll have to pay Dahveen's tab in a minute or two. Hope he has enough. The boy drinks like a camel."

"Thanks."

I wandered to the far corner, where Jeran and another boy his age were huddled over a barrel, both looking intense. A trio of carved bone dice sat on the barrel top; a moment later, Dahveen snatched them up, clattered them into a clay cup, and set the cup face down between them.

"Call," he told Jeran.

Triple Fang was a simple enough game; when the cup went down, players would gamble on how many dice showed the same numbers, and if they were even or odd. You might guess "double evens," and if the dice showed, say, a pair of fours, you would win. "Triple fang"—where all three dice showed ones—was the most sought-after combination. Calling it correctly was an automatic win, but if you called triple fang and the dice didn't cooperate, you forfeited all your winnings to your opponents.

Jeran chewed his lip, staring at the cup. "Double odds," he said finally.

Dahveen snorted. "You guessed that last time." Dahveen was a lean, shifty looking boy with oily hair and a thin mustache above a narrow top lip. "Why don't you just go ahead and pay my tab right now? Go away, Sparrow," he added as I came up. "I don't need your brand of jinx. Back off, we're almost done."

I smiled and stayed where I was, gazing down at the cup beneath his sweaty palm. "Triple evens," I said, making Dahveen scowl and Jeran glance up at me. "I just have a feeling."

"You and your feelings," Jeran muttered, and Dahveen's scowl grew darker.

"You already called," he told Jeran quickly. "You can't change your answer now. No fangs," he went on, meaning he thought there would be no matching numbers beneath the cup. It was his favorite strategy, the safe strategy, which was how he won against Jeran so often. He didn't take any risks. He lived life the same way, going after something only if it was reasonably safe to do so. Which was why he was an average thief, but not a great one. High risk equaled high reward. My tactics drove him crazy.

Dahveen lifted the cup. All three dice beneath showed a two.

"Oh, look at that," I said smugly, as Jeran shook his head and Dahveen let out an explosive breath. "Triple evens. Does that mean you buy my drinks for the next month?"

With a curse, Dahveen shoved away from the barrel and stood, snatching his dice and cup as he did. "I hate it when she pokes around our games," he told Jeran, who shrugged. "I swear she's cursed. She throws everything off."

"Or maybe Fate just likes me better," I said, knowing that would piss him off even more. He curled his thin, mustached lip at me and turned away, slipping the dice and cup into the pocket of his tunic.

"We're done," he growled. "I don't play with cheating harpies. Are we going to the Highmarket District or not?"

Jeran rose easily and stretched, not able to completely hide the smirk on his face. "Suns won't be down for another hour," he said. "We have time."

"Good," snapped Dahveen. "Then you two can wait while I grab another drink."

He stalked to the bar, pulling a waterskin from beneath his shirt and muttering to himself. Jeran shook his head and turned to me.

"Great, thanks for that. Now he's going to be an ass until his next winning streak."

"Mm-hmm, and how is that different than his normal personality?"

Jeran snorted and lowered his voice. "Did you get everything worked out with Vahn?" he asked, trying and failing to not sound curious. He knew he wasn't supposed to ask the details of any missions that came from the Guildmaster. "Are you in the clear for tonight?"

I nodded, feeling my stomach twist as Vahn's reaction to the tapestry and his words to me came rushing back. "It's been sorted," I told Jeran, pushing that scene to the back of my mind to deal with later. Even if I wanted to know what Vahn had been talking about, he wouldn't explain until he was ready to. "Let's go. I desperately need a distraction tonight."

Jeran's brow furrowed. "Are you all right, Sparrow?" he asked softly. "Everything okay with you and the Guildmaster?"

"Of course." I gave him a half grin, ignoring the persistent coiling of my insides saying that it was a lie, that everything was not okay. "Why? Were you hoping otherwise?"

"No." He crossed his arms and glanced away, looking strangely defensive. "I was just asking."

Our conversation was interrupted by an argument between Rala and Dahveen, with Rala informing him that, no, she wasn't going to add any more to his tab until he paid what he already owed her, and he could take it up with Vahn if he didn't like it. Dahveen returned with an even darker scowl on his face than normal and gave me a look that could wither stone. I grinned cheerfully back.

Jeran sighed, sensing uncomfortable times ahead. We left the tavern, slipped out the back door of the warehouse, and ducked through the fence. The air of the Docks District was hazy and dust choked as we tugged hoods over our heads, pulled scarves over our mouths, and headed into the city.

True dark in Kovass, where a sickly moon hung in the sky and the twin suns were nowhere to be seen, lasted about four hours. That was the span between Namaia fully sinking below the horizon and Solasti rising triumphantly over the dunes once more. Nights in Kovass were short, days were long, and evenings tended to linger, as if Namaia was reluctant to concede her spot in the sky.

Said sky was just beginning to turn pink as Jeran, Dahveen, and I made our way through the streets toward the Highmarket District. Not to be confused with the more bustling Market District, where the lower-class citizens peddled their common wares, like bread, baskets, and chickens. Where the air stank of livestock, smoke, and unwashed bodies in the sun, and pickpockets prowled the streets like sand wolves.

There were no bread vendors in Highmarket, no bleating goats or cries from a fruit peddler to peruse his stock of shriveled pears crawling with flies. There were no dirty, crowded booths, no heaps of limp vegetables or fruit or raw goat meat lying in the sun. No, Highmarket was where the rich sent their servants to procure what they needed. Where vendors stood in front of their shop doors, beckoning customers inside, out of the heat. Shouting matches between seller and buyer haggling over prices were nonexistent. Instead, there were open streets lined with cloth overhangs for shade and shelter. There were stone benches to rest on if the rich grew tired of walking. There were strategically placed potted plants beside shop doors, adding a bit of life and greenery to otherwise stony facades. And there were guards, both private and city, patrolling the streets or stoically flanking their masters. Had it been a normal day in Highmarket, the presence of three dusty, lowborn street rats like me, Jeran, and Dahveen would have drawn the gaze of every guard in the area. At best, they would've been be instantly wary. Maybe threatened us with words or gestures to keep our fingers to ourselves, or else. At worst, we might've been run out of the district.

Thankfully, the firedancer circus had come to town, and the large open square in the center of the district was already filled with people of all shapes, sizes, and classes. Any bodyguard would be hard-pressed to keep the crowds away from his patron; there were just too many bodies jammed together, all eager to watch the show. Easy pickings, had we come for that.

"Ugh, there's so many people already," Jeran muttered, hanging back from the edge of the square. He didn't share my fondness for crowds, even though it was easy to hide in a large mass of people, becoming invisible in the throng. Jeran gazed at the mob surrounding the square and wrinkled his nose. "I guess we'll have to get closer," he grumbled. "We won't see anything from here."

I rolled my eyes at him. "How long have you been a guild member?" I gazed pointedly at the rows of shop rooftops lining the square. First rule of observation: If you couldn't see anything at ground level, get above it.

Dahveen made a face. "Risky," he said, purely to be obstinate, I thought. "The guards won't like it. If they see us, they might chase us out."

"Then don't let them see you," I told him. He glared at me, and I shrugged. "Stay here and miss the show, then. I'm going up top."

I started walking toward a line of stone buildings behind us, hearing Jeran and Dahveen follow reluctantly. I secretly hoped Dahveen would stay behind just for spite, but he trailed after, muttering under his breath. We ducked into an alley between a rug tailor and a jewelry shop, deftly avoiding the gaze of a guard stationed by the doorway. The rug shop was a couple of stories high, with rough sandstone walls and a flat roof. Perfect.

"You're not going to climb that, are you—" Jeran began, but I was already moving, striding to the wall, then leaping for a windowsill, using momentum and the windowframe to propel myself upward. I scrambled to the ledge of the first floor, then continued up to the second, until I heaved myself over the wall and onto the roof. I heard Dahveen give a vehement curse and stifled a grin.

I walked to the opposite side of the rooftop, then froze. The view was definitely better from up here. The market square spread out below me, crowds of people ringing an open area where colorful dancers were already moving. Problem was, someone else had had the same idea. A figure sat on the edge of the roof watching the scene below, legs swinging over the wall.

His back was to me, so I couldn't see his face. But his head was uncovered, and in the light from the square, his tousled hair was the color of the dunes, a pale ashen gold. His garments were strange: a dark brown jacket over a white shirt, and trousers with several pockets and belts hanging off them.

He was definitely not from Kovass. I didn't know where he was from, actually. I had never seen anyone like this.

"Don't let me scare you away."

I jumped. His voice cut through the murmur of the city, clear and confident, with the hint of a smile beneath. He turned to gaze over his shoulder, and his eyes were the sapphire blue of the sky after Demon Hour. I took a wary step back. He was young, maybe a couple of years older than me and Jeran, but he held himself with the confidence of someone who had seen a lot and wasn't afraid of anything.

"You had the right idea," the boy said easily, as if we were the oldest of friends, not strangers who had just met on a random rooftop. "This is the best seat in the city. You don't have to run," he went on, holding out a hand. He wore brown fingerless gloves, I saw, the digits beneath them worn and calloused. "We were fated to meet here, after all."

"Uh." I blinked at him. "What?"

"Sparrow?"

Footsteps echoed behind me a moment before I felt Jeran's presence at my side. Like me, he immediately saw the stranger and tensed, his body coiling like a spring.

"Who are you?" Jeran demanded, and the hostility in his voice startled me, as did his fingers dropping to his sash, where I knew a knife was tucked into the folds. "What are you doing here?"

The stranger just smiled, holding up his hands. "Just a simple traveler, here to watch the circus," he replied. But his gaze wasn't on Jeran; it was still locked on me. "I am but a seed, a leaf, a grain of sand, blown on the winds of Fate."

"Well, the winds of Fate can blow you somewhere else now," Jeran said, his tone still hard. "This is our city, and our territory. Find another spot."

"Jeran." I frowned at him. "There's enough room up here for all of us."

"No, no." The stranger rose gracefully on the edge of the roof. "I know when I'm not wanted," he said with a shrug. "Nor do I think my fate is to be stabbed to death on a lonely rooftop, so I shall take my leave." He bowed, though his gaze was on me as he straightened. "Enjoy the circus," he said. "May Fate smile on you."

And with that, he stepped off the edge of the roof and was gone in an instant. The building was tall; *I* could have jumped off to the ground, but only because I'd been climbing buildings all my life and knew how to land safely. Blinking, I hurried to the edge and peered down, but the stranger had already vanished into the crowd.

Jeran snorted. "Tourists," he muttered, walking to the edge as well. "Good riddance."

Was he a tourist? Well, whoever he was, he's gone now. Turning back, I smirked at Jeran. "Like you really would have stabbed him to get him off the roof," I challenged. "You get queasy when you have to kill mice."

He shrugged, though his face remained dark. "Guess we'll never know, will we?"

I rolled my eyes. Jeran was a lot of things, but he wasn't a coldhearted killer. Though this was the first time I'd seen him act that aggressively. "Where's Dahveen? I thought he wanted to see the dance."

"Oh, well . . ." Jeran hesitated, scratching the back of his head. "He . . . decided he didn't want to come up here," he said with a very casual shrug. "He told me he would watch from the ground."

I frowned. That sounded suspicious. Had Jeran told Dahveen not to follow us onto the roof? Or was something else going on?

A hush fell over the crowd below, the air of anticipation and held breaths growing stronger. The show was about to start. I lowered myself to my heels, then sat down on the edge of the rooftop, swinging my feet over empty space. "Guess it's just us, then."

Jeran hesitated, then joined me on the edge, sitting with his elbows resting on his knees. Closer than I expected him to be. I felt the heat of his body, the shift of his sleeve against mine, and my stomach gave a weird little lurch.

Down in the square, a drumbeat started, thumping out a hollow rhythm. Four women in red and yellow danced in a circle, waving scarves the color of fire. As the dance continued and the drumbeat grew faster, the ends of the scarves burst into real flames, lighting up the square, and a roar went up from the crowd. The performance continued, with the dancers expertly whirling the scarves so that they traced a ring of fire around them. The audience cheered and clapped, gazes riveted to the swirling flames.

Warmth blossomed against the back of my palm, the lightest brush over my skin. I looked down to see that Jeran's hand had drifted next to mine, one finger hesitantly probing. A tingle raced up my arm to my shoulder. Swallowing, I glanced at his face and saw him watching me from the corner of his eye. Within his hood, the dancing firelight cast flickering shadows over his features, accenting his cheek and the strong curve of his jaw.

My stomach danced. The touch on the back of my hand was a question; I could pull back if I wanted, letting us both pretend it had been an accident. We could leave this place, and nothing would change between us.

I hesitated, weighing the consequences of this choice, then slowly turned my hand over. His fingers gently curled with mine, sending a ripple of heat through my stomach like molten gold.

Below us in the square, someone screamed.

Jeran and I jerked up, hands breaking apart, that faint warmth vanishing. Part of the crowd was surging back from a central spot on the ground. I shielded a hand over my eyes and peered into the square, trying to see the cause of the sudden commotion.

A man lay face down on the stones, legs and arms twitching in a death spasm, a bag of candied nuts spilled on the ground by his head. There was no blood, no wound that I could see, no obvious sign of what had killed him. But as I watched, he convulsed once more and went still, and I knew he would not be getting up.

The screams were spreading as everyone in the square started to realize what had happened. Citizens fled or froze in place, gaping stupidly at the body. Guards raced toward the commotion. Everyone's attention was riveted to what was happening in the square.

Without really knowing why, I looked at the rooftop directly across from me.

For a split second, I saw a figure. A hooded silhouette, pale against the surrounding stones. Just as it drew back and vanished into the shadows.

My stomach churned, a chill sliding up my spine. Instinctively, I knew who it was.

"Sparrow!"

I jumped. Jeran was on his feet, eyes narrowed as he gazed at the chaos below. "Come on," he snapped, holding out a hand. "Let's get out of here before the guards show up and start asking questions."

Standard thief procedure: Flee from any crime or disturbance, even if you had no part in it. No guild member wanted to deal with guards on a normal day; whenever there was trouble, our kind tended to mysteriously vanish into the cracks, crowds, or shadows. But I hesitated, heart pounding, searching the rooftops for a glimpse of that elusive figure. Even though I knew I would never find him.

"Sparrow!" Jeran's voice held a thread of desperation. I scrambled to my feet, as screams and cries of alarm continued to ring from the square below. Most everyone was fleeing now, except for the guards and a few brave, curious, or foolish citizens. The body lay motionless where it had fallen; a man of average height and considerable girth, his features hidden, planted into the stones. There was still no blood, no wound, nothing to show how he had died. Two guards stood over him with their swords drawn, glaring around the square as if they could somehow catch the one responsible.

Drawing back from the solemn sight, I turned and fled, following Jeran across the roof. We scrambled down the wall, sprinted across the road, and vanished into the darkness of the alleyways beyond.

We headed straight back to the Docks District like mice fleeing to their hole to escape the household cat, not stopping to think or talk. We nearly crashed into Dahveen in an alley, and the three of us continued to the warehouse without speaking until we were safely within its dingy walls.

Staggering into the tavern, we headed toward the corner barrel. My heart still pounded as I plunked into the seat, relieved to be back in familiar territory. Rala took one look at our panting, sweaty faces, set down a trio of mugs, and said she'd get the story out of me later.

Jeran downed the contents of his mug and set it on the barrel with a thump. "Well, that was interesting," he said. His tone was flippant; death was no stranger to any of us, but the sudden, unexpected way it had happened back in Highmarket had taken us by surprise. "They'll be talking about this for a while. Any idea who died back there?"

Dahveen snorted. "Some fat, rich noble," he muttered. "Probably choked on one of his candied palm nuts."

I sensed Jeran's gaze on my face, worried and appraising, and my cheeks warmed. "What about you, Sparrow?" he asked. "You've been awfully quiet. What do you think happened?"

The iylvahn's face flashed through my mind, pale eyes cold and blank as he stood before the high priestess. *A kahjai in Kovass only invites death.*

But I couldn't talk about the iylvahn without revealing where I had seen him, which was strictly forbidden. "I don't know." I shrugged. "There wasn't any blood, though. No wound I could see. Maybe he *did* choke on a palm nut."

Vahn abruptly strode into the tavern, startling everyone. The Guildmaster rarely came here, preferring to spend most of his free time alone in his office. Glaring around the room, he spotted us in the corner and immediately headed in our direction. Jeran and Dahveen stiffened as he stalked toward us, his expression frighteningly intense.

"You three." His voice was sharp, making the other two flinch. Neither Jeran nor Dahveen looked him in the face, their gazes darting everywhere but to Vahn. I glanced up and saw anger in his eyes. Anger, but also a hint of fear, which made my heartbeat quicken. I had never seen Vahn react fearfully to anything. Something had shaken him to the core.

"You were at the firedancer circus tonight, correct?" Vahn asked, glaring around the table. "Did you see the murder?"

Dahveen shook his head, but Jeran and I both nodded. "We were on a rooftop when it happened," Jeran told Vahn, whose gaze sharpened. "We didn't see *how* it happened—one second, everything was normal, and then there was a body on the ground and everyone was running away."

"Did you see who did it?" Vahn asked, and though the question was for the group, his gaze was on me. From the corner of my eye, I saw Jeran's lips tighten, a dark expression crossing his face. But I couldn't focus on Jeran under the weight of Vahn's glare.

"I thought I saw . . . someone," I confessed. "On the rooftops across from us." For a second, I considered telling him what I had overheard in the Temple of Fate. The conversation between the high priestess and the iylvahn. But Jeran and Dahveen were right there, listening. I didn't want to get any of us in trouble by revealing things I shouldn't.

Vahn's gaze continued to pierce through me, expectant. And I was not going to disappoint him. Even if I wasn't certain of what I had seen. "I . . . couldn't really see them clearly," I began, stumbling over the words. "It was dark, and they were far away. But . . . it . . . it might've been . . . an iylvahn?"

Dahveen gave a snort of disbelief, but Vahn's face went pale. He straightened, gazing around the tavern, as if the iylvahn could be lurking among the barrels or under the countertop. "It's here," he growled, mostly to himself, though I felt a chill run up my spine at the words. "It's already in the city." His jaw clenched, and he glanced back at us, narrowing his eyes. "Do not leave the guild tonight, Sparrow," he said, making me blink. "That's an order. Understand?"

Bewildered, I nodded. "What's going on?" I asked, but Vahn had already turned away. I watched him stride back through the tavern and duck out the curtained doorway, and tried to ignore the feeling of anxiety spreading through my chest. I considered running after Vahn to ask him more questions, but I knew the Guildmaster. Until he was ready to explain what was happening,

I would have to wait and try not to worry about it.

Dahveen blew out a breath and gave me a disgusted look. "You did not see an iylvahn tonight," he accused. "Stop lying—everyone knows the iylvahn hardly ever leave their hidden city. Why would one be here in Kovass?"

I shrugged. "Maybe to kill a fat noble," I said, and he snorted again.

"You really saw one?" Jeran asked, sounding warily hopeful. "An iylvahn? You didn't just say that to impress the Guildmaster?"

I frowned. I didn't really care if Dahveen believed me, but Jeran's words stung. "I wouldn't lie to Vahn, Jeran," I said. "Especially when someone just died. You know me better than that."

His gaze dropped, and he immediately raised a placating hand. "You're right," he said. "Sorry. Forget I said anything."

I relaxed and gave him a forgiving nod. He and Dahveen continued talking, about the circus, the performers, and the unexpected death, for several long minutes. I sat there, nursing my drink, and thought about . . . other things. The iylvahn, the Circle, Vahn's ominous behavior and his order not to leave the warehouse.

But also, I thought of the brief touch Jeran and I had shared on the rooftop. The look on his face when his eyes met mine, and the strange fluttering in my stomach. And I wondered what might've happened, what might have started, had we not been interrupted.

FIVE

"Sparrow. Get up."

I jerked awake, muscles tensing to dodge or scramble back before my brain could even register what was happening. I was an extremely light sleeper, and my door creaked horribly, a defect I left unfixed so no one could sneak into my room while I was unconscious. Because nearly everyone in the guild could pick a lock, and because a locked anything announced to others that you might have something to hide or protect, no one bothered locking their doors. But the shadow looming over me had either opened the door without making anything squeak or had ghosted right through it and floated to my bed without touching the floor, because I hadn't heard so much as a whisper in my dreams.

"It's me," the shadow said before I could leap off my tiny cot and scramble upright. Hearing Vahn's voice, I relaxed, but only a little. He rarely came into my room, and never at night. Had something happened?

"Vahn?" I blinked at him blearily, then gazed at my boarded-up window. Through the slats, it was true dark; the stars glimmered like distant gems, and a thin crescent moon hung against the navy-blue sky. "What's going on?"

"Get up," Vahn repeated. "Come with me. Don't ask questions, and speak to no one. Let's go."

Even more confused and more than a little alarmed, I pushed myself off my cot and rose, shivering a bit in the chill. Demon Hour might scorch the skin from your bones, but once the suns went down, the temperature plummeted as well. Vahn said nothing else, just turned and glided silently from my room without looking back. Rubbing sleep from my eyes, I followed.

The guild warehouse was deserted as we made our way down the stairs and onto the first floor. Because nights were so short, guild members took advantage of the darkness while they could and planned jobs around the few hours of true dark. The lights of Rala's tavern gleamed orange in the corner, but no one sat at the tables or the bar. Rala herself was not in the tavern, either, probably catching a few hours of sleep while the place was empty.

I started toward the back entrance, but to my surprise, Vahn snapped his fingers at me, shaking his head. "Not that way," he said shortly.

I blinked. "We're not leaving the building?"

"I said no questions," he replied. "We're not leaving by the normal way, is all." He headed toward the back of the warehouse, then down a long flight of rickety wooden steps to the basement level of the building. This chamber was rarely visited and had been given over to storage. It was large, with dusty stone floors and a low ceiling. Stacks of crates, pots, pallets, and containers had turned it into a miniature maze, and it was impossible to see the farthest corners of the room through all the junk.

Vahn didn't hesitate, weaving through the labyrinthine aisles without pause, heading for the far end of the room. I followed until we came to the far wall, cloaked in heavy shadow.

Bewildered, I gazed around. There were no doors, no exits or entrances, no windows, even. Just crates of junk and flat, solid brick walls.

In the corner, Vahn paused, then turned to me. His dark eyes glimmered a warning in the shadows. "What I am about to show you is of the utmost secrecy," he said in a low voice. "Under no circumstance are you to reveal what you learn here to anyone, inside the guild or out. Breaking this rule will result in intervention by the Circle. Is that understood?"

A flippant reply rose to mind, but I knew better than to press Vahn when his eyes were hard and scary, so I just nodded. He turned toward the corner. One hand rose, and two fingers pressed into one of the many bricks along the wall.

There was the faintest *click*, and the brick Vahn was pressing slid back like it was some kind of large button. Part of the wall detached and became a door that swung slowly outward, making my breath catch in my throat. Beyond the opening, a narrow tunnel snaked away into the darkness.

My eyes widened.

Vahn pinned me with a narrowed gaze. "Remember, not a word of this, to anyone. This door, this tunnel, does not exist." He jerked his head at the dark space beyond. "Let's go."

Heart pounding with excitement and a tinge of fear, I ducked through the secret door into the dark tunnel beyond. "What is this?" I asked once Vahn had stepped inside as well. My voice echoed down the tunnel, making me shiver. "Where are we going?"

His jaw tightened, but he didn't chastise me for breaking the "no questions" rule again. Maybe he realized it was a lost cause.

"Beneath the city," he replied, taking a lantern from beneath his cloak. He lit it and held it up, casting a weak orange glow over the tunnel around us. "We'll be taking the sewers most of the way. Stay close—it's easy to get lost down here."

"Most of the way to where?"

He didn't answer, but I hadn't expected him to.

The narrow tunnel quickly led us into the sewers, which, in a city like Kovass, were a marvel unto themselves. Sewers required water, and aboveground, at least, water was nearly nonexistent. But eons and eons ago—so long ago that no one really knew exactly when—there had been a terrible cataclysm. Mountains crumbled, the earth split apart, and the ocean disappeared, draining into the cracks and sinking deep below the sands. For many years, it sat there, silent and untouched, as the world above withered and died beneath the merciless glare of the twins.

Obviously, life cannot exist without water, and necessity is the mother of invention. The underground sea was eventually discovered, and the ancient builders and architects of Kovass designed a vast network of copper pipes to pump the water from underground and distribute it across the city. It was stored in reservoirs and public fountains, where the citizens lined up each morning to fill their daily buckets and jugs. That water was used for cooking, bathing, drinking, and washing waste down the drains into the sewers below.

The sewers I found myself in now.

Vahn and I didn't speak as we continued through the maze

of tunnels, pipes, and narrow corridors. Unsurprisingly, it stank down there, and there was a chill in the air that I suspected wasn't present when the suns were up. Vahn moved quickly, giving me little time to look around, but I tried to memorize all the twists and turns in case I needed to find my way back alone. The sewers were sprawling and ancient, but for some reason, few in the Thieves Guild used them. Entrances were difficult to find and harder to access, and the sewer itself was confusing and not laid out well, according to some. I had a good memory when it came to remembering my surroundings, but I would have to concentrate if I ever had to navigate my way down here.

As Vahn and I continued on, I had the impression that we were moving downward, deeper into the undercity, into the belly of Kovass. We walked down a flight of stairs and descended a rusty ladder, and then, abruptly, the narrow tunnels opened up and I found myself staring at a large cavern. The chamber was man-made, its smooth walls and ceiling indicating this was not natural stone. The temperature had dropped sharply, probably because the cavern floor was filled with dark water, throwing off waves of cold as we stepped into the room. A narrow walkway cut straight through the middle of the cavern to a door on the other side.

"What is this place?" I asked Vahn, my voice echoing into the vastness above.

"An abandoned cistern," he replied. "Before the pipes and pumping stations were constructed throughout Kovass, water from the underground sea was stored here. Few come down here anymore. Fewer still remember that this place exists."

We passed through the chamber, the dark water lapping at the edges of the walkway and sloshing over the path. Icy droplets fell from the blackness overhead, hitting my skin with tiny stabs of cold. I stared out over the opaque water and felt the hairs along the back of my neck start to rise. It was probably my imagination, but I could almost feel something watching me from beneath the dark, chilly surface. Something old and terrible that could reach out of the water and drag me down into the darkness with it. I stayed to the middle of the walkway as much as I could, and was relieved when the chamber finally came to an end.

"Sparrow."

At the door, Vahn turned to me once again, his face a mask of stone.

"I know," I said before he could say anything. "Whatever I see, whatever is waiting for us beyond that door, tell no one what transpires here. This never happened."

His lips thinned, but he gave a short nod and turned away. I followed him through the doorframe and down another narrow, shadowy tunnel, and finally, into the last chamber.

Even though I had been bracing myself for what could lie down here, forgotten by the world, I still felt my stomach drop with amazement. The room we found ourselves in was dim, vast, and circular. A wide ledge surrounding the perimeter dropped down to a second level perhaps five or six feet below, a single set of roughhewn stairs leading to the lower floor. Stone columns, broken and crumbling, ringed the edge, and torchlight flickered from braziers surrounding the circle.

In the very center, standing around a large stone altar, five dark-robed figures turned to watch us come in. A quiver slid up my spine and lodged in my stomach. Their cowls were drawn up, but peering out from the darkness of the hoods were the bleached, hollow faces of skulls. After a moment, I realized that they were masks, that it wasn't really a group of living dead staring at us. Still, it was eerie and unsettling, and I suddenly wanted to find the nearest clump of shadow and disappear into it.

Vahn gave me no chance to back out. I felt his firm hand on my shoulder as he stepped forward, and I reluctantly let myself be escorted into the chamber. Down the steps, and before what had to be the infamous Circle, who stared at me with flat, hollow eyes behind their masks of bone. My heart pounded, and I dropped my gaze, staring at the altar. Almost immediately, I wished I hadn't. Suspicious brown stains covered the flat surface, and though it was hard to tell exactly what they were in the flickering torchlight, the implications made my skin crawl.

"Guildmember Sparrow."

I swallowed hard, raising my head to meet the cold gaze of the figure who had spoken. The eyes behind the skull mask were human, but the ruthless contempt they held made me bristle and cringe at the same time. I wasn't a person to this figure, I was an asset. "Long have we waited for this moment," it rasped. "Long have we searched for the one who steps outside the Weave. Now you are here. Now it is time to truly prove your worth."

Steps outside the Weave? What did that mean? Did it have anything to do with stealing the Tapestry of the World? And if that had just been a test, what supposedly impossible task did they have in store for me now?

"Guildmember Sparrow," another voice broke in, female, though no less eerie. "The Circle has called you here to give you a momentously important task. You have proved your talent by retrieving the Tapestry of the World from the Temple of Fate. Now it is time to undergo the mission you were born for."

"And what is that?" I asked in a quiet voice. I was no longer intrigued. I no longer wanted to impress the Circle. I just wanted to leave this chilling place as soon as possible.

"Are you aware of the city that lies beneath Kovass?" the first voice whispered.

I nodded. Kovass had its sewer system, and below the sewers lay the vast, sunken ocean. But there were even darker secrets lurking below everyone's feet, unknown and unexplored. According to Vahn, there had been a city before Kovass. A sprawling metropolis that towered into the sky and made Kovass look like a poor hamlet compared to its glory. It was gone now, of course. The same cataclysm that had drained the sea had also swallowed the mighty city, burying it beneath the sands. Kovass had been built on the bones of an ancient metropolis, and everyone had conveniently forgotten that below their feet, an entire dead civilization slumbered in the darkness.

"The First Kingdom," the voice went on as if I hadn't replied. "The time of the Deathless Kings. And it's most glorious city, the most beautiful in the world, now lies destroyed and forgotten beneath the sands."

"But not by all," whispered the female voice. "We remember. We hold the memories of the First Kingdom close. We have made it our mission to never let its glory fade into nothingness. But now we need your help, Guildmember Sparrow."

The Deathless Kings again. I snuck a furtive glance at Vahn and saw him staring straight ahead, his eyes hard and his face giving nothing away. I wished he'd given me a bit more instruction on what to do when meeting the most powerful, dangerous members of the guild. I didn't know if I should speak up or just continue waiting in silence. Fortunately, the members of the Circle did not seem to expect me to answer, and after a heartbeat, the male voice spoke again.

"There is a vault," the Circle member rasped, "that lies deep within the sunken city. Within the vault is a small stone, no bigger than your finger, marked with runes."

I swallowed. This seemed like a dangerous mission to undertake for a single item the size of my finger. I suspected curiosity was not encouraged here, but I summoned the courage to ask, "And what is this stone?"

The Circle stared at me. I could feel the disapproval in their flat, unamused gazes. Clearly, I was not supposed to ask questions. But if Vahn didn't want me to talk, he should've said something earlier. Finally, one of the skulls replied in a stiff voice, "It is a memory stone. It holds the final recollections of the Deathless King who ruled the city. If we can retrieve it, we will understand more about the First Kingdom and the people who lived there."

Suspicion and doubt flickered within. The Circle ran the Thieves Guild, the largest institution of organized crime in Kovass. They weren't scholars or academics or historians. They weren't interested in preserving the past; they were concerned with things like power, profit, and personal wealth. Unless they were going to sell this memory stone for a ridiculously high price, I couldn't understand why they would be so eager to get it.

I wasn't going to ask them to elaborate. That would certainly be pushing any amount of luck I had. I figured I could get away with one more question before the Circle decided I wasn't worth the hassle and left my broken body down here for the roaches.

There was a shifting of cloth, and one of the figures drew a rolled-up parchment from beneath its robes. An emerald ring glimmered briefly on the third finger before the hand set the parchment down and vanished back into the folds of cloth.

"This is a map of the undercity," the skull told me. "You will need this map to find your way through the sewers to your target, and then through the city to the vault itself. Beware," the voice added as I reached for the scroll. "This will not be a simple stroll through an empty kingdom. The Deathless Kings built their cities on ancient magic and protected their riches with traps and powerful curses. I would advise caution at all times. The city swallows any who are not supposed to be there."

Oh, this just sounds better and better. Now I have to be on the lookout for traps and ancient curses as well?

"Succeed, and your reward will be great," droned the female skull. "Fail, and your reward will be death. Return with the stone as soon as you are able. Do not disappoint us, Guildmember Sparrow. Yours is not the only life at stake." The eyes behind the mask flickered, very briefly, to Vahn, standing quietly at the edge of the dais. My blood chilled, but the figure's robed arm lifted in a dismissive gesture. "Now go," she rasped. "And let us hope you fare better than your predecessors."

I gave a small bow and turned away, searching for Vahn. He was already striding out of the room without a backward glance. I hurried to catch up, feeling the gazes of the Circle on my back the entire way.

I waited until we had crossed the walkway over the ancient cistern and were firmly back in the sewers before I quickened my pace to catch up to Vahn. He strode resolutely down the tunnels without looking at me, as if determined to pretend I didn't exist.

"Vahn—"

"Don't," he said shortly, still not looking at me. "Your mission with the Circle is strictly between you and them. I'm not allowed to tell you anything about it, or the Circle members, so don't ask."

"I know," I said. "I wasn't going to. Just . . ." I remembered the look on his face when I'd presented him with the tapestry, the words that had haunted me ever since. *You have no idea what you have set into motion. Soon, everything you know—your entire world—is going to change.*

And then, the final words of the female Circle member: *Let us hope you fare better than your predecessors.*

"There have been others before me," I said, and watched the faintest grimace cross Vahn's face. It had been mostly a guess, but that tiny flinch confirmed my suspicions. "Others have tried what I'm about to attempt, haven't they? And I'm guessing none of them came back."

Vahn didn't answer. "And you knew," I accused him, almost jogging to keep pace now. "You knew what the Circle was going to ask. Maybe not the details, but you knew they were going to send me to a place no one has come back from. So what makes you think I'll be able to—"

"Sparrow." Vahn whirled around abruptly and took me by the shoulders. I flinched as his rough grip squeezed my skin. His expression was conflicted and angry . . . almost haunted.

"I'm sorry," he murmured. "I didn't want this for you. When I took you from that hovel, I wanted only to save you from a life of misery. I never imagined that you would be the one to—" He broke off, his jaw tightening, then sighed. "You will succeed, Sparrow," he told me, as if willing the words to be true. "You *must* succeed. Even if everyone before you has failed, you will be the first to open the vault and retrieve whatever lies within. I've seen you work. I've watched you from the moment you took on your first job. You have something no other thief has."

Unable to meet his intense stare, I dropped my gaze. "Luck," I muttered, managing to dredge up a smirk.

"There is no such thing as luck," Vahn said. "Even if there was, what do I keep telling you? Don't rely on luck—it's more fickle than the sands. No, you have something more—something unlike anything I've seen. It's almost as if . . ." He paused, deliberately stopping himself.

I frowned. "As if what?" I asked softly.

"It doesn't matter." Abruptly, he straightened and turned around, slamming the door on the conversation. "You have your mission," he said as we started walking again. "Be sure you have everything you need to complete it. I'll come for you tomorrow, after Demon Hour. Take whatever resources you require from the guild—you have access to anything you think you'll need."

"Really?" Despite my disappointment and repressed fear of the upcoming mission, I grinned. "So those crates of explosives Amal and Neem stole from the quarry warehouse..."

I didn't expect him to answer, but when he did, it did not assuage my fears. "Whatever you want," Vahn said softly, "as long as you come back with the stone."

SIX

The guild was still fairly empty when we returned in the wee hours before dawn, its members either still out on other jobs or sleeping away the last minutes of night. Vahn immediately went to his office, shutting and locking the door behind him. Clearly, he did not want to talk to me. I stared at the closed door for a long moment, trying to gather the courage to step up and pound on it with a fist; surely *that* would get Vahn's attention, if not his approval. But the seconds ticked by in agonizing silence, and I finally turned away. Annoying the Guildmaster wouldn't get me what I was looking for, and I had other things to worry about now.

I wandered to my room, sat down on my cot, and tried to plan out a strategy for traversing the undercity. That sounded like a good idea; Vahn was always saying I needed to plan more, instead of my usual tactic of jumping into a heist headfirst and hoping things worked out. Which, to be fair, they usually did. But my mind kept spinning in circles, and fear crawled along the edge of my thoughts, making it hard to concentrate. I did not like being underground. I much preferred the rooftops and open sky; the higher and more open, the better. Going into the sewers with Vahn had been bad enough—how was I going to survive an ancient, cursed city and the buried vault of a Deathless King?

A soft tap on my door made me blink and glance up. Wondering if it was Vahn, I rose and walked across the room to crack open the door.

It wasn't Vahn.

"Hey," Jeran greeted, almost shyly. His smile was crooked, and he scratched the back of his neck in an atypically uncertain manner. "I saw you come back with Vahn, and Rala said you were out all night. Everything okay?"

"Um . . ." My heartbeat picked up, and my mouth was suddenly dry for a different reason. "Yeah," I managed, taking a step back and opening the door. "I'm fine. Vahn . . . had something he needed to show me. You want to come in?"

He did, stepping over the threshold and fully into my room, causing my stomach to start those crazy cartwheels again. What was happening here? Jeran had been in my room before; this wasn't anything new. Why was I having such crazy reactions to his presence? Because of that one moment on the rooftop? That had just been a second, and nothing had really happened.

Maybe something would happen now.

Jeran's dark eyes studied my face. "You sure you're all right?" he asked. "You look . . . scared." One hand rose and gently brushed a strand of hair from my cheek, sending a tingle all the way up my spine. "Anything you want to talk about?"

My heart thudded in my ears. He was so close; his clothes smelled of dust and the spiced wine he liked to order at the bar. His long fingers moved from my hair to the edge of my hood, starting to brush it back.

Fear prickled the back of my neck, the anxiety of having my

face exposed rising to the surface. I stepped away quickly, taking myself and my hood out of his reach. I couldn't think about *this* now; I had to be completely focused for what I had to do. Distractions would get me killed. "It's nothing," I said, and Jeran immediately dropped his arm. "I have another job, that's all."

"Another job? From the Guildmaster?" Jeran shook his head, his demeanor turning sullen. "Must be nice," he muttered. "Years of working for the guild, doing everything he asks without screwing up, and it's still not enough for him to take notice. Maybe if I was a girl, he'd pay more attention to me."

"Jeran . . ." I sighed. I wasn't in the mood for this. I had my own troubles to focus on without having to listen to his jealousy issues. "Trust me," I told him, "I'm not at all eager to do this next job. I'd trade it to you in a heartbeat if I could."

"So why don't you?" Jeran asked. I blinked at him, and he shrugged. "Give the job to me," he reasoned. "We'll say we did it together. I'll even share the credit with you."

I grimaced. "I can't do that."

"You mean you won't." Jeran's voice was morose again. "Because you like the attention. Because it means you keep getting to be the Guildmaster's favorite."

"Goddess, will you stop with the hard-on for Vahn," I snapped. "It's not like that at all. This job isn't even from him, anyway."

Oops—I hadn't meant to say that. I desperately hoped Jeran would drop the whole subject out of embarrassment, but his eyes narrowed and he instantly pounced on my last statement.

"Wait. If you're not doing it for Vahn, who are you doing it for? He's the Guildmaster. He gives the . . . oh."

Jeran was smart. Or at least, incredibly perceptive when it came to rank and prestige within the guild. I could see him putting two and two together and guessing the identity of the mysterious client. His expression darkened even more, and his eyes went cold.

"Jeran," I began, but he looked away and took a step back.

"I get it." His voice was flat, sounding like a stranger's. "So even *they're* taking notice of your accomplishments now. Congratulations." Even angry, he knew better than to openly discuss the Circle with anyone. "You're really moving up in the guild. Be sure to remember us petty thieves when you get rich."

I ground my teeth, wanting to tell him that working for the Circle was not the prestigious position he thought it was. It was, instead, quite terrible and frightening, and I would give anything not to have to do the mission they were sending me on. But there was nothing I could say that would salvage this conversation, so I simply said, "I think you should go now, Jeran."

"Yeah." For the briefest of moments, a glimmer of regret, maybe even shame, crossed his face. Taking another step back, he paused, as if he was going to say something else. But then he ducked his head, left the room, and shut the door behind him.

Confused and, for some reason, a little sad, I sat down on my cot again and scrubbed a hand over my face. Jeran had always teased me about being "the favorite child" in the guild, and though his pokes were sometimes sharper than they needed to be, we'd never actually fought about it. He'd sounded more than irritated tonight; he'd sounded bitter and angry, as if he truly resented me.

Lying back on my cot, I stared at the ceiling, my brain swirling in aimless, chaotic circles. Eventually, out of sheer frustration, I hopped up and went down to the tavern, hoping I wouldn't meet Jeran or Vahn on the way.

"A bit early for beer, little dust sparrow," Rala said, smiling as she slid a tankard across the counter toward me. I grabbed the mug and emptied half of it immediately, feeling it hit my empty stomach like a rock. It did nothing to drown the fear coiled around my insides.

Lowering my arm, I found Rala watching me in concern. Her kind brown eyes took in my face, my messy, tousled clothes, the half-empty tankard in my hand, and her expression softened. "Another job?" she guessed.

I nodded.

"Something for Vahn?"

"Sort of."

Her nails drummed the counter. "Jeran was in here earlier, drowning himself in d'wevryn ale. Boy was in a sulk that put Dahveen to shame. I assume he knows?"

I nodded again, feeling a fresh bloom of annoyance, confusion, and hurt at the reminder.

Rala sighed. "Sparrow," she said, and hesitated, as if debating whether to share whatever information she had. "Jeran is . . . well, he is crazy about you, you know that, right?"

I snorted. "No, he's not," I protested. "I've known him forever. If he is, he never shows it."

"Of course not," Rala said. "He's a boy. A very confused boy, trying to reconcile his feelings for you with his desire to be the very best in the guild. He tries so hard to be noticed, to get Vahn to see his accomplishments. Unfortunately, there is someone standing in his way."

"Me," I said glumly.

Rala chuckled. "So humble, this one," she mused, shaking her head. "But yes. You are both his muse and his rival. You have the attention of the Guildmaster, something he desperately craves. Every time you succeed, he feels himself falling further behind."

"So what am I supposed to do about it?" I muttered.

"Nothing." Rala put a hand on my arm. "Keep doing what you do best, little dust sparrow. And don't worry about Jeran. This is his insecurity to work through, not yours. If Fate wills it, it will happen. If not . . ." She shrugged. "Then his ambition will eventually drive him to madness, and you won't have to worry about it any longer."

She meant it as a joke, but I winced. "Thanks, Rala. I feel so much better now."

"Anything for you." She smiled, and I felt my spirits lift just a little. "Now, are there any other pressing life choices I can help you with?"

Only if you know how to obtain a memory stone from a dead city without getting skewered by traps or activating an ancient curse.

I sighed. "Nothing else I can think of."

Vahn came for me right after Demon Hour.

"Ready?" he announced after I opened my door to his brusque knock. I nodded, and he quickly scanned my outfit: work gloves, rope and grapple, and the satchel over my shoulders that held a few extra things—flint and steel, bandages, waterskins. "You have everything you need?"

I shrugged. "We'll know soon enough. I didn't have time to run to the docks and pick up a curse-protection talisman from Nabba, so..."

Vahn managed not to roll his eyes, though I could tell he wanted to. Nabba was a barely tolerated member of the guild, a weaselly little man who sold "protection" and "anti-curse" talismans to unsuspecting souls coming off the sand striders. They were as effective at warding off evil as rotten fruit was at repelling flies.

I dredged up a weak grin. "I'm as ready as I'll ever be."

"Let's go, then," Vahn said quietly. "The entrance we want isn't far."

We left the warehouse, walking into the streets of the Docks District, haze thick on the air. People were just beginning to return to work; dock loaders and sailors passed us on their way to the piers, moving slowly as the air was still chokingly warm. I kept my hood low and my scarf over my lower face as we continued through the dust-filled streets.

Vahn led me to a deserted section of the docks, over a crumbling stone wall to the edge of the Dust Sea itself. Below an abandoned, broken pier, a large stone drainpipe jutted out of the wall. A trickle of greenish water dribbled from the pipe, only to be swallowed by the dust waves below.

"The grate is open," Vahn said, hanging back from the edge of the pipe. Six feet below us, the great Dust Sea lapped against the wall, the constant haze making my throat itch. "Follow the pipe into the sewers. The entrance to the underground ruins is marked with a door. You can't miss it. Once you're in the ancient city, pay special attention to the path marked on the map. You don't want to become lost down there. Any questions?"

So many. But none he would be willing to answer. I chewed my bottom lip a moment in thought. "What do I do when I have the memory stone?"

"Come straight back to the guild," Vahn replied. "Don't stop, and don't talk to anyone. Do not show the stone to anyone but me, understand?"

"Yeah."

He shifted, facing me dead-on. The suns overhead cast his face in shadow, and his eyes were haunted as they met mine. "You can do this," he said, his voice softer than I'd ever heard it before. "I know you can. You will succeed where everyone before you has failed." His arms rose, and his thick, calloused hands gently gripped my shoulders. "You can do this," he repeated, more of a mantra to himself than to me. "You will succeed, and you will come back. I believe in you, Sparrow. Promise me that you won't fail."

My throat closed. I took a quick breath to open it and managed a shaky, defiant grin. "Fail?" I repeated. "I don't think I know what that means. Maybe you could tell me? Because I've only ever done it once or . . . oh, wait. Never. I've done it never."

Vahn didn't smile. I sighed and put one of my hands over his, gazing up at him seriously now. "I've got this," I told him. "I won't fail, Vahn. When have I ever not come through before?"

He still didn't smile. His grip on my shoulders tightened, and he seemed on the verge of pulling me into a hug, something he had never done before. Not once. Even when I was a toddler, the closest he had ever come to showing affection was a quick arm squeeze or a pat on the head. Tears were not encouraged in the Thieves Guild. Moments of weakness were shunned and ridiculed, so I had learned to never let anyone see me cry. I had been hugged once in my entire life, by Rala, who had found me crouched wet-faced and sniffling behind the bar for some reason I don't even remember now. She had knelt down and held me tight, and I remembered first the shock and confusion of being that close to someone, followed by the feeling of never wanting to let go.

I had been five years old at the time. And sometimes, I wished Rala had never found me huddled behind the bar that evening. If I'd never learned what being hugged felt like, I wouldn't miss it. I wouldn't hold my breath every time Vahn stepped close, wondering if this would be the day his perfect control would crack. So far, it never had.

It wouldn't be today, either. Dropping his arms, Vahn gave me a brisk nod and stepped back, avoiding my eyes. Disappointment fluttered my stomach, but I squashed it down. "You have your mission," he said shortly. "I'll see you when you return to the guild. Fate be with you."

I didn't answer, and for half a heartbeat, he paused, as if wanting to say something more. Something . . . personal. That he was proud, perhaps. That he never doubted me. But then he turned and walked away, up the embankment, and disappeared over the wall. He didn't look back.

I clenched a fist and swallowed the sour feeling in my throat. From here on out, I'd be on my own.

I hooked my fingers into the mesh grate covering the pipe and pulled. It swung open with a rusty screech, revealing a dark, narrow stretch of tunnel beyond. After double-checking my person to make sure I had everything I needed, I stepped into the pipe and closed the grate behind me, slipping from the light into the darkness of the underground.

The sewers reeked. Especially right after Demon Hour, when everything had had time to fester in the heat. I pulled my scarf over my nose and mouth—it worked almost as well for lessening smells as it did for filtering out dust—and unrolled the scroll the Circle had given me. The first part of the map contained only instructions: *From the pipe, go due north until you come to an intersection, then head west. Keep walking. You'll know the door when you see it.*

"Very cryptic," I muttered. "At least this part is easy."

Easy, but not pleasant. I hugged the tunnel's narrow walkway, avoiding the water that flowed through the center channel. Eventually, it would empty into the Dust Sea and be swallowed in the sand. Out of sight, out of mind. Overhead, life in Kovass went on, the bustle of daily life filtering through the drains above and echoing down the endless tunnels. Vendors shouted, civilians milled on the streets, and guards patrolled, the stomp of their boots ringing over the stones. No one suspected that a lone dust rat was creeping through the tunnels below their feet.

I didn't like it. I wanted to see the sky over my head; the

cramped, claustrophobic tunnels made me jumpy. Also, it really, *really* stank down there.

I walked for a long time, eventually reaching the intersection marked on the map and turning due west. The tunnel went on, seemingly endless, as I kept looking for the cryptic "door." Nothing stood out to me, and after a while, I began to worry that I had become lost. Had I missed it somehow? The instructions didn't give me a lot to go on, but I hadn't seen any doors, mysterious or otherwise, on my journey through the sewers.

The tunnels grew darker, the walkway I was on getting even more narrow and crumbling. I was on the verge of turning around and retracing my steps when I heard something in the passage beyond.

Freezing in place, I held my breath and listened. Footsteps, walking quietly toward me down a side passage. Someone, or something, was coming toward me.

I closed a hand around one of my daggers, easing back a step. I hadn't expected to run into anything down here except rodents and bugs, but all sorts of stories existed about things living in the sewers—everything from deranged madmen that ate human flesh to giant roaches mutated on waste and filth. Not that I believed those stories, but none of them sounded pleasant.

I teetered on the verge of fleeing. Of slipping down a side passage and avoiding whatever was coming toward me in the tunnels. But I was also afraid that if I left this particular passage, I would never find it again. I would lose my way in this labyrinthine sewer system where all the tunnels looked the same. And then I would either have to return to Vahn empty-handed, or start over from the beginning. Neither was an appealing option.

Pressing my back against the crumbling stones, I waited.

The footsteps grew louder, and a voice began drifting through the tunnels, low and mumbling, too soft to make out the actual words. A normal person who had somehow gotten lost in the sewers? Or a disease-ridden cannibal who had lost all semblance of sanity? My heart pounded, and I tightened my grip on my dagger. The person might be harmless, but in my world, it was better to be safe and assume the worst than to be wrong and dead.

I waited until the footsteps were just around the corner, then, with a yell, I lunged, aiming my dagger at what I hoped was neck-height of the stranger. I caught a split-second glance of a startled face, sun-bleached hair and wide blue eyes, before my brain registered that I knew this person. Or at least, I'd seen him before.

"Aagh!" the stranger yelped, smoothly leaping back from my blade. His reaction was immediate; he moved so quickly, I wouldn't have been able to stab him even if I was truly trying. "Wait wait wait, don't hurt me," he said, backing away with both arms raised. "I don't have anything that you want, I swear."

"You!" I exclaimed, lowering my weapon. The boy from the rooftop blinked at me, looking just as surprised to see me as I was him. "What are you doing down here?" I demanded.

"What am I doing here?" He shrugged, and that bright grin came creeping back as he recognized me. "Just going where the threads of Fate take me."

"Fate took you into the sewers?"

"Well, I took me into the sewers." He laced both hands

behind his head, looking nonchalant. "But I was following where Fate told me to go. I'm a Fatechaser, you see. That's what we do."

I shook my head, confused. The Fatechasers were an enigma to pretty much everyone. They wandered the kingdoms and the lands beyond, chasing their fates. Whatever *that* meant. How could you chase your own fate? It made no sense to me, but I wasn't going to ask him to explain. It was widely stated that talking to a Fatechaser about Fate was akin to repeatedly bashing your forehead against a brick wall, something I wasn't eager to experience. "But why are you in the sewers in the first place?" I asked instead.

"I really have no idea." The Fatechaser grinned, completely at ease with the idea. "I just had the strangest feeling that I needed to go into the sewers today. But now the answer seems obvious." He cocked his head, regarding me in a curious, appraising manner. "I was fated to run into you. That's the only reason I can see for being here. So here we are."

"Here we are," I agreed, and took a step back. I didn't have time for this, whatever *this* was. "And here I go. So now you can find the nearest ladder out of here and head on back to the surface. It's not safe down here."

"Leave?" He seemed genuinely surprised. "Oh no, I can't leave. I was supposed to find you. We were supposed to run into each other."

"What?"

"Our first meeting on the rooftop? That was no coincidence. And now I run into you again, wandering through the sewers?" He shook his head with a smile. "There are no accidents, not with me. Our fates are intertwined, our paths connected, and we have to follow them wherever they take us. There's a reason I ran into you."

"No, there's not," I insisted. I couldn't have this boy following me into the city of the Deathless King. He would certainly get himself killed. "You can't come with me," I told him. "Not where I'm going. Leave now."

"Sorry," he said cheerfully. "I don't question what Fate points me at. Unless you're going to kill me here, I'm afraid you're stuck with me."

I scowled. I didn't want to hurt this boy, but if I didn't scare him off and keep him from following me around the city, either he would die, or I would. He might be a Fatechaser, but he had probably never ventured into a mysterious underground city filled with traps, strange magics, and ancient curses. He didn't seem the type to pick his way through locks, avoid enemies, and keep himself hidden. Or . . . maybe he was? I admittedly knew very little about Fatechasers, but it didn't matter. I could not, under any circumstances, fail this mission. Which meant I wasn't going to be able to look out for him or pull him out of danger if he needed help. I did not need this distraction, even if he was strangely charming.

I was going to have to drive him away. Even if I didn't want to. He was just going to get us both killed, otherwise. Raising my dagger, I stepped up and pressed the blade against his sternum, the point just shy of drawing blood. "That can be arranged," I said, feeling him stiffen. "You can't follow me if you're dead."

His piercing blue eyes met mine, unafraid, and the smile he offered held the barest hint of resignation. Raising both hands from his sides, palms turned out, he continued to smile and hold my gaze. "If it is my fate to die in a sewer today, so be it," he said calmly. "Not the glorious end I would've hoped for, but at least my killer is beautiful."

I felt my cheeks grow hot. He wasn't being honest, of course; people would say anything with a knife at their throat. But he *was* entirely serious about dying in a sewer if that was his fate.

Dammit. Well, he had called my bluff, and I certainly couldn't kill him now. Not that I was going to, anyway, but it would've been impossible with those blue puppy-dog eyes gazing at me without a shred of guile or fear. Stepping back, I lowered the blade with a sigh and glared at him in exasperation.

"Fine," I said. "Do what you want. Just remember, you're on your own. Don't expect me to save your skin if we run into something dangerous."

He gave a very flashy bow, grinning brightly as he straightened. "You won't regret it," he promised. "You have Halek the Fatechaser with you today, and fortune smiles on me more than most. So shall we go and see what Fate has in store for us, Lady . . . ?"

Despite myself, I felt a smile tug at my lips, but I quickly shut it down. Halek the Fatechaser wouldn't be around long enough for me to get to know him. "I'm no lady," I told him. "But you can call me Sparrow."

"Sparrow," he repeated, and gave a single nod. "It is an honor and a pleasure," he said seriously. "Shall we go, then? I will follow you, until Fate dictates otherwise."

"Sure," I said, turning away. "Just try to keep up."

I didn't tell him that he was probably going to die down here.

SEVEN

As luck—or Fate—would have it, we found the door not long after.

Halek was never completely silent. Even when he was just following me through the tunnels, he sang softly or hummed under his breath. He did have a very nice singing voice, I noticed, but I was uneasy at how much attention we could be drawing to ourselves. Maybe in the sewers, all we would've attracted were curious rats, but down in the undercity, anything that took notice of us would probably be very dangerous.

"Tell me about yourself, Sparrow," he urged after a few minutes of walking. "What do you do? Have you lived here long?"

I eyed him warily. "Why do you want to know?"

"Just curious." He shrugged with that disarming smile. "I meet so many interesting people on my travels. I like to get to know them a bit before moving on."

"I've never left Kovass," I said, deliberately ignoring the other question. "I was born in the city, and I've lived here my whole life."

"Oh," Halek said. His tone was faintly sympathetic. "No desire to go anywhere else? See what other places are out there? See what lies beyond the Dust Sea and the Endless Dunes and the Broken Plateau?"

I hesitated. Many times, I'd imagined myself hopping aboard one of the sand striders and traveling across the Dust Sea to the lands beyond. I thought of the small box of treasures in my room, holding my dreams of someday getting out of the Thieves Guild. But I knew they were just fleeting daydreams. There was no way I could leave Kovass. I belonged to the guild, but more than that, I was a simple thief. That was my fate, my place in the Weave. I didn't know how to be anything other than what I was.

But it was too hard to explain all this to Halek, so I just shrugged and said, "Not really."

"Pity." Halek didn't elaborate. "Well . . ." He shrugged. "If you ever get the desire to leave the city and see the world, I know of several places that shouldn't be missed."

"I'll keep that in mind," I muttered, then came to a dead stop in the middle of the passage. Across the channel of dark, sluggish water, a narrow door was set into the stones. The faded image of a skull wearing a pointed crown had been painted on the wood.

You'll know the door when you see it, the instructions had said. This had to be it.

"Well, that's interesting," Halek commented, observing the door with mild curiosity. "If I were by myself, that would definitely be a door that begged exploring."

"Lucky for you," I said, moving toward the edge of the walk, "that's exactly where we're going."

"Oh, well, Fate continues to smile on me today."

We hopped across the channel, Halek easily leaping the distance. At least he was fairly agile, from what I'd observed. I didn't know if he could keep up with me over the rooftops, but he could jump a gap without falling in.

At the door, I hesitated again, glancing at my companion. "Are you sure you want to keep following me?" I asked. "This leads into the undercity, where they say a Deathless King used to rule. The whole city is under an ancient curse. I don't know what we'll find down there, but I do know it'll be dangerous. You really should leave now."

I was trying, again, to scare him away. Usually, mention of a curse would make even the most stalwart hesitate. Unfortunately, I'd forgotten that Fatechasers did not react to danger like normal people.

"Undercity? Deathless King?" His eyes practically glowed with excitement. "I had no idea. I was intrigued before—now a pack of wild sand wolves wouldn't be able tear me away."

I ground my teeth. "All right, fine. But no singing."

The door was locked, but the lock was weak and simple and I had it open after a few minutes. I pulled the door back. It gave a rather ominous groan, and an eerie breath of wind whispered out of the opening, ruffling my hair and smelling of dust and decay. Beyond the doorframe was a tiny room with a trio of rusty copper pipes running from floor to ceiling. Beside the pipes, a circular hole with a metal ladder descended into the unknown.

My skin prickled, the hairs on my neck standing up. But the feeling wasn't coming from the hole. Stepping away from Halek, I turned back and gazed down the tunnel we'd just come through, peering into the gloom and shadows. The passageway was empty, but my heart beat faster, a chill crawling up my spine like a spider. I couldn't see anything in the clinging darkness, but fear suddenly clutched at my heart with icy fingers.

Something was coming. I didn't know how I knew, but I was absolutely sure I didn't want to meet it.

"Sparrow?" Halek touched my elbow, making me jump. I wasn't used to being touched, especially by strangers, but his blue eyes showed only concern. "Are you all right?" he asked. "You've gone pale. Do you hear something?"

I silenced my churning stomach and turned back to the doorway. Years of following my gut told me I shouldn't ignore the instinct, but I couldn't turn around and go home. "I'm fine," I told Halek, ducking through the frame. "Come on, let's go."

"Right behind you."

Stepping to the edge of the hole, I peered down. It plunged straight into pitch darkness, and I couldn't see any sign of the bottom. On impulse, I dropped my torch into the hole. It fell for a long, long time, becoming a mere spark in the darkness before hitting the bottom and instantly snuffing out.

"That's a long way down," Halek commented. "And it's very dark."

"Hang on," I muttered, reaching into my pack. "I have another torch."

He put a hand on my arm, startling me again. He touched so easily, without thought; it was a little disconcerting, but at the same time, completely without malice, so I didn't mind it as much as if it had been someone else. Growing up with thieves, pickpockets, and petty thugs had taught me the value of keeping my distance.

"Just a moment," he told me. "I have something better."

Reaching into a pouch at his belt, he withdrew something small and round on a cord. A yellowish stone, but translucent, like it was made of honey. Cupping it in his hands, he blew on it gently, and a soft orange light began radiating from the tiny stone, giving off a very lanternlike glow.

Smiling, he handed it to me. "A glowstone from the underground kingdom of the troblin," he said as I stared at the stone in amazement. It pulsed softly in my palm like an enormous firefly. "If the light starts to fade, just breathe on it again. It's triggered by the heat of your breath."

"Thank you," I murmured. How valuable was this stone? I'd never seen anything like it. I'd only heard stories of the troblin, a race of short, green-skinned people who lived in caves and tunnels so the sunlight wouldn't hurt their eyes. "I'll be sure to give it back," I told him, though I was extremely tempted to keep it. Our fence would probably faint if I brought this little gem into his office.

Halek chuckled and shook his head. "I have a dozen of them," he said easily. "Keep it. That one is yours."

I tied the cord of the glowstone onto my belt as Halek pulled out a second one and draped it around his neck. With the lights of the little stones throwing off a comforting glow, I stepped onto the ladder and began the descent into the pitch blackness.

The shaft continued for a long time. And for a while, the only sounds were our breathing and the clunk of our boots against the metal rungs. Several were broken or missing, causing me to kick frantically in the near blackness for the next rung.

The air turned colder and began to smell of salt and brine. I took the next step down and my boot plunged into icy water that made me yelp and jerk my foot back up.

"What's wrong?" Halek called from above me.

I peered down. The ladder ended in a pool of black water that glimmered dully in the light of the glowstones. Gazing around, I saw a stone tunnel half submerged on the opposite side of the shaft. Judging from how much of the tunnel was still visible, the water level was only a few feet deep. Still, I hadn't expected to have to get wet today.

Gritting my teeth, I stepped off the ladder, sinking past my knees in cold, brackish-smelling water.

"Was that a splash?" Halek wondered aloud, just as he too reached the end of the ladder and dipped a foot into the water. "Oh, that's cold! Why is there water down here? Have we hit a lake or something?"

"It must be the underground sea," I murmured. Glancing at the tunnel, I grimaced. It looked like it slanted downward. "We're going to get even wetter."

"Well," Halek said cheerfully, landing next to me with a splash, "it's a good thing I know how to swim."

I didn't know how to swim. Halek aside, I didn't know anyone who knew how to swim. There was no body of water anywhere near Kovass large enough that you would have to worry about drowning—there was only the Dust Sea, and if you fell into *that*, you were doomed to suffocate and lie at the bottom until the waves of dust and sand stripped the flesh from your bones.

Halek glanced at me and smiled. "Don't worry," he assured

me. "If we get into trouble, I won't let you drown."

It was an odd feeling, walking through the tunnel. The water in the passage reached my waist and was colder than anything I had ever experienced before. Dripping echoed through the passage, and the waves from our passing sloshed against the stone wall. After several minutes of walking, my body adjusted to the temperature and wasn't quite so cold. It did not adjust to the unsettling feeling of being underground in a narrow tunnel full of water.

"I think I see a light ahead," Halek said at length.

Which should've been impossible, because nothing lived down here, but he was right. There was a faint glow in the darkness ahead of us, not orange like torchlight or candlelight; this was ghostly blue-white luminance. Warily, we kept going, pushing through the water until the tunnel abruptly opened up and we stood at the edge of something impossible.

"Oh," Halek breathed behind me. "By the Weaver, it's beautiful."

We were at the edge of an enormous cavern, so huge I couldn't see the ceiling overhead. Glowing lichen and fungi grew on the walls and floor, lighting the space with an eerie, ethereal glow. Spores drifted through the air like blue-white fireflies, showing us the marvel we had stumbled onto.

A city sprawled around us, broken, crumbled, half sunk in the lapping water. Walls leaned against each other, columns lay shattered or stood half erect, domed roofs jutted out of the water like the tops of enormous mushrooms. Buildings lay half submerged beneath the surface, chillingly frozen in time.

"The fallen city of the Deathless King," Halek whispered, his eyes huge as he took it all in. He blinked, then turned to me with a curious look. "So what are we here for, anyway? I didn't dare ask before, but I'm guessing we didn't find that door by accident. Did you come down here to explore the city, or are you looking for something special?"

I shivered and pulled the map from my satchel, then unrolled it with shaking hands. In the eerie spore light and the pulse from our glowstones, I studied the scroll before me. "We must be here," I muttered, tapping a circle drawn on the parchment in red ink. "And here"—I traced a finger north on the map to the prominently marked *X* at the top—"is where we have to go."

"And . . . where is that?" Halek wondered.

"I have no idea," I confessed. "And by the way, yes, I *am* looking for something in particular. I just can't tell you what it is."

The Fatechaser nodded, seeming unconcerned. "Fair enough." He smiled. "Well then, shall we go and see for ourselves?"

We climbed from the ditch onto the streets of the ancient city, still gazing around in wonder. Kovass was the largest city this side of the Dust Sea, a sprawling behemoth of wealth, industry, and power. Because of the underground ocean, the city possessed the one thing that no one could live without: an infinite supply of water.

This city, broken, crumbling, and shattered, made Kovass seem small. In its prime, it must've been staggering.

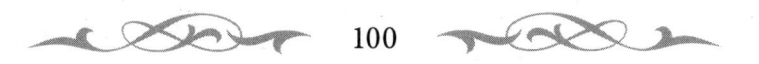

"This is amazing," Halek mused as we walked down one of the raised streets. He kept his voice hushed, barely above a whisper. The city around us was eerily silent and dead, but I couldn't shake the feeling of eyes on me, watching from hidden nooks and crannies. "Can you imagine what it would've looked like at its peak? I wonder how many people lived here."

"And what happened to them when the city fell," I muttered.

The street emptied into a large square, shattered white stone columns surrounding the perimeter. I couldn't be certain, but the stones beneath our boots felt like marble. Which would've been ludicrously expensive. I'd heard that the king's palace in Kovass had floors made of marble and gold, but us poor commoners had to be content with limestone and mud.

In the center of the square stood an enormous statue of what I thought was a person, though it was hard to tell, as the top half of the figure was missing. I looked down at the map again, Halek peering over my shoulder.

"I think we're here," he said, pointing to a spot on the map that did look like some kind of open square. "Looks like we're getting closer."

A breath of wind smelling of dust and dry leaves whispered through the square. It slithered across my skin and raised the hairs on my arms. At my waist, the glowstone flickered and went out.

My stomach turned, and I instinctively looked around for a place to hide. The openness of the square made my skin itch. It felt like the eyes of the city had turned inward, searching for the intruders in its midst. I darted across the stones to the nearest clump of shadow, leaving Halek to scramble after me.

Reaching one of the broken columns, I ducked behind it and peered out at the square. Halek pressed close, his heat and nearness making my nerves prickle.

"Did you see something?" he whispered. He had smartly closed his hand over his own glowstone, dousing the light. I pressed a finger to my lips and scowled at him, and his other hand went to cover his mouth.

A sound drifted across the stones—faint, shuffling footsteps, like someone dragging a wounded foot behind them. Biting my lip, I watched as something emerged on the other side of the square.

It was humanoid, and at first, that was all I could see. Wrapped in tattered gray rags, it limped slowly across the ground, dragging a long strip of cloth behind it.

My skin crawled, and an icy chill crept up my spine. There was something inherently... *wrong* about this creature. Not natural. As it continued across the square, drawing closer to our hiding place, the dragging cloth caught on a jutting corner of rock. The creature was jerked to a halt, but with a tearing sound, the cloth tore away, revealing dry, bleached bones underneath.

I bit my lip to stifle a horrified gasp. There was no skin, no flesh, just stripped leg bones that somehow still carried the shuffling body across the square, its top half still wrapped in rags. I could see why it was limping now—its left foot was missing. The broken ankle joint made faint clicking, scraping sounds as it hobbled over the stones and then vanished into the shadows.

Behind me, Halek let out a slow breath. "Undead," he whispered. "I've heard rumors that sometimes, in the darkest, most cursed places, they still walk." He paused, as if pondering that statement, then flashed a wry grin. "This is indeed a cursed city. I *am* lucky I ran into you today, Sparrow. Just think of what I would've missed."

I wrinkled my nose at him. "You have a strange idea of luck," I whispered back. My voice shook, but only a little. Walking skeletons? Cursed undead? Neither Vahn nor the Circle had prepared me for *this*. And the thought of running into more undead made my blood curdle. How many more skeletons roamed the broken streets and crumbling alleyways of the undercity? I didn't want to find out.

"Come on," I whispered to Halek. I was not having fun on this mission. I no longer wanted to prove myself to Vahn or the Circle; I just wanted it to be over. "Let's go. The sooner we find what I came for, the sooner we can leave this place."

We continued into the dead city, much warier now. I scanned every shadow, nook, and dark cranny for skeletons, straining my ears to hear the scrape of bones on rock. The streets remained silent and empty as we picked our way through ruined buildings and over crumbling walls, the smell of stone and the faint scent of decay clinging to everything.

As we made our way over a cracked stone bridge spanning a yawning chasm, the stones under my boots trembled and an ominous rumble echoed through the air. Instinctively, I leaped forward, just as the entire section of the bridge I had been standing on crumbled and fell. Behind me, Halek gave a yelp and tried to lunge to safety, but he was in the center of the crumbling section and wasn't able to move fast enough. He plummeted with the falling rocks, but at the last second, his hands hit the edge of the hole, jerking him to a halt and leaving him dangling over a drop into nothing.

"Halek!" Heart pounding, I knelt and grabbed one of his wrists to stop him from sliding into the abyss. I set my jaw and pulled as Halek kicked and scrabbled and finally clawed his way back onto what remained of the bridge.

I fell to my backside on the stone, pebbles digging into my palms, and Halek dropped to his knees, sucking in air as we waited for our heartbeats to return to normal.

"Well." Halek looked up at me with a weak grin. "That was exciting," he panted. "Nothing like a near-death experience to make you feel alive. Though it would've been embarrassing if my fate was to fall to my death in an abandoned city." He grimaced and sat back on his heels, regarding me with solemn blue eyes. "I think I owe you my life."

I shook my head, waving it off. "Don't worry about it." I didn't like to be owed things. Sometimes people got strange about debts, and I didn't want the attachment that came with them. "Just buy me a drink later and we'll call it even."

Halek nodded and glanced at the section of missing bridge. "I'll do that. Though it looks like we'll have to find another way back," he observed wryly. "I could probably jump that gap, if something nasty was chasing me, but I'd rather not have to."

He stood and dusted off his knees, then held out a hand to help me up. I took it, but as he pulled me to my feet, I caught something from the corner of my eye.

Across the destroyed section of bridge, back in the direction we'd come, a figure was watching us from the shadows.

I jerked, wrenching my hand from Halek's grip, and spun toward the end of the bridge, squinting into the shadows.

Nothing was there.

Halek gazed at me in confusion, then turned as well. "Do you see something?"

My heart thudded in my ears. The shadows were nearly impenetrable, but I knew there had been someone—something—watching us across the chasm. That same frisson of fear and dread crept up my spine, and the section of bridge we stood on suddenly felt very exposed. I needed to get back into the darkness and shadows, out of sight of whatever was hunting us.

"Halek," I ventured, after we were safely away from the bridge. "You know a lot about other kingdoms, right?"

He cocked his head at me. "A bit," he replied with an easy shrug. "More than most, I'd say. Why?"

"What do you know about the iylvahn?"

His brow furrowed, and then he smiled. If he was confused by the randomness of the question, he didn't say anything. "Ah, the iylvahn." He sighed. "I've only met a couple of them on my travels—they don't leave their homeland all that often. They're an aloof, secretive people, but their songs can bring tears to your eyes. One of my dreams is to see their great city in person—I've heard so many stories and rumors about it—but sadly, it remains as elusive as its legend."

"But what of the iylvahn themselves?" I asked. "Have you heard of something called a . . ." I had to think a moment. That conversation in the Temple of Fate had happened only yesterday, but it already seemed so long ago. "A kahjai," I finished. "Do you know what a kahjai is?"

Halek sobered. "The kahjai," he repeated. "I've heard a few stories of them. Much like the city, the truth about the kahjai is elusive, and is clouded by rumor and speculation.

"The iylvahn have a different view of Fate," Halek went on. "Very unlike Kovass, where it is believed that every person has a single place in the Tapestry of the World, and once you are born into your fate, you cannot leave it. Beggars are beggars, kings are kings, farmers are farmers, and so on."

Thieves are thieves, I added silently, and nodded.

"The iylvahn still revere Maederyss," Halek continued, "though she has a different name in their language. But they believe that Fate is less a tapestry and more of a tree. A beautiful, endlessly growing tree, with individual lives as branches that sprout and grow in different directions. You cannot change the Tree of Fate, but you can . . . nurture it, shall we say? Cultivate it along a certain path. Like trimming a bush of dead branches to help it flourish. Are you following me so far?"

"I think so."

Halek nodded. "The iylvahn are said to follow a seer," he continued. "One who can read the threads in the Weave, or the branches of the Tree of Fate, or whatever you want to call it. They can see which branches are blighted, or which threads are weak. If these spots are left unchecked, they might affect every branch or thread around them. A limb could die, or an entire section of cloth could unravel. The kahjai are the ones sent to remove these problems before they affect the whole."

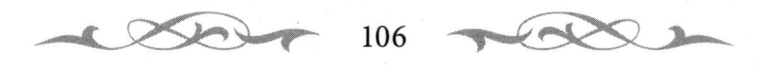

I drew in a slow breath of realization. Suddenly, that conversation between the high priestess and the iylvahn in the Temple of Fate made a lot more sense. *A kahjai in Kovass invites only death.* "So what you're saying is, the kahjai are assassins," I said.

Halek grimaced. "I don't know if they see themselves as such, but... yes. More or less," he admitted. "The kahjai are sent by the seer to kill individuals before they can negatively affect the world around them. Snipping the weakened threads from the cloth, or pruning the blight from the tree, so to speak." He shrugged, and that wry grin came creeping back. "Again, these are only stories I've heard, in places I really wasn't supposed to be. Honestly, with what I know, I'm surprised a kahjai hasn't been sent for me yet. The iylvahn are quite secretive, after all."

An assassin. I remembered the night of the circus, that fleeting glimpse of a figure on the rooftops as the man in the square twitched and died. Could it have been the iylvahn, sent to murder that man, even in a crowd?

Or had he been sent here to kill someone else?

Had he been sent here for me?

"But why this interest in the kahjai all of a sudden?" Halek wondered. "That's a bleak subject. If you want to hear about the iylvahn, I can tell you much more fascinating stories."

"Maybe later," I muttered. I didn't want to hear about the iylvahn, unless it was how to escape a ruthless assassin who might be chasing me through an ancient cursed city. Anything else, I really didn't care about.

"You have to wonder, though." Halek's voice drifted over the empty streets and bounced off shattered walls and crumbled buildings. Even his hushed tones seemed to echo in the dead silence of the ancient city. "This city is enormous. Bigger than Kovass, from the looks of it. It must've been thriving once. A few of these buildings alone would've held hundreds. So . . ." He looked at me, a question in his eyes.

I blinked back. "So what?"

"So where are all the people?" Halek waved a hand at the streets. "Their remains, I mean. We've been walking for a while, and we haven't seen a single bone, skull, or scrap of cloth. Except for the one that was shambling around, anyway." He grinned, somehow making light of a terrifying situation. "But where are all the others?" He gazed around the street, where a building had collapsed on top of another, crushing it fully. "This city wasn't just abandoned and forgotten," Halek mused, sounding more serious than he had before. "Something happened to it a long time ago. Something catastrophic. People would have died. Large numbers of them. It would have been chaos. Not that I want to see a bunch of skeletons lying in the streets, but there are no signs that anyone lived here."

I shivered. He was right, and the realization just made the ancient city that much eerier.

As I was imagining what kind of disaster had struck the ancient city, and what it must've been like for everyone who lived here, we pushed our way through a hole in a stone wall and came upon a massive palace.

I froze, and Halek sucked in an awed breath. In Kovass, I had seen the king's palace atop its hill, looming over the city. The striking blue-domed roofs could be seen from nearly anywhere in Kovass. I had never been there, of course. The high gate and the guards kept out the riffraff so that no unworthy commoner could touch the seat of the king.

Like the rest of the ancient city, this palace dwarfed the one in Kovass.

It was eerily intact, a looming behemoth of marble and stone surrounded by the remains of a dead city. Some of the walls had cracked with age, and several of the huge columns marching up to the doors were shattered and broken, but the palace itself stood like an indestructible giant at the end of the road. Gazing up at the domed roofs far, far overhead, I saw a glimmer of metallic yellow in the drifting spore lights, and realized they were gilded gold.

"Wow," Halek murmured beside me, also gazing up at the ludicrous amount of wealth and power on display. "The palace of a Deathless King. Can you imagine what this looked like when it was inhabited?"

I shook my head numbly. How had this place survived for so long without anyone knowing it was here? Well, except the Circle. Perhaps rumors that it was only a legend kept it safe. Or maybe the undead things wandering around the city killed anything that ventured too far in. Whatever the reason, I suspected my mission was about to get even more difficult.

"I bet no one has seen this place in a few hundred years," Halek said, his voice taut with excitement. "Maybe a few thousand. Please tell me we're going inside."

I glanced at the gaping doors, then down at the map, just to be certain. The X hovered at the top of the map, indicating a spot past the palace doors.

"Yeah," I said. "Whatever we're looking for, it's somewhere inside the palace. Through those doors."

"Perfect," Halek said, staring up at the palace with his hands on his hips. "And I'm sure there are no traps or curses or nasty surprises waiting for us at all."

I could appreciate the sarcasm, even though we were probably going to die.

EIGHT

Stepping through the doors of the ancient palace was like stepping into a tomb.

The city had been silent; except for our own footsteps and muted voices and the shuffling, undead thing, there had been no sounds as we made our way through the empty streets. But walking into the palace of the Deathless King felt like stepping into another world. The very air was oppressive, heavy with the stillness of time and laced with the scent of death. The chamber we entered was huge, with enormous pillars marching down either side. Statues stood in every corner, though many were shattered and lying in pieces on the floor, only the feet and calves still upright on their plinths. Rubble was piled along the walls and strewn across the floor, and bones were scattered throughout, bleached and white. I caught a glimpse of a forearm with a skeletal hand lying smashed beneath a column, and shuddered.

"There are your people," I whispered to Halek, who gazed through the door with a solemn look on his face. "At least some of them."

"Probably the guards who lived in the palace," Halek muttered. "Take a look at what they were guarding."

I followed his gaze and drew in a slow breath. A massive throne on a raised dais loomed against the far wall. It was made of marble laced with gold; even from across the chamber I could see it glimmering faintly around the back and arms. I had never seen a throne before, but this throne did not seem like the seat of a mere human. Perhaps a god had sat there once, gazing down on their tiny subjects below. A pair of statues flanked the throne, and though nothing remained but their legs, I could imagine their stony faces glaring down, warning the unworthy to keep their distance.

The entire chamber had been built to impress and intimidate, and it did that well. Goose bumps rose along my back and arms, a tremor creeping up my spine.

As I took a cautious step forward, a cold wind hissed through the chamber and a billow of thick dust rolled toward us out of the gloom. It flowed over us, heavy and choking, clogging my throat and stinging my eyes. It smelled . . . awful. Like bones and grave dirt and ancient, rotting rags. A whisper slithered through my head, wriggling in my ears and causing every hair on my body to stand straight up.

Leeeeeeeeaaaaaaaaaave.

The wind faded, the dust cloud dispersing in the air. Halek was bent over, one sleeve held to his nose, coughing violently. I sucked in a labored breath, feeling like my mouth was coated with ashes and my throat had been scraped dry.

"Ugh." Halek coughed once more and straightened, shaking his head. "Agh. Well, that was unpleasant. I'm assuming you heard that whisper, too?"

I nodded. "Something definitely doesn't want us here."

"And that's likely our only warning," Halek agreed. He

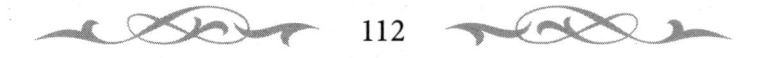

dusted off his hands, and a cloud billowed from his palms and drifted to the floor. "In tombs and ancient places like this, you usually get one indication that you should get out," he went on. "After that, things get intense." He paused, glancing at the shadow-cloaked halls beyond the chamber, and gave me a sober look. "I don't know what you've come here for, but I won't think less of you if you decide to turn back. I've heard the stories. If this is truly the palace of a Deathless King, anything is possible. We're talking ancient magic, after all."

I swallowed the scratchy dryness in my throat. Even if I wanted to, the Circle wouldn't let me abandon the mission. My choices were simple: succeed; die here; or forfeit not only my own life, but Vahn's as well.

More than that, I would not fail Vahn. I'd promised him I wouldn't. "No," I told Halek. "I can't turn back. It's not an option. I have to keep going."

Halek grinned, and for a moment, his smile lit up the room. "I was hoping you'd say that." He gestured toward the throne. "Shall we?"

We picked our way across the rocks and shattered stones. The air was heavy and stale, as if it hadn't moved in thousands of years. I felt eyes on me and glanced over to find the head of a statue staring up at me from the floor with a flat, stony gaze.

We came to the foot of the throne and stopped at the edge of the dais, gazing up at the huge marble chair. Not only was gold laced in intricate patterns through the white, but bits of turquoise and gemstones winked at us from beneath the layer of dust that had settled over everything.

Halek shook his head. "These Deathless Kings certainly liked to show off," he murmured. "Look at this. There's enough coin embedded in this chair to make you a merchant prince."

If thieves were allowed to become such things, I thought, staring at the throne. My fingers itched at the amount of wealth just paces away. Sapphires, emeralds, rubies, turquoise, and, of course, gold. What I could do with a literal fortune. I could finally buy my way out of the guild. Maybe secure passage aboard a sand strider and travel to the other side of the Dust Sea at last.

If I was willing to pry it off the throne of a Deathless King.

The gemstones twinkled in the darkness, seeming to mock me. Setting my jaw, I unsheathed one of my daggers and, before I could think too hard about what I was doing, inserted the point beneath the edge of an emerald set into the throne.

"Sparrow, wait," Halek hissed.

I dug the blade beneath the gem. The stone came loose, popped out, and clinked to the floor as the echo of Halek's warning died on the air. I bent down and grabbed it, then held it up to my face The gem was cool between my fingers, glittering with its own inner luminance. A breath seemed to echo through the chamber, wafting along the ceiling and dispersing into the unseen rooms beyond.

I held my breath and waited, but seconds ticked by and nothing happened. After a few heartbeats, Halek let out a puff of air and relaxed.

"Whew, okay," he breathed. "Looks like we're in the clear. Just be careful. You never know what will happen when you touch ancient treasure. I've heard stories of people who were struck down or cursed just for opening the wrong door."

I glanced at the gem in my palm. It seemed like a small, foolish thing to risk my life for now, but I closed my fingers around it and smirked. I was a thief. This was what I did, and not even the treasures of the Deathless King were off-limits. "I guess we got lucky."

"Seems that way." Halek ran a hand along the arm of the throne and shook his head. "At least the Deathless King isn't too touchy about his throne."

A hissing sigh rippled through the room, swirling dust eddies into the air. Along the wall closest to the dais, something moved.

I backed away, the emerald still clutched in my hand, watching as a bundle of rags and bones slithered over the rubble pile and spilled onto the floor. It wriggled for a moment, then started to rise. Bony hands emerged from the cloth, a rib cage gleamed through the rags, and a humanoid shape staggered forward on slender leg bones.

My stomach twisted so hard it felt like I'd been stabbed. The head beneath the tattered cowl was the bleached skull of some kind of canine, its narrow muzzle filled with sharp teeth. Hollow eye sockets fixed on me, and the jaws opened in an eerie parody of a howl, though no sound emerged.

Halek and I staggered back, as scraping, slithering sounds echoed all around us. More skeletons were crawling out of the rubble, dragging themselves across the floor before rising slowly to their feet. Bony jaws opened and closed with snapping, gnashing sounds that echoed through the chamber.

Halek grabbed my arm. "There!" he gasped, pointing across

the room, where an open doorway had once stood. It was half covered by a large rubble pile, but I could see the gap beyond. Unfortunately, there were also two skeleton creatures between us and the open door.

With a rattle, one of the skeleton creatures near us lunged, coming at me with jerky, almost frantic movements. A bony claw swiped at my face, and I leaped back with a yell.

"Go!" Halek cried, and we sprinted across the chamber. Skeletons lunged at us, but they seemed disoriented from being reborn, their movements sporadic and confused. We reached the doorway; the two creatures guarding it gnashed their teeth when they saw us and leaped forward with gaping jaws. I spun aside, barely dodging the fangs that snapped shut inches from my ear. Halek dove forward as the second skeleton raked at him, hitting the ground with his shoulder and rolling to his feet behind the guard. We darted through the opening into the darkness of the hall beyond.

The skeleton creatures chittered behind us. Sprinting down the hallway, we turned a corner and ducked into the first dark room we could find. At one point, it might have been a small library, perhaps filled with forbidden scrolls and ancient tomes. But part of the ceiling had collapsed, and books were scattered everywhere among broken shelves and rock. Halek and I squeezed under a bookshelf leaning against a corner and waited, listening to the scrape and scrabble of bones in the hall. None of the creatures came into the room, but we huddled there, our hearts pounding together, until their snarling faded away and silence throbbed in our ears once more.

Halek drew in a slow breath, cautiously poking his head out from beneath the shelf. "I think they're gone," he whispered.

I slid out behind him. My hands were shaking, but my fingers were still curled tightly around the gemstone. The thing that had apparently triggered the rising of the skeleton creatures. The meaning was very clear. *Do not touch the king's belongings.* Even in death, he had cursed any who would attempt to steal from him.

I slipped the emerald into my satchel. No use in putting it back; the damage was done. We would have to avoid the skeletons wandering through the palace now, but at least they didn't seem very intelligent.

"Where to now?" Halek wondered once we had confirmed that the room and surrounding hallways were empty.

I consulted my trusty map. Briefly, I wondered how the Circle knew so much about a city that had been lost for thousands of years, but the instructions on the back were crystal clear. *Find the vault*, the spidery handwriting said, *in the crypts below the palace.*

"Crypts," I muttered, rolling up the map up again. "Fantastic. Nothing terrifying in the crypts, I'm sure."

Halek chuckled, appreciating the sarcasm. "If we survive this, remind me to tell you about my venture into the burial mounds of the siha."

The palace went on, an unending labyrinth of hallways, rooms, corridors, and vast chambers. Time, it seemed, had either been frozen or didn't flow normally here. Carpets still stretched down corridors, intact except where the floors had cracked beneath them or the walls had fallen on them. Colorful tapestries lined the walls, depicting scenes of flowers, animals, and people, with a towering figure in white and gold looming over everything. Books were unchewed by rodents or insects, paintings unfaded. A bathing chamber still held crystal clear water that was icy cold to the touch, though the tiled floor around the pool was shattered. The air remained deathly still, as if the very walls and floors were holding their breath. But now we weren't alone. Shambling skeletons wandered the halls, and a few times Halek and I had to duck into a room or find cover and wait until an undead monstrosity had hobbled past. They never stopped or paused to look around, patrolling the halls with mindless fortitude. Probably cursed to march a set route forever. I hoped nothing more intelligent waited for us in the shadowy halls of the crypts.

Following the main hall, we slipped farther into the palace, making our way past more wandering undead, collapsed hallways, and empty rooms until we abruptly came to a place where we could go no farther. An entire section of floor had fallen, leaving behind a huge, gaping hole, at least thirty feet wide and maybe fifty feet across, completely blocking our path forward.

I walked to the edge and peered down. The darkness made it impossible to see the bottom, but it wasn't a sheer drop into the void. The sides were slanted enough that we would be able to make our way down, carefully. If we slipped, we would probably break our necks at the bottom, but the walls were scalable.

I looked at Halek. "The map says the vault is below the palace," I said. "This is probably the quickest way down, but it won't bet the easiest."

He shrugged. "Not the first giant hole I've flung myself into."

A rattle at the end of the hall made us glance up just as a skeleton creature shambled into the corridor. Without thinking, I stepped off the edge and dropped several feet into the gaping hole.

Halek followed, the light of his glowstone pulsing weakly in the gloom. The hole grew narrower the farther down we went, the air turning colder.

I dropped onto a ledge and came face-to-face with a skull, grinning at me from the wall. With a shudder, I continued picking my way down, the faint light from above dying around me, until my boots finally hit what felt like solid stone. Gazing around, I found myself in a partially collapsed stone tunnel with long, narrow shelves carved into the walls. A bony foot poked out of one, and a shattered piece of a spine lay on the floor beneath it.

Halek dropped beside me and took in our surroundings with a glance. He wrinkled his nose. "Well, we are definitely in the crypts," he whispered. "Amazing that even this much survived when the city fell." His gaze went to the skeletal hand poking out of the stone shelf. "We should be careful. This is most definitely a place that could be cursed. And there are a *lot* of skeletons down here. If they start crawling out of the walls, it's going to be interesting."

With that lovely image in mind, we started into the crypts.

Thankfully, despite Halek's ominous observation, none of the skeletons crawled out of their alcoves to attack us. Perhaps it was only the guards who were cursed to protect the palace, even in death. It was still eerie making our way through narrow, claustrophobic tunnels, the bones of the dead on either side.

"I know you can't tell me," Halek whispered as we ducked into yet another low-roofed tunnel. "But if what you're looking for is down here, it might be difficult to find in this mess. I hope what you're searching for isn't small."

I swallowed. "It's the size of a finger," I whispered back, and he winced.

"We could be here awhile, then."

"There's supposed to be a vault." I gazed down the tunnel at the seemingly endless shelves of bones. Hopefully, the vault would still be intact, not broken open, as Halek was right: We would never find the memory stone if it had been lost in the crypts.

"A vault," Halek repeated. "Well, that's something. If there's a vault, I guess we'll know it when we . . ."

He trailed off, stopping at a crumbled section of wall half blocked by a pillar. I paused, too, edging forward to peer through the gap, and my stomach curled. Beside me, Halek released an awed breath.

"Maederyss's mercy. I think we found it."

My heart beat faster. A breeze whistled through the gap and into a massive chamber, soaring up into the darkness. Similar to another cavern I had recently been in, this one was circular, ringed with stone columns that vanished up into the void. In the center, an enormous platform rose out of a pit that seemed to drop straight into the center of the earth, vanishing into blackness. A narrow stone bridge led to the edge of the platform, and at its very center stood a pedestal.

Something glimmered on the pedestal, something small yet clearly powerful, pulsing with a glow that seemed to suck in the light instead of reflecting it. A chill slid up my back, and I suddenly knew—this was what I had come for.

Ducking under the pillar, I stepped into the room.

I tensed, gazing around the cavern, waiting for a rush of choking air to sweep through the chamber or a voice to hiss that I was doomed. But nothing happened. No wind, no voices, no sudden arrival of skeleton guards, clawing themselves upright to destroy me. The chamber remained silent, my pulse and the faint drip of water somewhere in the void the only sounds I could hear.

This doesn't feel right. I was a thief, and in my world, no one left a vault unguarded.

Halek eased his way through the hole and looked around, blue eyes wary as he scanned the cavern. He, too, was tense, not trusting the apparent stillness. "Well," he ventured, "I don't like that nothing has jumped out at us, but I guess we should take advantage of it while we can."

Carefully, we walked to the bridge. It arced slightly away from us before coming down at the edge of the platform. I peered into the pit and saw what I'd suspected—a straight plunge into absolute darkness. If I let my imagination run wild, I could imagine thousands of eyes peering up at me and Halek from that abyss. With a shudder, I wrenched my gaze away and studied the pedestal in the center of the platform.

"Be careful, Sparrow." Halek's voice was uncharacteristically somber. His warm hand came to rest on my arm, making me start. "I don't know what that is," the Fatechaser went on, "but I've been in a few cursed places in my time, and this place . . ." He shook his head with a shiver. "Just . . . be careful," he finished, dropping his hand. "I'll stay here, in case you step onto the platform, get hit with a nasty curse, and need someone to pull you back."

My stomach churned. And suddenly, I didn't want to do this. I was the best thief in Kovass, was chosen for this job by the Circle because I was literally the only one who could do it, and . . . I did not want to grab that stone.

"Or you could let me do it," Halek offered. I glanced at him in surprise, and he gave a wry grin. "I've dodged a couple curses in my time," he said. "If it's not my fate to die here, not even the curse of a Deathless King can kill me. If it is, well, there's nothing *I* can do to prevent that." He gave a casual shrug, as if the thought of his own death was truly of no concern to him. "So if you want me to march up there and grab that stone, I will. Just say the word."

"No." I shook my head. I trusted that Halek was *probably* not someone who would snatch the treasure and run with it, but still, this was my mission. If anyone was going to pick up the memory stone and whatever curse came with it, it had to be me. "I've got it, Halek."

He nodded. "All right. I'll stay here, then. If you feel yourself turning into dust or a centipede, just yell."

"Yeah. Thanks for putting that thought in my head," I muttered, and started across the bridge.

The feeling of eyes on me grew stronger as I crossed the

narrow arching pathway, and I couldn't shake the sensation that we weren't alone. As if hundreds of *things* were clinging to the underside of the bridge, mere inches from the bottom of my boots. I kept walking, putting one foot in front of the other, refusing to look down, until I stepped off the bridge onto the platform.

Still nothing. A breath of wind circled the chamber, stirring up dust eddies and smelling of death, but nothing happened on the flat surface of the platform. I set my jaw, locked eyes on my target, and started toward it.

A foot from the pedestal, I paused, staring at what I'd been sent to retrieve. The tiny black stone hovered over the stand, the ominous dark glow surrounding it sucking in the light. It seemed to pulse like a heartbeat, and with every beat, tiny crimson runes appeared on the jet-black surface, making my eyes burn when I looked at them.

This was what the Circle wanted. This was what I had to retrieve, though every instinct I had was telling me not to touch it. Normally, I listened to my instincts; they had kept me alive when otherwise I would've been captured or killed. A suspicious deserted alleyway that held thugs waiting to ambush me. A normal-looking empty window that actually held a guard with a crossbow, ready to shoot first and ask questions later. Sometimes I got lucky—luckier than most—but sometimes, I kept myself out of trouble by listening to my gut. And my gut was telling me everything about this was wrong.

But this was my mission. I couldn't return to the surface empty-handed. I knew how the guild worked well enough to know the Circle would kill me, and Vahn, if I failed. I was a thief. This was my place in the story.

Taking a deep breath, I stretched out my hand toward the glowing rock.

"*Stop!*"

NINE

The deep voice echoed through the chamber. I spun, looking past Halek to the entrance of the vault, and my blood chilled.

A figure was striding toward the bridge, long legs rapidly eating the ground between us. His hood was up, obscuring his face, but I recognized him immediately. I knew him from the Temple of Fate, from the rooftops over the crowded market the night of the firedancer circus. My stomach dropped. The iylvahn assassin had come.

Halek hovered at the edge of the bridge, watching the figure approach. I saw him stiffen; he knew what the iylvahn was, especially since I had asked him about the kahjai. But he raised a hand in casual greeting as the figure drew closer. "Hey, friend," he called cheerfully, putting himself between the stranger and the bridge entrance, I noticed. "This is an odd place to meet one of the people of the Hidden City. You're a long way from home."

"Get out of the way, Fatechaser." The iylvahn's voice was ruthless. Without slowing his pace, he reached over his shoulder and drew a curved sword with a raspy screech, sending a chill up my spine. "I'm not here for you."

He is *here to kill me.* I looked frantically across the platform, but there was no bridge on the other side. Just a sheer plunge between the platform and the narrow ledge around the cavern.

I might be able to make it with a running jump, but it would be close. The black memory stone hovered over the pedestal before me, but the echo of the iylvahn's shout was still ringing through my head. If I left the stone where it was, would he let us go?

"Hey, hold on just a second, now." Halek backed up several steps, moving onto the bridge, and raised a hand to the approaching assassin. I saw his other hand slip casually into his belt; recognizing the classic sleight-of-hand diversion, my heart beat even faster. "We can talk about this," he said as the assassin reached the foot of the bridge. "This doesn't have to be unpleasant—this doesn't have to be a fight. Look, we can just run away!" And he hurled something to the stones between them.

A flash of brilliant light exploded in the air right in front of the assassin, turning the entire chamber white for a split second. The assassin reeled back, one arm covering his eyes, and Halek immediately sprinted up the bridge toward me.

"Sparrow, run!"

Run? The kahjai was on the bridge, between us and the only exit off the platform. Did Halek expect us to leap off the other side? "Where?" I shouted back, as Halek reached the end of the bridge.

"Anywhere away from him!"

The second Halek's boot touched the edge of the platform, a shudder emanated from the pedestal. It flowed across the stones and over the edge of the platform, and a terrible noise rose from the darkness of the pit, like thousands of insect wings buzzing all at once.

I grabbed the stone from where it hovered in the air, and a

stab of complete, absolute terror lanced through me like an arrow to the heart, taking my breath away. For a moment, I couldn't move, feeling an ancient gaze—cold, intrigued, alien—staring into my soul. I could feel it probing my mind, easily stripping away all defenses. In a frigid moment of clarity, I felt it smile.

"Sparrow!" Halek grabbed my wrist, yanking me away from the pedestal just as a curved blade struck its surface with a metallic clink. We scrambled back, and the assassin stared at me over the pedestal, his pale blue gaze moving from my face to the pulsing black stone in my hand. If possible, his expression grew even colder, and he strode forward with death in his eyes.

Halek and I swiftly backed away from the assassin stalking us. But there was nowhere to run; he was still between us and the bridge, pressing us toward the edge of the platform. Around us, the buzzing noise was growing louder, becoming nearly deafening.

Something terrible and many legged crawled over the edge and onto the platform. A huge beetle, its carapace shiny black, scrabbled up and turned the hollow eyes of a human skull toward me. It hissed, its curved mandibles opening, and then dozens more beetles with human skulls were pouring over the edge in a black wave that swallowed the side of the platform.

Terror spiked through me. I turned back and instantly had to duck as the assassin's blade swished over my head. The skull beetles were coming from everywhere, from all sides of the platform, even dropping from the ceiling overhead. I leaped back from the horde, somehow avoided another slice from the iylvahn's blade, and bolted toward the bridge with Halek beside me.

The platform was nearly swallowed in beetles now. The only clear space was around the pedestal, and it was rapidly shrinking. I glanced back and saw the iylvahn, surrounded by beetles, sweep his sword along the ground and send several flying off the edge. Between us and the bridge was a writhing carpet of black, swarming ever closer.

"Halek, we're not going to make it," I panted, leaping over a beetle that fell into my path. "There are too many of them!"

"Keep going!" he replied, and his hand dropped to his belt again. "And don't look directly at the flash when it hits."

He leaped onto the pedestal, vaulted into the air, and threw a trio of small white orbs at the ground in front of us. I looked away as the orbs exploded in a blinding flash, drawing a cacophony of screeches from the mass of skull beetles. They skittered back, confused, turning in circles. Several fell off the edge of the platform, dropping into the void, and the way to the bridge was clear.

I didn't look back again. I didn't know if the assassin had been pulled under by the skull beetles, if they were chewing off his skin, or if he was somehow hanging on. I didn't want to know. Halek and I just ran, across the bridge and into the crypts, then wove through tunnels and passageways until we finally reached the hole up to the palace. I bloodied my hands in my scramble to the top, tearing my skin and clothes in my haste to get out.

The palace was in a frenzy when we emerged. Whatever had happened down in the crypts had alerted the skeleton guards as well, and they were frantically marching up and down the palace corridors, the clicking of their bones reverberating off the walls. Halek and I darted through the palace, playing hide-and-seek with the horde of snarling, frenzied skeleton creatures.

We rounded a corner, and a trio of skeleton guards spun, turning their hollow eyes on us, their muzzles opening in chilling howls. As we tensed to flee back the way we had come, a tremor ran through the ground, and cracks shot up the walls from below. I looked up and saw them spreading to the ceiling directly over us, and my stomach clenched.

Without thinking, I grabbed Halek's arm and pulled him forward, toward the trio of skeleton guards. They snarled at us and lunged, teeth snapping. Releasing Halek, I ducked, rolling beneath the gnashing fangs, hearing the click of their jaws as they snapped shut inches from my head. Halek also dove forward, somehow managing to avoid two sets of teeth, and rolled to his feet beside me.

With a roar, the ceiling behind us collapsed. Dust and pebbles filled the hallway, raining from above and billowing into the air. Halek and I staggered back, coughing, the ground beneath us still trembling and bits of rock stinging our skin where they hit. When the dust cleared, the corridor was completely filled with rubble and the skeletons that had been chasing us were buried under several tons of stone.

I glanced at Halek and saw that his face was ashen in the dim light of his single glowstone.

"Halek." I touched his elbow and he jumped, turning wide blue eyes on me. For a moment, he looked stunned and terrified, a shocking change from the grinning, seemingly fearless Fatechaser I had come to know. Apparently, *this* near-death experience had affected him more than all the others. "Come on,"

I panted, taking a step back down the hall. "We're almost to the throne room, and then we're free. Let's get out of here."

He shook himself, glanced once more at the collapsed hallway, then back to me. "Right," he breathed as we began to sprint down the passage, the echoes of our footfalls ringing off the stones. "We've definitely overstayed our welcome."

TEN

I could probably jump that gap, if something nasty was chasing me, Halek had said earlier, when the section of bridge leading to the palace had collapsed. *But I'd rather not have to.*

We had to.

With a group of skeleton creatures clacking and skittering behind us, we rushed at the gaping hole in the center of the bridge and hurled ourselves into space. I saw the sheer drop below us, the plunge down to the rocks beneath, before I hit the other side and rolled painfully to a halt on the crumbling walkway.

Grimacing, I pushed myself to my elbows and saw Halek pushing himself to his knees with a groan. Glancing back at the other side revealed the bridge was empty; it seemed the pack of undead weren't able to make the jump. But I could see more skeletons pouring out of the palace, swarming into the open like huge bony insects. Scrambling to our feet, Halek and I fled the palace of the Deathless King and vanished into the city.

In a narrow alley a few blocks from the palace, we finally stopped to catch our breath. Collapsing against the rough wall, I gasped air into my lungs, watching as Halek bent over with his hands on his knees, heaving. Neither of us was able to speak.

Finally, Halek straightened, raking a hand through his shock of yellow hair, and cast a solemn glance back toward the palace. I expected him to say something flippant—*Well, that was a close one, wasn't it?*—but ever since the collapsed hallway, his demeanor had changed. He hadn't spoken at all, his gaze troubled and faraway.

"Halek?" I pushed myself off the wall, watching him with concern. "You all right?"

"I . . . don't know." He took a step back, brow furrowed, and raked a hand through his hair again. "For a second, I had the strangest feeling . . . that I was supposed to die in there," he muttered. "That my fate was to not make it out of the palace."

I blinked at him. "You must've been mistaken," I said. "You're still here. Granted, that whole thing was pretty terrifying, and we both nearly died, but we made it, Halek. We're alive."

He shook his head almost frantically. "You don't understand," he said. "The stories are true! I wasn't sure if I believed it or not, but . . ." He paused, taking a deep breath, as if realizing I had no idea what he was talking about. "There are legends," he began, "rumors, that claim Fatechasers know when their fate has arrived. We can't see the future, of course, and we don't know what Fate has in store for us, but the moment it happens, we understand that this is it. This is our fate. And we accept it."

He glanced at me, the expression in his blue eyes almost anguished. "I had that feeling in the palace," he whispered. "When the ceiling collapsed. For just a moment, I knew. That was my fate. That was how I would die. But . . ."

Now he scrubbed both hands through his hair, making it stand on end.

I frowned. "I don't understand," I said. "Not meeting your

fate... that's a good thing, right? You're alive. You didn't die back there."

"Is it?" He ran a hand down his face. "Maybe. But now everything I thought I knew has changed. I've always been confident in my choices, because I knew when Fate did find me, there was nothing I could do about it. If my fate was to die in the palace, and I'm still here, what does that mean? How can I go on, knowing I've cheated my destiny?"

"Take it as a second chance?" I offered. "I don't know about you, but for me, I would always rather be alive than not. I will always try to cheat death. If it was my fate to die, and I didn't, that's another day I get to live."

"Maybe you're right," Halek said, but he didn't sound confident. He sighed and turned away from the palace, as if not wanting to think about it anymore. "In any case," he went on, with a hint of his old confidence, "there's an iylvahn assassin back there who is probably very angry with both of us right now. I suggest we try to lose him before he catches up and we *both* meet our fates."

I shivered. "You think he's still alive?" The last I'd seen of the iylvahn, he was surrounded by skull beetles in the center of a crumbling platform. It was hard to imagine anyone surviving that.

"You haven't heard the stories of the kahjai," Halek said. "Once they have their target, they don't give up until their mission is done. They're relentless, unyielding, and nearly impossible to kill—the perfect assassins. So the stories say." He gave me a sympathetic wince. "I think we have to assume that unless we've actually seen a body, the kahjai is still coming. And that you're his target."

Fear crept up my spine. Halek was right—the iylvahn wouldn't die so easily. He was still coming for me.

No, I suddenly realized. *Not for me.*

"I'm not his target," I muttered.

Reaching into my satchel, I withdrew the black stone and held it up. It pulsed in my hand like a heartbeat, and the shadows around us grew darker as it sucked in the light. "This is," I whispered. "He was after this."

Halek made a face, leaning away from the throbbing stone. "I've seen my share of relics," he said, crossing his arms as if loath to touch it, "and that one is about as cursed as they come." He tilted his head, pondering the stone for a few heartbeats before adding, "You know, if you offered it to the iylvahn, he might take it and let you live."

"Or he might kill me anyway." I slipped it back into my satchel. The suggestion made me bristle with defiance. I didn't bargain, and I wouldn't be frightened into giving up my treasure, even if it was to a terrifying kahjai assassin who would hunt me down to get it. Besides, even if the iylvahn didn't kill me, the Circle certainly would for returning empty-handed. And Vahn would also suffer for my failure; I wasn't going to let that happen. "I'm not giving it to him," I told Halek, firmly closing the satchel. "That's not an option."

He nodded. "Then we should keep moving. Quickly. Because I think our friends are coming after us."

I jerked and glanced back toward the palace. The streets and shadows were empty, but then, with a ripple of bones, a skeleton shambled out of the darkness, swinging its bony muzzle from side to side. Halek and I quickly melted back into the alley and tiptoed away.

The ancient city was no longer still. Whatever had happened at the palace seemed to have had a ripple effect that had stirred everything to life. Skeletons wandered the streets and skull beetles skittered over the walls and ruined buildings. When one of the beetles blocked our path through a narrow alley, I discovered, by terrifying accident, that they could actually fly: The creature had spotted us, but instead of rushing forward over the ground, it opened its shell and spread translucent wings, then zipped at my head with a high-pitched buzz. I might've let out a shriek as I ducked.

After what seemed like an eternity, we finally reached a part of the ancient city that felt familiar.

"There's the door," Halek whispered, pointing across an open square. The path dropped into the shallow ditch of water, and I could just make out the door, halfway submerged in the side of the cliff face. Beyond the door was the ladder back up to the sewers. "We made it."

But even as he said those words, I caught a shadow at the corner of my eye, making my blood run cold. I didn't get a clear look, but I didn't need to. Grabbing Halek's sleeve, I pulled him back into the shadows.

"The kahjai is close," I whispered.

His puzzled frown turned to alarm in an instant and he gazed back toward the exit. "Are you sure?" he whispered back. "I don't see anything."

"I'm sure." It had been only a ripple, a split-second glimpse, but I had no doubt. "I don't think he saw us, but I know he's there."

Halek chewed his bottom lip. "If he *is* out there, he'll be waiting for us to run for the door," he said thoughtfully. "He knows it's the only exit out of the city. Or at least, it's the only one *we* know of."

I clenched a fist to stifle my rising fear. "How are we going to get around him?"

Halek was silent, scanning the darkness between us and the door. Finally, he took a deep breath, nodded once, and turned to me. "The assassin is after you," he said, as if I weren't acutely aware of that fact. "If you go out there now, you won't make it halfway to the door before you meet him. Or maybe he's waiting on a ledge with a crossbow aimed and ready. We won't be able to outwait him. Like I said, the kahjai are ruthless. They don't give up until their mission is done."

"Then what are we going to do?"

"*You* are going to stay here." Halek put a hand on my arm, smiling. "I'll lead him away. When the path is clear, run. Run to the door and get back to the surface."

"Halek . . ." I couldn't explain the sudden desperation rising inside me. I was a thief. In the Thieves Guild, you looked after yourself and no one else. If you were with a crew and the situation went bad, you got yourself out first and trusted that the others would do the same. We didn't stick our necks out for each other. We didn't risk our skins for someone else. If a thief couldn't take care of themselves without relying on others, they were of no use to the guild.

I didn't know Halek. I had been with him only a few hours. And yet he was willing to confront a kahjai, one of the most dangerous people in Arkyennah, so I could escape.

Why?

"It's all right." Halek gave me a reassuring grin. "Don't worry about me. If it's not my fate to die at the hands of a coldhearted killer, a dozen kahjai won't be able to run me down. If it is . . ." He shrugged, though his smile faltered. "There's nothing I can do to stop it, anyway.

"So wait here," he went on. "And when you're sure it's safe, *go*. Like I said, don't worry." That crooked, charming grin came creeping back. "Meetings like this are never by accident. I get the feeling our paths will cross again."

I didn't know what to say or feel, so I just nodded. Halek drew back, peering out at the shadowed streets once more. "This is going to be interesting," I heard him mutter. "I'm guessing wherever the iylvahn is, he can probably see the whole area. I can't be too obvious, or he's not going to be fooled."

Reaching into his belt pouch, he pulled out a white cloth, then wrapped it around his head like a shawl, hiding his hair. "Not the greatest disguise I've ever worn," he said wryly, tucking the ends of the cloth into his collar. "But at least I'm not dressed as a Ragnian sword swallower this time."

My stomach twisted. "Be careful, Halek," I told him. I was worried, I realized. Halek was still a stranger, but I didn't want him to be killed. He might be a bit too fatalistic, but he was kind and brave, and he hadn't vanished on me the second things got dangerous.

For a moment, a prick of anger filtered through the fear. *This is why you keep things distant and professional. This is why you do not get attached.*

"I will be." The blue-eyed Fatechaser glanced at me once more and winked. "Fate be with you, Sparrow," he whispered. "And don't cry for me. If the Weaver is kind, our paths will cross again."

He darted out of the alley, keeping to the shadows, and vanished from sight.

Biting my lip, I drew back, crouched down in the darkness, and waited.

I didn't see the iylvahn, but I knew he was watching for us, invisible, silent, and deadly. He must've come straight to the door after getting out of the palace, rather than wasting time tracking us through the streets. A smart tactic; if I hadn't caught that fleeting glimpse of a moving shadow, I wouldn't have known he was there at all. How he had beaten us to the door, I didn't know, but the implications were terrifying. It was pure chance that my gaze had been in the right place at the exactly right time.

At least my luck was holding.

Minutes passed. I didn't see movement in the shadows, from either Halek or the iylvahn. I didn't hear anything. No footsteps, voices, or anything to indicate the assassin had taken the bait and gone after Halek. The silence throbbed in my ears until it was deafening.

After a few excruciatingly indecisive moments, I slowly rose and stepped to the mouth of the alley. On the other side of the street, across the shallow pool of water, the door to the surface beckoned. So close. And yet it might as well have been on the other side of the Dust Sea.

Move, Sparrow. You can't stay here forever.

I took a quick breath and tensed to run, but as I did, a cry echoed somewhere in the alleys behind me. A sound of pain, fear, and alarm that made my stomach clench. I couldn't tell if it was Halek, the iylvahn, or something else, but in that moment, I had a choice. Turn back and try to find Halek, or keep going.

I bolted for the door.

Guilt clawed at me, but I kept running. If Halek had met the iylvahn, he was probably dead, and nothing I could do would change that. I tried not to think about it as I splashed through the water, shoved open the door, and stumbled blindly down the tunnel, hoping I wouldn't feel a knife in my back at any moment. I hit the ladder and started climbing, the darkness of the shaft closing around me. My glowstone still hung dead and lifeless at my waist, and I didn't dare light it up again for fear of being seen.

Gasping, I reached the top of the ladder and scrambled onto solid ground. Heart pounding, I dared a peek down the shaft, wondering if I would see the cowled head of the kahjai ascending after me. But the chute remained dark and silent, and I backed away from the hole and fled the room, slamming the door as I did.

I wove my way through the sewers, not daring to stop, until I finally had to pause at a small alcove to catch my breath. Leaning back against the damp stone, I closed my eyes and tried to comprehend everything that had happened.

With shaking hands, I reached into my satchel and pulled out the black stone. It pulsed steadily against my fingers, cold and ominous, and holding it caused my insides to squirm. This was the thing everyone was after. The Circle, who'd sent me down there to get it. The iylvahn, who was willing to kill for it. What was this thing? I wasn't ignorant. I was a thief, and I knew that the more rare, dangerous, or valuable an item was, the more people wanted it. And the more atrocities they were willing to commit to get it. It couldn't be just a memory stone.

Regardless, I had a job to complete. That hadn't changed, and I'd be relieved to get it over with. Once I delivered this thing to the Circle, my part in their plan, whatever it was, was finished. And hopefully, once I'd handed it off, I wouldn't have to worry about iylvahn assassins climbing through my window to murder me in my sleep.

Kovass seemed different when I finally climbed out of the enormous drainpipe and back into the fresh air. The sky was dark, and the moon hung low over the Dust Sea, a brief visitor to Kovass before the twins chased him away. The district was deserted, the residents sleeping while they could, unaware that deep below them, a cursed city lay forgotten, slumbering like an ancient giant, its own residents waiting in the darkness for unsuspecting fools to cross their paths.

"Sparrow."

I flinched, nearly bolting across the street before I recognized the voice. "Jeran?" I said, as a figure stepped out from behind a fence and waved to me. "What are you doing here?"

"I followed you." He looked sheepish, but only for a moment. "I saw you and Vahn leaving the guild and I was curious, so I decided to tag along."

"Tag along? Have you been here all day? You're lucky Vahn didn't spot you." I gave him an incredulous look. Guildmaster business was deadly serious, and if you weren't directly involved, then you didn't need to know. Vahn did not tolerate insubordination and would not find Jeran's "curiosity" amusing. Even if a tiny part of me was happy to see him. "That wasn't very smart, Jeran," I finished, shivering as a cold breeze whispered through the streets, tugging at my damp clothes. "You could've been kicked out of the guild."

Jeran shrugged, a defiant, almost sullen gesture. He stared at me, and for a moment, his eyes were hooded, but then he blinked and seemed to go back to normal.

"Yeah, probably. I was just . . . worried about you." He scratched the back of his head and gave me a somewhat forced smile. "If you were going on a dangerous mission for the Circle—"

"Jeran!" I cut him off with a sharp gesture. "Not here, you idiot." You didn't discuss the Circle openly in the streets. Actually, you didn't discuss the Circle at all. You pretended the Circle didn't exist. "What are you doing?" I hissed at him. "What's wrong with you lately?"

He ground his teeth, then made a visible effort to calm down.

"I'm sorry." He raked a hand over his face. "I just . . . Look, Sparrow, can we talk? There are some things I have to say."

"Now?" It really wasn't a good time. I wanted to deliver the memory stone to Vahn, get it out of my possession. The sooner I did that, the sooner I could be done with this whole ordeal. "I'm on my way back to the guild," I told him. "Let me deliver something to Vahn, and then we can talk."

"No." He held out an arm, surprising me. "We don't need to go back to the guild. This won't take long." I gave an impatient huff, and his expression turned desperate. "Please, Sparrow. I won't keep you, I promise. I just . . . I really need to talk to you."

I clenched my jaw. After everything I'd gone through, I wanted to get this delivery over with. But Jeran had been acting strange lately, and I did want to talk to him about what had happened in my room the other night. Maybe he wanted to apologize for being a jealous sand ass.

"Fine." I sighed. "But only a few minutes. I really do need to get back to Vahn."

He glanced around, then nodded at the door to a warehouse across the road and beckoned me forward. "Come on, we can talk in here."

I followed, impatient. The memory stone throbbed in my satchel, as if it could sense something had changed. The warehouse was empty, and we slipped into a corner behind a row of rotting gray shelves.

Jeran turned to me. In the shadows of the warehouse, he suddenly looked like a stranger.

"I'm leaving the guild," he said without preamble.

I gaped at him. Of all the things he could've said, I never expected this. My heart gave a little stutter of despair, and I swallowed quickly to open my throat. "Why?"

He turned away, his expression caught halfway between a grimace and a scowl. "Dahveen and I have been spending a lot of time at the Golden Chalice," he muttered, referring to the largest gambling house in the city. I knew Dahveen was a regular there, but Jeran had no interest in high-stakes gambling. Or so I'd thought.

Instantly, I knew where he was going with this, and a knot formed in my stomach. "Jeran..."

He grimaced. "Dahveen said I could make it big," he said, gesturing helplessly at nothing. "He kept pushing me, saying I was one step away from a big score." His lips tightened, and he shook his head. "Guess I'm not as good with dice as he is."

I winced in sympathy. "How much did you lose?"

"Pretty much everything. But that's not the point." He hesitated, glancing to the side and not meeting my gaze. "I kept going back to the Golden Chalice," he admitted at last. "Dahveen and I went nearly every evening for weeks." He bit his lip, and his voice dropped to a strangled murmur. "I... haven't paid my guild dues in four months."

A ripple of horror went through me, and I stared at him in shock. You didn't cheat the Thieves Guild—that was one of the defining rules. You could steal from everyone else, but you did *not* steal from the guild. Even I, the Guildmaster's prodigy, had to pay the tithe.

"Vahn gave me a choice," Jeran continued in a low, dull voice. "Pay what I owe, or leave. And you know what that means."

I did. Leaving the guild wasn't just exile from the building. It meant being banned from the Docks District entirely. It meant never setting foot in buildings that were guild-operated. And it meant you were forbidden to ply your trade in any place that the guild considered its territory. The Thieves Guild did not tolerate competition, especially from former members, and those who broke the rules soon received a visit from someone like Bassig, who made certain they wouldn't have the dexterity or fine motor skills to continue their work.

"You should've told me," I said, watching Jeran's mouth tighten. I didn't know if the squeezing in my gut was anger that he hadn't come to me sooner, or a desperate need to stop him from leaving. "I could have talked to Vahn. I could've helped you, Jeran."

He stared at me, his eyes narrowed. "You can help me now." His gaze flicked to my satchel, as if he could sense the memory stone pulsing within. "Give me what you retrieved for the Circle," he demanded. "Let me deliver it to Vahn. If I do that, I know he'll wipe my debts and let me stay."

I recoiled. "What? No!"

"Please, Sparrow." Jeran took a step forward. "I need this. I can't survive out there without the guild. You'll be all right. You're the Guildmaster's daughter—the Circle won't do anything to you." His mouth twitched, as if he were trying not to curl his lip, and a shadow of resentment crossed his face. "Let me take it to Vahn," he continued. "I'll say we did it together, and you decided to let me go on ahead."

"This is for the *Circle*," I hissed at him, more terrified than angry now. "It doesn't work that way and you know it, Jeran."

His face darkened, his eyes going cold and sullen, but he didn't say anything.

Putting a hand on my satchel, I backed away from him. My stomach twisted, and I felt pulled in two different directions, but I couldn't waver. Vahn was counting on me, too. "I can't give this to you," I told Jeran. "I have to deliver it to Vahn, and only Vahn. Look, let me get rid of this thing, and then we'll figure something out together. There are other ways we can clear your debts—I'm the best thief in Kovass, remember?" I tried to smile at him, but he just stared at me, stone-faced and silent. I sighed, briefly closing my eyes, and turned away. "I have to go," I said, feeling his bleak gaze on the back of my neck. "Vahn is waiting for me. I *will* help you, I promise, but not like this. I'm sorry."

As I started for the door, I heard the scrape of wood from a nearby shelf. "I'm sorry, too," Jeran muttered, almost too low for me to hear. Puzzled, I turned back—and saw him lunge at me, a broken plank held in both hands. Then wood filled my vision, and I knew nothing else.

ELEVEN

Cold water splashed against my face.

Coughing, I opened my eyes and winced. They were blurry with water, and I tried raising a hand to wipe it away.

I couldn't move.

I was sitting in a chair with my arms tied behind the chair-back, my wrists bound tightly and secured to the wood. My ankles were also bound, lashed together and tied to the chair legs, rendering me immobile. After a moment of panicked confusion and futile struggling, I blinked the last of the water from my eyes and looked up, my heart pounding in my ears.

The iylvahn crouched in front of me, pale blue eyes staring from beneath his hood. Up close, he looked even more beautiful and alien, with high cheekbones, charcoal-gray skin, and strands of silver-white hair hanging over his eyes. He watched me, neither smug nor threatening, just silent. Calculating.

"Where is it?" he said at last.

I tried to swallow my fear, but it stuck in my throat, making my voice raspy and breathless. "What?"

"The soulstone." The assassin's voice was ruthlessly calm. "The thing you took from the crypts in the ancient city. The black stone with runic markings. Where is it?"

"I . . ." My thoughts spun. I was suddenly cognizant of a

horrific pounding in my head and the feeling of dried blood in my hair. "I don't know."

The assassin moved, so swiftly I wasn't even aware of it. One second, he was crouched in front of me; the next, his face was only a foot from mine and something cold was pressed against my throat. I could feel the razor edge of his blade barely touching my skin, and knew that if it moved just a hair closer, I would be bleeding.

"You can tell me now," the iylvahn said, still in that same calm, deadly voice, "or you can die here. Those are your only options."

"My satchel," I whispered.

"Your satchel was empty," the iylvahn said. "It was the first thing I checked. The soulstone is gone, taken by whoever knocked you out and left you here." He leaned back, thankfully taking the blade from my neck, though his gaze still seared a hole through my face. "Who are they? Where are they taking the stone?"

Jeran. I bit my lip. Saving my own skin was one thing; selling out a fellow thief whom I'd known all my life was another. Even after everything, even after his betrayal, I wasn't going to give Jeran to this killer. He might've deserved it—he might've even sold me out had the situation been reversed—but he was still my friend, and a fellow thief. I didn't want him to die.

"What makes you think I know where they are?" I asked the iylvahn, daring to look up at him. "It was a random attack by a random lowlife—if you hadn't noticed, there are a lot of them around here." His expression didn't change, and I tried to give a careless shrug. Difficult to do with my hands tied behind my back. "I wasn't being careful, and they got the drop on me. I don't even know who they are, much less where they went."

"You're lying," the iylvahn said quietly. His blade came up again, not against my throat, but held between us. "I've killed a lot of people." The assassin said this as if he were discussing the weather. "I study my targets, and I know them very well. And you . . ." Those pale blue eyes narrowed to slits. "I tracked you through the ancient city. I hunted you in the crypts below the palace. You were my target, and yet you managed something none have ever succeeded at. You escaped. You literally slipped through my fingers, and nothing I tried, despite my years of experience and hunting down the most dangerous men to ever walk the sands, was successful in catching one slip of a human girl."

I swallowed. "I was lucky," I said, dropping my gaze. "It's something I've been blessed with." *Or cursed with*, I thought, upon reflection. The iylvahn didn't move, and I looked at him again. "I'm not special," I told him. "I'm just a thief who gets lucky from time to time."

The kahjai shook his head. "It's more than luck," he said simply. "You shouldn't have been able to even reach the soul-stone. The curses and ancient guardians kill any trespassers who set foot in the palace. But you were able to move through the palace untouched. Like a shadow, or a mirage."

"Hardly untouched," I argued. "Or didn't you see the mobs of skeletons and skull beetles chasing us?"

"I did," the iylvahn agreed, nodding. "And I saw that they stirred only after the Fatechaser stepped onto the platform or touched something he was not supposed to touch. You, however . . ." He paused, regarding me with a look that was frightening in its intensity. "They couldn't sense you. They couldn't see you. As if you weren't even there."

"Halek." I suddenly remembered the Fatechaser who had offered to lead the assassin away so I could escape. "What did you do to him?" I asked the iylvahn, suddenly afraid I knew the answer. "Where is he?"

"I don't know where the Fatechaser is," the iylvahn said. "He led me on a merry chase, but when I finally caught up and realized you weren't with him, you had already gone."

"You didn't kill him?"

The assassin shook his head. "I don't kill those who are not my targets," he continued, making me slump in relief. "The Fatechaser is either still in the undercity, or he made it back to the surface. Or he died trying to leave. Whichever way, he is not my concern.

"Regardless"—the iylvahn's blade came up, the tip pressing into my cheek, his gaze focusing on me once more—"I followed you back to the surface as quickly as I could. And after doing a quick search of the area, I found you here. Without the soulstone."

"Like I said." I tried to ignore the cold steel against my flesh. "It was a random attack. I was careless."

"No."

The iylvahn leaned close again, his eyes hard. "You are not one to be negligent," he said firmly. "Not once in the underground city did I see you let your guard down. Luck is one thing, but you would not have survived this long as a thief if you were careless." His eyes narrowed to pale blue slits. "I'm guessing that you knew your attacker," he went on, making my stomach twist. "Perhaps it was a fellow guild member. A partner in crime, maybe even a friend. And you followed them in here because you trusted them. Only to find, as is often the case with humans, that greed and desperation easily overpower loyalty. They struck you down, and they took what you had, either to sell, or for some other reward it would bring. And you're here with me now because even though you are skilled, crafty, or even lucky enough to escape a city full of curses and horrors, you are still naive when it comes to human betrayal."

My throat felt tight, and to my horror, there was a stinging sensation behind my eyes. I ducked my head, breathing deep to banish the tightness. I would not let this assassin see me cry. I wouldn't give him the satisfaction. Even though I was exhausted, in pain, and reeling from the horrors of the night and Jeran's betrayal, I would not let him see my weakness.

There was a sigh, and, to both my surprise and dismay, the assassin brushed back my hood, letting it fall behind me. Instantly, I cringed, feeling even more exposed and helpless. Now there was nowhere I could hide, and the iylvahn's piercing gaze seemed to stab right through my head.

"So young," he murmured, more to himself than to me. "And likely just a puppet that the ma'jhet would use and throw away." He sighed again, running a hand over his eyes, before looking back at me. "You don't even know why you were sent for the soulstone, do you?"

I ground my teeth, banishing the last of the tears, and made sure my voice was steady. "I'm a member of the Thieves Guild. When they tell you to fetch something, you don't get to ask why. You just do it. So, no. I don't know why the Circle told me to go down into a cursed ancient city crawling with monsters, where I very nearly died, to fetch some rock for them. I guess you're going to explain why this thing is so important that you would kill me to get it?"

The iylvahn's jaw tightened, but not in anger. His gaze shifted to the grimy, dust-encased windows on the opposite wall, as if weighing his choices. "I don't have a lot of time," he finally murmured. "None of us do now. But maybe if you understood what's at stake . . ." He rose and paused, then shook his head and turned to me. "How much do you know about the Deathless Kings?" he asked.

The Deathless Kings. It all came back to them, didn't it? What the Circle wanted, why the iylvahn had been after me. It all had something to do with what I'd taken from the city of the Deathless King. "They were the rulers in the age before this one," I answered. "Several thousand years ago. They built great kingdoms, and their cities stretched to the edges of the world. But then there was a great cataclysm. The kingdoms collapsed, and the cities sank into the sands."

I stopped. The iylvahn waited quietly, as if he expected me to go on. "That's all I know," I told him.

"So, not a lot," the iylvahn murmured. "Certainly nothing that matters."

I clenched my fists behind my back. "That's as much as

anyone knows," I said defiantly. "The stories of the Deathless Kings are so old, they're mostly faery tales. Shadows and bogeymen mothers threaten their children with." Ignoring the fact that I had just been in one ancient city of the forgotten kingdom. And the monsters there had definitely not been mere stories.

The iylvahn's face went cold and terrifying as he loomed over me. "Then let me tell you the true story of the Deathless Kings," he said in a deep voice that sent chills racing up and down my back. "Long ago, several thousands of years past, the lands were ruled not by one, but thirteen souls of immense power. Each of these kings, or queens, had their own cities, their own subjects, their own government. And their kingdoms, as you said, stretched to the edges of the known world.

"Back then," the iylvahn continued, his voice almost lyrical in its storytelling, "the world was different. It was not endless sand and blasted rock—it was lush. Green. Imagine valleys not of dust or stone, but of ferns. Deep forests instead of wasteland. Hills of rolling grass, not empty dunes where nothing can survive. The Dust Sea was an ocean of water, filled with life, reaching all the way to the horizon and beyond."

Listening to him, I felt breathless, amazement and disbelief fighting a battle within me. A world that was green and lush, covered in plants and filled with water? *That* sounded like a faery tale; I couldn't even imagine it. But the iylvahn sounded dead serious. *He* didn't think this was a children's story.

"For many eons," his voice continued, "the immortal Deathless Kings ruled their world without opposition. They were more than rulers, more than kings; they were very nearly gods. In some very old legends, the Deathless Kings were the ones who created all the races of man, bringing to life a people in their own image, whose only purpose was to serve them. Whether or not this is true, none of the ancient people could stand against the Deathless Kings. Their power came from life itself. They drew from the life forces around them to fuel their magic, and with this power, they could do anything. But the more power they drew in, the more life around them withered and died. A single Deathless could turn an entire forest to dust if he pulled enough energy into himself. An angry queen could suck the life from her subjects in a heartbeat if she willed it, leaving nothing behind but bones and ash. All life—anything that lived, and grew, and breathed—could be taken by the Deathless to fuel their power.

"Fortunately, it was difficult to be worshiped in an empire of dust and bones, and the Deathless Kings were careful to balance their power with the need for life. But with that much power, and that many godlike immortal beings sharing a world, the kingdoms were only a breath away from destruction at any time. And eventually, that is what came to pass.

"The Deathless Kings began to war with each other. No one remembers how this war started, but it soon escalated into a nightmare of death and chaos. The kings rained calamity down on the other kingdoms. Mountains crumbled, forests burst into flame, seas rose up to swallow whole towns, and horrific creatures that none had seen before clawed their way out of the earth, destroying everything in their path. The people, of course, perished by the thousands, only to reappear as undead soldiers in their king's army, denied release even in death. The land withered as the warring kings drew in more and more life energy to fight their endless war. Deserts replaced forests. Wasteland supplanted once-vibrant fields. The sea itself drained away through a massive fissure one king opened beneath a rival's city. And yet the Deathless continued to war with each other, until one day, they looked around, and there was nothing left. No life. No subjects. Nothing but sand, and dust, and emptiness.

"And then the Deathless Kings discovered the truth about themselves: That without life, without the energy to fuel their power, they were no longer immortal. And so, like the very lands they had scoured to nothing, the now mortal Deathless Kings withered away until they, too, were nothing but dust and bones, and faded from existence.

"As the Hourglass of Time turned, and the suns set over the once flourishing world, the age of the Deathless Kings finally came to a close. And very slowly—because even after the world ends, there are always a few survivors—life returned. The land would never heal. The kings had drained it of everything, and it could not return to the green landscape it once was. But humanity's will to live is ever constant. The survivors built new settlements on the bones of the old kingdoms, and gradually, some of those settlements became villages, then towns, then cities. Wars were fought, new monarchs struggled for power, kingdoms rose and fell, and the Deathless Kings were eventually forgotten."

My pulse was racing like I had just run through the district with a trio of guards on my tail. Sweat had gathered under my clothes, and a terrible fear had lodged itself somewhere below my stomach. I had never heard this story, and I suspected that the worst was yet to come.

"But that is not the end of the tale," the iylvahn continued, before I could take a breath. "The age of the Deathless Kings might be past, but that does not mean they are truly gone. In the final days of the war, one of the kings realized he could not win against the others. So he decided to seal a portion of himself, of his soul, into a special container. As long as the seal was not broken, his consciousness would remain, even if his body withered and died. With the last of his power, he then buried his own city and its subjects deep beneath the earth, so that no trace of him would remain on the surface. And so the king slept for generations, waiting for the day when he could return to the world. The knowledge of where the king hid his soul container was lost for many years, but it was rumored to lie somewhere deep below his palace, protected by guardians and ancient curses, so that his enemies could not come and destroy it."

The assassin paused, looking down at me, and ice spread through my veins as I realized what he was saying. That the stone I'd taken from the crypt held the soul of one of the Deathless Kings. An immensely powerful godlike being who had, long ago, played a part in destroying the world.

"Do you understand now?" the iylvahn asked quietly. "Why I could not allow you to take the stone? Why it should never have been returned to the surface?"

"I'm starting to," I said, making him frown. "I think I'm missing something, though. Assuming this story is even true, what does it matter if the stone is taken from the city? The

Deathless King hasn't come back, so I'm guessing he can't just pop out whenever he wants."

The iylvahn sighed. Clearly, he found my ignorance trying. "I forget that the other races have virtually no memory of the Deathless Kings," he murmured. "Am I correct in assuming that you do not know who the ma'jhet are, either?"

"Yes," I answered. "I mean, no. I don't know who they are."

He shook his head. "The ma'jhet were the closest confidants and advisors of the Deathless Kings," he explained. "They served the kings, but they were also allowed to rule over the commoners and make choices when the kings couldn't be bothered to. I suppose they were the closest thing to nobles within the Deathless courts.

"When the kings fell, the ma'jhet vanished," the iylvahn continued. "Perhaps they knew they would be hated in this new world without the kings. No one knew what happened to them, but there were always rumors that they lurked on the fringes and underground of society, waiting for the day the Deathless Kings would return. And, in many stories, working tirelessly to bring them back."

A terrible, yawning pit opened in my stomach as finally, all the pieces clicked into place. "The Circle," I whispered. "The Circle are the ma'jhet. And they sent me to retrieve the soulstone..."

"Because they are planning to resurrect the Deathless King," the iylvahn finished. "*Now* do you understand?"

Numbly, I slumped in the chair, trying to process everything I'd learned. My mind was spinning, my thoughts fractured, but I did manage to piece one question together. "What will happen," I whispered, "if the Deathless King comes back?"

"I don't know," the iylvahn replied. "But life has returned to the world. There is a whole city of souls to draw power from, and no rival Deathless to pose a challenge. Whatever you think might happen, the reality is likely a hundred times worse."

The assassin knelt in front of the chair, his gaze intense. "I need you to tell me where the soulstone is," he said. "This isn't about riches, or wealth, or power. This is about preventing a Deathless King from returning to this world. You won't just be saving your friend—you'll be saving the entire city, and possibly the kingdoms beyond."

I bit my lip, using the pain to clear my mind. I felt like I was drowning, in way over my head. I was just a thief trying to complete a mission for her leaders. Leaders who, according to the kahjai, were attempting to summon a legend straight out of the history scrolls. Because of me. And if they succeeded, it would be on my head.

"The thief that took the stone," I said shakily, "he doesn't know anything about the Deathless Kings or the soulstone or the ma'jhet. He just . . . needed a way to impress the Guildmaster. He took the stone to the guild."

"To the Guildmaster."

I nodded, hoping he wouldn't ask me who the Guildmaster was. I was already betraying Jeran and the entire guild. I couldn't betray Vahn, not for anything.

"The Guildmaster won't keep the stone there," the assassin

continued thoughtfully. "He'll be taking it to the Circle. I suspect they're in a panic because one of their members has already died. They know I'm close. They'll want to perform the ritual straightaway." His piercing gaze rose to mine again. "Do you know where they are?"

I hesitated. The iylvahn waited patiently as I fought a battle within myself. I had already betrayed the guild. But now I faced leading a stranger—an assassin—directly into Circle affairs. They would kill me if they found out what I was doing.

But . . . if what the iylvahn said was true, if the Circle really was trying to resurrect an ancient, godlike Deathless King . . .

"I can take you there," I told the assassin slowly, "on one condition." I took a deep breath and met those impassive blue eyes. "The thief and the Guildmaster . . . they're not part of the Circle," I said. At least, I desperately hoped Vahn was not. "They're being used, same as me," I continued. "If I take you to the Circle, I want you to promise that you won't kill either of them."

"My mission is to stop the Circle," the iylvahn replied. "And to prevent the rising of the Deathless King at all costs. If you say these two are not part of it, I have no reason to kill them."

That wasn't exactly the ironclad promise I was looking for, but I had a feeling the iylvahn wasn't going to change his answer. "All right," I said, feeling an invisible hand grab my stomach and twist. "I'll take you to where the Circle meets. We'll have to go through the guild, though. I don't know any other way."

"Through the guild." The assassin's eyes narrowed. "I don't think you'll be this foolish," he said, his tone cold and dangerous, "but just in case you are planning to betray me once we are inside, I would very much advise against it. I promised I would not kill your friend or the Guildmaster. Others will have no such protection."

I clenched my jaw and nodded. "I know how this works."

He crouched in front of the chair, the dagger in his hand again, and sliced through the ropes around my ankles. Then he stepped behind me, and a moment later, my hands were free as well.

Rubbing my wrists, I stood and quickly pulled up my hood, feeling a swell of relief as it settled over me, hiding my face from the world again. I was in a room with the deadliest of assassins, and I had just agreed to take him inside the guild. I did not want to be seen by anyone.

"Are you ready?" the iylvahn asked. "Is there anything you need before we attempt this?"

"Just one thing," I said, turning to look up at him. "What do I call you? I mean, you don't have to give me your name, but I don't want to have to yell 'Hey, assassin!' the whole time we're together."

He blinked. I got the strange feeling that he almost smiled. "You can call me Raithe," he answered. "Not my real name, of course, but it's better than 'iylvahn' or 'assassin.'"

"Raithe," I repeated. It fit the dark, silent figure at my side. "All right. Let's go."

His arm came up, stopping me. "And what about you?" he asked.

"What?"

"Your name," he went on. "What do I call you?"

"Oh." For some reason, that surprised me. I didn't think the cold, deadly iylvahn assassin would be interested in knowing my name. "It's Sparrow," I told him. "And yes, that is my real name."

Again, that hint of a smile went through his eyes. But he simply nodded and turned toward the door. "Lead on, then. The Circle might be well into the ritual by now. I pray that we are not too late to stop them."

TWELVE

It was a surreal feeling, striding through the Docks District with the iylvahn beside me. Everything around me looked normal. The haze hung thick in the air, and dock workers shuffled down the street, hoods up and cloths over their noses and mouths. High overhead, Solasti blazed in the cloudless sky, alone for a few more hours until her sister joined her for Demon Hour.

For a brief moment, I wondered what would happen if I ran. If I darted into a nearby alley and lost the iylvahn in the crowds. After all, he hadn't been able to catch me in the underground city, and I knew these streets like the back of my hand. I could abandon the assassin sent to kill me and go warn Vahn about the Circle and the Deathless King myself. And then maybe we could leave the city together, take a strider across the Dust Sea to start a new guild on the other side of Arkyennah. Far from the Circle, scary iylvahn assassins, and terrifying Deathless Kings. Vahn wouldn't want to leave Kovass, but he had always been practical; if I told him what the Circle was planning, surely he would see the writing on the wall. We were thieves, and this wasn't our fight; if a godlike Deathless King really was about to be summoned, the smart thing to do was to be far, far away when it happened.

Assuming, of course, that the assassin didn't chase me down and slit my throat the second I decided to run.

The iylvahn—*Raithe*, I reminded myself—walked silently next to me, his head slightly down. At first glance, he looked like everyone else, dressed in loose, light-colored clothes with his hood raised to keep off the sun. But as I continued to sneak furtive glances at my dangerous companion, I noticed he moved with a predatory grace the crowds around us couldn't match. Perhaps it was glaringly obvious only to me, because no one gave us a second look as we made our way through the narrow streets to the old warehouse at the end of the docks.

My heart pounded in my ears as I led the iylvahn through the front yard and around the back to the single door. Bringing strangers into the guild wasn't unheard of, but I had to play this just right. Stepping up to the door, I gave the secret knock and waited as it creaked open just enough for a bloodshot eye to peer out at me.

"Just me, Bassig," I announced as casually as I could.

His eye narrowed as it swept from me to the hooded figure at my back. "Who's he?"

"New client," I said immediately. "Vahn wanted me to escort him to his office. Is he here?"

Bassig's head swung back and forth. "Vahn went into the basement about an hour ago," he said. "Took that skinny friend of yours with him. Thought it was a little strange that he was taking him and not you, but hey, it ain't my business to question the boss."

Jeran. I felt a prickle of mingled worry and anger. Worry for my misguided friend who didn't know what he was getting into; anger because my head still hurt like crazy, I had been tied up and threatened at knifepoint, and I was now in the company of an iylvahn assassin who still might kill me if he had the mind to. I was not happy with Jeran at the moment, but at the same time, I understood. Even though we had a code, we were thieves, and life on the street was hard. In his situation . . . well, I probably wouldn't have done the same, but I'd have been tempted.

"Also," Bassig went on, eyeing the silent figure at my back again, "Vahn did say not to let any non–guild members inside, for any reason. So your friend is either gonna have to leave, or wait until he gets back."

My heart sank, but I sighed and gave the door guard an exasperated look. "Bassig, come on," I said. "It's me. Don't make us stand outside. Demon Hour is going to be here soon."

"Ain't my decision," Bassig said stubbornly. "It's what the boss told me."

Before I could think of anything else, the iylvahn stepped forward. For a heartbeat, I was afraid he was going to kill Bassig, but his posture was relaxed and nonthreatening as he moved beside me. "The king's crown is on the altar," he said in a low voice, making Bassig's bushy eyebrows shoot up. "And the stone in the center is green."

"Ah." The big man gave Raithe a half-wary, half-puzzled look. "New client, then. Right." He stepped back, opening the door a bit wider, and waved us through. "Go on in. You'll have to wait for Vahn to come back, though. Sparrow can show you to his office."

"Thank you," Raithe said easily, and stepped through the door. Trying not to let my astonishment show, I followed.

Once inside and out of earshot of Bassig, I gave the iylvahn a sidelong look. "Have you been to the guild before?" I asked in a low voice. "I wasn't even aware of that passcode. How did you know what to say to Bassig?"

The faintest hint of a smile crossed his face. "I'm observant," he said, equally softly. "I've been trained to blend in, which means taking on the mannerisms of those around me. The Circle, as you call them, runs the Thieves Guild of Kovass, among other things. Which means I learned everything I could about the guild and its practices before I came here. And one ma'jhet was kind enough to tell me the code before he died."

My awe—and fear—of the man increased. I wanted to ask him more, but I saw Rala gazing at us curiously from behind the bar, and I hurried across the floor to the steps on the other side.

Down in the basement, I stared at the brick wall, trying to remember which one opened the door to the sewers. I had an excellent memory, but I hadn't known I should be paying attention when Vahn pressed the secret brick, and it had happened so quickly, it was over before I could really focus on what he was doing. Raithe stood quietly at my side, patient and unhurried, as I stared blankly at the flat wall. After a long moment, he tilted his head as if listening for something.

"Someone is coming," he said in a low voice. He didn't tell me to hurry or ask what was taking so long, but the implication was crystal clear: I needed to get us out of there now.

Taking an educated guess, I stabbed my fingers into a random brick and nearly broke them as the brick remained just that: an immovable brick. Gritting my teeth, I moved my hand over a couple of spots and tried again, and this time, there was a scraping sound as the brick moved and a *click* sounded from somewhere beyond the wall.

With the grinding sound of stone on stone, the narrow section of wall slid back, revealing the darkened tunnel beyond. But a new noise echoed behind us—the thump of footsteps on the stairs. Immediately, Raithe and I ducked into the passageway as the door began to close. Through the gap, I saw Rala descending the stairs and looking around in confusion. The gap disappeared a moment later, plunging us into absolute darkness.

I cursed myself for not thinking to grab a lantern, but then remembered Halek's glowstone. It was still tied to my belt, and I quickly untangled it, feeling guilt gnaw at me as I thought of the Fatechaser. Hoping it wasn't broken, I raised the stone to my lips and breathed softly, and the tunnel was instantly bathed in a faint orange glow.

I looked up at the iylvahn, whose pupils had constricted sharply in the unexpected light. "An escape tunnel," he mused, gazing down the narrow corridor. "Clever, but I expected nothing less. Where does this lead?"

"I don't know, exactly," I replied. "A big cistern, somewhere underground. I've only been there once, with Vahn, when the Circle asked me to get the stone."

He nodded, indicating that I should take the lead, and in the faint light of the glowstone, we started down the tunnel.

I remembered the path well enough and soon began seeing familiar signs. When the tunnel opened into an enormous room with dark pools of water on either side of a walkway through the center and pillars reaching up to the ceiling, I knew we were close.

I started forward, but suddenly felt a firm hand on my shoulder, fingers tightening in warning. "Careful," Raithe breathed, his pale eyes sweeping the room. "This place feels wrong."

As he spoke, an eerie sensation crept over me, as if hundreds of tiny, invisible spiders were scuttling beneath my clothes. My skin crawled, and I cringed, fighting the urge to flap my arms and beat at my clothes. But almost as soon as the feeling struck, it faded, leaving me shivering and strangely cold. Raithe, if he had felt anything, showed no signs of it at all.

"Magic," he whispered, his voice gone hard. "It's starting. We have to move, quickly!"

We were halfway across the room when around us, the water started to ripple.

Nearly a dozen skeleton creatures broke the surface, rising from the glassy water, and the smell of decay filled the chamber as they turned their hollow eyes upon us. They were different from the ones in the ancient city; these were much bigger, their canine jaws capable of crushing my skull. They wore the tattered remains of golden armor and carried shields in one hand and curved swords in the other. They didn't shamble across the room; they moved with smooth, lethal intent, stepping from the water onto the narrow stone path, blocking our way forward.

I cringed. Raithe drew his blade and shoved me behind him as the monsters stepped toward us, their jaws gaping open in silent snarls. Pinpricks of green light glimmered in through their eye sockets, slowly growing into dancing flames. "The king's elite guardians," he muttered. "The Circle must've raised them to protect the ritual."

I glanced toward the exit, wondering if we should run, and saw more skeletons had stepped onto the path behind us. "We're surrounded," I told the assassin, who didn't turn around. "Should we run?"

A tremor went through the chamber, spreading ripples through the water and causing dust to rain from the ceiling.

"There's no time," Raithe said grimly. "The ritual is happening." He brandished his sword. "I'll deal with these," he said. "You get to the ritual site. Do whatever you can to stop the summoning, or at least stall it. Remember, if the Deathless King is resurrected, everything you've ever known will end. We cannot allow the Circle to summon him back into the world."

The closest skeletons were almost upon us; I could hear the scraping of bones as they raised their shields before them. The stink of death was overpowering; I stifled the urge to gag and tried to focus on what the assassin was telling me.

"Sparrow." Raithe spared me a split-second glance. "Do you understand? You have to stop the Circle. Everything will fall if the Deathless King rises again."

"Yeah." My mouth was dry with terror, but I forced the words out. "I get it. Stop the Circle. I'll try."

And the monsters lunged.

They came in silent and fast, with none of the clattering of the skeletons in the ancient city. I barely had time to blink before one was upon me, sweeping its sword down in a lethal arc. Instinctively, I ducked, and felt the blade catch the very top of my hood and knock it back. Staggering away, I saw the monster forward, raising its sword again, but Raithe whirled, sweeping his own blade at its neck. The skeleton quickly raised its shield. The iylvahn's sword hit the shield with a ringing *clang* that echoed through the chamber, and his pale eyes flashed to me.

"Sparrow, go!"

I went, darting around the monster as it turned toward Raithe, and splashed my way to the other side of the room. In the doorway, I looked back and saw that five of the creatures had surrounded the assassin, eyes blazing as their swords rose and fell, but so far, the kahjai was holding them off.

Wondering if this would be the last time I saw the iylvahn alive, I turned and fled into the tunnel.

Fear clawed at me as I crept down the passageway, trying to breathe normally and not in short, panicked gasps. My heart was pounding, and my palms were clammy with sweat. How was it that just yesterday I was sitting on a rooftop, watching the circus with Jeran and not thinking of anything that had to do with soulstones and forbidden cities and Deathless Kings? Now an iylvahn assassin expected me to stop the rising of an ancient godlike being by . . . doing what? I was just a thief. This was way out of my league.

I came to the end of the tunnel, and the circular chamber surrounded by pillars came into view. I ducked behind one of the columns, and when I peeked out into the chamber beyond, a chill like nothing I'd ever felt before infused my whole body.

Six Circle members in robes and skull masks stood around the stone altar, arms raised, chanting in unison. One tall, robed figure stood at the head of the altar, and his skull mask was the terrible visage of a demonic-looking horned creature. The other Circle members had their heads raised, but the horned skull stared down at what was before him on the altar.

Jeran lay shackled to the stone surface, eyes wide and terrified as he struggled against the chains. I bit down a gasp, my hands flying up to cover my mouth. He had been gagged, and his muffled cries were drowned out by the chanting of the robed figures around him. The black soulstone hovered a few feet above his chest, seeming to suck in the torchlight as it floated there. My insides twisted, horror flooding through me like a wave, and my legs nearly gave out beneath me.

The horned skull figure paused, observing the prisoner before him. Slowly, as the droning chants seemed to reach a crescendo, the figure raised its arm, a curved dagger with a serpentine blade as black as night glittering in its hand. My heart clenched, and I lunged from behind the pillar.

"Wait!"

I staggered into the torchlight. The droning voices abruptly stopped, and six pairs of hollow eyes turned on me. On the altar, Jeran looked up, his own eyes flaring with hope. He tried calling out, but his voice was muffled by the cloth.

In the silence, I seemed to stand in a spotlight, all eyes focused in my direction. What was I supposed to do? *Stop the summoning,* the iylvahn had said. *Or at least stall it.*

"What's going on here?" I asked, grateful that my voice didn't tremble as I spoke. "What are you doing to Jeran? Where's Vahn?"

"She's here."

It wasn't the horned leader who spoke, but one of the other robed figures, its cowled head turned to stare at the skull at the head of the altar. "The Fateless has come," it said, nearly hissing the words. "Now we can finish what we were supposed to finish tonight. The sacrifice does not matter, any life can be traded, but before the king returns, the Fateless must die."

Fateless? I didn't have time to puzzle out what that meant, and fear was suffocating my mind. "Where's Vahn?" I asked again, trying to speak clearly. "Does he know what you're doing? Jeran is part of our guild—the Guildmaster is not going to be happy if one of his members is hurt or killed."

"Sparrow."

At the head of the table, the horned figure raised his arm, took hold of the skull mask, and pulled it away. A familiar face stared out from beneath the hood, eyes dark and solemn, and my heart froze.

"I'm sorry, Sparrow," Vahn said as I stared at him in disbelief, not wanting to accept what was in front of me. "I hoped it wouldn't come to this. I didn't think, when I brought you to the guild all those years ago, that *you* would be the one to usher in the new age."

"Vahn?" I shook my head, my mind reeling. "No. You're part of the Circle?"

He smiled without humor. "A good ruse, was it not? No one suspected a thing. But it was necessary. The Guildmaster can see everything that happens in Kovass. I needed to be Vahn the Guildmaster so I could watch for the arrival of the Fateless." He sighed then, a furrow creasing his brow for just a moment. "I had begun to suspect it might be you, Sparrow. I hoped it was not. I hoped that you were just a talented thief whose luck defied all odds. But when you returned with the Tapestry of the World, I could no longer deny it. You were the one who could breach the ancient city, defy the curses and guardians who protected it, and retrieve the soulstone of our king."

He gazed at the body on the altar, and the coldness in his eyes filled me with dread. "Jeran said that you gave the soulstone to him," Vahn went on, as Jeran shook his head violently, his gaze pleading. "And that you told him to deliver it for you. It was obvious that he was lying. Still, in a way, I am glad. I would rather he be lying here, that the life I end to bring back the true ruler of the empire is not yours."

Horror flooded me as I realized what he was saying. That would have been me on the altar. If Jeran hadn't ambushed me and Raithe hadn't found me tonight, I would be the one chained to that table. My reward for bringing back the soulstone.

I felt sick. Everything I knew had been turned upside down. Jeran had betrayed me. Vahn had been lying to me my whole life. He was not only a member of the Circle, he was its leader.

"We waste time, Vahn," one of the Circle members hissed. "We are so close. We have the soulstone. We have the life that must be traded. The king *will* rise tonight—we have waited too long to fail now. Now there is only one last thread that must be cut." He pointed a withered finger at me. "The Fateless must die. She is a threat to our king's new empire. Kill her. You know it must be done."

"The last time I checked," Vahn said, his voice colder than

ice, "*I* led the ma'jhet, not you. We have a sacrifice. We have the soulstone. The Fateless is a fly, a thorn, a speck of dust in the glory of the Deathless King. The instability she could bring to the empire might never come to pass."

My heart pounded. It sounded like Vahn was trying to convince himself. Hope fluttered within me. I had to believe that even in this horrible situation, he wouldn't go through with whatever the Circle was planning.

"She is Fateless," a woman's voice droned, hard and unyielding. "You know what that means. You know we cannot risk it, Vahn. We are the last of the ma'jhet. Family, children, partners, everything we love must be sacrificed to the king if he calls for it." Her skull mask turned toward me, hatred shining through the hollow eye sockets. "You know what must be done."

"Vahn." I met his gaze, saw the conflict within. "Don't," I whispered. "Please. You're the only family I have."

He hesitated, a muscle working in his jaw. For just a moment, a ripple of emotions crossed his face: sorrow, anger, regret. I remembered all the moments I'd had with him; the times he had looked at me with pride, the small gestures of affection and love.

Vahn closed his eyes, and when he opened them again, a stranger stared back at me, cold and resolved. "I am sorry, Sparrow," he said again, and raised his arm. I caught the glint of metal and wood in his hand, a crossbow, pointed at me, and went numb with disbelief. "I truly wish that you had not been the Fateless."

Suddenly, something lunged in front of me, filling my vision. I heard a metallic clang as the crossbow bolt struck the copper shield of an elite guardian. Held by the iylvahn. Raithe straightened, and though I couldn't see his face, I could picture his searing, icy gaze on the Circle members below.

"*Kahjai!*" one of the robed figures screeched, sounding almost panicked. "The Fateless led it here! Traitor!"

Raithe darted forward in a blur, leaping onto the altar. His sword flashed, and the Circle member who had spoken toppled backward, his head leaving his shoulders halfway down. The skull mask hit the ground, shattering against the stones, and pandemonium erupted.

My heart lodged in my throat. I needed to run, but my legs were frozen, my body numb from what I'd just seen and heard. As Raithe stepped forward, plunging his sword into the back of another robed figure who had turned to flee, Vahn raised his head, his dark eyes shining with terrible determination. Raithe spun on him, raising his bloody sword, as Vahn calmly drew the knife across Jeran's throat.

No! My stomach heaved, and everything around me seemed to slow. On the altar, Jeran's body spasmed. He made a few strangled choking sounds, red liquid bubbling from his lips and running down his neck, before his eyes glazed over, staring up at nothing.

The black soulstone pulsed once, and for a split second, everything—light, heat, emotion—seemed to be sucked into it. I felt cold, as if all the warmth had been drawn out of me. The torches guttered, casting flickering shadows over the room, and in the eerie light, I saw Raithe spring across the altar over Jeran's motionless corpse and aim his sword at Vahn's neck. I cried out just as the torches flickered and died, plunging the chamber into complete darkness.

The black soulstone flared, casting everything in an eerie red light. Vahn stood in the same spot, his own sword now raised to meet the iylvahn's, their blades pressed together.

"You're too late." Vahn's tone was soft, triumphant; he stepped back, smiling, and the red light turned his face into a terrifying mask. "The king has come."

On the altar behind Raithe, Jeran's body dissolved, his flesh turning to dust and leaving behind only a skeleton. The particles rose in a glittering cloud and swirled around the soulstone, which was pulsing like a frantic heartbeat. Raithe spun, his blade flashing, and struck the glowing stone from the air. Instead of shattering, it flew to the edge of the altar and stopped as if it had hit a wall. The cloud of dust followed, swirling into the shape of a man, tall and broad shouldered, his features were blurred. Within the swirling cloud, the soulstone pulsed one final time and then shattered, sending shards of black rock flying in every direction.

A ripple of power went through the room, causing the floor to shake and the walls to tremble. I felt the vibrations through my boots, felt the ground heave under me, and staggered back. Cracks slithered across the floor and snaked up the walls, sand rained from the ceiling, and chunks of rock began smashing into the altar from above. The three remaining Circle members, who had scattered to the edges of the chamber when Raithe attacked, fell to their knees.

"He comes." Vahn's calm, triumphant voice reached me through the chaos. He wasn't talking to me, but to the iylvahn, who stood at the edge of the altar, gazing up at the swirling cloud. The look on Raithe's face chilled me; one of dismay and weary resignation. "You've failed, kahjai. The king rises, and he will destroy this world and remake it in his own image. Run now, iylvahn. Run while you can. Soon, it won't matter where you go."

Raithe's eyes hardened. He glanced back at Vahn, as if contemplating whether to attack him, and my stomach twisted. Vahn simply smiled, half raising his arms, as if inviting him to try.

At the edge of the chamber, one of the Circle members screamed. His hood fell off as he arched back, mouth open in a tortured wail. Abruptly, the skin of his face dissolved into dust, which was immediately sucked into the swirling cloud over the altar. The skeleton beneath the robes collapsed to the floor. I dug my shaking fingers into the pillar to keep myself from bolting from the room.

Raithe made his decision. Spinning from Vahn, he leaped from the altar and ran for the door at my back. As he passed the dust storm, I saw a grimace cross his face, as if he expected to be struck down, turned to dust and bones himself in the blink of an eye. But he passed the swirling cloud without incident and continued across the room.

The dust solidified, and a man stepped down onto the altar, naked except for a gold loincloth belted around his waist. He was very tall, standing virtually head and shoulders over everyone else. Jet-black hair fell to his shoulders; his skin was a darkened bronze, and his physique was powerful. He turned his head, observing the scene around him, and his eyes were two fathomless black pits, empty of pity or understanding.

As I backed away, Vahn's gaze met mine across the chamber. Regret glimmered there, but only for a heartbeat before it vanished and cold determination took its place. In that moment, the Guildmaster of Kovass, the man who had raised me and taught me everything I knew about being a thief, vanished—only the leader of the ma'jhet, the elite advisors to the Deathless King, remained.

Then Raithe was leaping up the stairs, his eyes telling me to run, and I did. We fled the chamber of the Circle and the Deathless King, the images of Vahn's cold eyes and Jeran's corpse seared into my mind forever.

THIRTEEN

When we slipped back through the secret door, we found the guild's basement was in shambles. Rubble littered the ground, and pieces of the walls and roof were strewn across the floor. I didn't understand what was happening until the ground beneath me trembled, causing several shelves to crash to the ground and spill their contents everywhere.

"Maederyss forgive me." Raithe leaned back against the bricks, his eyes blank, his expression dazed. Slowly, he slid down the wall until he was sitting, resting his arms on his knees and bowing his head. "I tried, but I couldn't stop it."

Seeing the calm, stoic assassin like that should have shaken me to the core, but I couldn't feel anything. Now that we were away from the immediate danger, everything I'd just experienced crashed down on me all at once. Jeran was dead. Vahn had killed him to bring the Deathless King back to life. He would have done the same to me. Without thought. Without remorse. Everything I thought I knew about him was wrong. I didn't know what to think, or feel.

I did know one thing. This wasn't Raithe's fault.

It was mine.

"What do we do now?" I whispered.

The assassin shook his head wearily. "There is nothing we

can do." He sounded resigned. "At least, not here. You cannot slay a Deathless—not even the kings of old could destroy one of their own. They draw life energy from everything around them. Only when there is no life left do they become mortal."

I shuddered. Only now, when it was too late, did I understand. Why Raithe had been so determined to stop the summoning. Why he would track someone through an ancient underground city filled with monsters and curses. Why he would kill to prevent the soulstone from being disturbed. The Deathless King couldn't be slain. There was nothing that could stop him from doing whatever he pleased within Kovass.

And all of this could have been prevented, had I never set foot in the undercity. .

"I . . . I have to get home." On the floor, Raithe stirred and pushed himself to his feet. "I have to get back to Irrikah and warn the queen that . . . that I've failed."

"Where is home for you?" I asked.

"Very far from here." Raithe took a breath, and some of his composure returned as he straightened. "Across the Dust Sea and over the Barren Steppes is Irrikah, the city of my people. It's time I returned." Raithe paused, and his pale blue eyes slid to me, narrowing. "You need to come with me, Fateless."

I recoiled. There was that word again. *Fateless.* "Why?"

Another tremor went through the floor, shaking dust loose and sending several pebbles plinking down around us. Raithe's expression hardened. "Because this city is doomed," he told me. "Do you want to stay here when the Deathless King makes himself known?"

"I've survived this long," I said, feeling almost hysterically stubborn. "That's all I know how to do, really. I'll keep surviving, by myself." Vahn's face swam before me, smiling and amused one moment, cold and blank the next. A stranger. Jeran, laughing and full of life, dead in the next heartbeat, dark eyes staring up at nothing. "If this taught me anything," I went on thickly, "it's that I can't trust anyone but myself. I probably will end up leaving the city, but I'll do it alone."

"No, you will not." Raithe took a step toward me. I tensed and cast a quick glance at the stairs, judging the distance between us. "Don't run," Raithe warned. "You won't make it far."

I glared at him. "What are you going to do—tie me up again and stuff me in a sack?"

"I would prefer not to have to do that." Raithe clenched his jaw, then, to my surprise, lowered his head and pushed back his hood. His face, fully exposed, was beautiful and haunted as he met my gaze.

"Sparrow." His voice, low and feather-soft, sent a shiver racing up my back. "I don't want you as my prisoner, or my enemy. But you must return with me to Irrikah. Our queen will want to meet you. Because you are the Fateless."

"Why do you keep calling me that?" I demanded. "Vahn and the Circle said I was Fateless, too." I remembered the robed figures pointing at me, hissing at Vahn that the Fateless had to die. And Vahn raising his crossbow in my direction, his eyes hard and cold. "They were going to kill me because of it," I went on. "Why? What does it even mean?"

Raithe hesitated. I could see him struggling with what to say.

Whatever the Fateless was, he didn't want to reveal it. "It's not my place," he said at last. "The queen is the best one to explain it."

Which meant I had to go with him to the iylvahn city across the Dust Sea. Away from Kovass and everything I'd ever known. Dread filled me. I had dreamed of leaving, but not like this.

Another tremor shook the ground, and this time, it didn't stop. The walls of the basement swayed, more dust and stones raining down from the ceiling. Cracks appeared in the walls as the earthquake continued to rumble. I staggered and winced as a large clay pot fell from the shelf and smashed to the floor, shattering into a thousand fragments.

Raithe and I rushed up the stairs. I cast a glance at the tavern as we sprinted for the doors, hoping to catch a glimpse of Rala. But the bar was empty as we passed, the tables deserted. As we ducked outside, I sent up a quick prayer to Maederrys that Fate would be kind to Rala, that whatever else happened, she would somehow survive what was to come.

Though I had the horrible feeling that many would meet their fate this day.

The district was in chaos; people were scrambling through the streets and coughing in the haze, which had been stirred into a nearly impenetrable fog. Dust stung my eyes and clogged my throat, and Raithe quickly pulled up his hood. The air had reached the thick, searing temperature that heralded Demon Hour. Shielding my face, I gazed at the sky, squinting through the haze and the dust, and my stomach turned. The color was an ominous orange, and my vision filled with swirling clouds that blotted out the suns.

Someone slammed into me, knocking me back with a grunt. They continued to stagger down the street, not even looking where they were going. I winced, rubbing my bruised shoulder, and saw Raithe's eyes narrow.

"We need to get to higher ground," he said, and took two steps back, gazing up at the large building across the street. "I'm going to the roofs. Will you be able to keep up?"

A tiny spark of my old defiance emerged, fighting through the horror and the numbness and the fear of what was happening around me. "I could ask the same of you," I answered, and darted across the street. I vaulted onto the stone wall of the building and dug my fingers into the cracks between loose bricks, finding handhold after handhold until I finally scrambled onto the roof.

Raithe, of course, was right beside me, and together, we straightened and gazed over the rooftops of the city. The heat beat down on my head, but the scene before me drove anything else from my mind.

From the docks to the Temple of Fate to the palace high on the hill, the entire city was surrounded by a whirling sandstorm. I couldn't see the horizon line, or the desert beyond; I couldn't see anything beyond the city's edge. The howling storm, massive and impossible, encompassed all of Kovass, blotting out the light and turning the air red.

In the center of it all, floating above the rooftops, was a figure with bronze skin and eyes like the Void, jet-black hair snapping in the wind. My stomach twisted at the sight, and I heard Raithe draw in a sharp breath as the Deathless King slowly turned, surveying the city around him.

This is the world I return to.

The voice echoed in my head, heavy with fury and disgust, seeming to ripple through all of Kovass.

Sand and dust and short-lived insects crawling over one another. Pathetic. A filthy shell of the shining kingdom that used to be. You do not deserve life. You do not deserve my glory. But I will grant it to you regardless, insects. I will show you what you have been longing for all this time. Let the shining kingdom rise once again and bury the filth beneath it in the majesty of your new god!

The Deathless King raised his arms, and the tremors turned to shaking. I staggered as the ground heaved like the waves of the Dune Sea. When I straightened, my legs went numb and I vibrated with horror. Buildings swayed, rocking like branches in the wind, and then several of them collapsed to the ground in a muffled roar of stone and dust.

The roof beneath me cracked, one corner falling away and smashing to the street below. Screams rose up from below us, and the stones under my feet shuddered and began to fracture.

"Come on!" Raithe held out an arm, indicating the edge of the roof. "The whole building is falling apart. Let's go!"

We scrambled to get clear, leaping off the roof and grabbing the wall of a shorter building. I pulled myself up onto its roof, then backed away from the edge, watching the Docks District shake and heave like a sick animal. "What's happening?" I gasped.

"The Deathless King is raising his empire," Raithe said grimly.

I frowned in confusion, until I realized what he meant, and my mouth dropped open. "You don't mean . . . the *ancient city*?"

"I told you." The assassin's blue eyes met mine, bright with anguish and helpless fury. "No one can stand against the Deathless King once he rises. He'll destroy Kovass and replace it with his kingdom, and there's nothing we can do but flee before it consumes everything."

One street over, the ground collapsed with a roar that made my ears throb, sending a plume of dust into the air. The house that had stood there vanished as well, breaking apart and disappearing into the pit. As I stared, cracks spread across the road like spiderwebs, and the pointed spire of a tower began rising from the hole.

"Sparrow!" Raithe's voice made me jump. The iylvahn held out a hand, his gaze stern and yet almost pleading. "The city is lost," he said, and the truth of his words turned my heart to ice. "Kovass has fallen. We have to get out of here before it crushes us, too. You know the city better than me. Where is the best place to go?"

"The docks," I whispered. There was no way we would get through the gates; we'd be crushed under buildings or swallowed by the earth before we made it out of the district. "The striders might still be operational. We have to get to the docks."

We fled across the rooftops, leaping from building to building and feeling them shake under our boots. Around us, the city continued to collapse, clouds of dust rising into the air as one structure fell and another pushed its way to the surface. The new buildings were huge, blotting out the suns as they soared into the air. The scale of destruction left me breathless; the sheer power of what was happening around me was incomprehensible. Raithe hadn't exaggerated when he'd said the Deathless Kings were nearly gods. I wished I had listened to him sooner, but it was far too late for regrets.

As I followed the assassin, leaping onto another roof, the stones beneath me crumbled. I dropped, but managed to throw out my arms and catch what remained of the edge. My legs dangled over the street as I tried to claw myself up, feeling the entire building tremble beneath me.

Strong fingers clamped over my wrist, and the iylvahn pulled me onto the roof. Surprised, I met those pale eyes for just a moment. I hadn't expected him to help; none of my teammates in the guild would've come back for me. The unspoken rule was every hood for themselves, and if you couldn't keep up, you weren't fit to be there in the first place.

"Are you all right?" the iylvahn asked. He sounded breathless, too. I nodded, feeling another tremor quiver through the ground beneath us, and he turned away. "Keep moving, then. We're almost there."

The docks were a madhouse. People were scrambling over each other, blindly shoving others out of the way, trying to escape the chaos. Waves of sand smashed into the rocks, sending geysers of dust into the air. Figures swarmed the piers like ants, several tumbling into the roiling sea and being immediately swallowed by sand.

On the farthest dock, at the end of the pier, silhouetted like a great wood-and-metal insect against the sky, one last strider crouched. Mobs of people rushed it, scrambling over the docks and sending more figures tumbling into the churning sea, shoved or thrown over the edge by the panicked and the desperate.

A grinding sound reverberated through the air, echoing over the voices of the mob. A shudder racked the strider's body and it rose from the sands, as if it were standing up.

"It's getting ready to leave," Raithe said, and leaped down to the docks. "Hurry!"

We ran for the pier, dodging multitudes of bodies. Thankfully, I had a lifetime of practice weaving through crowds, and Raithe seemed to be an expert as well. People stumbled, pushed, shoved, and jostled around us, but we dodged and wove our way through the human sea until we hit the last dock.

The strider began to move. People were still flinging themselves at it, reaching for the rope ladder that was quickly being drawn up the side. Some leaped for its legs, missing and plummeting into the sands below. A few managed to cling to its sides, hanging on for dear life as the wood-and-metal beast continued down the dock.

Raithe narrowed his eyes, gauging the distance between the strider and the pier. "We're going to have to jump," he muttered, glancing back at me. "Can you make it?"

"Yes," I gasped, but my voice was drowned out as, with the thundering of a landslide, the earth broke apart and a great tower surged into the air at the edge of the docks. Shedding sand and boulders, it loomed over us, its gilded roof flashing a dull gold in the eerie light. Raithe grabbed my wrist and yanked me back as rocks rained onto the pier, smashing into planks and crushing civilians. Most of the crowd vanished into the waves, screaming. We pressed back against a wall as chunks of stone continued to rain down, sending up massive plumes of dust as they crashed into the sea.

The strider wobbled, lurching to the side as stones bounced off its body. The ground beneath it heaved, and a huge wave of sand smashed into it, causing it to stagger even more. I watched it lean to the side in seeming slow motion, shedding figures that went flailing helplessly into the waves. A metallic scream pierced the air as one of its legs buckled under the unnatural weight. With a groan like the dying howl of a great beast, the strider collapsed into the churning waves. A swell rose up to swallow it, and then it was gone, taking my heart to the bottom of the sea with it.

Raithe and I staggered away from the wall and stared at the harbor, at the empty spot where the strider had gone down. The docks were in shambles, wooden planks smashed apart and floating on the waves. Bodies lay everywhere, struck by falling rock or crushed under the feet of their fellow humans. The boats and sand skiffs had long been taken, and the last strider lay in a crumpled heap at the bottom of the Dust Sea. No way out, except to go back through the collapsing city to try to reach the gates, clear on the other side.

I knew for a fact we weren't going to make it.

"Sparrow!"

I jerked at the sound of my name. Nearly inaudible, it floated to me through the chaos around us. It hadn't come from the harbor or the streets behind us, but from somewhere in the ocean of sand.

The bow of a sand skiff crested a wave, sails flapping wildly in the gale, and moved toward us. A figure stood at the rudder, trying desperately to make the little boat go where he wanted. Blond hair gleamed in the suns and deep blue eyes flashed as they met mine.

My own eyes widened, and I gasped. "Halek?"

The Fatechaser waved at us, then quickly grabbed the rudder again as the sand skiff lurched to the side. "Come on!" he cried, steering the vessel toward the broken remains of the dock. A wave caught the boat, nearly tossing it into the air, and he winced. "I can't bring it much closer. You're going to have to jump!"

I glanced at Raithe, and we sprinted over the shattered dock, leaping broken planks and bounding from post to post. Sand swells rose frighteningly high, and waves slapped against my legs, filling the air with grit. Raithe reached the end of the dock and sprang over the roiling sand, landing in the boat with room to spare. Halek's gaze snapped to him as a swell caught the boat, pushing it farther from the docks just as I reached the end.

"Sparrow!" Raithe lunged to the very edge of the skiff and held out an arm. "Jump!"

I jumped.

The Dust Sea boiled beneath me, hot wind and sand blasting my face. My eyes stung, blurring with tears as I fell, and I reached out blindly with one hand.

Once more, strong fingers closed around my forearm and yanked me forward, and I fell into the skiff. I landed on top of the assassin, feeling his rigid body against mine as I pressed him into the boards.

Panting, trembling, I raised my head and met that pale blue gaze, the face within the hood a breath away from mine. The expression staring back at me wasn't anger or even unease; it was calm, plus the barest hint of relief peeking through the stoic features.

A muffled roar echoed behind us. I rose and stumbled to the back of the skiff, then watched the docks shrink rapidly from view as we sailed away. I could barely see Kovass through the massive dust storm swirling around it, but the hazy silhouettes against the sky were not familiar.

My legs buckled, and I sank to my knees on the deck. Kovass—my city, the only home I'd ever known—grew smaller and smaller beyond the waves. I thought of the guild and the people I'd known my whole life: Rala, Dahveen, Shadyr, Jeran. All gone. Maybe *someone* had survived, but I had seen the utter chaos in the streets as the city collapsed, and knew they were probably dead. Swallowed in the fall of the city. Or killed at the hands of someone they knew.

And Vahn. The one I'd trusted the most. Who'd taught me everything, raised me to be the best. Who'd been planning the rise of the Deathless King and the fall of Kovass from the beginning.

But Vahn wasn't responsible. The Circle wasn't even responsible. There was only one person who could have gotten the soulstone and brought it back to the surface. If I hadn't gone into the ancient city, if I hadn't been so determined to prove myself to Vahn, Kovass might still be standing. Everyone I knew might still be alive.

I heard Halek's voice at my back, asking if I was all right, but I couldn't answer. Raithe was silent, but I felt his eyes on me, appraising and concerned. I didn't turn around. The skiff bobbed on the waves, the suns beating down overhead, and I continued to stare at Kovass until it became a smear of dust on the horizon and finally vanished altogether.

PART TWO

FOURTEEN

"Sparrow. Get up."

I groaned. The mattress beneath me was soft, the blankets warm and comfortable. Sinking farther into the pillow, I pretended not to hear the voice of the Guildmaster, even as I knew he wouldn't let this go.

An impatient sigh. "Fine. Sleep away the morning, lazy child. I suppose you don't want the gift in my office, then."

I opened my eyes. "Gift?"

"Aha. I thought so." Vahn shook his head in amused exasperation as I sat up, more curious than anything. The times Vahn had gifted me with anything could be counted on one hand. If I wanted something, I was expected to get it myself.

"It's nothing big," he went on, "but the client was impressed that you managed to get into Rul Fadel's bedchambers to acquire the item from his nightstand. She left you a gift from her private collection in thanks."

"Ooh." I hopped up, grinning. "I'm awake," I told Vahn, who raised a brow at me. "I'm ready for my gift. Maybe it will make dodging guards and hiding from a pack of attack dogs worth it."

A reluctant smile flickered over his features. One hand rose and rested briefly atop my head. "You did well last night," he said, and a warm glow ignited in my stomach. "That was a difficult job. I don't know if anyone else could've pulled it off so easily."

The warm glow spread through my whole body, but I shrugged. "As if there was any doubt. I *am* the best thief in the guild, after all."

Anyone else, especially Jeran, would've rolled their eyes or made some comment about my lack of humility. Vahn, however, simply chuckled.

"Yes," he muttered, and turned away, leaving me to follow. "Let's hope that stays true for a while longer."

I stirred, opening my eyes slowly, the dream fading into a searing white light as consciousness returned. For a moment, I wondered where I was. The surface against my back and legs felt hard yet unstable, bobbing rhythmically beneath me. I raised my head, seeing the edges of a small wooden skiff with two figures sitting against its sides, one dozing with his head on his chest, one gazing out over nothing. And then everything came rushing back.

Kovass had fallen. Jeran was dead. Vahn had betrayed me. And the godlike, immortal Deathless King had returned to the world. Because of me.

My stomach heaved. I turned, dragged myself to the edge of the skiff, and emptied its contents into the churning sands, which swallowed the mess instantly. My eyes burned, my vision going blurry, as I gagged and tried to suck in enough breath not to be sick again.

"Sparrow."

I felt Halek's presence beside me, right before a gentle touch pressed into my back. "Easy there," he murmured as I panted and tried to compose myself. "This is probably not the best time to mention this, but you should try not to waste any liquid. It's going to get really unpleasant in a couple hours."

Blinking away the last of the tears, I looked up, and my stomach threatened to rebel once more.

The endless expanse of the Dust Sea surrounded us all the way to the horizon on every side. Dust eddies swirled along the sand, dissolving into nothing before forming again. Heat waves shimmered off the surface, making the air look like water. No matter where I turned, I couldn't see anything but shifting sand and dust, stretching on and on until it touched the sky.

And then I saw Solasti, directly overhead, and I realized what Halek was talking about.

Demon Hour was coming.

Dread filled me. There was no shelter out here, no shade, nothing to protect us from the burning glare of the twins. The air on the Dust Sea was already like an oven, thick and oppressive; once Demon Hour hit, we would be like meat on a skillet.

As Halek said, things were about to get really unpleasant.

I glanced at Raithe, sitting on the edge of the skiff with one foot braced on the bench, and found the iylvahn watching me. "Any ideas?" I asked weakly. The inside of my mouth felt rancid and dry; I desperately wished I hadn't vomited precious liquid over the side.

The iylvahn closed his eyes. His face, I suddenly noticed, looked haggard beneath his hood. "Pray," he said, opening his eyes. "And hope that the winds of Fate blow a little harder in this direction."

We drifted.

The Dust Sea stretched on, endless and eternal. Unchanging. Time was measured by the appearance of Namaia, poking her head over the horizon, and how far she had climbed to join her sister overhead. When Namaia first appeared, the heat was unbearable. By the time she was halfway into the sky, I knew we weren't going to survive the next hour. Eventually, our boat would be found bobbing in the waves somewhere, with three baked, shriveled corpses lying in the bottom. Halek, Raithe, and I worked together to take down the sail, positioning it so that it cast a bit of shade over the boat, providing a little relief from the glare of the twins. But it wasn't enough, and as Namaia climbed ever higher, it was all I could do to lie motionless on the deck, Halek and Raithe beside me, expending as little energy as I could.

It was hard to breathe. The air scraped my throat, passing over lips as dry and cracked as a brick wall. I couldn't summon any saliva to wet my lips; my mouth felt like a desert, filled with dust. On either side of me, Halek and Raithe lay like the dead, Halek on his stomach with his face buried in his arms, Raithe on his side, facing away from me. The skiff was small, so we were crushed together, but there was nowhere else to lie, and sitting on the edges of the boat was impossible. Occasionally, I felt one of them shift, or heard a breath that told me they weren't dead. Idly, I wondered when that would change. When their movements would cease and there would be a pair of lifeless bodies lying next to me. Or would I be the one they tried to rouse and couldn't?

On my left side, Halek shifted so that his face was turned toward me. My hood was pulled down as far as it could go to protect me from the sun, but even without seeing him, I could hear the faintest grin in his voice. "Fate has . . . a funny sense of humor, I've found," he whispered, his voice coming out raspy and dry. "Escape the literal fall of a city . . . only to be roasted alive on the Dust Sea. But I can't . . . cry about it—literally—so I . . . have to laugh."

He was trying to cheer me up, but smiling would split my lips open, which would be painful. Besides, I didn't think I would smile again for a long, long time. Maybe Halek could laugh in the face of death, but when I closed my eyes, I could still see Jeran bleeding out on the altar, and Vahn's flat, emotionless stare. I could see the city crumbling, crushing thousands, including the people I'd known all my life. And I could see the black soulstone hovering in the air above the pedestal. If I had simply turned around and left it where it was . . .

Beside me, I felt Halek raise his head a little more, though how he had the energy to do even that, I didn't know. "Hey, kah-jai," he called weakly. "Raithe, was it? Are you dead?"

There was a pause, long enough to send a ripple of fear through my stomach; maybe the deadly iylvahn assassin *had* died and I was lying next to a corpse. But then there was a breath, and Raithe's voice drifted up, raspy and hoarse. "No."

"I feel . . . we got off on a bad foot," Halek went on. "This might not be the time but . . . if it is my fate . . . to die here on the Dust Sea, I want my conscience to be clean." He took a breath, as if gathering the remains of his energy. "I . . . appreciate that you helped Sparrow," he went on, "and that you ... didn't kill me when you had the chance. So ... thank you."

Raithe made a tiny sound that might've been a sigh. "Save your strength, Fatechaser," he said, not unkindly. "If it eases your conscience, I am not your enemy. I appreciate that you came by when you did, though I fear the end result will be the same."

I'm sorry. My eyes burned, and I squeezed them shut. I had no tears to cry, even if I wanted to. *All the death, the fall of the city ... it happened because of me. I was the catalyst for everything.*

Now Kovass was gone. And I was going to die here, on a lonely boat in the middle of the Dust Sea. It seemed my luck had run out at last. Maybe the Weaver had finally gotten tired of my hijinks, but Raithe and Halek didn't deserve this fate.

Somehow, Halek gave a raspy chuckle. "Maybe we'll be ... eaten by a dust serpent," he wheezed, referring to the legends of the enormous snakes that prowled the Dust Sea. "It would be over fast, I would think. At least then ... we'd be out of the suns."

Raithe hesitated. I could sense him struggling with himself, debating whether or not to say something. "If ... you like," he began at last, "if you want the pain to end, I can make it quick."

My stomach twisted. He was offering to kill Halek, to end his suffering quickly instead of letting him die a lingering death. For just a moment, it was tempting.

But Halek gave another painful-sounding chuckle. "Much ... as I appreciate the thought, assassin," he rasped, "it's against the Fatechaser code ... to orchestrate your own death. For good or ill, when our fate does come for us ... it's because it was meant to happen. Trying to stop it, or hurrying it along ... goes against the entire ideology of a Fatechaser."

Raithe didn't say anything to that, and another moment passed in silence. "Sparrow?" the assassin murmured after a few heartbeats. "Are you awake?"

I nodded, knowing he would feel it, not trusting my voice at the moment.

"I am sorry for Kovass," he went on, making my throat close and my eyes burn even more. "And your friends. I know that's of little comfort now."

He wasn't expecting an answer, and talking seemed like too much effort. His next words, though, caused my stomach to twist and sent a clammy chill up my spine, despite the heat.

"I suppose not even the Fateless can escape everything."

I didn't care about whatever this Fateless thing was. But hearing him say that, disappointment and regret heavy in his voice, made me lift my head an inch to gaze at the back of his head.

"What?" My voice scraped my throat; my tongue felt huge and awkward in the dusty cavern of my mouth, but I forced words out anyway. "What do you mean by that?"

He was silent for so long that I thought he had passed out or simply wasn't going to answer. I had stopped paying attention when he finally muttered, nearly to himself:

"The Fateless wasn't supposed to die like this."

A tiny spark of anger and defiance emerged, though it was feeble, and almost immediately snuffed out by the heat. "I am ... not dead yet," I whispered.

This time, he didn't answer.

Demon Hour intensified. I drifted helplessly, sliding in and out of consciousness as the suns continued to blaze down, relentless and unyielding. Snatches of dreams tormented my thoughts: Jeran, Vahn, and the Circle, leering at me from the edges of darkness. They shouted at me, words I didn't understand but that were filled with anger and rage. The Deathless King floated toward me, smiling a terrible smile. He opened his mouth, and thousands of winged insects burst forth, swarming, buzzing. They swirled around me in a black cloud, the drone of their wings making my ears throb. I could suddenly feel them in my nose, my mouth, burrowing beneath my skin, and I thrashed myself out of the dream.

I was staring at the inside of my hood, still pulled over my face, but for a moment I didn't know if I was still dreaming or not. I could still hear the faint buzz of wings in my ears, a remnant of the dream. Only, it didn't fade. Instead, it grew louder and louder, until it sounded like a massive swarm of insects droning right above the skiff.

I must still be dreaming. More curious than anything now, I pushed my hood back with leaden arms and cracked open one swollen eye to squint into the suns.

A massive black shape hovered in the air before me, silhouetted against the searing blue of the sky. My vision was blurry, but I could make out multiple jointed legs, a chitinous segmented body, and two long antennae curling into the air. A pair of transparent wings, moving so quickly they were nothing but a blur, droned in my ears.

"Hey," the giant insect said, its sultry voice distinctly feminine. "You in the boat. Are you still alive?"

Definitely dreaming, I thought. Closing my eyes again, I let my head drop back, and hoped my next dreams would be pleasant ones.

Sparrow. Jeran staggered forward, throat cut, blood glistening wetly down his neck, staining his clothes crimson. *You let me die*, he said accusingly, turning hollow eyes on me. *I'm dead because of you.*

You were a tool. Vahn turned a cold smile in my direction, eyes empty of any warmth or recognition. *Never a daughter. I always knew it would come to this.*

The Circle surrounded me, bleached skulls floating in the darkness. *The Fateless must die*, they whispered. As one, they stepped closer, serpentine knives gleaming in their hands, dripping blood to the stones. *The Fateless must die for the Deathless King to rule the world!*

The circle of knives rose . . . and stabbed down at me all at once.

I jerked awake with a gasp.

The world had changed. I was lying down, not on the deck of the tiny skiff but on a cot in the corner of a small room. The walls of the room were strange, not stone or wood, but metallic with a coppery sheen. The air was cooler, breathable now; I no longer felt the relentless heat of the suns scorching down on me.

I was also naked, though a light sheet had been draped over my body and a wet cloth had been pressed to my forehead. I felt a stab of panic at being so vulnerable, and quickly sat up to look for my clothes.

The room and everything in it spun wildly. I closed my eyes, waiting for the dizzy spell to pass, gritting my teeth against the sudden bloom of nausea in my stomach.

"Ah, so you're up now, are you?"

I opened my eyes. A woman had entered the room carrying a stack of towels with a bowl set atop the pile, the door swinging shut behind her. She was a head shorter than me, which was saying something, and her shoulders were twice as broad.

A d'wevryn? I hadn't seen many d'wevryn in my years in Kovass, but I knew they piloted most of the striders that journeyed across the Dust Sea. They had an affinity for machines and mechanics, and nearly all striders had at least a couple of d'wevryn workers as crew. Reddish hair was pulled into a no-nonsense bun atop the woman's head, and a pair of copper-tinted glasses sat on the end of her large nose. She paused at the side of the cot, setting down the towels and the bowl perched atop it, then shook her head at me.

"Welcome back to the world of the living," she said in a wryly amused tone. "I expect you must feel like a strip of sun-dried jerky right now. Let's see if we can't fix that."

She withdrew a mug from the bowl and pressed it into my hands. "Slowly," she warned, with a glower nearly as frightening as Vahn's when he was annoyed. I glanced down and saw the mug was half full of water. "Drink it too fast, and it'll come right back up," the strange woman warned as I immediately pressed it to my lips. It was lukewarm and slightly salty, but it could've been vinegar and I wouldn't have cared. "That's right," the woman nodded, satisfied, as I took deep but careful sips. "I didn't spend the last hour putting liquid into you for you to puke it all over the floor."

Finishing the water, I handed the mug back to the woman and eyed her warily. I was grateful, of course, and happy that I wasn't floating in the middle of the Dust Sea being turned into human jerky, but I still didn't know who she was, or where I had been taken.

"Ah, now, save your breath, girl," the d'wevryn said, seeing me eye her with suspicion. "I know that look, and don't you worry. You're safe. You're on Captain Gahmil's strider. We were on our way to Kovass when our scout happened to spot your boat. Good thing she did, too—a few more minutes and there'd have been nothing but two cooked humans and an iylvahn in the bottom of that skiff." She gave a slightly guttural chuckle. "Thankfully, you were only half cooked when she found you."

"The others," I whispered, after swallowing several times to get my throat working. "They're all right?"

The woman snorted. "Last I checked, the human had charmed the nurse halfway out of his pants, and the iylvahn was trying to convince the doctor to let him speak to the captain." She shook her head with another huff. "I don't know why you lot were on a sand skiff in the middle of nowhere—any fool who's been on the waves can tell you a skiff isn't meant for the open sea. I'm surprised you didn't capsize or get yourself eaten by something bigger than your boat, but it seems Fate was on your side today."

I drew in a sharp breath, which scraped my still painfully dry throat and made me cough. "Here, now," the woman exclaimed, snatching another mug of water from the bowl. "None of that. Drink, and stop breathing so hard."

I took two quick swallows, letting the water soothe my throat. "Kovass," I whispered, gazing at my reflection at the bottom of the mug. "Are we still headed that way?"

She frowned. "As far as I know. Why?"

My stomach clenched in fear. "Just curious," I said, handing the mug back to her. She gave me a suspicious look, as if I were plotting something. I was, and if she knew *what* I was planning, she would try to stop me. One did not give away their intentions to complete strangers, even if they were being helpful. As soon as she left, I would find my clothes, sneak out, and search for Halek and Raithe. Once I found them, we had to come up with a plan for getting off this strider. Even if it was just to steal supplies and a lifeboat, and take our chances on the Dust Sea again. If not, we'd be walking straight into Kovass. Straight to the Deathless King.

There was a tap on the door, and it creaked open a few inches. "Tahba," said a male voice from the other side, and I quickly snatched the sheet from where it had fallen to my lap. "Sorry to barge in, but is the girl awake?"

The d'wevryn, Tahba, stomped to the door, wrenched it back, and stepped through. Scowling, she closed it firmly behind her, presumably with the intention of yelling at whoever was on the other side. I had the feeling they were about to get an earful.

Time to go.

Quickly, I searched the room, finding my clothes, neatly washed and folded, in a basket in the corner. I slipped into them and pulled up my hood, and the comforting sensation of anonymity descended. Now I just had to find my companions, and we could get off this death trap. Facing Demon Hour again wouldn't be as deadly with adequate water and shelter from the heat; we just had to plan accordingly. Better that than marching merrily into Kovass, or what was left of it, and facing the sheer terror of the Deathless King. Ironic, that my first experience of actually being on a strider would be the one time I was desperate to leave.

Unfortunately, before I could slip out of the room, the door opened and Tahba stepped through. I tensed, wondering if she would scold me for being up and order me to lie down again. I would comply, but I'd be gone the second her back was turned.

Tahba's brow creased when she saw me up and dressed, but she didn't scold or point to the cot. Instead, she sighed and gave me a worried, half-apologetic look. "If you're well enough to walk, you can follow me to the bridge," she said. "The captain wants to see you."

The inside of a strider wasn't what I had expected. Gazing at them from the streets of the Docks District, I'd thought they seemed so large, so majestic. I had thought the inside would be bright and spacious, with travelers seated at tables on thick silk cushions, luxuriously sipping wine as they gazed through the windows at the endless sea surrounding them.

The reality was not like that at all.

The hallways of the strider were dim and narrow, with low ceilings and flickering lights. Copper pipes were everywhere, snaking along the roof, the walls, even the floor. Occasionally, they would hiss and leak a thin curl of steam. You could feel the strider's movements with every step it took, a sort of lurching stride that rocked you back and forth. The air was warm and humid and smelled vaguely metallic.

The narrow corridor continued past several wooden doors on either side of the hall. Curious, I stood on tiptoe to peer into one tiny round window in one door and saw a ridiculously small room with three sleeping alcoves lined with bedding set into each wall. *This is where people sleep—piled atop each other, with no personal space.* I shuddered and hurried after Tahba, my fascination with striders fading a little. Though it made sense, if I thought about it; striders carried a lot of things across the Dust Sea. Every inch of space had to be utilized.

I followed Tahba up a long stairwell that wound its way through several floors, until we reached a final door at the top. As she pulled it open, sunlight flooded the landing, and a blast of hot, dust-scented air hit me in the face.

"The captain is on deck," Tahba told me, jerking her head at the open frame. "You'll know him when you see him. Stay inside during Demon Hour from now on, you hear? I don't want to see you pale and shriveled up in my sickroom again."

I gave her a half smile. "From now on, I'll try very hard not to die."

She snorted. "One of those," she muttered, and walked past me to the stairs. I listened to her footsteps clunking down the stairwell, then turned and slipped through the open door.

The breeze on deck was dry, chafing my lips, but at least the entire platform was shadowed by thick canvas squares, protecting it from the relentless glare of the twins. I glanced over the railing and saw the Dust Sea stretching to the horizon in every direction, and my willingness to be a tiny speck in that vast emptiness faded a little.

"Sparrow!"

I looked up. Halek was striding toward me across the planks, sunlight gleaming off his hair and a bright smile on his face. Without any hesitation and before I realized what was happening, he crushed me to him in a sudden embrace.

Strangely, though I was surprised, the abrupt closeness didn't set off alarms in my head. I could feel the desperate relief in Halek's embrace, and I tentatively hugged him back, feeling hard muscles through his shirt.

"There you are." Pulling back, the Fatechaser gave me a relieved, beaming grin. "I told them you would make it. Surviving Demon Hour on the Dust Sea only to die in a bed just wasn't your fate. Though Tahba was quite worried. Apparently, it was touch and go for a while."

"Really?"

He nodded somberly. "You should have seen our iylvahn friend—while he was waiting to see the captain, he stalked outside your room until Tahba got so fed up, she banned him from the hallway." Halek gave a soft chuckle and shook his head. "Ah, d'wevryn tenacity. She wasn't at all afraid of his kahjai mysteriousness. Pushed him right out and closed the door in his face. It was quite the sight to see."

Raithe was worried about me? That seemed odd. I glanced over Halek's shoulder and saw a pair of figures near the center of the deck, watching us. One was a stout, red-haired d'wevryn, his beard pulled into tight braids, probably to combat the wind. He wore a rust-red coat trimmed in copper, the image of a cog stitched onto one shoulder, and a turban atop his head. Most definitely the captain, as Tahba had said.

A familiar hooded figure stood beside him; as our gazes met, I caught the flash of a pale blue eye and, for a moment, open relief on the iylvahn's face. It made my stomach do a funny little dance, and I quickly looked away.

"Ah, and here's our last lost traveler." The captain gave me an appraising nod as he walked up, Raithe trailing behind him. I caught a glint of metal beneath the captain's coat and realized that he was wearing armor under his clothes. "I am pleased that you are well again," he went on. "My name is Captain Gahmil, and this is my strider. We were on our way to Kovass for a standard passenger and supply run, but then these two"—he glanced at Raithe, looming behind him, then at Halek standing beside me—"show up with the news that Kovass has fallen. Is this true?" He held up a thick hand as Raithe joined us, looming over the captain's shoulder. "Forgive me, I don't mean to imply untruthfulness, but an iylvahn and a wandering Fatechaser are not citizens of the city on the Dust Sea." His dark gaze shifted to me again and narrowed. "You were born in Kovass, or so they tell me. Is the city lost? Has a Deathless King truly returned?"

I gave a solemn nod. "We fled the city as it was falling," I told the captain, whose mouth thinned until it vanished into his beard. "The Deathless King lifted his own ancient city from beneath Kovass, and everything else crumbled. Honestly, I don't know what has happened to Kovass, how much of it is left, if anyone survived. I just know that the Deathless King is there now, and I don't want to go anywhere near him again."

"We told you, Captain," Raithe said quietly from behind the d'wevryn. "Turn this vessel around. If you keep going, you're putting yourself and all the lives aboard in danger. A Deathless King is not something you can survive."

"I know what the Deathless Kings are, iylvahn," said the captain, a bit shortly. "Your kind are not the only ones with long memories. The d'wevryn have our own legends of the Deathless, and our grudges last forever. We remember, even though the troblin and the humans have forgotten. We know what it was like under the heel of the Deathless Kings." He glowered at Raithe, then sighed heavily. "I just have a strider full of cargo and investors and passengers bound for Kovass. If I'm going to turn this vessel around, I'd better have a damn fine reason to endure the screaming and wailing that's going to come from this."

"A fallen city and a risen god seem like a pretty good reason to me," Halek said.

"Indeed." The captain's jaw tightened. "I will make the announcement." He sighed. "Right after our scout returns. I sent her to investigate Kovass from a distance, and I wish to hear her report." He raised his head and gazed at the sky. "In fact, I believe she is coming back now."

I followed his gaze. A black spot hovered in the sky, silhouetted against the cloudless blue. As it drew closer, a droning sound began to vibrate in my ears. With a shock, I realized that this was the creature in my dream, the great black insect with transparent wings and curling antennae, descending from the sky like some kind of terrible nightmare. My skin crawled, and I tensed, but Halek put a hand on my arm and squeezed gently.

"Don't panic," he whispered with a secret grin. "That's Rhyne. He's a rock beetle. I know he looks terrifying, but he's actually very well mannered." His grin widened, and he lowered his voice even further. "The one you should be afraid of is his rider."

Rider? Utterly confused, I looked back just as the massive insect touched down on deck. It wasn't completely black, I realized. The translucent membranes of its wings were a shimmering emerald, and a faint metallic green tint covered its shell. A huge horn, nearly four feet long, protruded from its face, curving into the air.

"Captain!"

Part of the huge beetle suddenly detached from the rest, and a figure leaped down from its back, making me start. Only then did I see the ridiculously small saddle strapped behind the insect's enormous head. I hadn't seen the rider at first because they wore chitinous black-and-metallic-green armor that blended into the shell of their mount. A helmet with the same curving black horn as the beetle covered their face.

"Kysa." Captain Gahmil stepped forward, brow furrowing. "Report," he said sharply. "What have you seen? Were you able to get to Kovass?"

"Get everyone inside." With one hand, the rider stripped off their helmet, revealing the face of a young woman. Her voice, low and smoky, was the one I'd heard on the Dust Sea when I'd thought I was dreaming. Straight black hair fell to her shoulders; her eyes were dark and her skin was pale, as if it rarely saw the sunlight. She looked only a couple of years older than me, but the hardness in her eyes and the set of her mouth hinted that she was the same kind of dangerous as Raithe. She had seen fighting, and death, and was no stranger to either.

"Get everyone below deck," the woman repeated, making the captain frown. "Quickly! It's coming."

"What? What is coming?" the captain sputtered, clearly flustered but trying not to show it. The insect rider ignored him and turned to her mount, fiddling with the saddle straps. Captain Gahmil scowled. "Kysa, I am your captain," he said in a voice of forced calm. "I order you to slow down and tell me exactly what is going on."

A hollow *thump* rang out, echoing over the strider, and the entire vessel shuddered as something huge struck its side. A shiver went through me as well.

The insect rider turned, a spear in one hand and a terrible look of grim resignation on her face. "Too late. It's here."

Hurrying to the railing, we peered over the side.

Something was crawling up the vessel. Something massive, with a segmented body the color of sand and eight jointed legs that nearly spanned the length of the strider. It wasn't a spider, or an ant, or a scorpion, but some terrible, blasphemous mix of the three, with a bloated, pale abdomen, four serrated mandibles half the size of its face, and a pair of shiny black eyes atop its head. It peered up at us, a soulless, alien predator, before its jaws opened in a piercing hiss and it skittered up the side.

FIFTEEN

My vision blurred as a wave of terror flooded me. I nearly passed out, but then survival instinct kicked in and I found myself lunging back from the railing before I even knew what I was doing. Around me, I was aware of bodies moving, voices shouting, the flash of steel in the sun. From the corner of my eye, I saw the insect rider jam on her helmet and swing herself onto her mount. The beetle's back carapace split open, and its translucent wings hummed as it lifted them into the sky.

"Maederyss's mercy, what is happening?" Halek gasped as we backed swiftly away from the side of the ship. Beyond the railing, I could hear the scrapes and thumps of the creature scaling the strider. "What is that thing?"

"An abomination that should be extinct." Raithe's eyes were steely, his gaze never leaving the opposite railing. As I watched, a long, jointed leg rose over the edge, followed by another, and the hideous bloated form of the monstrous insect crawled onto the deck with a shriek that chilled my blood. Captain Gahmil stood at the center of the deck, his face white as he stared up at the thing looming over him. His hand shook as he groped for the blade at his belt. "Get out of there, Captain," Raithe growled. "Don't try to be a hero."

Faster than thought, the monster darted forward and pounced, seizing the d'wevryn in its jaws. Captain Gahmil let out a single shout as the mandibles closed, severing the d'wevryn's body into several pieces. Blood rained onto the deck and spread rapidly into a pool, and the mangled mess of Captain Gahmil vanished down the monster's gullet. One severed arm thumped to the wood and lay there, twitching.

Gore dripping from its jaws, the abomination turned, multiple legs moving, and fixed its beady eyes on us. Halek and Raithe tensed beside me, but my limbs felt numb with absolute terror. As the creature scuttled forward, a spear flew through the air and struck it in the face. The monster staggered back, legs flailing, as the insect rider and her mount buzzed overhead. Kysa shouted something at us as she passed, probably telling us to get inside, but her words were lost in the wind and the drone of wings.

"Sparrow." Raithe stepped forward, curved sword at his side; despite the horror on deck with us, his voice was calm. "You and Halek get inside. Try to keep the passengers from coming up. Don't come out until you know it's safe."

"Raithe . . ." My mouth was dry with terror, but realizing what he was about to do filled me with a different dread. "Don't."

He shook his head without taking his gaze from the monster. "These things can burrow through solid rock. If I don't kill it now, it will start chewing through the hull to get at the people inside." His pale blue eyes met mine. "Don't worry about me—just keep yourselves safe. Even if I'm not there to guide you, you have to find your way to Irrikah and meet the queen."

The spear in the monster's head finally came loose, falling to the deck with a clink. Lunging forward, the creature pounced on it, seizing the weapon in its mandibles and snapping it into pieces. The insect rider swooped overhead and the monster reared up with a hiss. One long front leg came up, swatting at the beetle and striking a glancing blow. The beetle wobbled in the air, almost falling, and the monster followed it relentlessly across the deck.

"Go," Raithe told us, and sprinted toward the abomination. Racing up behind it, his sword flashed as he struck one of its chitinous legs. It didn't sever the joint or even seem to hurt the creature, and the monster spun on him with a scream.

Halek's eyes narrowed. Setting his jaw, he stepped forward, making my stomach clench. I quickly grabbed his arm. "Halek, what are you doing?" I gasped. "The door is this way."

He gave me a half-serious, half-apologetic look. "I can't let Raithe and Kysa take on that thing alone. It wouldn't be right." One gloved hand came up, gently prying my fingers from his arm, and he nodded at the door. "Get inside, Sparrow. We'll deal with this oversize cricket. I might not be a warrior or an assassin, but I'm really good at being distracting."

"You can't! What if it kills you?"

That familiar wry grin came creeping back. "You already know the answer to that," the Fatechaser said quietly, and stepped away. "Protecting innocent people from a massive abomination? That's the best fate I can hope for."

And before I could say anything else, he whirled and sprinted away toward the battle and the towering monster in the center of the deck. I watched as he charged fearlessly up to the massive predator and hurled something at its injured face. There was a burst of fire and smoke, not large, but the abomination turned with a snarl to face this new enemy.

I bit my lip and ran for the door.

Screams followed me, the enraged shrieks of the abomination grating painfully in my ears. I clenched my jaw and didn't look back, praying the monster wouldn't notice me. I put on a burst of speed and reached the door at last, my fingers closing over the handle.

And then . . . I stopped.

The battle raged behind me, the hisses of the abomination mingling with Halek's explosions, the clang of Raithe's sword, and the drone of beetle wings. The three of them fighting not only for their lives, but for the lives of everyone aboard. And here I was, running for safety once again. Abandoning them to their fates.

My fingers tightened on the handle. I wasn't a warrior. I wasn't a fighter. I was a thief, and in my world, it was everyone for themselves. When a guard appeared, you hid. When a patrol spotted you, you ran. You didn't worry about the others. You didn't go back for them, even if they were caught. Vahn and the guild had taught me this. Take care of yourself first, and let others do the same. A brave thief was a dead thief.

But there had been no hesitation on Raithe's part. Even when faced with the scariest, most terrifying creature I had ever seen, he hadn't fled. Neither had Halek or the insect rider. They were all fighting to protect everyone on the ship, and to make sure I could escape.

If they die, where will I be? I have no one. Everyone else is gone.

I raised my head, took my hand off the door handle, and turned.

Immediately, I saw the huge creature in the center of the deck, and terror stopped the breath in my throat. It seemed even bigger than it had a moment ago, its movements frighteningly quick. Raithe and Halek were doing a good job of keeping its attention split between them as Kysa and her giant beetle harassed it from above, but the three of them looked like ants trying to take down a scorpion.

I breathed slowly, trying to think. The creature's legs were armored, and its body was massive. My thin daggers would do very little if I charged in from below. Maybe if I came at it . . . from above.

My gaze fell to the strider's center mast and the swaths of canvas stretched over the deck to protect it from the sun. The network of ropes and cloth was high enough that the top of the monster's head cleared them with room to spare, but anyone dangling from those lines would be within easy reach of its serrated jaws. If I was noticed, my choices were to risk the long drop to the deck, or watch my bottom half fall away as I was bitten in two.

Fear crawled up my spine. Before I could think too hard, I ran for the mast. Toward the abomination and the three souls still fighting it valiantly. Reaching the ladder, I started to climb.

Heaving myself to the top of the mast, I peered through the gaps in the cloth at the pale, segmented body of the monster below. Now that I was closer, I saw that I'd been right; the back and legs of the monster were heavily armored with chitin, which turned away most sword blows. And the hairy, bloated abdomen, though it had been cut several times and was leaking a greenish fluid onto the deck, was so large that the small gashes weren't slowing it down. Only its face, where Kysa's spear had first struck, seemed vulnerable.

It was also the closest point to those grinding, gnashing jaws.

My heart roared in my ears. I could see its eyes, black and shiny, protruding from the top of its head. They twitched... and then fixed right on me.

Instantly, the abomination broke away from Raithe and Halek, spinning around and rushing toward the mast. I threw myself across the network of ropes, feeling them sway under my feet as I scrambled away from the horror now crawling toward me. The huge arachnid easily scaled the mast and crawled onto the ropes, its multiple legs balanced on the lines as easily as on a web. I saw its jaws working, grinding against each other, as if it could taste the prey just within reach. My thoughts fractured in utter terror as I stared into the face and soulless black eyes of death.

"Sparrow! Cover your eyes!"

Halek's voice rang out behind me a moment before something small and round flew through the air and hit the side of the monster's head. The blinding flash that followed caused the abomination to shriek and whirl around to search for its attacker.

The buzz of wings droned as the huge black beetle appeared overhead, its rider holding out one armored hand as they swooped in.

"Jump!"

The monster whirled back toward me, jaws gnashing as it lunged. I leaped for the insect rider's outstretched arm, grabbing her wrist, and the beetle rose swiftly away. The abomination's face filled my vision, serrated jaws coming for me as it rose after us, legs waving to either side. I kicked, and the toe of my boot struck the inside of one mandible as the beetle pulled me farther into the air.

Raithe scaled the mast, leaped onto the ropes beneath the monster, and plunged his sword into its abdomen.

In an eyeblink, the abomination curled in on itself, serrated fangs working as it sought to destroy the iylvahn now trapped beneath it. For a second, it was directly below me, head bent as it scuttled in circles trying to get to Raithe. It was horrifically quick, its movements frantic as it pursued its prey. Once more, I had a split second to make a decision.

I let go of the insect rider's hand.

She gave a dismayed shout as I fell, the enormous, hairy body of the abomination rushing up at me. I hit the monster's head with a *thump* and instantly felt the creature respond. One long jointed leg came up, raking at its head. I felt the bristly hairs of its legs brush my shoulder as it passed. The other appendage did the same, swiping at the intruder who had hitched a ride, barely missing me. I flatted myself against the monster's carapace, ignoring the hairs that pricked my skin, knowing that if I fell or was scraped off, I would be chewed into pieces.

Heart racing, I reached to my belt, curled shaking fingers around the hilt of a dagger, and pulled it free. I could see the monster's eyes, shiny with fury as they glared at me from atop its head. The legs continued to flail; one bristly hair caught in my clothes, pulling me down a few inches and making my heart stop.

No time to think, Sparrow. Just do it.

I aimed for one of those bulbous eyes, still glaring at me like pods from hell, and plunged my dagger straight down, sinking the blade in as far as I could. The eye burst, black ichor spattering my face and staining my hands, and the abomination went crazy, screaming, hissing, all its legs flailing at me. I closed my eyes, shoved the dagger down even farther, and clung to the hilt for dear life.

I lost track of time, or maybe I passed out for a split second, because when I regained my senses, things seemed calm. My eyes were closed, and I was too scared to open them, though I could feel my dagger under my fingers, something warm and slick covering the hilt and my skin. Beneath me, the abomination was quiet, swaying gently with the rocking of the strider, but I still kept my eyes tightly shut, as if everything would shatter into chaos if I opened them.

I felt a touch on my shoulder and instinctively flinched away.

"It's all right." Raithe's voice, low and breathless, nearly made me sob with relief. "It's safe, Sparrow. It's dead. You killed it."

Cautiously, I opened my eyes. My dagger, sunk to the hilt in the monster's head, was smeared with black, as were my hands.

Raithe knelt beside me on the dead abomination, looking haggard and spent himself. But his pale blue eyes, fixed on my face, were shadowed with concern, relief, and . . . something I couldn't put my finger on. Awe? No, that was silly; nothing about me was awe-inspiring. Most likely, it was surprise that I was still here. That I hadn't gotten myself eaten by a giant spider abomination. Truthfully, I was shocked myself.

"Are you hurt?"

I shook my head, not trusting my voice just yet. Raithe held out a hand, and I unclenched my fingers from their death grip on the dagger. I reached for the offered hand but then hesitated, seeing the filth that stained my skin, not wanting to get it all over the iylvahn.

Raithe reached out and curled his long fingers over mine. The contact sent a shiver all the way from my spine to the bottom of my toes. His grip was steady as he helped me off the dead abomination, holding me up as my legs shook on the wobbly network of rope and canvas. The monster hung lifelessly in the web, legs dangling through the gaps. Its terrible serrated jaws were open in one last, silent scream.

I dropped to the deck and nearly fell, my legs threatening to give out, but Halek was already there, arms around me, pulling me close. I felt the roar of his heartbeat through his shirt, felt him shaking against me, and let myself relax. Halek and Raithe, at least, were safe. And the monster was dead.

"Goddess, you scared me," he whispered as we pulled back. "I thought you had lost your mind for a second. And when you fell, I thought it was over." He paused, and that faint, familiar grin crept across his face once more. "That was recklessly, stupidly heroic, and that's coming from *me*. Are you sure you're not a Fatechaser?"

"Positive," I choked out, and managed a weak, shaky smile.

"I'm not heroic," I told him, as Raithe and the insect rider stepped forward to join us. "I was terrified the whole time."

"We all were." Kysa had stripped off her helmet again and was regarding me with dark, appraising eyes. "Bravery isn't having no fear," she said, as Rhyne huffed and shoved his massive, blocky head against her side. "It is being afraid and doing something regardless." She nodded at me solemnly. "Today, you've earned this warrior's respect."

I dropped my gaze, unable to meet her eyes. "What was that thing, anyway?" I asked no one in particular. Glancing at the dead abomination, hanging lifelessly amid the rope and canvas, I shuddered. In death, it looked no smaller or less horrifying than it had in life. "There's always been tales of monsters on the Dust Sea," I went on, "giant serpents and sand sharks, but everyone knows they're just sailor stories. Raithe, you said this thing was extinct."

"It should be," the iylvahn replied grimly. "Its kind haven't been seen since the age of the Deathless Kings."

Halek drew in a sharp breath. "You don't think . . . ," he began, and stopped. We all looked at him curiously, and he grimaced. "You don't think . . . it was *sent*, for us?"

Raithe and I stiffened. The insect rider frowned. "Why would something like this be sent after you?" she wondered aloud. "And who could harness such an abomination?"

"The Deathless King," I whispered.

A piercing scream interrupted anything the others were going to say. The door to the lower decks had opened, and a small group of people stood staring up at the dead monster in horror.

One woman, her face ashen and her eyes huge, opened her mouth and screamed again, before they all turned and fled back down the stairwell.

Everyone, including me, winced at nearly the same time. "Weaver's mercy," the insect rider sighed, and shoved the helmet over her face again. "Things are about to get chaotic. We need to find Captain Gahmil's second-in-command and explain what has happened before this turns into a full-blown panic."

I cringed inside. Talking to figures of authority, particularly when they had the power to detain me or toss me in a cell, was something I tried to avoid at all costs. "You won't need me for that," I said, intending to slip down to the lower decks and lose myself in the crowds and shadows.

Unfortunately, both Halek and Raithe moved up on either side, stopping me from fleeing. "Oh no," Halek said, putting a hand against my back. "You can't run away now, Sparrow. You're the hero of this story, after all."

"I'm not," I protested. "The three of you were fighting it, not me. My plan was to sneak up and stab it in the back while it was distracted."

"You saved my life," Raithe said, very softly. Heart pounding, I glanced up at the iylvahn, who regarded me with an unreadable look on his face. "I didn't think I would survive that encounter," he said. "If you hadn't killed it when you did, I wouldn't be here."

That ended the argument, though I still wasn't keen to talk to the second-in-command about it. In my experience, even if we weren't somehow blamed for the attack and the death of the captain, it was still attention on me—attention that I didn't want.

I was a thief. It was very hard to be a thief and do thief-y things when everyone recognized you.

"I know the second-in-command," Kysa said as we all started back toward the door. I could still hear screams and shouting somewhere below us, and my stomach turned. "He's a reasonable d'wevryn. With any luck, we can have this whole thing sorted and be on our way back to the city of Damassi before nightfall."

One last time, I glanced back at the body tangled in the ropes, and felt a fresh prickle of fear as Halek's words echoed in my mind. *It was sent, for us.* The abomination was dead, but if the Deathless King had sent it for us—for me—what else might still be coming?

SIXTEEN

I sat on a cot in a tiny room, knees drawn to my chest and the lights off, listening to footsteps scurrying and pounding outside my door.

Arham, Captain Gahmil's second-in-command, hadn't been pleased. When he first saw the dead abomination and the captain's severed arm, still lying in a congealing pool of blood, his face had gone white, and he'd had to stagger away to collect himself. When he returned, he had a lot of questions for all of us, demanding to know where we came from, why we had fled Kovass, and how Captain Gahmil had died. It was clear that he wanted someone to blame for the debacle, but after a long interrogation in his—or, rather, Captain Gahmil's former office, he reluctantly let us go, with the assurance that the strider would be turning around and heading back to Damassi straightaway.

When we emerged from the office, we found a crowd had gathered outside, all shouting and talking at once. Word of the abomination and the captain's death had spread like wildfire through the strider, and passengers were demanding to know what was going on. We left Arham with the unenviable task of explaining the situation and retreated to our quarters to hide from the ensuing rage and panic. At least, that had been *my* intention.

A tap came at the door, rousing me from my thoughts. The door was locked, of course, bolted from the inside. I hesitated, listening for what would come next. I didn't want to talk to anyone right now, especially a stranger. I'd had my fill of talking and explaining for the day. If I didn't answer, anyone who wasn't Halek or Raithe would assume I was asleep or not available and leave. If it was Halek, he would certainly let me know it was him. Raithe . . . I wasn't sure.

"Sparrow." The iylvahn's voice drifted quietly through the door. "It's me. I need to talk to you."

My heartbeat quickened. Suddenly, I both wanted and didn't want to see him. After a moment's hesitation, I pulled myself to my feet, walked to the door, and shoved back the bolt.

He stood at the threshold as I pulled the door open, his face half hidden in the shadows of his hood. Moonlight filtered through one of the tiny round windows on the wall, casting him in a strange aura of silvery blue. Seeing him, feeling those pale eyes on me, my stomach gave a weird little flutter. I wanted to find a dark shadow to slip into, but in this tiny room, there was nowhere to hide.

Raithe stood there, quietly waiting. I swallowed these sudden strange feelings and gazed up at him, frowning. "Well? I'm here. What did you want to talk about?"

He blinked slowly. "I would prefer to do it out of the open," he said in a low-pitched voice. Someone passed behind him in the hall, hurrying by with their head down, and Raithe went perfectly still until they had gone. "We can go to my room to talk, or somewhere more private if you wish, but not in an open hallway where anyone can overhear us."

Alone in a room with the iylvahn. The last time I was alone with him, he had been threatening me at knifepoint. Granted, he'd had good reason, but that didn't change the fact that Raithe could kill someone as easily as swatting a fly. If he wanted to murder me in this tiny room, I'd be dead before I knew what was happening.

Perhaps sensing my thoughts, Raithe narrowed his eyes. "I mean you no harm, Sparrow," he said seriously, though there was no edge to his voice at all. "You will be safe in my presence, I promise."

I sighed and stepped back through the door. "Come on in, then," I said. "Just watch your head. There's not a lot of room."

I perched on the edge of the cot as he ducked his head and came through the door, then closed it firmly behind him. For a moment, he stood there, head bowed, as if gathering his thoughts, then turned to face me.

"I spoke to Arham again," the iylvahn said, leaning against the opposite wall. "Well, technically, I suppose he's Captain Arham now. The strider has officially turned around and is on its way back to Damassi. It has just enough fuel to reach the city. It will be several days before we get to the other side of the Dust Sea."

I nodded, excitement and nerves prickling my stomach. I had never seen Damassi, but I had imagined what it was like countless times.

"Damassi sits at the edge of the Stoneshard Mountains," Raithe continued. "And beyond them are the Barren Steppes. It is a wasteland of rock and flat earth, but Irrikah, the city of the iylvahn, waits on the other side. That is my destination. Once we reach the steppes, I'll be heading home." He hesitated again, regarding me with those pale blue eyes from the shadows of his hood. "I need you to come with me, Sparrow."

I blinked at him. "I thought you weren't giving me a choice."

"I won't force you." Abruptly, Raithe pushed himself off the wall, stepped close, and knelt so that we were eye to eye. My pulse jumped at his nearness; this close, I could reach out and brush the silver strands of hair hanging over his forehead.

"You saved my life." Raithe's voice, low and soft, made my heart thud in my chest. "We survived the Dust Sea together. If you decide to leave us when we reach Damassi and set off on your own, I won't stop you. I am asking—if not as a friend, then as someone who faced down the Deathless King with you and lived—will you come with me to Irrikah and speak to the queen? I am not exaggerating when I say the fate of the kingdoms could depend on it."

I swallowed the lump in my throat. This was somehow worse than being threatened at knifepoint. There was no way I could refuse, not with those pale eyes pleading up at me. Besides, Raithe might be an assassin and a killer, but, at least for now, our goal was the same: Stay away from Kovass and the Deathless King. That seemed like a good reason to keep him around.

"I have nowhere to go, Raithe," I said at last, feeling a sharp pang at the truth of those words. "My whole life was in Kovass, and . . . it's gone now. Everyone I knew . . ." I paused, taking a moment to breathe as memories crowded in, familiar faces that I doubted I would see again, even if they had somehow survived.

"So, yes," I finished, "I will come with you to see your queen. Might as well." I gave a twisted little smile. "It's better than meeting the king who wants me dead."

Raithe sighed, his lean shoulders slumping in relief. "Thank you," he said simply, bowing his head. "And I promise I will protect you on the journey. No matter what we run into. Even if we meet the Deathless King himself."

I squirmed at the sincerity in his voice. "Unless we run into another abomination," I said lightly, and dredged up a smirk. "Then I might have to protect *you* again."

"Perhaps." His faint smile was wry. "I underestimated you," he said, gazing up at me. "I met a thief in Kovass and thought she was only that. Clever and cunning, but only interested in possessions and what she could steal. Unwilling to put herself at risk to save others. Today . . ." He paused. "Today, I saw, for the first time, someone who could truly be the Fateless."

Now I was even more uncomfortable. I still didn't know what this Fateless was, I just knew it wasn't me.

Strangely, it wasn't the thought that I was the Fateless that bothered me. I knew what I was: a simple thief. That had never been a concern. But the thought that Raithe would be disappointed when he realized the truth—that I wasn't Fateless, or brave, or special—for some reason, *that* made my stomach twist. It was unnerving; the only person I had ever strived to make proud had been Vahn, and look how that had turned out.

A banging on my door made me jump. Raithe rose swiftly, hand already on his sword, as voices echoed through the wood from the other side.

"Is she here? The one who killed the giant monster?"

"I don't know. These are the guest quarters."

"Well, she has to be here, then. Knock louder."

I grimaced, shrinking back against the wall. This was what I hadn't wanted to happen. I hadn't wanted people to learn I had killed the abomination, but word of the battle had spread. And now people were looking for me.

I gave Raithe a desperate look, and his jaw tightened. He crossed the room in a single stride and pulled open the door, revealing a pair of men on the other side. They jumped when they saw the motionless, unamused visage of the iylvahn staring at them with cold eyes.

"Oh." One of the men took a step back. "The iylvahn. You were in the battle as well, yes? I am looking for the young woman. Is she here?" He rose on tiptoe, trying to peer over Raithe's shoulder.

Raithe didn't move. "What do you want?" he asked in a voice of stiff politeness.

"Ah, well. You see, I would like to hire her. All of you, actually." The men retreated another step, now that it was clear that Raithe was not letting them into the room. "Allow us to introduce ourselves. We are businessmen from Jorlan, the closet neighbor to Damassi."

I wrinkled my nose. *Businessmen* was another name for the merchant princes, the elite class of traders who had gotten so rich from their various dealings that they rivaled the nobility in wealth and power. They were despised by nearly everyone. The commoners hated them because they acted like nobles, and the nobles looked down on them for daring to be prosperous. But since the merchant princes controlled much of the trade between cities, they weren't too worried about either side.

"We saw the abomination before it was dumped back into the Dust Sea," the other man went on. "Magnificent, and terrifying. To kill a creature like that must have taken a great amount of skill."

"Is there a point to this?" Raithe asked. Still coldly polite.

The first man cleared his throat. "Well, you see, a creature like that, even dead, must be worth a great amount of money to someone. If I understand correctly, those beasts were thought to have gone extinct ages ago."

"Yes," Raithe agreed. "The Deathless Kings brought them to life in the war that destroyed the world, and they disappeared when the kings faded away."

"Yes, yes, yes, if you believe those old legends," the other man said, waving a hand. Raithe didn't reply, but I could almost feel the air around him grow colder. "The point remains," the man went on, "that they are extremely rare creatures. And the rarer the creature, the more valuable it is. There is a fortune to be made if we can track another one down and kill it."

"Once we reach Damassi, we're planning to put together an expedition of hunters and beast killers," his companion broke in. "We would be honored to have you at the head. You and the girl, since you have successfully killed one already. The insect rider would have been helpful, but she has rather foolishly turned down the offer. We will pay you, and of course, we are willing to share a percentage of the profits—"

"You are both fools."

Both merchants stiffened, but Raithe's stare remained cold and flat. "Fools, and shortsighted ones," the iylvahn continued. "The abomination is a sign that a Deathless King has returned. You will have much larger things to worry about when the king starts his conquest of the kingdoms."

"Deathless King?" The merchant princes exchanged glances. "The boy did not mention that," one muttered, making me stiffen. "Abominations, Fateless, and now Deathless Kings? How are we to separate the truth from rumor and faery tales?"

Raithe went very still. "How do you know of the Fateless?" he asked, in a voice that made my skin prickle with fear. I wondered if the merchants knew how very close they were to death at that moment.

One of the men seemed to realize the danger, for his face paled and he clamped his jaw shut. The other did not. "The boy," he muttered, waving a hand. "The one who was with you. Who calls himself a Fatechaser. We approached him first, to see if he wanted to be part of our expedition, but he was so drunk he could barely see straight. He was sobbing about 'Fateless' and 'missed destiny.' Obviously we had no idea what he was rambling on about. He told us to find the iylvahn and the girl if we wanted to talk business."

"Halek . . ." Raithe clenched a fist. He sounded furious, and worry for the Fatechaser twisted my insides. It was hard to imagine the smiling, aggressively cheerful Halek sobbing and drunk in the strider's tavern. Something had to be wrong.

"So are we to assume you are not interested in joining the expedition?" the first, somewhat oblivious merchant asked Raithe.

"I urge you to consider the offer carefully—imagine the profit you could make! Girl," he added, peering past Raithe into the room, "you came from Kovass, yes? If the city is truly gone, think of the potential. You could make enough coin to start a new life somewhere else—"

Raithe shut the door.

Indignant sputters came from the other side, and I almost smiled. Raithe shook his head and turned back to me. "I *am* correct in assuming that you did not want to be a part of their expedition?" he asked.

I gave an emphatic nod. If I never saw one of those spider-scorpion-demon things again, it would be too soon.

After a final shout that we were making a grave mistake, and that if we changed our minds, we could find them in Damassi, the voices at the door faded. I listened to the merchants' footsteps shuffling away and was pretty certain everyone on that expedition was going to die.

When they were truly gone, Raithe sighed. "Fatechaser," he muttered, reaching for the door handle. "We're going to have to have a talk."

I sat up quickly. I didn't *think* the assassin would track down Halek and kill him, but I didn't want to take any chances.

"Raithe, wait. I'm coming, too."

The strider's tavern was located on one of the lower decks. A dimly lit, dingy room with a low ceiling, grated metal floors, and no windows, it smelled strongly of grease and working-class citizens packed too close together. Nobles and merchant princes didn't venture this low into the strider, not for drinks, anyway; the tavern was obviously built for the d'wevryn who lived and worked on the vessel.

Raithe and I stepped inside, scanning the booths and beat-up tables scattered throughout. The iylvahn nearly had to duck his head to avoid scraping it on the ceiling, which barely cleared the top of his skull. A few patrons were seated at the bar, while two d'wevryn sailors and a human sat at a central table, throwing a familiar set of dice. It seemed Triple Fang was popular no matter where you went.

A familiar bright-haired figure was seated in a corner booth, elbows on the table and head in his hands. Mugs were scattered around him, and the entire corner smelled of cheap ale. He wasn't alone. Kysa sat across from him, arms crossed, a look of sympathetic confusion on her face. She glanced up, raising a slender brow as we approached, then gave a resigned shrug.

"I admit, I cannot understand most of what he is saying," she told us as we stepped to the edge of the table. "The ways of the Fatechasers are foreign to me. But as we fought a great evil together, I figured I would lend a listening ear. Perhaps you can better comprehend his dilemma—he has said both your names multiple times." Her dark gaze flickered to Raithe and narrowed slightly. "He also kept saying that you were going to kill him, iylvahn."

Raithe sighed. "Halek," he said, staring down at the still motionless Fatechaser.

Halek's shoulders flinched. "I know," he groaned, burying his head deeper in his hands. "I'm sorry. I wasn't thinking straight.

I didn't mean to tell those men about the Fateless." He looked up, his eyes red and bloodshot, and my stomach twisted. It was obvious he had been sobbing, hard, and for a long time. "If you're here to kill me, go ahead," he told Raithe. "I have no idea what Fate or destiny are anymore."

"I am not going to kill you," Raithe said in a low voice, glancing at the patrons milling around the tavern. "Life is sacred. I take it only when I must. Accidentally revealing a secret while in the throes of drink and grief is not cause for death." He paused, glancing at Kysa, who gave a solemn nod of respect, then turned back to Halek. "The three of us survived the fall of Kovass, the Dust Sea, and an abomination that was possibly sent to kill us all. I am not about to slay one of my allies. I am just curious as to where this sudden lapse of judgment came from."

"Lapse of judgment," Halek repeated, and groped for a half-full mug of ale beside him. "I guess you can call it that. If a life-altering, belief-shattering realization is a lapse of judgment."

"Halek, what is going on?" I asked, sliding into the seat beside him. "This isn't like you. What happened in the fight with the abomination?"

He gave me a mournful, blue-eyed stare, then let out a heavy sigh. "I guess it's not your fault," he murmured, staring into his drink. "You're the Fateless, whatever that means. I don't know much about it."

"I don't know anything about being Fateless," I told him in a whisper. I could feel Raithe's eyes on me and deliberately did not look at him. "I don't even know what a Fateless *is,* much less if I am one or not. But what does that have to do with whatever is happening here?"

Halek continued to stare into his mug. "I think . . . no, I'm pretty certain that monster was supposed to kill me," he finally confessed. "I could *feel* it. While the three of us were fighting, before you came back, I suddenly knew. And for just a second, I was relieved. I thought I had cheated it, back in the ancient city."

Kysa frowned. "Cheated what?" she asked. "Death?"

"My fate," Halek said, looking up at the insect rider. "Fatechasers know when their destiny has come," he explained. "Like I told Sparrow earlier, we can't predict how it happens, but we do know it when it arrives. I was ready this time. I was prepared. I had already cheated it once—this was just Fate catching up with me."

Kysa shook her head. "I apologize," she murmured, looking both bewildered and incredulous. "The ways of the Fatechasers make little sense to me."

"It's all right. You're in good company." Halek gazed at me again, and his eyes were haunted. "I was ready to meet my fate. But then . . . you came back. And just like that, it was gone. I'm still here and . . ." He swallowed. "My fate is still out there, waiting for me."

I frowned at the implied accusation. "I'm not sorry that you're alive, Halek," I said. "I would help you again, if it came to that."

"I know. And I don't want you to apologize. This isn't your fault, Sparrow. I just . . ." Halek paused, and the mug between his fingers shook as he stared at it. "I'm afraid now," he whispered. "I've never feared my own death before, but I have this terrible feeling that I have somehow cheated Fate and thrown off the balance of the world. And the longer I'm alive, the worse my fate will be when it finally catches up."

I put a hand on his arm, making him flinch, though he didn't look at me. "How close is it now?" he whispered. "Am I going to step out of this room and be impaled by a guard chasing down a thief? Or will the shelf above my cot snap and crush my skull in my sleep? Maybe I'll just get tossed overboard by a random gust of wind. Anything could happen."

"Anything could happen," Raithe agreed. "To any of us. At any time. Every step, no matter which direction we go, brings us closer to meeting our fate. *How* you take those steps is what matters."

"Yes," Kysa broke in. "The iylvahn understands. A warrior steps proudly, unafraid of what Fate puts in their path. Will you let this so-called destiny paralyze you into not moving at all?"

"I . . ." Halek scrubbed a hand through his shock of blond hair. "You don't understand," he muttered. "I have never been afraid of death. I've never shied away from what could be the end for me. But now I feel that I've somehow . . . missed what I was supposed to do. I've cheated Fate, and the repercussions are coming. They could be lurking around any corner, and the uncertainty is driving me mad. How can I keep going, knowing that? If it didn't go against the entire Fatechaser creed, I'd throw myself overboard right now and save Fate the trouble."

"Or . . ." I bumped his shoulder with mine. "You could keep living, keep defying Fate, for as long as you can. You know it's coming. You'll be ready when it arrives. But until then, each day is a blessing you didn't have before. You can do things Fate or destiny never expected."

Halek blinked, staring at me for a long moment. "That's an . . . interesting thought," he finally mused. "A Fatechaser who defies their fate? Who dodges when it comes for them?" A shadow of his old grin crept across his face. "It's almost blasphemous."

I shrugged. "It's what I would do."

"Of course you would. You're Sparrow. The Fateless. You don't—" Halek suddenly sat straight up, his eyes going wide. "Oh," he breathed. "I get it. I understand now."

I frowned. "What are you talking about?"

"*You're* the reason." He turned, his face so close I could see myself in the deep blue of his gaze. The hint of alcohol lingered on his breath as he smiled. "Every time I was about to meet my fate, you appeared, and it vanished. You're my lucky charm, my protection amulet. As long as you're here, Fate can't get me."

I leaned back. He was obviously drunk and not thinking straight. "I don't know if it works that way, Halek."

"It doesn't," Raithe muttered beside us.

"No, it makes perfect sense!" Halek threw an arm around my shoulders, pulling me close. Strangely enough, I didn't mind. "You and me, Sparrow," he slurred, lifting his mug in a drunken toast. "Nothing can stop us. We'll laugh in Fate's fate . . . face Fate . . . Fate's . . ." He coughed. "We'll laugh at Fate together. You're stuck with me now."

I met Kysa's gaze across the table, and she shook her head. "The ways of outsiders are strange indeed," she mused.

SEVENTEEN

It would take six days for the sand strider to reach the port of Damassi on the other side of the Dust Sea. To pass the time, I wandered the strider's innards, familiarizing myself with the vessel, from the upper decks to the deep lower bowels where most of the d'wevryn crew lived and worked. I memorized the layout, taking note of good escape routes, hidey-holes, and places I could lose any potential attackers in the labyrinthine corridors of the strider.

Evenings were spent either in the tavern or the common spaces with Halek. Sometimes, Raithe joined us, and on rare occasions, Kysa would appear, when her duties as a scout permitted. The insect rider seemed fascinated with us, and me in particular; she would often ask me about Kovass and its fall to the Deathless King. But talking about Kovass and my life before brought up painful memories, and I avoided the subject when I could. But the insect rider was persistent.

"You know you cannot keep running forever," she told me one evening. We were back in the cramped, dingy tavern, the smell of grease and pipe smoke thick on the air. Halek had been roped into a game of Triple Fang by the d'wevryn regulars, and I pitied their ignorance. The Fatechaser had nearly the same uncanny luck as I did when it came to dice. The difference was, he was charismatic and well liked enough to get away with it.

I smirked to hide the unease tracing a cold finger up my spine, and leaned back with a shrug. "I can give it my best shot."

"The Deathless King will come for us all," the insect rider went on, ignoring my last statement. Apparently, the Scarab Clan had their own legends of the Deathless Kings. "If everyone runs away, his empire will only grow, swallowing kingdoms like a sandstorm. If there is no resistance, the Deathless King will not stop until every living thing is consumed. There will be nowhere to run. Better to face him, to slow that tide, than to cower in fear, waiting for him to find you."

I cringed. She hadn't been there when the king was resurrected. She hadn't seen the king's terrible power, enough to pull down an entire city and replace it with his own. "I'm not a warrior," I told her. "If I stand against the Deathless King, I'm going to die. Anyone who faces him is going to die."

"And yet it must begin somewhere." Kysa's voice was unyielding. "The Scarab Clan will not submit. We will not be subjugated. If we must die protecting our lands and our freedom, so be it. We are not afraid to make that choice. And perhaps our sacrifice will inspire others to stand and fight as well."

"I hope so," I said. "Because I'll be hiding in the deepest hole I can find. Or in the farthest reaches of the farthest kingdom. Maybe if I put enough dust oceans between me and the Deathless King, he'll decide one insignificant thief is not worth the hassle."

The insect rider raised a brow. "I seem to remember this 'insignificant thief' returning to strike the killing blow on a legendary abomination."

"Yes, and I hope never to do it again." Kysa still looked dubious, and I shrugged. "I'm a thief," I told her. "That's what Fate decided. That's my place in the Tapestry of the World. We all know we can't change our fates."

"You are very confusing," Kysa said bluntly. "Wasn't it you who convinced the Fatechaser to defy what Fate has in store for him?"

I winced. She had me there. "I convinced him to try," I said, shrugging. "And it's different for Halek—he's not doing anything he wouldn't already do. I know what I am, Kysa. I'm not a warrior. I'm not a hero. I've made it this far because surviving is what I'm good at. In the guild, it was every hood for themselves. You stick your neck out for someone, you just get your head chopped off."

"Then I'm glad you made an exception for us the other day."

Everything inside me cringed as Raithe's low, quiet voice drifted into the conversation. His tone wasn't angry or accusatory, but it still made me want to slip away into a dark corner so I wouldn't have to face his disappointment.

Wait, why do you care what he thinks of you? A spark of defiance made me frown. *He's a kahjai who has probably taken dozens of lives, maybe hundreds. You've always known what you are. You won't ever be what he wants.*

"Don't get up on my account," Raithe told Kysa, who had shoved back her chair. "I didn't mean to intrude."

"I was just about to leave, anyway." Kysa rose with elegant grace, her black hair shimmering in the greasy tavern light. "Rhyne will be impatient for his dinner," she said, as Halek waved to her from his table. "If I don't feed him in a timely manner, he starts chewing his stall." She rolled her eyes in an affectionately exasperated manner. "That's the problem with having a mount that can eat literally anything. Once I was forced to ration his food, and he chewed a cart-size hole in the lower deck."

"That would be amusing," Raithe said, "if it wasn't also terrifying."

Kysa chuckled. "Remind me to tell you the story of Rhyne in the shipyard one day."

She walked off, chitin boots clicking against the metal floor of the tavern. I noticed several male patrons stop what they were doing to watch her leave. Including Halek.

Raithe sat down in the chair next to mine. I avoided his eyes, drawing farther into my hood, but felt his gaze on me all the same. Was he angry? Disappointed? Regretting that he had ever made the promise to take a lowly thief to his grand iylvahn city?

"I heard that Bahjet and his associate were waiting for you outside your room the other day," Raithe said, referring to the pair of merchant princes we'd met earlier. They *had* been lurking in the hall one morning, cornering me as soon as I'd stepped through the door. I'd given them the slip, but they were persistent, chasing me down the corridor while shouting the wonderful benefits of joining their venture.

"They won't be bothering you again," Raithe went on. "And no," he added as I peeked up, "I didn't kill them. I did make it very clear that you were not interested in their offer, and that further inquiries would be very bad for their business."

"Thanks," I muttered. "I was planning to never use my front door again and just pry up the floorboards, but that works, too."

A faint smile crossed his face, which made my stomach do that weird little flutter. "I'll pretend I didn't hear that," he said, still smiling. "I have enough on my mind without having to think about people scurrying around beneath my floor."

A snicker escaped me, which was a bit surprising. After all that had happened in Kovass, I hadn't been certain I would ever laugh or joke again. "Just tell yourself it's mice," I said. "Really, really big mice. Nothing to worry about at all."

"Mmm." He narrowed his eyes. "I keep hearing rumors about some kind of creature ghosting around the machinery decks. Some of the workers are even starting to whisper that Captain Gahmil's spirit has returned and is haunting the lowest floors. You wouldn't happen to know anything about that, would you?"

I shrugged. How the striders worked had always fascinated me. I wanted to see the gears and machinery for myself, despite signs proclaiming *Danger!* and *No entry* in certain areas. "Probably really big mice," I told Raithe.

He gave a resigned chuckle, making my insides squirm again. "Well, I hope they're careful mice," he said. "We don't want anything happening to them this close to Damassi."

"They're very careful mice," I assured him. "No one will ever see them at all."

"What? Are we talking about mice?" Halek asked as he joined us, plopping into a chair across from me. "I think I have a couple living in my wall. By the way, do not play Triple Fang with Rhulac over there—I'm pretty sure his dice are weighted."

"You seemed to be doing pretty well regardless," I said, remembering the stack of coins on Halek's side of the table.

He shrugged. "Oh, I definitely won most of the time. I'm just saying he was probably cheating. Weird, right? Anyway..." Halek gave both me and Raithe a serious look. "We're only a couple days from Damassi. Where are we going after we reach the city?"

"'We'?" Raithe frowned. "I was under the impression that we would part ways once we reached the coast. Sparrow and I will be traveling across the Barren Steppes toward the Maze, the steep cliffs and canyons that surround Irrikah. It's a hard, dangerous journey, even for one of the iylvahn. I can navigate the Maze well enough, but I cannot promise you would be allowed into the city, Halek. They might turn you away at the gates."

Halek started to answer, but suddenly, my skin crawled, and the hairs on the back of my neck stood straight up. Instantly wary, I looked around the room, searching for anyone whose gaze lingered on our table, who seemed far too interested. No one was watching us; even Rhulac at the center table was drowning his losses in drink and ignoring everyone around him. Still, I couldn't shake the intense feeling that something was staring at me.

"Sparrow?" Raithe leaned toward me, lowering his voice. "What is it?"

"I don't know," I muttered. "I feel like we're being watched."

Raithe swept his gaze around the tavern without moving his head. "There is no one observing us," he murmured, as Halek casually leaned back with his hands behind his skull, also scanning the room. "Are you certain of this?"

"Yes," I whispered. The feeling wasn't abating; in fact, it was getting stronger. Though Raithe was right—no one in the tavern was paying any attention to our table. "I know it's strange, but—"

A needle of pain lanced through my temple, making me suck in a sharp breath. Clenching my jaw, I pressed a hand to the side of my head, expecting to find a dart or something sharp protruding from my hood. Almost as soon as the pain began, however, it vanished. As it disappeared, I thought I heard the faintest of echoes in my head, and a hint of satisfaction so fleeting, it might've been my imagination.

There you are.

"Sparrow. You okay?" Halek's worried voice cut through the fading agony. I glanced up and saw him leaning forward, blue eyes concerned. Raithe, too, was watching me, though he had gone dangerously still, as if waiting for an enemy to show itself.

"I'm . . . okay, I think." The pain and the strange feeling were gone, like they had never existed. "I don't feel anything anymore. I guess I was just being paranoid."

"Are you sure?" Raithe said in a low voice. His tone was calm, but his eyes and posture were still dangerous. I nodded. Everything was normal again, and I wasn't going to admit that I was starting to feel mysterious pains and hear voices in my head. They might think the stress was getting to me, or worse, they might believe me and want to investigate further. And I was generally opposed to anyone prying into my life.

Don't rely on anyone was one of Vahn's favorite sayings. *If you start depending on others, they'll let you down, and then where will you be? The only one you can fully trust is yourself.*

Thinking of Vahn made my throat close, a heavy weight

settling deep in my chest. "I'm tired," I told them, pushing back my chair. "I think I'm going to turn in early. Halek, if you ever want to double-team someone in Triple Fang, let me know. I bet we could clean out the whole tavern."

"Sparrow."

It was Raithe's voice that reached me as I turned away, not Halek's. "If you feel you are in danger, don't hesitate to tell me," he said as I glanced back. "I promised to keep you safe, but I need to know what I should be protecting you from."

I smiled at him. "I'm fine, Raithe," I said. "Trust me, if I see any shadowy assassins lurking in the halls—well, besides you, anyway—I'll be sure to let you know."

He didn't smile back. "I do not lurk," he told me, though a hint of reluctant amusement bled through his voice. Halek stifled a snort, managing to turn it into a cough, and Raithe sighed. "Just promise me you'll be careful," he finished, holding my gaze. "Sometimes, physical threats are not the most dangerous. The ma'jhet were known to wield forbidden magics. They were not as powerful as the Deathless Kings, but could be deadly all the same. If you see or feel anything strange, come tell me. I will keep you safe, but you have to give me the chance."

I wanted to believe him. I wanted to think that I could rely on the iylvahn, that he would be there like he promised. But relying on people was dangerous. Raithe was interested in my safety only because he thought I was this Fateless. I wasn't. I was just a thief, nothing more. And when Raithe figured that out, he would disappear.

Like everyone else.

I drew back from the table. The iylvahn's pale, worried gaze followed, making my stomach twist. "I will," I told him, and left quickly before he could see I was lying.

That night, the dreams were worse.

Vahn's face loomed above me, cold and dispassionate. In one hand, he held the black soulstone, pulsing with its eerie nonlight. In the other, he raised a serpentine dagger, the hilt dark and shiny with blood. I lay on a stone altar, iron shackles around my wrists, and could only watch as the blade rose, a sliver of bloody light shining against the darkness.

The Fateless must die, the robed, hooded figures around me hissed. *The Fateless and the Deathless cannot exist in the same era. Kill her, and rid our world of this plague.*

Vahn looked down at me, and for just a moment, his face softened, and he was the person I'd once known. "I'm sorry, Sparrow," he murmured. "But you should've known this was coming. You cannot trust anyone. We are mortal. Betrayal is in our blood. This is the way of things. Everyone you know will turn on you in the end. Really," he whispered, and the dagger turned, angled at my heart, "it's better this way."

The knife plunged down, and I closed my eyes.

I jerked awake, heart pounding and cold sweat trickling down my back. My tiny room was dark; the copper lantern hanging from the ceiling was either broken or had run out of whatever fueled it. Panting, I leaned against the wall, the shadowy visages of Vahn and the Circle fading into the darkness.

Shivering, I pulled my knees to my chest and pressed my face to them, waiting for my heartbeat to return to normal. Just a nightmare. Vahn wasn't here, and I wasn't chained to a table with the Circle screaming for my death. Though Jeran was still dead, Kovass was still gone, and the Deathless King was still out there. All because of me.

"Sparrow?" A quiet tap came at my door, and a low voice drifted into the room. "Are you awake?"

Raithe again. My stomach cartwheeled, and I swung my legs off the cot. Pulling up my hood, I rose and took the two steps to the door. It groaned as I swung it back, revealing the dark hallway and a figure silhouetted in the frame, and my heart seized up in terror.

A dead Raithe stared down at me, his eyes shriveled pits in his face, the flesh on one side of his head rotted away. I could see bones and teeth through the holes in his jaw. The smell of decay filled the room, clogging my throat, as what was left of the assassin's arm shot forward, bony fingers latching onto my sleeve.

I twisted on instinct, feeling my clothes tear as I wrenched myself out of the skeletal grip. Undead Raithe pressed forward, raising his other arm. I saw his curved blade coming at my head and ducked, hearing the steel bite into the doorframe. Diving beneath his arm, I lunged past him into the hallway.

I nearly ran into Halek, who stared at me with glassy eyes, maggots wriggling through his wasted flesh. He clawed at me, and I leaped back, stifling a scream, as up and down the corridor, doors began creaking open and rotting corpses spilled forth. They moaned as they saw me, staggering forward with arms raised.

Halek lurched toward me, his jaw hanging at an odd angle, held in place by exposed tendons and strips of flesh. "Run, Sparrow," he whispered through rotted teeth. "Run."

Raithe stepped out of my doorway, chillingly graceful even in death. The hollow pits in his skull found me in the corridor, and his lips twisted in a ghastly smile.

I ran.

The halls of the strider were filled with corpses, reaching for me with bony hands, their eyes blank and staring. Drifts of sand lay in corners and along the edges of the walls, and my boots kicked up dust clouds, turning the air hazy and thick. My breath rasped, dry and gritty in my throat, and the overwhelming stench of decay made my stomach turn and my eyes water.

I reached the stairs, intending to go down and lose myself in the nooks and shadows of the lower decks. As I started down the steps, though, my heart lurched with terror. The bottom of the stairwell was choked with bodies, pressed together in a moaning, shambling horde. When they saw me, they howled and surged forward, clogging the cramped space even further. I turned and fled back up the stairs.

Raithe's terrifying visage suddenly appeared, blocking the floor I had just left. I threw myself aside as his blade swept down, missing me by a hair. The metallic clank of steel against the wall echoed up the stairwell, sending a chill through my whole body. I dodged the dead kahjai and continued toward the upper decks of the strider.

Bursting through the door to the outside deck, I gasped, raising an arm to shield my face. Wind tore at me, shrieking in my ears, scouring my flesh with sand. Past the railing, I couldn't see anything through the swirling, raging sandstorm surrounding the deck. Just like when Kovass fell. I could hear sand beating the sides of the strider and ripping the canvas sails to ribbons.

A thump behind me made me glance back. Rotting faces and bony limbs pressed forward up the stairs, as if they were one terrible creature of heads and arms and limbs. My heart seized, and I staggered onto the deck.

Sand lashed my skin, ripping at my hair and clothes. The mob of corpses burst out of the stairwell, flooding onto the deck with moans and howls. They staggered as they stepped onto the deck, wind and sand scouring dead flesh from their bones, making them even bloodier and more skeletal. But they still shuffled toward me, uncaring of the pieces they were losing, their eyes blank with hunger.

Fateless.

Across the deck, past the horde of shambling corpses, a fifty-foot head rose slowly over the side of the vessel. It was made of sand, but even blurred and featureless, I recognized it immediately. The Deathless King, come to massive, terrifying life, opened depthless black eyes and gazed down at the tiny insects far below.

Come to me, Fateless. The giant's lips didn't move, but his voice echoed in the winds, everywhere around me. A hand the size of a cart rose over the deck, fingers clenching into a fist. *You have no place in my new world. I will crush you like an ant beneath me and feast upon your life as you wither to dust. There is no escape.*

The dead shambled closer, trapping me against the railing. The looming mass of the Deathless King towered over the ship. My heart roared, and my breath came in short, panicked gasps as I backed away. No escape. Nowhere to run. I would die here, torn apart by the bony fingers of the undead or crushed in the grip of the Deathless King.

The wooden railings pressed against my back, and the howl of the sandstorm echoed around me. Everywhere I looked, I saw death, a creeping tide that would eventually suffocate me.

I leaped onto the railing, dropping my weight to find my balance as the ship lurched and the winds tore at me. With the howling storm and raging sands, the Dust Sea was obscured from my vision, but I knew it was there, far, far below. What would be worse? To be ripped apart by a mob of undead, or to suffocate in the unforgiving waves of the Dust Sea? At least with the latter, I would choose how I died.

The mob was nearly upon me. The terrifying visage of the Deathless King leaned over the ship, raising its massive fist. I glanced once more down the side of the ship, gathering my shattered courage for the jump. It would be over quickly, I told myself. After that final gasp that filled my lungs with sand, there would be nothing.

And then Raithe's horrifying figure lunged through the horde and grabbed me around the waist.

I shrieked, fighting in his grasp. I smelled the death that clung to him, felt the steely tendons locked around me as he dragged me from the edge, back toward the mob. Desperately, I twisted, pulled my dagger from its sheath and stabbed it at the corpse's face with all my might. He jerked his head back and grabbed my wrist with one hand, stopping the blade from slicing his cheek open.

"Sparrow, stop!"

His voice startled me; it sounded so normal. But his rotting, leering face loomed in my vision as he grabbed my other wrist, pulling me closer. I twisted my head away, fighting to get free, the blade of my dagger held helplessly between us.

"Sparrow, look at me!" He gave me a shake that jolted my head back. "You're dreaming," he went on as I staggered and my vision went fuzzy. His voice suddenly seemed to come from a great distance away. "This is a dream. Open your eyes. Wake up!"

I gasped and opened my eyes.

Raithe's alarmed, haggard face filled my vision. Normal, living, unrotted. Panting, I looked around, searching for the horde of the dead. We were on the upper deck of the strider, a few feet from the railing that prevented a sharp plunge into the Dust Sea. The night was clear and still. The deck, save for the two of us, was empty.

"Sparrow." Raithe's voice shook a little. His fingers were still clamped tightly around my wrists, the blade of my dagger still gleaming in my hand. "Talk to me. Are you here?"

I started to shake. My knife dropped from my hand and clattered to the planks between us as I realized what had almost happened. How close had I been to dying, to leaping from the strider into the open arms of the Dust Sea?

My legs gave out beneath me. Nothing felt real. I sagged in Raithe's grip, my breath coming in short, panicked gasps. He knelt with me on the deck and drew me close, letting me feel the strength in his arms, the solid thump of his heart against mine. This was not a dream. This was real, and right now, no nightmares, not even the Deathless King, could touch me.

"You're safe." His voice was low and steady, soothing my fractured, spinning thoughts. "Breathe, Sparrow. I've got you."

Gradually, my muscles unclenched, the shaking calmed, and my breath returned to normal. Raithe waited until the trembling had faded before his arms loosened and he shifted, gazing down at me. "Can you tell me what happened?"

"I . . . it started as a nightmare," I began, and to my relief, my voice was steady. "But it was one I've had before. And then I was alone on the ship, and everyone else was dead. But not the kind that stay dead—the kind that get up and come after you. Even you and Halek. You were all chasing me through the ship.

"I came up here," I continued, feeling my heartbeat pick up again. "And I saw *him*. The Deathless King. He was towering over the strider, staring right at me. He told me there was no escape, that I had no place in his world. And the dead were all here, reaching out for me. There was nowhere to go, except . . ."

My gaze flickered to the railing. Raithe's arms tightened around me again.

"I'm sorry," he murmured. "This is on my head. I knew something was wrong this evening. I suspected the ma'jhet were looking for you. I just didn't expect them to use that kind of magic this soon."

"That was magic?" I whispered.

Raithe nodded. "Almost certainly. That type of dream spell

was common in the age of the kings, so much so that charms and runes were crafted to protect against them. In a dream, they could make a person experience anything. It was a dangerous type of magic that could drive one to self-harm, madness, or even death." His jaw tightened. "But it hasn't been used in centuries. I though that type of magic had died out, but it seems the ma'jhet have kept it alive. And now they're using it against you."

I shuddered. Even with an ocean of dust between us, I wasn't safe from the Circle or the Deathless King. Or Vahn, I realized. Vahn was still trying to kill me.

Raithe must've sensed my dismay, or perhaps he felt the shiver that went through me, for he bent his head close, curling his body protectively around mine on the deck. "There are things we can do to shield you from the ma'jhet," he murmured. "My people are experts on the age of the Deathless Kings and their magic. I will protect you, Sparrow. You have my promise."

I raised my head and met his piercing gaze.

His expression was intense, relief, anger, regret, and determination shining in equal parts from those pale blue eyes. A thin stream of blood trickled from a shallow gash across his cheek; I realized with horror that the wound was from me, from the knife I had stabbed blindly in his direction.

Shame and guilt flared. Before I knew what I was doing, my hand rose and gently touched his face. His eyes closed, a soft breath escaping his lips, as my fingers traced the side of his jaw, brushing his cheek.

The buzz of wings overhead made me jump and caused Raithe to jerk up his head and scan the sky. With a loud droning, the enormous, bulky mass of Rhyne the rock beetle descended and landed on the deck with a thump.

"Raithe? Sparrow? Are you well?" Kysa peered down at us, worry written clearly across her face. Her spear was clutched in one hand, ready for action, as she leaped from the saddle, joining us on the deck. "Is the girl hurt? What has happened?"

I rose quickly, and Raithe did the same. "We're fine, Kysa," I told her, which made her frown. "I just . . . had a nightmare, and . . ." I faltered, unsure if Raithe wanted me to say anything, not really certain what I would say myself.

"There was an incident." Raithe stepped forward, drawing the rider's gaze. "Involving magic, and the ma'jhet. They're looking for the Fateless."

Kysa's gaze narrowed sharply. "What kind of magic?" she asked.

"Based on what Sparrow said earlier, I would guess some kind of scrying magic," the iylvahn replied. "They're not here now," he went on, as Kysa looked around warily, "but we need a plan on how we can prevent certain attacks in the future. Where is Halek?"

"Probably still in the tavern, swindling workers out of their hard-earned wages." She shook her head. "It is fortunate that everyone seems to like him—I've seen d'wevryn sailors stuff gamblers into empty ale barrels and roll them down the stairs if they lose too often." The insect rider rolled her eyes, then sobered quickly. "If this involves the Fateless, I would like to be a part of it," she told Raithe. "I know I am not part of your group, nor am I from Kovass, but this is worrying for me and my people." She glanced at me, her smooth brow furrowing. "I also might have a solution for this magic concern, if you will hear it."

Raithe nodded. "You are welcome to join us, Kysa."

She turned toward her beetle, who was huffing and tossing his horned head. "I've just finished my last patrol, and Rhyne is an impatient beast," she told us, swinging into the saddle again. "Let me get him settled and I'll join you in the tavern."

With a drone of wings, Rhyne and Kysa took to the air. I watched them fly across the deck, then drop from sight over the railing. The buzz of wings faded, and we were alone again.

Raithe looked at me, and there was something different in his eyes. A hint of realization that thrilled and terrified me all at once. The last time someone had looked at me like that, I'd wound up unconscious and tied to a chair, while the person I thought I knew took a cursed soulstone to the Circle to claim the reward for himself.

I couldn't deal with that again. It wasn't that I didn't trust Raithe . . . right now, in this moment. He had vowed to protect me, and I believed him, but only because he thought I was the Fateless. That protection and trust would end the moment we reached the iylvahn city and spoke to the queen. I couldn't forget that. I had trusted Jeran, too. I'd let down my guard, let myself think that we might have something special, and ended up with a figurative knife in the back. Raithe was a kahjai. How much easier would it be for him to slide a very real knife between my ribs from behind?

And still, despite all that, I found myself wishing we could reclaim that moment on the deck before Kysa found us.

"Sparrow," the assassin murmured, still watching me intently, "are you all right? Were you hurt?"

I shook my head. "I'm fine," I told him. "Do you think Kysa can really help us when it comes to magic?"

He inclined his head. "The insect riders, particularly the Scarab Clan of the Eastern Wastes, are an honorable people. They're also very suspicious of magic. The stories of the rider clans stretch all the way back to the age of the Deathless Kings. In the war of the kings, millions died, and countless races were wiped out, but it is believed that the riders were among the first to flee their empire as it was falling. They vanished, and it was thought they had gone extinct, like many other races. Only within the past hundred years have they returned, and they are very tight-lipped about how they managed to stay hidden from the world for so long." He took a step, closing the distance between us, though he didn't touch me. His eyes were conflicted as they met mine. "The ma'jhet want you dead, and I can't fight them if they're using magic against you. I think it's wise that we hear what she has to say."

EIGHTEEN

"Magic nightmares." Halek shook his head, furrowing his brow. We were in the tavern once more, sitting at a corner table in the nearly empty room. "That sounds unpleasant. So the Circle are playing dirty, eh? What do we do? How are we going to protect Sparrow?" He glanced at me, a faintly evil grin crossing his face. "I guess we could always tie her to the bed."

I smirked back. "And then you'll have to explain to Tahba how you ended up with a knife in the groin."

He winced. Kysa rolled her eyes and turned to Raithe, who sat quietly at the end of the table with his fingers laced below his chin. "Tell me about this magic," she said in a practical voice. "You mentioned that you recognized it."

Raithe uncurled his fingers and sat straighter in the chair. "The Deathless Kings weren't the only creatures with magic," he explained to us. "They were undoubtedly the most powerful, and the most destructive, but all magic comes from the same source."

"Life," Kysa said solemnly.

Raithe nodded. "Yes. You can't create something out of nothing—the magic has to come from somewhere. The Deathless were able to take it from the world around them, whether from plants, insects, or their own subjects. But some members of the ma'jhet figured out a way to work small magics by sacrificing living creatures. Sometimes animals, but usually people, trading that life to fuel their power, if only for a short time."

"Blood magic," Halek muttered, wrinkling his nose. "I've heard of these so-called sorcerers. There's a reason magic is banned in nearly all civilized societies. Like Raithe said, it has to come from somewhere."

I shivered. The thought that something had been sacrificed because of me turned my stomach. I could see Vahn standing over the altar, knife in hand, ready to end the life of whatever was below him. I hoped to the goddess that it hadn't been another human.

"To cast a scrying spell like the one that was probably used on Sparrow," Raithe continued, "you have to have something belonging to that person. Commonly, a strand of hair, or a piece of clothing. Even a single drop of blood might be enough to find them."

My insides did another cartwheel. "Everything I owned was in my room in the guild warehouse," I said, recalling my private collection. My nest of treasures. Even those were being used against me. "Vahn has no shortage of things that were mine."

Kysa's lips thinned. "Then we are running out of time, indeed," she murmured into the grim silence. "I might have a solution, if you would hear it. It would require drastic measures."

"If it keeps away nightmares and stops me from sleepwalking off the edge of the strider, I'm more than willing to hear it," I said.

Kysa nodded. "One moment," she said, and reached across her body with one arm, sliding her fingers underneath the shoulder of her armor. There was a *click*, and the chitinous shell came loose from shoulder to wrist. Laying the armor aside, she placed her arm on the table, wrist up. Vivid green tattoos covered every inch of her bared skin in elegant, swirling runes. They were written in a language I did not recognize, and swept up her arm in an almost hypnotic pattern.

"When our warriors complete their initiation," Kysa began as we stared at the mesmerizing swirls of ink on her skin, "they are expected to travel the world for a year. Among my people, this is a fairly new development. We were hidden and isolated for so long, our paranoia and fear of outsiders nearly destroyed us. Thankfully, a few wise elders realized we could not hide from the world forever, and now we wish to learn as much as we can to make up for those centuries of isolation. These"—she traced the runes on her arm with one slender finger—"are meant to protect our warriors from evil. To keep them safe, even when they are far from home."

I gazed at the swirling tattoos, my mind spinning at the thought that magic existed, and that I was being targeted by such power, at least according to Raithe. "Do they work?" I asked Kysa. "Can they shield you from magic as well?"

"It is mostly tradition now," Kysa told me. "Long ago, every member of the clan was inscribed with these tattoos. It has been many centuries since that era, however. Now only our warriors receive them, to prove they have been found worthy of being a rider. But . . . yes." Her dark eyes met mine over the table. "They are for protection against evil magic. Whether they would work for you, I am not certain," she said, pulling her arm back. "Nor am I certain if our lore keeper could inscribe them onto an outsider, or if the clan would even allow it. But I am willing to ask. We are only a few days out from Damassi. I could send a message to my clan tonight and hopefully have an answer before we reach the city."

Suspicion reared its ugly head. "Why are you doing this, Kysa?" I asked. "You've only known us a few days."

She cocked her head at me. "Is that a reason not to help someone?" she asked. "If you see a traveler sinking into devouring sand, do you try to get to know him before pulling him out?"

"Well, no," I stammered. "But this is different."

"Not so much," Kysa said. "It is a warrior's duty to offer aid to those in need. Besides," she continued softly, "things are happening in the world. A monster appeared that was extinct for centuries. A Deathless King has apparently returned from legend. And I keep hearing you referred to as 'Fateless,' over and over again." She glanced at Raithe, who raised an eyebrow but didn't respond.

"I suspect that, willing or not, you are going to be embroiled in the center of whatever is happening," Kysa went on, watching me with dark, appraising eyes. "There is a storm coming, and you seem to be the catalyst. My people need to know of it, lest they be swallowed themselves."

"I don't have any money," I told her. "I won't be able to pay for any of this."

Her eyes narrowed. "We would not ask you to pay," she said in a slightly offended voice. "This is not a service we offer to outsiders. As I said, only our warriors are inscribed with the protection markings. However, receiving the tattoos would mark you as a warrior of the Scarab Clan. If the clan agrees, you *will* have to go through the warrior's initiation to prove yourself worthy."

I swallowed. "What kind of initiation is it?" I asked.

"I cannot say." Kysa's gaze darkened. "It is forbidden for me to tell outsiders the rites of our clan. But if you wish to receive the tattoos, you will have to pass the test."

I looked at Raithe. "What do you think?" I asked him.

He regarded me seriously before answering. "If the Guildmaster is truly the one using magic against you, I think it's a good idea to have as much protection as you can," he replied. "But it's your decision, Sparrow. I don't know what the tattoos will do, if they do anything. Ultimately, the choice is yours."

I swallowed. I didn't like asking for help. And if this test was dangerous, I didn't know if I would be able to pass. I wasn't a warrior like Kysa or Raithe. But I couldn't fight magic. I couldn't run from my own dreams. Vahn had all he needed to turn my dreams against me every night. If I wanted to make it to the iylvahn city alive and sane, I had to fight back somehow. I couldn't do this alone.

Glancing at Kysa, who waited patiently, I nodded. "All right," I told her. "Yes. If your clan is willing, I will undertake this test of theirs."

She gave a solemn bob of her head. "I will send a message now."

"Quick question," Halek broke in, raising a finger. "How are you going to send a message, exactly? We're in the middle of the

Dust Sea—it's not like there are any courier huts around."

The rider's lips twisted in a faintly mocking smile. "Courier huts," she repeated, somewhat disdainfully. "I don't know why the cities use such ponderous creatures to send missives. Our messenger bugs are ten times faster, and they have wings."

"I'll come with you," Halek offered, pushing back his chair. "I want to see these amazing messenger bugs you speak of."

"Just don't put your fingers too close to their cage," Kysa warned as they left the table. "You might lose them."

I glanced at Raithe and found him watching me, his expression caught between relief and concern. The intensity in his pale blue gaze made my stomach flutter. I forced a grin. "You know, I haven't had the best luck with giant insects lately. I hope their test isn't something like 'tame a wild rock beetle naked.'"

Raithe blinked, and it might've been my imagination, but his cheeks seemed to color slightly. It was hard to tell. "Just make certain you want to do this," he said, choosing to ignore my previous comment. "The Scarab Clan live in a harsh environment, and many of their people are warriors. This test might be very difficult, Sparrow."

I nodded. "I think I have to try," I told him. "I can't hide from Vahn and the Circle if they're using magic to find me. And I know Vahn—he won't stop. The Circle will continue to come after me, which puts the rest of you in danger, too. If Vahn knows where we are, the Deathless King knows, as well. Based on that . . . I'll risk whatever this test is to keep us safe."

From across the room, the d'wevryn bartender caught my eye with a frown. "Oy, are you two nearly done?" he called gruffly.

"Contrary to popular belief, we're not open all night. I'd like to close up sometime before suns rise."

I glanced at Raithe and smirked. "I think we're being kicked out."

"It would appear so," he agreed, and rose gracefully from his chair. "I'll walk you to your room."

"I don't need an escort," I protested as we left the tavern. "I doubt there are any assassins of the Circle waiting for me in the corridors."

He raised a brow, which made me instantly regret my statement. If someone like Raithe was after me, they wouldn't let an ocean of dust stop them from getting to their target. And if they had magic at their disposal, who knew what they were capable of. Maybe there *were* assassins on the strider, watching us as we spoke. I suddenly felt a lot safer with the iylvahn at my side.

"Humor me," Raithe said, and thankfully did not point out the obvious flaws in my logic as we made our way through the halls and back to the guest quarters.

Thankfully, there were no more attacks on me that night, nor on the next two nights. My nightmares were of the standard variety, the kind from which I would wake, sweaty and frightened, as images of Vahn, the Circle, Jeran's corpse, and the Deathless King faded from my thoughts. I did not wake up somewhere else, about to throw myself overboard or into the turning gears and pistons of the strider. Though on that first morning, I did find Raithe keeping watch at my door when I stepped into the hall.

Apparently, he wasn't about to let me nearly sleepwalk to my death a second time.

Three days after my terrifying encounter with the nightmares of the Deathless King, Halek strode into the tavern, an excited grin stretched across his face.

"We're almost there," he said when he reached our table. "You can see Damassi on the horizon now."

I rose, and together we hurried to the upper deck, where a small crowd had already gathered. Peering over the railing, I squinted against the suns and watched as a dark blot grew larger and larger against the horizon.

Kovass had been a very flat city. It was built atop the desert sands, and except for the king's palace on the hill, most of the districts were on the same level. Damassi, I saw, had been built at the feet and into the sides of the mountains that bordered the coast. Square stone buildings perched atop ledges and precipices, and one enormous structure sat on a flattened rise in the very center. Roads snaked up through the different layers of the city, and a bustling network of docks sat at the edge of the Dust Sea, with dozens of skiffs and a handful of striders waiting in the harbor.

Behind the city, the jagged peaks of the Stoneshard Mountains rose into the air, looming over everything.

"Ah, Damassi," Halek said, sounding wistful. "City of temptation and gateway to the Barren Steppes, though most people never get that far." He gave me a sideways look and a grin. "You were with the Thieves Guild. You know all those illegal goods you could get for a price in Kovass? Well, they're not illegal in Damassi. And the things that *are* illegal?" He shook his head with a short breath. "They'll knock you on your ass for a week. If they don't kill you, that is."

"I would advise against sampling Damassi's selection of indulgences," Kysa warned, joining us at the railing. The other passengers, I noticed, either pretended not to notice the armor-clad rider walking across the deck or stared at her with blatant interest and awe. Some of their leering smiles turned my stomach and made me want to pull my hood up even farther. Kysa, for her part, ignored them completely.

"I was able to get a message to my clan," she told us in a low voice, turning her back on the cluster of passengers milling about the deck. "They have agreed to meet with us at our seasonal stopping grounds, a place called Carapace Basin. The journey isn't far, but it can be harsh for those unfamiliar with the steppes. I suggest getting a mount in the city before we embark."

The strider continued making its ponderous way through the sands, never hurrying or changing pace, and the city of Damassi grew steadily closer. Sometime before we reached the docks, Raithe joined us, appearing without any warning that he was coming. When I glanced up and found him standing beside me, his gaze on the approaching city, that tiny prickle simmered in the pit of my stomach.

"When the strider docks, we won't have a lot of time before Demon Hour," he told the rest of us. I gazed at the sky and saw that he was right. Solasti stood directly overhead; soon her sister would begin the climb to join her. "We'll need to find shelter as soon as we get into the city."

"Not to worry," Halek said. "I know a lovely little tavern right on the edge of the docks. It'll probably be a bit crowded during Demon Hour, but the food is good and they serve the best redseed ale in the kingdom."

Kysa took a step back. "I need to speak to Captain Arham to finish my service here," she said. "And I'll need to prepare Rhyne for the journey." She looked to the iylvahn. "I assume you will be taking the northern pass when you leave Damassi? It's the closest way into the steppes from the city."

Raithe nodded. "There's a sand dragon stable right outside the gate," he replied. "My plan was to acquire mounts before we head into the pass."

I perked up. Sand dragons were not the literal dragons of legend, with great sweeping wings and devastating, fiery breath. These were a species of squat, short-necked lizards with mottled scales and large horns sweeping back from their heads. They were popular mounts for desert travel, as they stored fat in their tails and could go for months without food or water. They were also infamously ill-tempered, and stories of sand dragons suddenly and unexpectedly taking a bite out of their handlers were not uncommon.

"I know those stables," Kysa said, though from the slight wrinkling of her nose, it was obvious she thought the desert lizards an inferior mount to the rock beetle. "I will meet you there tomorrow, before suns rise. If we leave at dawn, we should have enough time to reach the first shelter before Demon Hour."

The strider finally came to a grinding, moaning halt at the end of a long wooden pier, and Halek, Raithe, and I joined the crowd of tired, relieved passengers disembarking into the city.

The tavern Halek directed us to—the Sand Dragon Den—was noisy and crowded, filled with patrons who were also looking to avoid Demon Hour. Claiming a table in a corner, I sat with my back to the wall and watched the many strange and different people milling around the tavern. Kovass had its share of different races and cultures, but sitting as it did in the center of a sandy wasteland, it was fairly isolated and human-centric. Here on the coast, a stone's throw from the Barren Steppes, Damassi attracted people of all shapes and sizes. I saw several d'wevryn sailors playing Triple Fang with a pair of troblin, the sharp-toothed, green-skinned people who lived in caves and tunnels underground. A lone insect rider, his hair dyed a shocking crimson, nursed a drink in the corner, and across the room, I caught a glimmer of eye shine from a malkah, a race of warriors with feline qualities, the most prevalent being their glowing eyes and retractable claws.

Halek nudged my shoulder with a grin. "Is it everything you hoped it would be?" he asked around a mug of redseed ale.

I shrugged. "It's certainly different."

"We'll spend the night in the city," Raithe said, watching as an argument broke out between the d'wevryn sailors and the troblin. Thankfully, it didn't escalate into a full-blown fight but ended when one of the troblin snatched his dice off the table and stomped away, muttering under his breath. Raithe casually took his fingers off his sword hilt and continued to scan the room and its patrons like a sand hawk. "I have a contact here who can shelter us for a few hours. Tomorrow we'll meet Kysa at the northern gate and figure out how we're all going to make the journey into the pass. I left a mount at the dragon stables near the gate when I first came through Damassi, but I didn't think I'd be returning with companions."

"If you're worried about what I'm going to do, don't." Halek waved a hand airily. "I'm sure I have something a reputable stable master would be willing to trade for. My bigger concern is, shouldn't we be talking to someone instead of hiding out in the docks?"

"Talking to someone about what?" I asked.

"Oh, I don't know," Halek said, and dropped his voice to a whisper. "Maybe about Kovass falling and the Deathless King taking over? There could be an unstoppable army sailing across the Dust Sea as we speak. That seems like something the other kingdoms should know about."

"Captain Arham will let the trade council know about the attack on Kovass," Raithe replied, also in a low voice. "If he chooses to mention the return of the Deathless King, that is his prerogative. My mission is to get the Fateless to Irrikah. It is not my place to warn the other kingdoms—that decision is the queen's.

"The Deathless King is powerful," Raithe continued as Halek frowned, seeming on the verge of arguing. "But even he cannot mobilize an army in a single day. Especially after he just decimated a city and replaced it with his own. I suspect that is why the ma'jhet have been using magic against Sparrow, not the king himself. He expended a massive amount of power that day, and is perhaps trying to forge and rebuild Kovass to his liking. I think we have time before he starts casting his gaze on the other kingdoms. Not much time, but a little."

Halek sighed. "I don't like it, but I guess there's not much we can do. It's not like I can march up to city hall and demand to see the council. From what I've heard, if they agree to see you inside a month, you're lucky." He glanced out the door, where, judging by the intense sunlight gleaming off the pale stone walls, it was very close to peak Demon Hour. The air within the dimly lit stone tavern wasn't unbearably stifling, but it wasn't cool, either. One of the barmaids was drawing wooden shutters over the windows to prevent light from trickling into the room. It was strangely comforting. Even across the Dust Sea, on the other side of the kingdom, Demon Hour was the same.

Climbing a narrow road that wound its way up the side of a rocky cliff was a new experience for me. In Kovass, even if I traveled by rooftop, the city itself was as flat as the surface of a mirror. I was impressed by the efficiency with which Damassi had been built; homes and buildings covered every horizontal space, poking out of walls and perching atop ledges. If there was no space for a structure, they managed to build one anyway.

Halek let out a sudden breath and leaned against a rocky outcropping that protected him from the suns. "Ah yes, Damassi's wonderfully steep roads. I'd forgotten about them," he panted, and glanced at Raithe. "Why are we going this way again?" he asked. "There's nothing up here but the temple."

I blinked. "Maederyss has a temple here?"

"Not exactly," Raithe said. "The worship of Maederyss as a goddess is a mostly human tradition. In Damassi, she has many names and many forms. Most other races here still believe in Fate and the Weaver, but they see her as more of a servant of Fate instead of the goddess herself."

"Oh." I frowned. "But the Weaver is the one who determines your place in the Tapestry of the World," I said. "Once it's set, you can't do anything to change it."

A faint smile crossed the iylvahn's face. "Try telling that to the troblin, who believe they can defy what Fate has planned if they burrow deep enough. Or the skin shifters, who change their names, their careers, their appearances, their entire lives several times a year, just to keep the Weaver guessing." He glanced at Halek, still leaning casually against the outcropping. "Or the Fatechasers, who don't wait for their destiny to come to them, but seek it out and embrace it themselves. Whatever it might bring. Do they take their fate into their own hands? Or are they simply following the path already set for them? No one, not even the Fatechasers themselves, knows for certain."

"And believe me," Halek said with a grin, "we've stopped trying to figure it out. The number of times I've caused a scholar or professor of Fate to pull his hair out would make your head spin."

My thoughts felt tangled, and at that moment, reality seemed very fragile. I had always known what I was: a simple thief. I would never be a merchant, a noble, a warrior, a scholar, anything but a member of the Thieves Guild. I'd accepted that long ago. And not only had I accepted it, I'd excelled at what Fate had decided for me. I wasn't brave. I wasn't a hero. I was a survivor. Until a few days ago, that had been enough. Now I didn't know what I was, or what I *could* be.

"The Temple of Fate sits atop this hill," Raithe went on, gazing up the steep and narrow path, which zigzagged ever higher until it reached a massive rectangular building at the top. "The keepers there know the kahjai very well. We'll be safe to spend the night and head out in the morning."

Damassi's Temple of Fate was very different from the one in Kovass. For one, it was far smaller, as space atop the mountain plateau was limited. It was also much less grand; there were no ruby-eyed statues peering down from the roof, no golden candlesticks in the corners, no enormous statue of Maederyss holding the Tapestry of the World in the main hall. As we stepped inside the front chamber, a robed figure in white greeted us, her smile faltering when she laid eyes on Raithe. But she remained stiffly polite, telling us we were welcome in the temple and that there were rooms where we could spend the night if we wished. After leading us down a hall to a pair of simple wooden doors, she departed quickly, the hem of her robe swishing against the stones.

I glanced at the iylvahn. "The priestess didn't seem happy to see you."

Raithe shrugged one lean shoulder. "They never are. But there is an ancient agreement between the Temples of Fate and Sahmessyia, the iylvahn queen. The priestesses know that from time to time, a kahjai is sent into the world to remove a weak thread from the tapestry, to stop the corruption before it can take hold. They know it is necessary, and so the Temples of Fate will shelter the kahjai, should they need it, but the kahjai are required to announce their presence to the temple if they are going to be doing work in the city."

"Oh," I said, remembering several things at once. "So that's why you were talking to the high priestess in Kovass."

One brow arched. "I thought I felt another presence in the temple that day," he mused with a faint smile. "So that *was* you, after all." His soft chuckle made my stomach twist. "Somehow, I'm not surprised."

That night, tired as I was, I couldn't sleep.

The cot the temple provided was hard and uncomfortable, but I was used to that. The room was small, with narrow slits for windows, but compared to the tiny quarters on the sand strider, it was more space than I'd had in a while. But the thoughts swirling through my head refused to calm. So much had happened in a short amount of time. I was in Damassi, on the other side of the Dust Sea. Somewhere back beyond the sands, Kovass lay in ruins, along with everything I'd ever known. My old life was gone, and there was no returning to it. If I wasn't a thief anymore, what was I?

My eyelids were heavy. Sleep tugged at me, but I resisted. I knew what would be waiting for me when I finally succumbed: Jeran's lifeless body, the Circle surrounding me, calling for my death, and Vahn, standing there with the cold eyes of a stranger. It was strange; the Deathless King was terrifying, all-powerful, and I feared him the most, but when the nightmares came, Jeran, Vahn, and the Circle were the images that haunted me.

My chin dropped to my chest, and for a moment, my eyes closed. But then a soft tap on my door caused my heartbeat to intensify. Only Raithe would be knocking on my door this late.

I swung my legs off the cot, walked to the door, and pulled it open with a squeak of hinges.

"Hello, Sparrow," said Vahn, smiling down at me. "I think we need to talk."

NINETEEN

I staggered back from the door, my heart no longer pounding but literally racing around my chest. All my survival instincts were screaming at me to run, but in the tiny room, there was nowhere to go. Vahn blocked the door, and the windows were too narrow for even me to slip through.

"You can relax, you know." Vahn's face still held that amused smile as he watched me; he knew exactly what I was thinking. "I wish only to talk to you."

"How are you here?" I hissed at him. "There's no way you could have crossed the Dust Sea that quickly."

"That would be true," Vahn agreed, "if this wasn't a dream. I just had to wait for you to fall asleep, which you finally did, so thank you for that. It is far easier to control the environment this way. If I had arrived at your door in the middle of the night in person, your assassin friend would not take that well."

"Oh really? I wonder why." Anger flared through me, a hot, burning rage. Suddenly, everything I had been through crashed down on me all at once, searing and painful. "Maybe because you summoned a literal god demon that destroyed our city and killed thousands of people," I spat at the figure in the doorway. "Maybe because you've been lying to me for seventeen years, and everything you've done has been to resurrect the Deathless

King. You sent me into a city crawling with monsters and curses to get that soulstone, you slaughtered Jeran in cold blood, and you were about to *sacrifice* me to your demon god! Oh, and let's not forget that abomination you sent after us, and the time you tried to sleepwalk me off the side of a ship with one of these harmless little dreams. I can't imagine why he wouldn't like you," I snarled at Vahn, who remained stone-faced but silent. "I can't imagine why *I* might be a little resentful. And I can't imagine anything you could say that would make any of this better. But go ahead . . ." I stepped back and waved a casual hand at him. "Please explain why you think all this death and chaos is justified."

"The iylvahn has been lying to you," Vahn said calmly. "He is not what you think, and he is taking you to his queen so that she may use you to bring herself to power." His eyes narrowed. "What have I told you about trust, Sparrow? It is a weakness that will destroy you in the end. You trusted Jeran, and he betrayed you. You trusted me, and look what happened. The iylvahn and his people will do the same."

"He's keeping me safe from you and the Circle," I said, curling my lip at the Guildmaster. "He's helping me stay alive. Every night, I see the Circle in my dreams, chanting 'Kill the Fateless, kill the Fateless.' Every night, I watch you slice Jeran's throat open and realize it should've been me. Why shouldn't I trust Raithe, if it keeps me safe from you and your Deathless King?"

"You are being shortsighted." Vahn gave me that look that said he thought I was being foolish. He paused a moment, then sighed and turned away. "Walk with me a bit."

He started down the hall, not looking back to see if I was following. For a moment, I gritted my teeth and considered slamming the door on him, hoping it would wake me up. But if I did, I wouldn't know why he was here, what he wanted, or what he might know about Raithe and the iylvahn. The Guildmaster might be a murderous, scheming, lying bastard, and I'd never trust him again, but he never did anything without purpose.

Stepping into the hall, I froze. Raithe sat across the corridor in a hard wooden chair, arms crossed, chin resting on his chest. He wasn't awake, but he wasn't entirely asleep, either. I wondered what would happen if I shouted at him as loudly as I could, right there in the hallway.

"He can't hear you," Vahn assured me. He looked at the dozing iylvahn, eyes narrowed, his anger toward Raithe peeking through. "I realized that after you managed to escape the first dreamwalking, the iylvahn would probably take precautions against a second attempt. To him, you are safely asleep in your room right now, so don't worry. We won't be interrupted by a vengeful kahjai this time."

With a last baleful glance at Raithe, Vahn turned and continued down the corridor. I set my jaw and stalked after him.

The temple was quiet as the two of us walked silently down the narrow passageways, passing closed doors on either side. No one roamed the halls of the Temple of Fate; I wondered if it was this quiet in real life, or because Vahn wished it to be.

"The iylvahn is deceiving you," Vahn said again. "Do not let yourself believe his reasons are altruistic. His queen wants you for the power you represent. She sacrifices her own people to keep herself alive. She will use you as well, make no mistake about that."

My stomach turned, but I narrowed my eyes at my former Guildmaster. "How is that any worse than what you did?"

He stopped and turned on me, his expression intense. "I brought the king back to life because this world is dead," he said firmly. "We live in an empire of dust and ash, where nothing grows and all life shrivels away under the twins. It was different when the kings ruled. The world was green, plentiful. No one questioned where they belonged. Everyone knew their place was to serve the Deathless. This misbegotten faith in Maederyss grew out of the uncertainty of people not knowing their purpose in life after the kings fell. Beliefs are fractured, and no one is certain of anything anymore. The Deathless King will put an end to that uncertainty. He will unite everyone under a common banner once more."

"Tyranny," I said, wrinkling my nose.

Vahn's lips tightened. "That kind of language is exactly how the wars first began," he said. "Because a group of peasants believed they deserved more. They betrayed their empire, deserted the king who gave them life, and sought sanctuary in another king's land. When the first king rightfully demanded that his people be returned, the other king refused. Thus, the War of the Kings—and the end of the world—began. Because a handful of commoners did not know their place."

"So is it my place to die?" I demanded. "Was it my place to stand there and let you slash a knife across my throat, like you did to Jeran? Sorry, I guess I ruined your entire plan when I didn't let myself be murdered like I was supposed to."

"Sparrow." Vahn sighed, and one hand rose to rub his brow. For the first time, he seemed . . . remorseful. "I regret that things happened the way they did," he murmured. "I truly did not want any of those things for you. I wish the child I had brought into the guild seventeen years ago could have been just that . . . a normal child. But you are the Fateless. Which means you are a threat to the stability of the kingdom." He dropped his arm, giving me a weary look. "I cannot ignore that, no matter how much I wish it were not so."

"I don't even know what being Fateless means," I said, frustrated once more. "Raithe won't tell me. He said the queen will have to explain it."

"Because the iylvahn knows exactly what the Fateless is," Vahn replied. "And if you realized it for yourself, you might change your mind about everything." He raised a questioning eyebrow, giving me a knowing look. "Do you wish me to tell you?" he asked. "It might be less painful to remain ignorant."

My heartbeat quickened. For a moment, I teetered like I was standing at the edge of a precipice, unsure whether I should take the plunge. Taking a deep breath, I looked up at the Guildmaster. "Tell me," I said. "I want to know. What does being Fateless mean?"

Vahn nodded, as if he'd known how I would answer. "It means that your thread is not present in the Tapestry of the World," he said. "All souls have a story and a connection to the millions of other souls bound into the Weave. Their lives, their stories, are interwoven, entwined. If one thread unravels or is cut, it affects every other thread around it. Except for yours." Vahn lifted his empty palms. "You do not have a thread. No one can trace your story. Maederyss herself is blind to your presence, because you are simply . . . not there."

"But . . ." My thoughts were tangled again. I tried to follow what Vahn was saying, with little success. "I don't understand. That doesn't make any sense—"

"Your thread is not present in the Weave," Vahn continued ruthlessly. "Your fate cannot be determined. However, even though they have no presence in the tapestry, the Fateless can affect the lives and threads of everyone they encounter. Shifting them. Disrupting them. Or, in some cases, removing them entirely. The Fateless ignore prophecy. They cannot be controlled, and they are shielded from the eyes of Fate itself. They are chaos incarnate, and because they exist, they can bring about the fall of entire kingdoms."

I swallowed hard, as my whole world seemed to be unraveling. "But if I don't have a thread in the tapestry," I began, as Vahn raised an eyebrow, "how can I even exist? The threads represent everyone's souls. Does that mean . . ."

"It has long been debated whether the Fateless are, in fact, soulless," Vahn said bluntly. "How else could they hide their presence from the goddess herself? The Fateless have no souls, and thus, no real concept of good and evil. Convenient for them, as they cause chaos and misery wherever they go. Everyone who meets them, everyone they touch, is in danger of having their fate unraveled." Vahn fixed me with a piercing stare. "Perhaps it *wasn't* Jeran's fate to die on the altar," he said. "But because he met you, events unfolded in a way no one could expect."

"No." I shook my head. "Don't . . . don't try to pin Jeran's death on me. That was all you. You and the Circle."

"Can you be certain?" Vahn's voice was ruthlessly gentle. "How do you know it wasn't your presence that doomed the boy from the start? How do you know that you were not the cause of the entire city's demise? After all, were it not for you, the Deathless King would not have risen."

I clenched my fists hard enough to feel my nails biting into my palms. "Why are you here?" I asked coldly, careful not to let the tremor in my arms and legs spread to my voice. "If you came just to tell me that you're going to try to kill me, you should've saved your breath. I'm not going to lie down and die."

"No." Surprisingly, Vahn smiled. One of his faint, old smiles, without malice. "I wouldn't expect you to. Not the Sparrow I know." He turned and started walking down the hall again, causing me to stride after him. "I will ask you this, though," he continued as we reached the inner sanctum of the temple. "What would you do to save the people around you from certain death? I know you care little for the kingdoms or the people within them, but what of those whom you consider your companions? The Fatechaser. The insect rider. The iylvahn assassin who tried to kill you. Are they important enough for you to want to save them?"

I eyed him warily. "Why?"

We had reached the front doors of the temple, which, oddly, were closed. I had thought they stayed open pretty much all the time. Vahn put his hand on one door but hesitated, turning to me with a look that sent chills down my spine.

"Because this is what will happen to all those who oppose the Deathless King," he said, and pushed open the door.

A wave of heat blasted me in the face. Beyond the doorframe, the sky was the reddish orange of an inferno. I heard the howl of flames and saw tongues of fire twisting and snapping at the few scraggly trees around the temple. Bodies were everywhere, charred and black, scattered down the steps and lying throughout the yard.

"This is just a dream," I whispered, taking a step back. "It's not real."

"True," Vahn agreed mildly. "This is not real. Not yet, anyway." He gestured to the stairway, to the railing separating us from the cliff's edge. "But it will be. Take a good look, and see what the future holds for everyone who defies the Deathless King."

In a daze, I walked to the railing and looked down at the city below.

Damassi was on fire. The valley looked more like an ocean of lava than anything resembling a city of thousands. Screams and wails rose into the air, mingling with the roar of the inferno and the crackle of things being consumed. The smell of smoke, ash, and burning flesh clogged the back of my throat and set me coughing.

"They will all die," Vahn said, appearing beside me. "Young and old, rich and poor, human, iylvahn, d'wevryn, it doesn't matter. Soon, the purge will begin. Soon, any who choose not to be part of the king's empire will perish in flame and blood and sand. There is no escape."

He looked down at me, his eyes dark and intense. "But you can save yourself," he said. "And your friends. It does not have to end in death for you." He lifted a hand to the doomed city far below. "If you stop running, if you return and pledge your loyalty to the king, this does not have to be your future. The king has spoken to me. He has told me that he would rather have a Fateless in his court than have to pursue her all over the empire." He held out a hand, as if presenting me with a priceless gift. "He wants you as part of his circle, Sparrow. Return to Kovass, and you can take your place among the ma'jhet. We can teach you the ancient magics. You can rule as one of us. And, most important, you will be safe. You will be spared when the Deathless King begins his conquest of the empire."

I swallowed hard. "And my friends?"

"The king does not care about individual lives," Vahn said, waving a hand. "Fatechaser, iylvahn, insect rider—they are as beneath his notice as grains of sand. As long as they swear their loyalty to the Deathless crown, they will be spared and forgotten."

"Sounds like a fine deal," I said sarcastically, "from a great and compassionate ruler and his circle of blood mages."

"Sparrow." Vahn paused; his brow furrowed as if in pain, then smoothed out. "I know what you think of me," he began, "and you are fully justified. I regret that I had to use you like I did. I truly did not want to kill you that day below the city. But that business is finished. The king wishes—no, the king *demands* that you come home. And when the Deathless King demands something, it must come to pass."

I hesitated. Return to Kovass? Go back to Vahn and my old

home like nothing had happened? Like I hadn't watched the Guildmaster kill Jeran in cold blood, and the Deathless King crush people by the thousands when he raised his city from beneath the sands? Pledge my loyalty to the king and save myself, Vahn said. Would that be better than this endless running, trying to find ways to hide myself from the ones who wanted me dead?

"It does not have to be painful," Vahn went on, his voice soothing. "You know the truth now. We could start again, no lies, no deception this time. I . . . I have always thought of you as a daughter." His voice faltered slightly, as if that had been hard for him to say. "Despite what you think of me, I have always been proud of you. You are the most talented thief I have ever seen, and your skills would be greatly valued in the Deathless King's court. You belong with us, Sparrow. Kovass has always been your home."

My eyes blurred, and I bit the inside of my lip to keep the tears back. *Why now?* I thought, not knowing if I was furious or stupidly relieved. *Why would you tell me this now? Why couldn't you have said it before, when I needed to hear it the most?*

I drew in a slow breath as something clicked into place. In all the years I had known him, Vahn had never begged, bartered with, or cajoled anyone. He'd laid out his terms clearly, and you either accepted them, or you didn't. This urging me to come home was new.

Because Vahn . . . was afraid. Of the Deathless King. Of what the king would do if he didn't bring me back.

Vahn stepped close and put a hand on my shoulder. "Think about it," he said. "You can stop running. You don't have to be afraid anymore." The fingers on my arm squeezed gently, making my stomach constrict as well. "Come home, Sparrow," Vahn murmured. "You cannot keep defying the inevitable. If you do, everything you know will be consumed."

The hand on my shoulder suddenly burst into flame. I jerked back, freeing myself, and saw Vahn wreathed in fire, flames snapping in his hair and burning his clothes.

"You can stop this," Vahn said, his voice as calm as ever even as the skin on his face bubbled and his eyes began leaking down his cheeks. "You can end the destruction, Sparrow. All you have to do is come home."

Pain seared my arms. I looked down and saw that the fire had spread to my sleeves and was crawling rapidly up my clothes. Gasping, I staggered back, looking desperately for something to put myself out, but I was surrounded by flame, ash, and death.

Before me, Vahn swayed on his feet, then crumpled, his head hitting the stones with a sickening *crack*. The fire consuming him flared, then sputtered out, leaving behind only a blackened skeleton, grinning sightlessly up at me.

The flames reached my neck, igniting my hair, and I screamed.

"Sparrow!"

I bolted upright, gasping, my heart thudding painfully in my chest. Immediately, the flames and burning sky faded to darkness, replaced with stone walls and the bright, concerned eyes of an iylvahn, hovering over me. His fingers dug into my shoulders, and the door behind him creaked on its hinges, letting soft orange light into the room.

"Breathe, Sparrow," Raithe urged, still holding me firmly by the shoulders, as if I might leap up and rush out the door if he let go. "It was a dream. You were dreaming again. You're safe now."

My breath came in short gasps, my vision blurring as tears streamed down my cheeks, burning like acid. I couldn't speak. I could still see Damassi in flames, Vahn staring at me as the skin on his face melted like candle wax. Raithe sat on the cot and pulled me to him, holding me close as I gasped and shook and tried to catch my breath, listening to the steady beat of his heart against my ear.

Raithe didn't say anything more; he simply held me as my pulse slowed and my breathing returned to normal. The horrific imagery continued to dance through my head, along with the sounds, smells, and feelings the nightmare had brought. But as the images faded, Vahn's words returned, echoing in my head like a litany of doom.

The iylvahn has been lying to you.

Your thread is not present in the Weave.

The Fateless have no souls.

You are an agent of chaos. Entire kingdoms could fall just because you exist.

I bit my lip, hoping the pain would clear my thoughts, but they still tangled hopelessly in my head. I had no reason to believe Vahn; he had lied to me—for my whole life, in fact. But doubts still crept into my mind, casting a shadow over my thoughts. Fateless. Soulless. Able to unravel the destiny of everyone I touched, for good or ill. I thought of Halek, and how twice now he'd thought he had missed his destiny, his fate. Because of me.

And Raithe. What was he really doing? I was starting to rely on him more and more, but really, everything he did was to get us to the iylvahn city to meet the queen. He knew what being Fateless meant. How could anyone want anything to do with me after that?

I pulled back from him, and he let go immediately, dropping his arms as I drew away. His eyes, however, were still concerned as he watched me. "Better?"

"Yeah." I stared at the thin covers of the cot, tangling my fingers in the fabric. "It was just another nightmare."

"Is that all?" His steady gaze never wavered. I could still feel it on me, but couldn't meet his eyes. "Sparrow?"

I clenched my jaw and didn't answer. He paused, and then brought one hand up to gently brush my cheek. I felt the tingle all the way down my spine, making my breath catch and my stomach squirm like crazy.

"Tell me," Raithe murmured, his voice softer than petals. "Was it the ma'jhet? If they are using magic again, I need to know to keep you safe."

My heart pounded. For a moment, I considered leaning into him once more, wanting to feel his arms around me, a shelter from the rest of the world. I wanted to tell him everything, about myself, and Vahn, and the Deathless King's invitation. I was tired of running and being scared. I longed to curl into Raithe, close my eyes, and let myself believe, if just for a moment, that I was safe.

I jerked up, shocked and terrified with myself. What was happening? I couldn't keep doing this. I trusted Raithe to protect us and get us to the iylvahn city, but as I had discovered with Jeran and Vahn, the more you actually cared for someone, the more devastating it was when they betrayed you. Raithe was a talented assassin, loyal to his queen, and I was—according to everyone—Fateless. Wanted by the Circle and the Deathless King. What if the iylvahn queen ordered him to kill me? Or, worse, used me as a bargaining chip to protect her own people?

I turned from Raithe, then stood and stepped away to put distance between us. He stayed on the cot, watching me, though I probably imagined the ripple of hurt and confusion that crossed his face. Folding my arms, I gazed out the narrow slit of a window at the navy blue of the sky over Damassi. Hearing the crackle of flames and the voice of the Guildmaster echoing in my head.

"I saw Vahn," I muttered. "Just now, in my . . . in my dream."

His expression sharpened. "The Guildmaster?"

I nodded once. Finally meeting his gaze, I narrowed my eyes. "When were you going to tell me the Fateless doesn't have a soul?"

He didn't ask how I knew. He was intelligent enough to put two and two together. Sighing, he closed his eyes, then looked up at me again. "I don't believe that piece of lore," he said. "I have seen soulless creatures. Demons. The summoned dead. You are not like that. You care for the people around you. You have compassion. It's buried, and a little hard to find . . ." The faintest of smiles crossed his face before vanishing in the next breath. "But I've seen it. You are not soulless."

My eyes stung. I turned my head away and took a quick breath so he wouldn't see. "You still should've told me, Raithe."

"Why?" He seemed genuinely puzzled, tilting his head at me. "Would it have made any difference on our journey?" he asked in a quiet voice. "What purpose would it have served? That kind of question can eat at you, keep you up at night, drive you mad, if you let it. I thought it better to save you that uncertainty. At least until we reached Irrikah."

"What about the rest?" I asked. "The parts about having no thread in the Weave, no part in the story of the world? Vahn said I could unravel destinies with just a touch, that anyone I encounter is at risk of having their fate vanish completely."

"That is all true." Raithe stood, rising elegantly to his feet. "And quite terrifying to some. Especially those who can see a bit of the future."

"Like the Deathless Kings?"

He nodded. "And the ma'jhet. And the seers. And the prophets of Fate who wander the empire. There are very few legends of the Fateless, but one tells the story of a great and respected fortune teller who tried to glimpse the destiny of one who was Fateless. He went mad, babbling about a great unraveling in the Weave, and threw himself into the Dust Sea soon after."

"Oh good," I said, hiding behind sarcasm once again. "So I drive people mad and cause them to kill themselves. I've always wanted to do that."

Raithe stepped closer. I held my breath, torn between wanting him to come close and taking a step back. "I'm sorry I didn't tell you earlier," he murmured. "I didn't want to put that burden on you. Once we reach Irrikah, the queen will be able to explain everything. But I think it's crucial now that we pay a visit to the Scarab Clan and see what we can do to shield you from the Circle's magic."

I nodded. That sounded like a good idea to me. I really could do without Vahn popping into my dreams and tormenting me whenever he felt like it. Briefly, I wondered if I should tell Raithe that the Deathless King wanted me to return to Kovass, but that might make my companions even more paranoid. Besides . . . I had to think about it. I had no intention of returning to the city now, but there might come a time when going home might be preferable to letting everyone be killed. Even if it was to face Vahn, the ma'jhet, and the Deathless King himself.

"Yeah." I sighed, leaning against the wall. "Agreed. I'll just have to find a way not to sleep until we get there."

Raithe frowned. I could tell he didn't like that idea, but he didn't protest, either. "It's still a couple hours till sunrise," he said, glancing at the tiny slitted window in the wall. "I take it you're not going back to sleep?"

"No." I shook my head. Even if Vahn wasn't waiting for me to go back to sleep, the dreams were. "No more sleeping for me tonight," I went on. "One heart-stopping nightmare an evening is enough, I think."

Raithe nodded. "Walk with me, then," he said, turning to the door. "It's a beautiful night, and the moon is full. Maybe it'll clear your head."

Clearing my head sounded nice. Right now, it felt like a tangled mess of uncertainty, fear, anxiety, and dread. I stepped out the door with Raithe, and together we walked down the silent temple hallway until we came to the main chamber. The large front doors still lay open, and silver-blue moonlight filtered through the opening.

As we walked down the temple steps into the courtyard, a cold breeze hit my skin. I shivered, pulling my hood up farther and crossing my arms to conserve heat. During the day the air was suffocatingly hot, but at night, when the suns fully disappeared, the temperatures plummeted as well. I gazed upward and saw a blanket of glimmering diamonds spread overhead, a sight rarely seen in Kovass, where the haze and the glow of millions of lanterns stifled the view of the sky. Reaching the courtyard wall, I leaned my elbows against the cold stones and gazed down at the lights of Damassi scattered below us. From way up here, the city seemed peaceful; no screaming, no snapping fires, no roaring inferno consuming everything in sight.

I felt Raithe beside me, also gazing at the lights and lanterns spread below. I realized that, just like Halek, he had probably been all across the world, seen cities and kingdoms that, with my sheltered Kovass upbringing, I'd never even imagined.

"What it's like?" I murmured, and felt him glance at me. "Irrikah, I mean. People know the iylvahn city is out there, and yet no one has ever seen it. No outsiders anyway."

"People have seen it," Raithe said, equally softly. "They just . . . forget about it, when they leave. It's part of the magic the queen employs to keep our people safe. Any non-iylvahn who leaves Irrikah will soon lose all their memories of the city—where it is, what it looks like, how it is laid out, everything."

"What is it like there?" I asked. "If you can tell me, that is."

"I can," Raithe said, turning to watch me intently. "But . . .

you'll forget what we talked about by tomorrow. You'll remember we *had* a conversation, you might even remember what it was about, but the details of Irrikah will fade from your memory and be lost. Some people can find that infuriating. I wanted to warn you first."

"Oh," I said. I'd never heard of that. "I'd still like to know," I went on, gazing up at him. "Even if I won't remember. What is it really like, from someone who has actually lived there?"

Raithe paused. Turning, he mimicked my pose, resting his arms on the stone wall and gazing down into the city. "Green," he said after a moment. His voice was soft, almost wistful. "Once you get through the Maze and past the gates, it's like you're stepping into another world. There are trees, and grass, and flowers; more color and life than you could ever imagine. Though it's taken hundreds of years of dedicated work to bring the land back from nothing."

A green city, full of life and flowers. Raithe was right—I couldn't even imagine such a thing. "You must miss it."

"I do," Raithe murmured, his gaze dark and far away. "Very much so. Every time I leave the city, I'm reminded of what the world is like for those outside. There are some iylvahn who have never seen the kingdoms beyond the Maze. They've never been outside the city walls, and have no desire to venture forth. I can understand that. Why would you leave a paradise to go into hell?"

"It's not *that* bad out here, is it?" I joked, making a corner of his lip twitch.

"A sun-scorched wasteland with demon abominations that

chase you down to devour you?" His voice was wry. "I can't imagine why I would think that."

I poked his elbow. "Hey, I'm the sarcastic one here. Don't let me rub off on you."

Raithe smiled, though his expression was serious in the next instant. Turning, he moved a step closer, pale eyes suddenly intense. My heartbeat quickened as he gently raised one hand toward my hood to brush it back.

I stiffened.

He stopped immediately, and a faint, puzzled furrow creased his brow as he gazed down at me. "Why are you afraid?" he asked.

I ducked my head, cheeks burning. "Because," I whispered, turning away. "If people don't see me, then I don't exist. I can be invisible, or a shadow on the wall. In my world, staying alive depends on my ability to blend in and be unnoticed. If people see me..."

I faltered, unable to voice my true thoughts. If people really saw me, they would realize what I was: A street rat. A thief. A girl who wasn't special, or pretty, or remarkable in any way. It was easier to be invisible and go unnoticed than for someone like Raithe to look at me and see there was nothing worth looking at.

"But I do see you," Raithe murmured. Stepping close, his fingers gently took my arm and turned me to face him once more. "I see a girl who I thought was just a thief, but who turned out to be so much more. I see someone who has survived a great tragedy, who looked a god of destruction in the face and lived. I've seen her cunning, and bravery, and intelligence. And even in our short time together, I've watched her change from someone whose only thought was of her own survival to a person willing to put herself in danger for others."

"Once," I protested. "I did that once."

"Would you do it again?"

"I . . ." I hesitated, really thinking about it. If another abomination attacked, if I looked down and saw a monstrous, eight-legged fiend crawling up the side of the mountain toward us, would I turn and flee? Vanish into the city and find shelter in the hundreds of cracks and hidey-holes where I'd be safe from the monster? Or would I fight, knowing Halek and Raithe—and Kysa, if she were here—would certainly stay behind and battle the creature to the death?

"I . . . yes," I whispered, dazed with the realization. I *would* stay and fight. Even if it meant my death, even if the very thought terrified me to the core, I couldn't run away and leave the others to die. "For you and Halek and Kysa, I would."

Raithe ran his hands up my arms, sending a shiver through my whole body. "That day on the strider, you saved my life," he murmured. "When you came back, that decision changed the fates of at least three people, maybe dozens more. There is no doubt in my mind." Once more, his hand rose to my hood, and this time, I let it fall back. The chill night wind ruffled my hair, lifting it from my shoulders, as I stared into the pale, beautiful eyes of the iylvahn gazing down at me.

"You are Sparrow," he whispered, bending close. The hand that had brushed my hood cupped the side of my face, warming my skin. "You are the Fateless."

And he kissed me.

His lips were soft and cool, and I closed my eyes, a thousand sensations sweeping through my center. Warmth bloomed in my stomach, spreading through me until I could no longer feel the chill, only the flickering heat between us, the gentle press of his mouth on mine. My hands crept up his shoulders and cupped the back of his head to pull him closer, and his arms wrapped around my waist in return. Disbelief and shock battled elation. Raithe, the deadly, long-lived iylvahn assassin, was kissing me; it felt more like a dream than anything real.

Because he thinks you're the Fateless.

That seed of doubt wriggled in, took hold, and began to spread. What if I wasn't Fateless? Would Raithe's interest in me dissolve? Would he be angry and disappointed if I wasn't what he hoped? What he had sworn to protect all this time? If, when we reached the iylvahn city, the queen took one look at me and declared that I wasn't Fateless, what would Raithe do?

Everyone you have trusted before has betrayed you.

The doubt spread, turning into fear. I'd thought I might have something with Jeran, only to lose him to jealousy and anger. I'd loved Vahn as a father, and right now, he was my greatest enemy. If I let myself fall for Raithe—which would be easy, I realized; I already depended on the iylvahn far more than I should—if I fell in love with him now, how devastating would it be if he turned his back on me? When he realized I was not Fateless, but just a human. A thief. A nobody.

I slid my hands down his chest and pushed, drawing back slightly. He didn't try to hold on, only let his arms drop as I pulled away, though I could feel his gaze as I stepped back.

"Sparrow..." His voice was soft, questioning.

"I'm sorry," I whispered, shaking my head. "I can't, Raithe. I just... I'm sorry."

Turning, I fled the courtyard, sprang up the stairs, and ducked back into the temple. I didn't look back until I reached my room, but I could feel his gaze on me the entire way.

TWENTY

The sand dragon stables reeked of dust, straw, manure, and, weirdly enough, saffron oil.

"Calms 'em down, it does," the stable owner told us when Halek made a comment about the odd yet delightfully fragrant smell in the air. "Any dragon owner worth his spit will keep a few jugs on hand at all times. The ones that don't? Well..." The lean, bald little man with the jagged scar across his skull held up his right hand, which was missing the last two digits. "They're either missing more fingers than me, or they're dead.

"Now, don't you worry," he went on, as Halek cast a concerned look at the stable of snorting, growling lizards. "I rub a fingerful of oil under their nostrils every morning, so any dragon you get from me will probably not take your arm off that first day. After that, however..." He shook his bald head. "I wouldn't turn my back on 'em, for any reason. Luckily, my special pots of calming oil are for sale, *if* you want to arrive at your destination with all your limbs still attached to your body."

"I think we'll be fine," Raithe said, though Halek looked ready to jump on the man's offer. I wondered if the Fatechaser was aware of just how expensive real saffron oil was. A tiny carafe sold for a small fortune on the streets of Kovass. "We appreciate the warning," Raithe went on, "but we'll take our chances."

"Eh, your fingers, not mine." The stable owner shrugged and shuffled toward the stalls, grabbing a pair of lead ropes as he did.

"Quite the salesman," I said in a low voice to the other two. "I bet he makes more money from fake saffron oil than he does selling lizards."

"Almost certainly," murmured Raithe with the hint of a smile. He hadn't said anything about our incident in the temple courtyard earlier. Both to my relief and disappointment, he acted as if nothing had happened between us. "Fortunately, sand dragons are not quite as dangerous as he makes them out to be," Raithe went on, "though you do have to be somewhat on your guard around them. Watch their eyes—if the pupils dilate and constrict rapidly, they're feeling aggressive and ready to bite. But they're usually only irritable when they're hungry, or if a female is in season."

Halek chuckled. "Well, that's most males," he remarked.

The stable owner returned leading two large sand dragons, one with dark brown scales and a creamy white underside, the other pale yellow with black spots mottling its back and tail. Both had impressive horns that curved back from their broad skulls and sharp, jagged teeth poking from their blunt muzzles.

"Two males, like you wanted," the owner said, though Raithe had told me most dragon stables sold only males, because having females around riled them up considerably. "These are two of my calmest," the bald man told us, with a wink in my direction, "seeing as we have a pair of new riders. They're not the fastest, but they should get you across the steppes in one piece. Hopefully."

He gave me the hint of a knowing smirk. "Sure you don't want a pot of calming oil? Just in case this one gets that look in his eye?" He patted the yellow dragon in an almost affectionate manner. "Dragon teeth are serrated, you know. They do more damage coming out than they do going in."

I smiled back. "I think we'll get along."

Raithe retrieved his own mount, a jet-black sand dragon with vivid yellow stripes and a hard, red-eyed stare that made me very nervous. I watched him swing gracefully into the saddle, then turned to my own lizard, peering intently at its eyes. The slitted pupils seemed normal, but then again, what was normal for a sand dragon? Taking the chance that it wouldn't immediately turn around and sink its fangs into my backside, I put one foot in the leather stirrup and heaved myself into the saddle. The dragon huffed beneath me, scratching the ground with its talons, but that was all.

"Good, good," the stable owner called behind me. "That's how you do it. Don't be nervous," he went on, as I looked to Raithe to see what to do next. "They can smell fear."

Raithe gave an approving nod that warmed my insides and turned his mount away. "Let's go," he told me and Halek, who seemed to be struggling a bit with his dragon. His mount was tossing its head and pawing at the ground, making him grab frantically for the reins. "Kysa should be waiting for us at the north gate," Raithe went on, moving steadily away. "We have to get through the pass and to the first shelter before Demon Hour, so we don't have a lot of time to waste."

"Easy for you to say," Halek said, as his dragon snorted and shook its head vigorously, making the reins jingle. "I think I got the broken one."

I gave my dragon a tap with my heels, and it started forward, easing into a long, loping walk that was surprisingly smooth. We left the dragon stables and headed toward the wall of mountains looming high overhead, and the city of Damassi soon faded behind us.

A familiar silhouette in sleek black armor waited for us at the city gates. She stood off the main road, leaning casually against Rhyne, who lay like an enormous shiny boulder in the dirt, his horn jutting into the air. Most passersby noticed her—it was hard not to see a beetle the size of a cart lying a few yards off the main road—but when they did, they quickly averted their gaze. As we approached, a pair of well-dressed aggressive-looking young men spotted her and elbowed each other with sly grins. But when Kysa raised her head and stared at them dead-on, they quickly seemed to lose interest and hurried away.

Kysa's hard stare turned into a smile as she saw us, and she pushed herself off Rhyne, raising an arm in greeting. The beetle stayed where he was, as immovable as a mountain.

"I received another message from my clan," the insect rider said as Raithe pulled his mount to a halt beside her. "The dust storms that blow across the steppes are volatile this season. If we are to reach Carapace Basin safely, we should hurry. However, I do know a few places we can duck into if the winds turn against us."

"We leave it to you, Kysa," Raithe said solemnly. "Whenever you're ready."

"Just remember that our mounts don't fly," Halek added with a grin.

Kysa nodded and gave a short whistle that caused Rhyne to heave himself to his feet and lumber over. I noticed several satchels, trunks, and saddlebags piled on his back and hanging from his saddle. It looked like about twice as much as our sand dragons were carrying, yet Rhyne didn't seem to notice the weight at all. "The journey across the steppes to Carapace Basin will take three days," Kysa told us, leaping gracefully atop her mount. "I hope you have everything you need, because you will not find it out there."

The north gate loomed before us, and beyond the gatehouse, the wall of the Stoneshard Mountains soared into the air, steep and treacherous. Two guards at the entrance watched silently as we rode our dragons beneath the gate; one of them gave Kysa a short nod, which she returned. Beyond the gate, a narrow pass cut through the jagged cliffs and snaked out of sight.

Halek craned his neck back, staring at the strip of sky above the pass. We had left the temple while it was still full dark, but now the heavens had turned pink, and the stars were fading.

"Solasti is coming," he said. "And I don't suppose the pass is any cooler during Demon Hour than the rest of the world."

"Actually, it's worse," Kysa said. She turned toward Halek with a small smile and gestured at the red-tinted cliffs on either side. "When Demon Hour comes, those walls radiate heat. It's like being inside a brick oven. Not something you want to experience."

"Ah no," Halek corrected her with a raised finger. "Again.

It's not something I want to experience *again*. I've already been broiled once by the twins on this journey—twice would turn me into a piece of shriveled jerky." He shook his head, a pained look crossing his face. "I have never wanted to die so much before my time, and that's coming from a Fatechaser who once fell into a nest of fire centipedes." He grimaced and shot a glance at Raithe. "If that happens again, iylvahn, I just might have to take you up on your previous offer. If we get caught in Demon Hour again, to clarify. Not the fire centipedes. Though getting bitten by a dozen fire centipedes is not pleasant, either, let me tell you."

"We're better supplied this time," Raithe said, as I shivered with the memory. Lying on the Dust Sea with Raithe and Halek, slowly burning away as we waited to die. "We know what we're walking into," he went on. "It won't be like Kovass." His gaze went to me, and the look in those pale blue eyes made my breath catch. "I won't let us be caught like that again, I promise."

"Can your . . . lizards move any faster?" Kysa inquired, as if she was trying hard to be diplomatic. "I know most landbound creatures cannot match a rock beetle's flight speed, but can they at least trot?"

Halek's laugh rose into the air and echoed off the rising peaks. "I think our good insect rider has just disparaged our mounts," he said, as his own dragon snorted and rolled its eyes back at him. "Shall we see how fast these lizards can run?" He grinned at us, eager and challenging. "Race you both to the bend in the road. Loser takes care of the other dragons for the whole trip."

I grinned back, but Raithe nudged his dragon forward with a sigh, making us pause. "I think you're both forgetting something," he said, casting a serious look over his shoulder. Halek frowned, expecting to be chastised.

"And what's that, iylvahn?"

The shadow of a grin went through those pale eyes. "Never bet against a kahjai," he said, and kicked his dragon hard in the ribs. The black lizard leaped forward with a snarl, leaving behind a cloud of dust as it skittered into the pass.

"Hey!" I yelled.

"That's a dirty trick, iylvahn!" Halek called at the same time, kicking his mount forward. Our dragons sprang after him, moving with a swaying, scuttling crawl over the dust and the stones. Moments later, there was the buzz of wings, and Kysa flew overhead, proving that the sand dragons could not, in fact, keep up with Rhyne. But this race was between the three sand dragons and their riders. The wind whipped at me, pushing my hood back and tugging at my hair, but with the hissing dragons, the shouts from Halek, and the rising adrenaline as we sped down the path, it didn't bother me. Rising in my seat, I lifted my head and let out a whoop that bounced off the canyon walls and echoed over the peaks.

Raithe won, of course. But only because he cheated.

Solasti stood directly overhead by the time we reached the first shelter Kysa had mentioned, a large cave that had been carved into the side of the cliff wall. It was spacious enough for all our dragons and Rhyne to fit inside, with pens and individual stalls to safely house our mounts while we waited for Demon Hour to pass.

"Here you go, Fatechaser," Raithe said, handing his dragon's reins to Halek as we stepped into the cave. "Make sure you remove their saddles so they can cool off through Demon Hour. An uncomfortable sand dragon is highly irritable, and more likely to take a finger when you're not expecting it."

"Oh, come on." Halek sighed, unhappily taking the reins. "I wasn't really serious about that bet, you know. This doesn't seem fair."

Kysa, already unbuckling the straps around Rhyne's massive bulk, smiled. "And yet a wager was definitely spoken," she said, not looking up from her task. "The last one to reach the bend in the pass was to care for the other mounts for the rest of the journey. The last to reach the bend was you. Or is it common for city dwellers to back out of promises that are inconvenient?"

Halek groaned. "Sparrow, help me out here," he said, giving me a pleading look. "I don't think a wager won by cheating is a fair wager, do you?"

"Oh, Halek." I smiled. "You're forgetting who you're talking to. I'm from the Thieves Guild. We *always* cheat to win."

And handing him my reins, I walked away, Raithe's laughter and Halek's sputtering protests echoing behind me.

A little deeper in the cavern, I found a pair of tables surrounded by stools, a stone bench next to a barrel that held a lantern, and a trio of rough cots against the far wall. Whoever had built this shelter for Demon Hour hadn't done so half-heartedly. Perching on the bench, I leaned back with a sigh, relieved to not be sitting in a bouncing, jostling saddle. I pulled out my waterskin and took a sip, hoping the relatively cool temperatures of the cave would hold through Demon Hour.

"Sparrow."

I looked up and saw Raithe's lean form hovering near the table's edge, watching me. As usual, I hadn't heard him approach at all.

"May I join you?" he asked, sounding strangely formal. Still calm and unruffled, but overly polite. I shifted on the bench and retreated farther into my hood.

"You don't have to ask, Raithe," I told him. "You're always welcome, no matter where we are."

"I would not presume," he replied, and I sensed, rather than heard, him move closer. Then there was a soft rustle of clothes as he sat beside me on the bench. "I wasn't sure if you wanted to be around me."

I swallowed as my heart began an erratic thumping in my chest. I wanted to fade away and hide, to remove myself from danger, but there was nowhere to go in this cave. Besides, this was Raithe. He wasn't going to turn around and stab me, even if I didn't know what being near him was doing to my heart.

"I apologize for last night," Raithe continued, and his voice had gone very soft. "I admit, I am not adept at reading human emotion, but I thought . . ." He hesitated, gazing down at his hands as if they were covered in something foul. "Was I wrong?" he murmured.

I bit my lip, and the frantic beating of my heart intensified. *Say yes, Sparrow*, I told myself. *Tell him he was wrong, that there is nothing between us.*

"No," I whispered. "You weren't wrong, Raithe, it's just . . ." I clenched my fists on my knees and stared at them. "It's hard for me to get close to anyone," I finally admitted. "The last person I tried with was Jeran and, well, you saw how that turned out."

"The boy who took the soulstone from you." Raithe straightened slowly. "He was your friend."

"I thought he was," I whispered. "And maybe, if things had been different . . ." I bit my lip, remembering Jeran's last moments, his eyes beseeching mine as Vahn drew the knife across his throat. "I'd known him for years," I went on. "We grew up together in the guild. I never thought . . ." I paused, and a tiny, bitter laugh escaped me. "But then I never thought Vahn would sacrifice me to raise the Deathless King, either."

"I am not Vahn," Raithe said, very quietly.

I bit my lip. *No, you're not Vahn. But still . . .* "Why does the queen want to see me, Raithe?" I asked. "What does she want with the Fateless?"

His jaw tightened, and he closed his eyes, making my heart sink. "I see," he murmured, and the warmth between us vanished. "You're right," he said in a flat voice. "There are things that I can't tell you. I suppose that is a good enough reason to hold me in the same regard as the Guildmaster."

He rose and walked away, leaving me alone on the bench, cursing myself and wishing I hadn't said anything.

"This is a dangerous game you're playing, iylvahn."

I opened my eyes blearily, hearing Kysa's voice echo behind me at one of the tables. One cot over, Halek dozed on his back with an arm over his eyes, snoring softly. I couldn't see the other cots without turning my head, and I didn't want to move and alert the speaker that I was awake.

I heard a heavy sigh that had to be from Raithe. "I know."

"She is human," Kysa went on, and though her voice was gentle, it was a warning. "She is young. I will not ask your age, but I assume it is in the hundreds."

"We don't look at age in the same way as you humans," Raithe said. "But yes, you would assume correctly."

"So why this girl? She is a survivor, yes. She knows how to take care of herself. And at times, she is reluctantly brave. The fight with the abomination proved that. But that does not make a warrior. Or a hero."

"Because I believe she can be those things," Raithe said, his voice a little more earnest than before. My stomach clenched and my throat tightened, hearing him speak like that about me. With a faith I didn't deserve at all. "I can see it in her," Raithe went on. "She *is* the Fateless. She just needs to see it herself." He sighed again, and I could almost see him raking a hand through his silver hair. "I wish I could get her to trust me."

"She shouldn't." Kysa's voice was brutally pragmatic. "You are an iylvahn assassin who has taken numerous lives for your queen. You are taking her to the city beyond the Maze and you won't tell her why. Why should she trust you?"

I'm sorry. My eyes went blurry. *I do trust you, Raithe,* I thought, surprising myself. *More than anyone. I'm just . . . I'm scared. I'm afraid you'll look at me and realize I'm not the person you thought I was.*

Raithe didn't answer, and after a moment, Kysa's voice came

again, low and calm. "Do you care for this girl?" she asked softly.

A long, long pause, and then a quiet sigh. "Yes."

"Then you should let her go," Kysa said. Everything inside me writhed itself into a tangled mess and I had to bite my lip to keep a gasp from escaping. "If she truly is Fateless, if she has any hope of surviving what is to come, she cannot have any distractions. She must consider the fate of millions, and how her decisions will affect them all. And there are few things more distracting than falling in love and worrying about the welfare of one individual soul."

I clenched a fist into the cot. Whatever they were talking about, whatever being Fateless meant, it was not something I wanted any part of. Worse, if Raithe expected me to somehow save everyone from the Deathless King, he was going to be even more disappointed when he realized I couldn't. Kysa was right; there were few things more distracting—and dangerous—than falling in love. I had no business hoping for anything with a beautiful, pale-eyed iylvahn assassin.

Once more, Raithe was silent, and after a few heartbeats, I heard a scraping sound as someone pushed back their stool and rose. "Demon Hour is almost over," Kysa said. "I need to saddle Rhyne—he takes twice as long to get ready as your lizards."

Raithe's voice was barely audible. "Thank you, Kysa."

The insect rider paused. "The truth is hard to hear sometimes," she said, as I swallowed the growing lump in my throat. "But my clan has always valued clarity over sentiment. It would be a disservice to you as a fellow warrior not to extend that same courtesy."

Halek suddenly gave a snort and rolled over on his cot. With a yawn, he sat up, scrubbing a hand through his hair and making it stand on end. "Aw, man, I was dreaming of the Desert Rose house in Tahveena." He sighed. "Instead, I wake up in a cave with lizard dung and giant beetles. Ah, well." He rose, stretching both arms over his head, and looked at Raithe. "I guess we're ready to go?"

"Nearly." I heard Raithe rise from his stool. "The dragons need to be saddled before we head out. I believe that's your job now, Fatechaser."

Halek groaned. "Dammit, if I ever get the urge to gamble with an iylvahn again, just stab me and save me the misery." He sighed, scrubbing at his face, then turned his head toward me. Quickly, I shut my eyes so I wouldn't be caught eavesdropping. "What about Sparrow?"

"Leave her be," Raithe said quietly. "Her dreams have been nightmarish of late, and the journey is only going to get harder from here. Let her sleep a little longer."

Halek walked off, grumbling about debts and cheaters under his breath, but I didn't hear Raithe leave. I kept my eyes closed, and a moment later, I felt a presence by my bedside. I inhaled deeply, both to keep my breaths slow and even and to calm the rapid thumping of my heart, which would surely give me away if he heard it.

"I know your life has been hard," Raithe whispered. My pulse spiked. Did he know I was awake? But he went on without acknowledging me. "I know you don't believe you could be Fateless, much less *want* to be Fateless. But . . . we need you, Sparrow.

You don't understand yet, but you will. Soon."

My heartbeat quickened. It was a struggle to keep my face neutral, to not respond to what he was saying. Even more so when cool fingertips touched my cheek, gently brushing a strand of hair from my face. Outwardly, I did not respond, though inside it felt like my stomach leaped up and curled itself into a ball.

"Whatever your decision," Raithe went on, "even if you can't trust me, I will protect you. I promise."

He walked away, leaving me inwardly gasping on the cot, both relieved and wishing desperately that he would return.

The next two days followed the same pattern: ride our dragons through the endless, snaking pass until Demon Hour forced us to take shelter in the caves and crannies carved out by those who had made the journey before. Sometimes Kysa would ride beside us, sometimes she and Rhyne would scout ahead, perhaps bored of our mounts' inability to fly. Halek told stories of all the places he'd been and often pulled me into friendly games of Triple Fang or cards. We didn't gamble, as I hadn't a coin to my name. But it was a way to pass the time while we waited for Demon Hour to subside.

Raithe was distant now. Outwardly, his demeanor didn't change; he was still polite and controlled, with a quiet confidence that infused everything he did. His faint, easy smiles didn't fade, and he maintained that subtle sense of humor that surprised you if you weren't expecting it. But he was definitely cooler toward me. Never cold or unfriendly, just . . . reserved. Sometimes, I thought I felt him watching me, but when I peeked up at him, his gaze was always somewhere else. I tried not to be affected by it; I tried telling myself it was a good thing. *Don't get close. Don't let down your guard. Trust leads only to betrayal. Love leads only to heartbreak.* But the mantras I continued to tell myself faded whenever I saw him smile or heard his rare, quiet laughter. I remembered the kiss, the look in his eyes when we were alone, and my emotions continued to swirl wildly whenever he was nearby.

On the morning of the third day, about an hour after the suns rose, the steep, vertical walls of the pass fell away and we found ourselves at the edge of a sprawling desert. The ground wasn't sand, but cracked red earth that rose in uneven steps and plateaus to the distant horizon. There were no trees, cacti, patches of grass, nothing green. A few scraggly bushes, barely more than clumps of thorns, dotted the landscape, poking up through clay and rock. The air shimmered with heat, causing the horizon to waver and strange shadows to dance across the plains.

"Welcome to the Barren Steppes," Kysa said, sounding both relieved and joyful to be home. Even Rhyne raised his head with a strange huffing sound that I took for happiness. "If we hurry, we should reach Carapace Basin by nightfall."

Raising an arm to shield my eyes, I peered across the endless expanse. To my mind, it was full of nothing, but I knew the different insect rider clans roamed the steppes, as well as groups of feral malkah who viewed everything, even sentient creatures, as prey. According to all the stories, it was a dangerous, barren, hostile land that did not take kindly to outsiders. Even the various rider clans did not tolerate intruders stomping through their territory. I was glad we had Kysa showing us the way.

"Just out of curiosity," Halek commented, squinting as he gazed across the barren landscape, "how are we going to avoid Demon Hour if we're out on the steppes? I don't see any caves we can duck into."

"There's an oasis not far from here," Kysa replied, gesturing northeast. "It's a small underground spring, and it's in neutral territory, so all the clans can use it. We can refill our water containers there." She gave Rhyne a tap with her spear, and he lumbered forward, going northeast without being directed. "Just watch out for stonebeaks near the spring," Kysa warned over her shoulder. "It's breeding season, so the males will kick you to death if they have a female."

"Oh," Halek said as we nudged our dragons and headed into the steppes. "So just like in Tahveena."

TWENTY-ONE

It was miserably hot out on the Barren Steppes.

I was used to heat. Heat was a way of life for everyone in Arkennyah. When the suns were up, it was hot. Sweat and sunburn and sweltering temperatures were normal, and everyone found ways to live with it. Be that wearing light-colored clothing, building a city with as much shade as possible, or sleeping through the worst of Demon Hour, life in the kingdom was all about working around the scorching rays of the twins.

But out on the Barren Steppes, the heat was a different story. There was no shelter. No cloth overhangs, no buildings to duck into, no trees to provide even the slimmest branch for shade. Solasti beat down on the hard-packed earth, unrelenting and unmerciful, and I could feel her gaze searing the top of my head, my back, my shoulders. I guessed I just wasn't used to it, because Kysa seemed fine, in good spirits, even. For her, this scorched, sun-blasted stretch of wasteland was home.

The steppes went on, barren and unchanging. No one spoke much, not even Halek. Sometimes, I thought I saw figures moving in the distance, but it was difficult to tell if they were real or mirages caused by the shimmering heat. Sometimes, we stumbled across the bones of large creatures, half buried in red earth and dust. I wondered aloud what kind of animals lived here, as I hadn't seen any signs of life besides us.

"Those are the bones of a stonebeak bird," Kysa explained, glancing at a large rib cage jutting out of the earth. "They're the primary source of meat for our hunters and all the larger predators that live out here."

"What predators?" Halek wondered, gazing around the barren landscape. "I haven't seen anything out here except us."

"They're around," Kysa assured him. "Nothing that lives in the steppes is active before Demon Hour. We might see a few at the oasis, but almost everything waits until dusk to start hunting."

"An oasis," Halek said. "That sounds nice. It's one of those oases with water and trees, correct? Not one of those havens with bandits and thugs and things that want to kill you?"

"Bandits, no," Kysa said. "I can't say anything about the things that want to kill you."

A couple of hours later, with Solasti directly above us and Namaia threatening to poke her head over the horizon, we spotted a tiny circle of trees in the distance. As we drew closer, I saw that the trees were growing at the edge of a shallow pool, the surface of which was so still, it looked like a giant mirror in the center of the barren expanse. A pair of large, flightless birds, their feathers so thin they resembled spines, watched us from the other side of the pool. These were stonebeaks, Kysa explained, but they were both female, so we didn't have to worry about an attack. I was relieved, as the two birds had powerful legs tipped with extremely long talons, and thick beaks that looked like they could crush rock with no effort at all.

The pool was barely a foot deep, but the water was cool and clear, fed by an underground spring, according to Kysa. I refilled my canteen and splashed water over my face and neck, resisting the urge to lie down at the bottom of the pool. A few paces down, Halek stuck his entire head in the water, then rose and tossed his hair back, flinging droplets everywhere. Kysa rolled her eyes and continued to unsaddle Rhyne in the shade of one of the trees.

I looked at Raithe. He had said very little since we'd ventured onto the steppes, and he now stood a few paces away, gazing toward the horizon with a distant, unreadable look on his face.

I paused, uncertain if he wanted—or was willing—to talk to me now. But he had always been polite, and his behavior had remained unchanged since the night in Damassi. Well, except for the kiss, of course.

I took a quick breath, then walked up beside him. "You all right?"

He gave a short nod, but it was more weary than brusque. "Just thinking of home," he murmured. "And what I'm going to tell the queen when we finally meet with her."

I blinked. "I thought it was your duty to bring me back, and that she's waiting to speak to us in Irrikah."

"That is true. However..." He paused, a pained look crossing his face. Taking a step back, he lowered himself onto a fallen tree near the edge of the water. Resting his elbows on his knees, he bowed his head. "I was sent to Kovass to uncover the evil lurking beneath the surface and put a stop to it," he muttered. "To find members of the ma'jhet and cut their threads from the Weave." Both hands curled into fists. "I failed. And because of that, the Deathless King is now loose in the world."

My heart clenched. Gathering my courage, I stepped forward

and sat beside him on the log, our knees just inches apart. "It wasn't your fault, Raithe," I said, staring at the horizon with him. "If anything, *I'm* the reason Kovass fell. I went into the ancient city. I brought the soulstone back to the surface. None of this would have happened if..."

I faltered. I was going to say *if I had refused the Circle's order to retrieve the soulstone,* but there was no way I could have refused, and we both knew it. Too much had been at stake; the knowledge that the Circle would kill me if I failed and my desire to prove myself to Vahn would have kept me going, even through the danger. There was only one way I wouldn't have brought the soulstone out of the ancient city.

Raithe gave me a shadowed look that said he knew what I was thinking. "If I had killed you," he murmured. "Down in the undercity."

My stomach churned, wondering if he regretted that now. Maybe my death would have been for the best. One unimportant thief dying to stop the rise of a Deathless King? It seemed a small price to pay.

Raithe gave a small, sad smile and faced forward again. "I'm glad I didn't," he said quietly. "I thank Maederyss that Fate—or luck, or whatever you wish to call it—was on your side that night. But the queen won't see it that way. I had a mission to stop whatever corruption was lurking beneath the city, by whatever means possible. By the time I knew what I was really dealing with, it was too late. And now I can only face the consequences of my failure."

"What will happen to you?" I whispered.

"It depends," he replied. "I . . . have never failed a mission before, so I'm not entirely certain myself. But on the rare occasion that a kahjai cannot complete what they are sent to do, they aren't usually punished." A bitter smile twisted one corner of his mouth. "Then again, those failures don't usually involve the destruction of an entire city and possibly all the kingdoms beyond. Because I didn't stop the Circle, thousands of people lost their lives, and millions more will meet the same fate. If the queen does see fit to punish me, I can't say that I blame her."

Fear and defiance flared within. Without stopping to think, I reached out and put my hand over his, making him blink and glance at me in surprise.

"If she does, she'll have to punish us both," I told him. "This is not your fault, Raithe. You did everything you could to stop it. I . . . *helped* it happen. She has more reason to blame me for the rise of the Deathless King than you."

"You're the Fateless," Raithe said quietly. "You're too important. She won't act against you."

That made my stomach do a weird little twist. He said it with such confidence. Raithe knew something about the Fateless that he wasn't telling me, but asking him about it now, when he was admitting something so painful, seemed wrong. I didn't know what I could do against the queen of the iylvahn, but if the Fateless was so important, I didn't have any problems leveraging that to help Raithe.

I squeezed his hand. "Well, if she wants my cooperation at all, she won't act against you, either," I told him. "You're the reason I'm here. I wouldn't have made it this far without you."

"Somehow, I doubt that," Raithe murmured. Leaning in, he touched his forehead to mine, and my heart leaped. "But thank you. I appreciate it."

"Aw, you two are so lovely together," Halek commented, making me jerk up. Raithe eyed him with weary annoyance. The Fatechaser grinned and took a sip from his waterskin. "Kysa says we're going to stay here through Demon Hour," he went on breezily. "She's setting up a tent for us so we don't get cooked. Just in case you want to help."

"Me?" Raithe lifted a slender eyebrow. "What about you, Fatechaser?"

"Oh, I already tried to help, but she shooed me away after I sort of made the whole thing collapse." He winced and gave a helpless shrug. "It's a very strange tent—I had no idea what I was doing, really."

Raithe shook his head and rose. I glanced over and saw Kysa under one of the few scraggly trees, working on a strange tent, indeed. It didn't look like it was made of cloth, but sections of transparent, shimmery green curtains strung together. Like the membranes of an insect's wing, only much, much larger.

As Raithe walked away, Halek sat beside me and handed me his waterskin. I nodded and took a sip of cold spring water, knowing the coolness wouldn't last. The Fatechaser watched me, then bumped my shoulder with his own, his grin mischievous.

"Stop it." I glared at him over the waterskin. "It's not what you think."

"No?" He leaned back, still smiling broadly. "So you *haven't* been sneaking glances at our good assassin for the past three days? And he *hasn't* been watching you like a mournful sand wolf cub when he thinks you're not looking? And Kysa hasn't been shaking her head and rolling her eyes at the both of you because you're both blindingly oblivious to what is happening? All that is just in my head."

I shoved the waterskin into his chest, making him topple backward off the log. "It doesn't matter," I said, as he landed on his backside with a grunt. "Nothing can come of it, Halek. He's an iylvahn and I'm . . . just a thief. Sooner or later, he's going to realize that."

"Sparrow." With a series of small grunts and huffs, Halek clawed himself upright on the log again. "You don't think he already knows what you are?"

"I don't know!" Frustrated, I scrubbed a hand down my face. "I don't know, Halek," I said in a softer voice. "Everyone keeps telling me that I'm the Fateless, that I'm special, though they won't tell me how or why. I don't feel special. I don't feel like I'm any of these things that they say."

I didn't know why I was telling this to Halek. Maybe because he had always felt safe and unassuming. Maybe because he always did just what he wanted, and Fate seemed to favor him even as he was trying his best to catch it.

"I'm not brave," I went on in a whisper. "I'm not a warrior. And I feel like Raithe expects me to do . . . something. Something big, involving the Deathless King. But I'm not that person. I'm a thief from Kovass. How can I be anything more?"

"Because you choose to be," Halek said simply. I glanced at him, and he gave me a strange half smile. "Destiny is a funny thing," he said. "I know in Kovass, they believe that your fate—what you're supposed to be—is set in stone. A beggar can't become a merchant, a merchant can't become a king, and so on. But what if you could?"

I blinked. "What do you mean?"

"What if a beggar *can* become a king?" Halek said, as if he wasn't casually blaspheming an entire belief system. "What's stopping him? Fate?" He shrugged. "That doesn't seem to apply now. Your story hasn't been written. You can change the destiny of everyone around you. Thief, warrior, hero, queen. You're the Fateless, Sparrow. Be whatever you want."

Whatever I want. It sounded so easy, though it went against everything I had been taught. To become something else. Could I really be more than just a thief?

The bigger question: Did I *want* to be more than just a thief?

It was strange under Kysa's tent. The shimmery green cloth or membrane or whatever it was looked thin and fragile but was surprisingly strong. It rustled when you brushed it aside, and though it seemed transparent, it repelled the sunlight quite well. We left Rhyne and the sand dragons tied up under the trees at the water's edge, and Rhyne immediately buried himself halfway in the mud, looking even more like a shiny black boulder. As Namaia rose over the horizon to join her sister, the four of us huddled under the rustling green tent to wait out Demon Hour.

As expected, it was warm in the tent when both twins stood directly overhead, but thankfully not unbearable. I sat against the side, being careful not to lean into it too much, and listened to Halek valiantly trying to coax Kysa into a game of Triple Fang, which the insect rider adamantly refused. Raithe sat across from me, an amused smile on his face as he watched the pair.

I yawned. The heat and the low murmur of voices were making me drowsy. Dropping my head to my chest, I relaxed and let my eyes flutter shut, listening to the voices of my friends.

"Oh, Sparrow. I'm almost disappointed."

Opening my eyes, I jerked my head up to find I was somewhere else.

I was back in the cistern, on the stone platform where I'd first seen the Circle. Where, so long ago, it seemed, Vahn had cut open Jeran's throat and released the Deathless King into the world. The altar was gone; in its place around me was a circle of painted red runes surrounded by candles and various items. Looking closer, I saw with horror that all the items had been mine, once; the knickknacks and small treasures I had collected during my years with the guild. All taken from my room and brought here. The runes they sat on glimmered wetly in the flickering candlelight; I had a horrible suspicion of what had been used to paint them.

Vahn stood just outside the circle of runes, shaking his head as he looked at me.

"You would think you would learn," he said. "Once you're asleep, your mind is vulnerable, and your dreams are open. I just need an instant to establish a connection. One moment of unconsciousness to bring you here. Demon Hour is so inconvenient, is it not?" He smiled at me without humor. "Nothing to do but rest, wait, and sleep until it's over."

I backed away from him but hit an invisible wall at the edge of the circle, preventing me from going any farther. "What is this?" I whispered.

"Quite impressive, don't you think?" Vahn stepped around the circle to face me. "I have scoured countless forbidden tomes—dozens of lost, half-burned books from the old kingdom—to figure out this spell. It would have been easier if I had your blood, but you did leave all your possessions behind when you fled the city. It was enough to bring you here."

"Vahn." I clenched my fists, searching in vain for a way out. The air between us shimmered, indicating the barrier surrounding the circle. "What do you want from me?" I asked in weary desperation. "Why these mind games? You were never this sadistic when we were in Kovass."

"I want an answer from you." Vahn narrowed his eyes. "I told you to return to Kovass, and yet you are still going in the wrong direction. This is your final chance to make the right decision, Sparrow. The king grows impatient. Are you going to return to Kovass, or are you going to make me drag you home myself?"

Anger flared. "I'm not going back, Vahn," I spat at him, and his eyes grew even colder. "I couldn't, even if I wanted to. Raithe wouldn't let me go, and besides, I stopped listening to you the second you decided to kill Jeran."

"Jeran." The Guildmaster of Kovass shook his head. "That boy was just the beginning. I regret that I had to sacrifice a member of the guild, but I would do it again to bring the king back. And now it seems you have found yourself a new guild, hm? A new little family to cling to." Vahn crossed his arms, his gaze suddenly hard. "The kahjai won't let you go, you say. Well, what if there was no kahjai to hide behind? What if you were alone once more? How quickly would you return home then?"

A chill spread through my body. "Leave them alone, Vahn," I growled. "They have nothing to do with this. Besides, you can't hope to stand against Raithe. He'd cut you down in a heartbeat as soon as he saw you."

"Yes," Vahn agreed, which did nothing to ease my alarm. "He would cut *me* down. But what about you? The Fateless whom he is duty-bound to protect? How far would he go to keep her safe?"

"What are you talking about?"

The circle of runes around me flared, bathing the chamber in red light. Vahn closed his eyes, raising his arms as the light snapped and flashed, throwing eerie shadows over the walls and floor. "I will be taking this consciousness for a little while," he murmured, making my stomach crawl with dread. "You stay there, and don't try to stop it. It will be less painful that way."

"What?" I whispered, but my eyes opened, and I was suddenly awake.

I was back in the tent, still hearing the murmur of Halek's and Kysa's voices a few steps away. It seemed only a second or two had passed since I had dozed off. Quickly, I tried to raise my head to warn Raithe and the others that Vahn was still there, still after me.

I couldn't move.

I told you, Sparrow. Vahn's voice echoed in my head, turning my blood to ice. *I will be taking over for a bit. Don't try to fight this—it's better to accept what is coming.*

No! I tried to make myself move, to shout a warning, anything. My body remained still, uncompliant. Vahn sighed.

It's useless to resist, he said, and my eyes closed, plunging me into darkness. *But this will be over soon, and then you will have no choice but to come home.*

My hand moved on its own, sliding down to my waist. I didn't know what was happening until I felt my fingers curl around the hilt of the dagger at my belt.

Oh no. Vahn, stop it. Please, don't do this.

This is for your own good, Sparrow. My eyes opened, though my head remained down, my face hidden by my hood. I lifted my gaze just enough to see Raithe, sitting a few paces across from me with his arms crossed. His attention was drawn to the discussion between Halek and Kysa, as Halek had given up on Triple Fang and was now trying to explain a card game to the completely disinterested insect rider. My fingers tightened on the dagger, and I felt myself tense to lunge.

No. Vahn, stop. Please not him. Don't do this. Raithe, look at me. Raithe!

"Raithe!"

My voice left my mouth in a strangled shout, and Raithe's attention jerked to me, just as I sprang at him and drove the dagger toward his heart.

He grabbed my wrist, stopping the blade from plunging into his chest, but the momentum drove us both through the wall of the tent and outside. Instantly, I felt the blazing heat of Demon Hour sear through my clothes. Raithe hit the ground on his back, his fingers still locked around my wrist. I straddled him, baring my teeth in a vicious smile as I tried to shove the blade toward his throat.

"Sparrow!" Raithe's other arm shot out and braced against my chest, keeping me from leaning my full weight onto the knife. His pale eyes, alarmed and beseeching, locked with mine. "What are you doing?"

"Sorry, kahjai," I heard my voice say through gritted teeth. My other hand gripped my own wrist, pushing down and adding its weight to the blade angled toward Raithe's neck. "But you have to die. You are in the way, and the king has plans for the Fateless."

Instant understanding dawned in Raithe's eyes before they hardened. Faster than thought, the hand not gripping my wrist shot up, grabbed my elbow, and yanked sideways as his body twisted with the motion, flinging me off him. I hit the ground hard, but Vahn rolled with the momentum and I came up on my feet, still holding the dagger between myself and the kahjai.

Raithe sprang upright like a sand cat, drawing his sword as he rose. As we circled each other, I saw Kysa and Halek come around the side of the tent to join him, and felt a rush of relief. Vahn was skilled, but he couldn't fight all of them. I felt myself swiftly back away, Vahn putting several paces between us and the others, as they stared at me in rage and wary shock.

"Sparrow." Halek looked between me and Raithe, his expression bewildered. "Uh, did I miss something? What's going on?"

"It's the ma'jhet." Raithe's eyes didn't leave mine as he answered. "They have her." He stepped forward, his gaze promising retribution as he glared at me. "Let her go."

I felt my lips curl in a cold smile. As Vahn answered with

my voice, I could hear his utter hatred for the kahjai before me. "What are you going to do, kahjai? Strike down your own Fateless? When you've worked so hard to keep her from us?"

"You can't fight us all." Raithe took another step forward as Kysa and Halek moved to the sides, spreading out around me. "Return Sparrow's consciousness and leave. You've lost this battle."

"Oh, have I? Well then." Vahn did not sound defeated or worried, and I felt my hand tighten on the dagger. "I suppose I should just give up."

My arm rose, and I felt the bite of steel against my skin as I pressed the blade to my own throat.

Halek let out a breath of alarm. Raithe froze, and Vahn turned a triumphant smile on him, forcing me to dig the knife in just a little deeper. I gasped soundlessly as blood welled and ran down my neck, and Raithe immediately lowered his sword.

Vahn shifted my body so he could keep all of them in his sights, the dagger never leaving its place below my chin. "What's the matter, kahjai?" he asked, addressing Raithe with a cold smile. "You look concerned. Did you think I forgot about you and what you did in Kovass? Do you think the king is not aware of your queen's machinations, and what she intends to do with the Fateless?"

My stomach clenched. Raithe didn't move, but a muscle worked in his jaw. "What do you want from me?" he asked in a low voice.

"Drop your sword."

Raithe immediately tossed his blade to the ground. It struck the hard-packed earth a few paces away and lay there glimmering in the searing light of the suns. I felt Vahn smile with my lips, though inside I was screaming at him to stop.

"Step forward," Vahn demanded, and Raithe obeyed, walking toward him until he was only a few feet away. On either side, Halek and Kysa were tense as they watched us, unsure of what to do.

"Stop," Vahn said, and Raithe did. I gazed into his eyes, saw the blank, fixed gaze staring back at me, and raged at my own helplessness.

Slowly, keeping his gaze on Raithe and the blade pressed to my throat, Vahn lowered himself until he was nearly crouched in front of the iylvahn. I felt him reach down with my other hand, to the inside of my boot, where I kept the small blade hidden for emergencies. My heart went cold as he grabbed the hilt and rose, the thin but deadly knife clutched between my fingers.

"How much does the Fateless mean to your people?" Vahn wondered as he straightened. "What is her life worth to you? If you could keep me from slitting her throat in front of you right now, what would you offer?"

He tossed the knife at Raithe's feet and took a step back. I glanced at the blade, glinting in the dust, and horror flooded me as I realized the implication.

No. Vahn, no. If you do this, I will never forgive you. I'll never come back to Kovass, and I will hate you for the rest of my life.

A price I'm willing to pay, Vahn said, though he sounded weary. *The king does not require love from his subjects. Just obedience.*

To the Void with the king! What about you and me?

Raithe hesitated, gazing down at the blade before him. For just a moment, several conflicting emotions crossed his face, before his eyes hardened and he looked up at Vahn again.

"If I do this," he said quietly, even as I wanted to scream at him, "how will I know you'll let her go?"

"Raithe," Halek said, sounding horrified. "Are you insane? Don't listen to her."

"You have my word," Vahn said, ignoring Halek. "As former Guildmaster of Kovass and high chancellor of the true king, I swear I will release Sparrow, unharmed and whole, to your companions and depart once the requirement is met."

No, I sobbed. *Don't do this, Raithe. Please. It's not worth it.*

Raithe paused a moment more, then slowly knelt and picked up the blade. "Sparrow," he murmured, and my stomach twisted at my name. "Can she hear me?"

"She can," Vahn said. "Currently, she is not happy with this decision, but once you're gone, I expect she'll come to see reason."

Raithe met my eyes, and there was no hesitation or regret in his gaze. I choked on a sob and my vision blurred, hot moisture running down my cheeks. I felt Vahn raise my other hand and wipe them away, keeping my gaze on the kahjai.

Raithe's brow furrowed at the sight of my tears, and he bowed his head. "I'm sorry, Sparrow," he murmured. "It seems I won't be taking you to Irrikah, after all." He observed the blade in his hand, and his face tightened. "I wish I could have told you everything," he went on. "For what it's worth, I'm glad I met you. Even though my thread may be cut, know that you changed it for the better."

No. Desperation, rage, horror, and grief rose up within me, a storm of boiling emotions. They pressed against the barrier around me, straining it. I sensed Vahn's surprise, then alarm, as I turned my fury on him, taking everything I felt and pushing outward. The wall around me shimmered and, like a tree bent to its breaking point, cracked.

I will not let you hurt him.

"Raithe, stop!"

My voice left my mouth as a ragged shout, as if invisible fingers were curled around my neck, crushing my windpipe. Vahn's grip on the knife didn't waver, but with all my will, I lifted my other hand and grabbed the blade at my throat, feeling it slice my fingers open as I squeezed.

Raithe reacted immediately. Springing forward, he grabbed the arm that held the knife and pried it away from my neck. I felt Vahn snarl, fighting us both and trying to release the fingers around the blade so he could stab it into Raithe.

Then Kysa and Halek closed in from the sides, and the last thing I saw was the blunt end of the insect rider's spear coming toward my head. I felt a blow to my temple, and then, mercifully, blackness.

TWENTY-TWO

Pain brought me back to the world of the living.

As I opened my eyes, a throbbing headache assaulted me. I was sitting against the wall of the tent, its shimmery folds rustling around me. The left side of my face above my eye felt hot and swollen, like someone had jabbed it with a needle.

I tried to probe it... and couldn't. My arms wouldn't move—because my hands were bound behind my back, wrists lashed together with rough cord. Which, given everything that had happened, didn't surprise me. Tentatively, I wiggled my fingers and found that my right hand was wrapped in cloth and bandages. They throbbed, but dully, as if the pain had been numbed or suppressed.

"Sparrow."

My stomach contracted. It was *his* voice above me, Raithe's voice, though I could suddenly feel all three of their gazes. Thankfully, my hood was raised, and I ducked my head even farther, afraid of what I would see in his eyes if I looked up.

"Can you hear me?" Raithe asked. His voice was neutral, carefully guarded, and my throat closed even as I nodded. If he despised me now, I wouldn't blame him.

"Yes."

"Come on." Halek's voice broke the stillness, sounding

pained and impatient. "She's awake. Cut her loose, already."

"We don't know if this is Sparrow or not." Kysa's tone was calm but wary. "It sounds like her, but the ma'jhet leader knows her. He knows exactly how to lower our guard, and one of us almost lost his life because of it. How are we to be sure this is Sparrow and not the imposter?"

There was a moment of silence, and I closed my eyes. I could tell them I was me again, but why should they believe anything I said? Besides, I couldn't muster any defense through the suffocating cloud of shame and guilt. I had almost killed Raithe. And yes, it had been Vahn acting through me, but that didn't ease the horror any less. If Raithe had died . . .

He stepped forward, sinking to a knee in front of me. And though I was terrified of what I would see in his eyes, I dragged my gaze up to meet his. His expression was carefully neutral, giving nothing away—the featureless mask of the kahjai.

"Tell me something only Sparrow would know," he murmured.

I swallowed. My mind spun as I tried to think of the words that would convince him. Raithe waited calmly, no change in his expression, though I could sense Halek holding his breath behind him. Kysa hovered at Halek's back, casually gripping her spear. If I didn't come up with a satisfactory answer, that spearhead might find itself in my heart.

Raithe still knelt before me, silent. Wetting my lips, I whispered, "On the sand strider, you told me some of the workers thought there was a ghost haunting the lower machinery decks, and I said it was just mice under the floorboards, but we both knew it was me." No change in Raithe's expression, and I dropped my gaze even as I went on. "And in the temple of Damassi, you said you missed home, that walking into Irrikah was like walking into another world. I remember thinking that I really wanted to see it, even though I'd forget everything about it when I left."

Raithe watched me in silence for another moment, before he rose and stepped smoothly to my side. I heard the rasp of a knife leaving its sheath, and a moment later the cord around my wrist dropped away.

Halek let out a sigh of relief. "Damn you three," he breathed, and raked both hands through his hair, making it stand on end. "I think my heart is about to explode from stress, and Fatechasers are famous for not worrying about anything. Sparrow, you okay?" His blue eyes met mine, and the genuine concern in them made my throat close up. I dropped my gaze, unable to answer.

Kysa stepped back. "Come," she told Halek, tapping his shoulder. "The dragons need saddling, Fatechaser. We've lingered here too long, and the twins wait for no one."

"Yeah, but—ow. Hey, watch the spear, ow! Okay, I'm going, I'm going."

The two of them shuffled out, the tent folds swishing shut behind them. I stared at my hands, still feeling Raithe's eyes on me, still uncertain of what I could say. I noticed that whoever had bandaged my hand had done so thoroughly; I remembered the moment the knife edge bit into my fingers, slicing them open as I grabbed the blade. I'd barely even felt the pain. I hadn't had much of a plan—my whole focus had been to hang on to the knife long enough that Raithe and the others could get to Vahn.

It chilled me now, how far Vahn was willing to go to bring me back. And how easily he could manipulate us all.

Raithe stepped in front of me again. Peeking up, I saw his open hand reaching down to me, a silent offer of support. It nearly made my eyes fill with tears, but I reached out and tentatively grasped the proffered fingers.

"I'm sorry—" I began. But my voice was lost as Raithe pulled me to my feet and into his arms, crushing me to him.

The tears and relief finally spilled over. Closing my eyes, I clung to him, hearing his breath, feeling the rapid beat of his heart against mine. I'd almost lost him. Vahn really would have killed him right in front of me, just like he killed Jeran.

"I'm so sorry, Raithe," I whispered into his shirt. My hands curled into fists against his back. "What I almost made you do..."

Raithe gently pulled back, looking me in the eye. "I'm still here," he said, cupping my cheek with one hand. "Still alive. And that wasn't you, Sparrow." His knuckles brushed my skin, catching the tears crawling down my face. "I don't blame you for anything," he murmured. "The ma'jhet's blood magic has always been insidious. I should have known..." He paused, a shadow going through his eyes as he shook his head. "I'm sorry. I haven't been able to shield you from any of this."

"Stop," I whispered. "I wouldn't even be alive if it wasn't for you, Halek, and Kysa. I'd be buried under Kovass, or the Dust Sea, or..." *Or dead on an altar with Vahn standing over me.* "Raithe, you're the reason I'm here," I said, not quite able to meet his gaze. "The reason I'm going to Irrikah to talk to a queen about what being Fateless really means. My whole life, I've been nothing but a thief. I ran from trouble and hid in the shadows when things got too dangerous. I didn't stick my neck out for anyone, because I knew they wouldn't do the same.

"But then," I went on, breathing deeply to hide the tremor in my voice, "I met you. And Halek, and Kysa. And for the first time, I want to be something more than just a thief. The thought of being Fateless . . ." My breath caught, and I shook my head. "I'm terrified. I don't know what I'm supposed to do, what anyone expects I *can* do. But I know I can't run away and hide from this. All of you showed me that. And now . . ." I finally peeked up at Raithe and found him studying me, pale eyes intense. "I have people I want to protect. I can't lose anyone else."

"You were never just a thief, Sparrow," Raithe said. "You were always something more—you just had to believe it yourself." One hand rose and gently traced my cheek, making my insides dance. "I never expected to find you in Kovass," he went on in a near whisper. "And I never expected . . ." He paused, his gaze dropping, as if the final words were hard to say. With a sigh, he closed his eyes, his brow furrowing slightly. "I never expected to feel this way," he finished, making my breath catch and my stomach curl in on itself. "Whatever you decide," he went on, "whatever Fate has in store for us, I'll be with you. No one can know their destiny, especially with the Fateless, but if you do have a thread in the Tapestry of the World, I think our stories are pretty well entangled."

My throat closed up. Suddenly, I didn't care about blame, or loss, or guarding my heart. I didn't care about the warnings Kysa had given, that I might or might not be the Fateless, that Raithe knew more than he was letting on. Right now, all that seemed insignificant. Doubt and fear still plagued me, the cynical street thief within me warning me not to trust or get close to anyone ever again. I ignored her. Raithe had been with me every step of the way since Kovass. And earlier, facing down the leader of the ma'jhet, he had been willing to trade his life for mine. For a Fateless whom he knew very little about, with only the slightest hope that she might be enough to change the world.

I reached out and trailed a hand down his jaw, and he shivered. He had gone very still, as if fearing I might pull back if he made any movement at all. Those pale eyes were open and gazing down at me, the longing in them clear. But he didn't move. This time, I would have to make the choice.

Be brave, Sparrow. For once, take a chance on something that matters.

The sound of someone clearing their throat made me freeze. Kysa stood just outside the tent, gazing in at us. Her spear was in her hand, but the look on her face was one of faint amusement.

"I am sorry," she said, without a hint of embarrassment, for herself or for us. "But Rhyne and the dragons have been saddled and we are nearly ready to go." She tilted her head, a slight, almost apologetic smile crossing her lips. "I do need to pack up the tent before we can depart."

Raithe slumped. I caught flashes of wry disappointment and resignation on his face as he pulled back with a sigh. "Of course," he murmured, glancing toward the insect rider. I set my jaw with a flare of defiance as he turned away. "I'll help you take it down—"

Reaching out, I caught his wrist, making him pause. As he glanced back, I stepped forward, snaked an arm around his neck, and pressed my lips to his.

He stiffened, breathing in sharply, and his hands came up to grip my waist. But only a moment passed before he relaxed and leaned in, his arms sliding up to hold me close. My pulse roared in my ears. I was really doing this, completely lowering my walls, offering my heart to an assassin who had once tried to kill me. But that was before everything. Before the soulstone. Before Vahn's betrayal, the rise of the Deathless King, and the fall of Kovass. Before I knew that the kahjai was one of those unique, beautiful souls who would cause me to question everything. I was Fateless. And for the first time, I was all right with that.

No more, I thought. *I can't be afraid anymore.*

Kysa shook her head at us as we pulled back, though her lips were curled in a wry smile. "If you are finished," she said, causing me to blush and the faintest of pink tinges to spread across Raithe's neck, "we do need to get moving. As it is, I doubt we are going to reach Carapace Basin before nightfall."

We pushed our mounts hard the rest of the afternoon, well aware of the passage of time and Namaia sliding farther across the sky. The heat was relentless, but we didn't stop, continuing across the steppes with one goal in mind: to reach Carapace Basin before Demon Hour the next day. I had already announced that I wasn't going to sleep until we reached the Scarab Clan. I wasn't going to give Vahn the opportunity to take control of me again, even if I had to stay awake all night and into the next day. If I wasn't asleep, he couldn't find me and force me to hurt my friends. I could tell my decision worried Raithe, but Kysa agreed that it probably was the best course of action, at least until I was protected from magical attacks. So until we were among the Scarab Clan, I would have to stay awake.

My thoughts and emotions were a tangled mess, flitting like agitated birds around my head. Guilt at what Vahn had almost made me do. Fear of what his next move could be. Apprehension about what the Scarab Clan would require, if they would even agree to help. And looming above it all, the knowledge that the Deathless King was out there, poised to make his move. We were just insects to him, and even across the Barren Steppes and the Dust Sea, his presence was still frightening.

But all those thoughts faded into the background whenever Raithe was close. My skin still tingled from the kiss, the memory seared into my mind forever. If I was honest with myself, I was still scared. The part of me that belonged to the guild, that had grown up with thieves and scoundrels in Kovass, that found it difficult to open up and put my trust in anyone, that part was still terrified.

But the other side wanted to trust him, to believe that he wasn't going to betray me, abandon me, or stab me in the back. To accept that I was safe—truly safe—with him.

And if I was the Fateless, whatever that meant, so be it. I didn't know what I could do, if a single thief from Kovass could do anything, but I wasn't going to run from it any longer.

Evening fell, and the temperature dropped as the suns dipped below the horizon. The dragons began to get antsy; we had ridden them hard all day, and they wanted to stop and rest. But we kept going, pushing on through the evening, as true night fell and the stars came out. Over the flat, empty steppes, they blazed brilliantly against the darkness of the sky, lighting up the plains and stretching on forever. I had never felt so small in my entire life.

Abruptly, my dragon came to a halt, raising its head and flaring its nostrils against the wind. With a snort, it began tossing its head and clawing the ground, making me grab for the reins to steady it. Halek's mount also began snorting and shaking its head, clearly agitated. I looked to Raithe, who had swung himself off his dragon and grabbed its bridle, speaking to it calmly. It growled and swished its tail, flaring its nostrils, but it didn't seem quite as nervous as the other two.

I yanked hard on the reins, and my dragon stopped digging gouges in the earth, though it continued to snort and toss its head. Beside me, Halek was having less luck getting his mount to calm down.

"Hey, dragon, do you mind?" Halek finally hopped out of the saddle, holding the reins as the lizard hissed and scratched at the earth. "Did you get a cactus pod under your saddle or what?"

"They sense something," Raithe answered, gazing warily around. Kysa and Rhyne had gone to scout from the air, so it was only us and the dragons. "Stay alert—something isn't right."

A droning of wings announced the arrival of the insect rider. Rhyne descended quickly from the air, and Kysa leaped off his back as soon as he landed.

"There's a storm coming," she announced, making my blood chill. "From the west, and it's traveling fast. We're not going to make it to Carapace Basin before it catches us."

I looked west, into the rising wind, and saw a dark smudge against the horizon. Halek let out a slow breath. "I guess we should find a place to hole up until the storm passes," he said. "Otherwise, we're going to be breathing sand."

Raithe looked at me, then at Kysa. "How far is it to the Scarab Clan camp?" he asked.

Her lips thinned. "If we hurry, we can reach it before dawn. But are you suggesting we go through the storm? Rhyne and I will be fine, but your lizards aren't going to like it."

"Neither am I, to be fair." Raithe glanced westward as well, his jaw tightening. "But we need to get Sparrow to your people as soon as possible. Waiting out the storm means she'll have to go even longer without sleeping, or risk falling to the ma'jhet's magic again."

"I'll be all right, Raithe," I told him. He looked at me, worried, and I shrugged. "It's not the first time I've had to go on no sleep for a few days. I'll be fine if we need to stop."

Though I *was* tired. The constant travel, the brutal temperatures of the steppes, the worry about Vahn and the Deathless King, even riding for hours on a sand dragon—it was all wearing on me. In fact, this entire journey, from Kovass to the strider to now, felt like one long, extended race for our lives. Weariness gnawed at me, the kind of exhaustion that was less physical and more like your very soul was tired.

And Raithe, watching me with perceptive eyes, knew it.

Kysa gazed between me and Raithe, her expression solemn. Finally, she gave a decisive nod. "We push through," she said, and

Halek groaned. She ignored him. "Tie a cloth around the lizards' eyes," she went on briskly, looking at Raithe. "It's the only place they'll be vulnerable to the sands. When the storm hits, walk single file behind me and Rhyne—we'll try to provide a little cover from the winds."

"You're not going to fly?" I asked.

The insect rider gave me a faint smile. "I said I would guide you through the steppes to my clan," she replied. "I will keep that promise, even if it is to be through a sandstorm. Besides," she went on, with an affectionate look at Rhyne, chewing a dead bush behind her, "rock beetles are typically hatched in the harshest regions of the steppes, where the wind and storms are much more severe. Unlike soft and fleshy mammals, sandstorms are nothing for them."

"What about you?" Halek asked. "I mean, I hate to break it to you, but you're a soft and fleshy mammal, too."

She snorted. "That's why I wear armor."

The winds grew stronger, gusting across the steppes and sending giant clouds of dust into the air. The dragons were too agitated to be ridden, continuing to toss their heads and claw at the ground. Kysa and Raithe wrapped strips of cloth around their eyes, and we led them into the wind.

"Here it comes," Raithe muttered.

I peeked up and saw a wall of sand coming toward us, swallowing the earth as it moved. Ducking my head, I braced myself as the storm front crashed into us, and everything vanished in a maelstrom of swirling sand and shrieking wind.

I kept my head low as waves of sand battered my clothes,

stinging my arms and the backs of my hands. Peeking up, I could just see Rhyne's large black bulk in front of us, trudging steadily through the wind. Sand curled around him, splitting on either side of his carapace as the giant beetle moved forward, shielding us from the worst of the storm. I glanced behind me and saw Halek walking forward with one arm raised in front of his eyes, a strip of cloth wrapped around his own face, covering his nose and mouth. Raithe brought up the rear, head down and shoulders hunched against the wind as he walked.

A strangled cry echoed through the swirling sands, and behind me, my dragon jerked to a halt. I turned, holding its reins tightly, as it threw up its head with a snort, baring its teeth and scratching at the ground. Its blindfold had come loose, and I saw that its pupils were razor-thin slits against the yellow of its eyes. Behind me, Halek's and Raithe's dragons were also rearing back and shaking their heads with alarmed snorts.

"Kysa!" I called, my voice muffled by the swirling winds. "Something is wrong! I think the dragons sense—"

With a shriek that sounded more terrified than angry, my dragon leaped backward, tearing the reins from my hands. Before I could react, it turned and bolted into the curtains of sand around us. Moments later, my blood chilled as a scream of pain and terror echoed through the gale, causing the other two dragons to go wild with fear. Halek's dragon lunged at him, fangs bared, and the Fatechaser dropped the reins as he jerked back to avoid the snapping teeth. The dragon instantly whirled and dashed away into the sands and darkness. But before it disappeared, several goat size shadows scuttled forward and swarmed the dragon. I heard another chilling shriek as the storm swallowed them and they vanished from sight.

"Kysa!" I turned, searching for the insect rider. "What's happening?"

Something came through the sands at me, something small and red, with six jointed legs and a pair of sickle-like jaws gaping wide to bite. It darted forward, horrifyingly fast, bulging black eyes fixed on me as it lunged.

A spear flashed through the air, striking the ant creature square in the head and pinning it to the earth. It lay there, legs still working, jaws clenching and unclenching weakly, as three more ant creatures scuttled out of the sands, crawled over their dying brother, and came at me.

Rhyne plowed into them, the massive horn on his face catching two and flinging them back. The third was crushed under the bulk of the rock beetle as the huge insect trampled it, leaving it squashed and broken in the dust. I gasped, staggering back a pace, as Kysa leaned down, yanked her spear from where it had impaled the first giant ant, and then held out a hand to me.

"Get on! Hurry!"

I leaped forward, grabbing her outstretched hand, and she lifted me onto Rhyne's back. Looking around frantically for the others, I saw Halek scramble onto a large boulder as several ants swarmed the place he had been standing. Raithe finally released his shrieking sand dragon, letting it go as he drew his sword, whirled, and sprang onto the rock with Halek. The unfortunate sand dragon tried to run but was instantly covered in a half dozen ants. They crawled all over it, sinking curved mandibles into its flesh, until the dragon collapsed with a final shriek.

From atop Rhyne's back, I gazed around in horror. The ground was vanishing at a rapid pace, replaced by swarms of giant ants that scuttled forward, gnashing their jaws. Rhyne swept his great head around, catching several and flinging them away with every toss, but there were always more. Halek and Raithe stood back-to-back on the rock, stabbing at and kicking away the ants that tried to climb up, but they would be overwhelmed in seconds.

"Kysa, get us out of here," I gasped, as the swarms around us grew thicker. "Grab Halek and Raithe and fly us away!"

"I am working on it." Her voice was far too calm for what was happening. She stabbed an ant crawling up the rock beetle's leg, then shouted an order to Rhyne. The rock beetle immediately put his head down and charged, scything through the ranks of ants like a giant wedge, knocking them aside. We drew alongside the boulder just as the carpet of ants swarmed up to cover it, and I held out my hand to Halek and Raithe.

"Jump!"

They did, Halek leaping first and grabbing my arm as he landed half on, half off the side of the rock beetle. Raithe stayed where he was a second more, cutting down another ant to give Halek time to get away before leaping and landing gracefully behind me. Halek kicked and clawed himself onto Rhyne's back, gritting his teeth as I dragged him up in front of me. Below us, the sea of ants tried to latch on to Rhyne as he barreled through, but their jaws scraped off the rock beetle's carapace or were knocked aside by his horn.

"Hang on," Kysa warned, as Raithe's arm curled around me

from behind, sending a ripple of heat through my stomach. "I don't know if Rhyne will be able to fly with this many riders, but we'll have to try. Rhyne, up!"

Behind the saddle, the rock beetle's shell split open, translucent wings unfurling from his carapace. With a drone that rang in my ears and made my teeth vibrate, the huge beetle rose into the air. For a moment, he wobbled in midair, as if adjusting to our weight. I looked down and saw a writhing, squirming carpet of ants climbing over each other as they tried to reach the hovering rock beetle. Thousands of curved jaws gnashed in our direction, thousands of black, bulbous eyes glared up at us, making my stomach turn and my skin crawl with fear.

The buzz of Rhyne's wings sounded labored. He drifted above the carpet of ants swarming frantically below, but couldn't seem to climb any higher.

"There are too many of us on him," Kysa muttered, as Rhyne sank a little in the air. Closer to the sea of jaws and skittering legs. "Cut the saddlebags, we have to lessen the weight."

I drew my knife, but suddenly, from the carpet of ants below, a chitinous red body flew at us through the air. I caught a split-second glimpse of an ant with long, backward-jointed legs like a cricket. It landed on Rhyne's back, drawing a yelp from Halek and a bellow from Rhyne, before Kysa spun and knocked it back into the squirming carpet with her spear.

"Stalker ants," she muttered, as Rhyne dropped a bit lower, wings buzzing frantically. "Get ready," she called back to us. "Don't let them land. If they start clinging to Rhyne, they'll pull us down into the horde."

"Kysa Tal'Rahhe!"

A shout echoed over the wind, followed by the drone of wings, and two rock beetles identical to Rhyne appeared through the curtains of sand. A pair of riders in familiar chitin armor peered down at us from the insects' shiny backs.

"We heard the fire jaws were swarming," one of them called, dropping his mount to hover beside Rhyne. "The hive mother sent us to warn you, though it appears you already know."

"I am aware," Kysa said dryly. "Perhaps you can take Rhyne's passengers before we all drop into the swarm?"

The other warrior nodded. "Quickly," he added, holding an arm out to me. "Before the rest of the stalker ants arrive. The hive mother is expecting you."

"Go, Sparrow," Raithe whispered behind me. I took a quick breath and leaped off Rhyne, grabbing the warrior's forearm, just as another chitinous red body flew through the air and landed on the back of the beetle with a hiss. The warrior gave a shout, releasing my arm, and I grabbed desperately for the saddle straps as the huge ant darted forward.

Raithe landed above me, eyes gleaming as he slashed his blade across the insect's face, making it reel back with a furious shriek. The beetle we were on let out a bellow and veered away, trying to shake off the unwanted passenger. I clenched my jaw, clinging to the saddle straps, and below me the living red carpet swarmed after us, chittering with hunger and rage.

The beetle rider managed to turn and drive his spear through the stalker ant's body, shoving it off his mount. With a shriek, it plummeted back into the swarm. Raithe reached down, grabbed my wrist, and yanked me onto the rock beetle's back. He was shaking slightly as he pulled me close.

The warrior gave his mount a command, and we soared over the horde. I glanced back and saw Kysa and Halek following us, leaving the swarm behind, and felt Raithe slump against me in relief. I had the strange musing that this was the second time we had been attacked by rather large insects who wanted to kill us, and I wasn't sure which incident was more horrific.

"I guess that makes us even," I whispered to the iylvahn behind me, and felt his soundless chuckle against my back.

"I suppose," he murmured. "Though I hope saving each other from giant carnivorous bugs isn't going to become a regular thing."

TWENTY-THREE

After only a few minutes, I understood Kysa's bias toward rock beetles.

The wind shrieked around us as we flew higher into the storm, and soon the ground vanished completely. As I hunched my shoulders, pulling on my hood to further shield my face from the driving sand, the wind suddenly stopped altogether. Blinking, I looked around and saw that we had risen out of the storm and were flying beneath a completely clear sky. Below us, the sands raged and howled, blotting out the land beneath, but up here, the stars stretched on forever, and the air was free of dust and grit.

"This should pass soon," our rider said, peering down at the choking cloud below. "The storms are volatile, but they never last long on the steppes. And once the winds die down, the fire jaws should return underground."

I shivered in the crisp, cold air, and Raithe drew me closer, shielding me from the wind. "Is there a reason these creatures come out during storms?" he asked the rider, who shrugged.

"No one really knows," he replied. "Why the fire jaws swarm during a storm has been a mystery of the steppes for as long as we've been here. Not all storms, either. In fact, it's pretty rare for them to get so aggressive. But every once in a while, when a storm blows in, the fire jaws come out of their tunnels in a frenzy and devour anything they come across."

"Then we are very lucky you decided to show up when you did."

"Our hive mother gave us the order," the rider said, nodding back at us. His sharp black eyes fixed on me, curious and appraising. "Kysa Tal'Rahhe is one of our most respected warriors," he went on. "It is ... unusual for our people to take a liking to outsiders, but the hive mother knows that any request from an elite warrior is not made lightly. I will warn you, however, that very few non-riders have seen the inside of our camp. There are a few who will be suspicious of your intentions."

Moments later, Kysa and Rhyne flew down in a buzz of wings, with the third rider following. "The storm is abating," she announced. Behind her, Halek met my gaze and offered a weak grin. I could tell he wanted to say something about our most recent brush with death, but it was hard to talk over the drone of the three beetles' wings. "We'll meet at Carapace Basin," Kysa continued. "I trust the council will be waiting for us."

"Of course," our rider said, and gave a wry smile. "We wouldn't want outsiders to think that we are barbarians."

The home of the Scarab Clan was unlike anything I had imagined.

From the back of the rock beetle, I watched the storm abate, the winds dying down and the sands settling over the steppes once more. As Solasti rose over the distant horizon, I saw what had to be Carapace Basin. The uneven steppes dropped away into a shallow, somewhat ovular bowl, not unlike the underside of a beetle wing. Dotted throughout the basin were enormous rock structures that, according to our rider, had been scoured so much by wind and sand over the course of millennia that they resembled large quills jutting up from the earth.

Nestled among the rocky spines and scattered in seemingly haphazard clusters throughout the basin were dozens of rounded clay houses. They seemed barely more than huts, though some had second floors that looked like they had been added on later. It surprised me; I had been expecting tents, like the one Kysa had used on the steppes. Something that could easily be packed up and moved. But this village of clay and stone houses seemed very permanent.

"I thought the Scarab people were nomadic," I said.

Our insect rider glanced over his shoulder and arched a brow at me. "We are," he replied, with a strange little smile. He swept the end of his spear toward the sprawl of houses below. "Look at our village," he said, still gazing back at us. "What do you see?"

"Houses," I answered. "Homes. Clay brick and stone, right?" I shrugged. "They don't seem like the easiest structures to pack up and move."

"No, but like most outsiders, you see only what is on the surface," the rider said, not unkindly. He gestured again with his weapon. "During the windy season, our village is here, sheltered through the worst of it. When the stonebeak flocks begin their migration across the steppes, we follow. When the oases dry up and the barren months sweep through this region, they will not find the village here. We will have already moved on."

"So you leave your homes behind and go to a new village?"

"No." The rider smiled. "The homes come with us."

The drone of wings interrupted him, and another insect rider swooped down before I could ask what in the Void he meant by that. "You've brought the outsiders," the new rider said, glancing at me and Raithe, then at Kysa coming in behind us. "The hive mother is waiting for them in the warriors' hall, along with the lore keeper and War Chief Vorkyth. You are to speak with her straightaway, Kysa Tal'Rahhe."

She nodded once. "Understood."

He turned and buzzed away. I looked down and saw a large, circular building in the center of the village, surrounded by a fence that looked like it was made of beetle horns. A group of children—boys and girls between ten and twelve years of age—faced each other inside the perimeter, holding long sticks in front of them. An older teen shouted something, and one line of children lunged, driving their weapons toward the others, who quickly stepped back, blocked, and returned with their own strikes. One boy took a vicious blow to the stomach and was knocked down. He lay there, gasping, until his opponent stepped forward and offered her hand, pulling him back to his feet.

As our beetle flew overhead, the group paused, shielding their faces to gaze up at us. Mouths dropped open, eyes widened, and they began whispering to each other, until the older boy strode forward and barked an order. The group quickly whirled back, bowed to him, and raised their sticks to each other again.

Our beetle rider touched down outside the gates, and I slid from the saddle, relieved when my boots hit solid earth again.

I tensed as I gazed around, and my heart began an erratic beat in my chest. We were deep in the Scarab Clan village now, surrounded by warriors and enormous insects. There was no place to hide, no place to blend in. What if the clan decided they weren't going to help? Or worse, what if they *did* decide to help, but I failed whatever test they required to prove that I was worthy?

Raithe dropped gracefully beside me a moment before I felt his steady hand on my arm. "Breathe, Sparrow," he whispered in my ear. "We're with you. You're going to be fine."

I nodded shakily, stifling the urge to slink away and find a dark corner to melt into. *Stop running, Sparrow,* I told myself. Raithe was with me, and Halek and Kysa were here, too. I wasn't doing this alone.

Through the gates, we came to the opening of the warrior hall. It didn't have doors, but a pair of shimmering, translucent green curtains hung in the doorway, opaque enough to block the view of whatever lay beyond. A pair of guards stood at the entrance, but they did not wear the full-body chitin armor worn by Kysa and the other warriors, just a helmet and a chest plate. They watched as we approached, eyes hard beneath their chitinous helms, but didn't move as Kysa swept through the fluttering curtains and led us inside.

My eyes adjusted quickly to the dim light. The interior of the room was simple, a circular space with a large stone table in the center. Three figures stood around that table waiting for us. A slight older woman, a figure with their head and face wrapped in a shawl, and a large man with chitinous black armor covering his whole body. The spikes on his gauntlets and shoulders jutted wickedly into the air, and the eyes beneath the helm were hard with suspicion.

"Kysa Tal'Rahhe." The older woman stepped away from the table and came forward. Her hair was steel gray, her face gaunt, with creases lining her eyes and mouth. Her arms, I saw, were marked with the same inky patterns I'd seen on Kysa. Pausing a few feet away, she swept fathomless black eyes over the insect rider and nodded once, as if whatever she saw pleased her. "You have returned to the hive. Welcome home."

Kysa knelt, briefly touching one knee and her fingertips to the floor. "Thank you, Hive Mother. My pilgrimage taught me much, but I am pleased to have returned to my clan."

"Is your mount well, warrior?"

This came from the armored warrior at the table, his deep voice echoing through the room. I couldn't see much of his face through the helmet, but his tone was a warning, as if Kysa's worth as a warrior was tied to Rhyne. And if the beetle had fallen, she was no longer worthy.

"Rhyne remains uncracked and unbowed, War Chief." A slight smile touched Kysa's lips as she rose, a note of pride shining through her voice. "He fought the fire jaws as they were swarming, and they were unable to pierce him."

"The fire jaws." The older woman blew out a short breath. "Fate was with you both indeed," she murmured. "To encounter the swarm on one of their rampages . . ."

The war chief gave a snort. "Foolish to be out in the storm in the first place," he growled. "One does not hope to fight a landslide and win." His dark gaze flickered to me and narrowed. "I can only assume that you were protecting these outsiders," he muttered with distaste. "Who are these strangers that you have brought to us, warrior? Two city dwellers and one of the long-lived race that hide in the Maze like dust mice."

"War Chief Vorkyth." The hive mother glared at the larger man, her voice calm but suddenly steely. "I would ask you to remember to be polite. We of the Scarab Clan no longer fear the outside world. We wish to welcome other cultures and people into our village, not shun them. The age of hiding ourselves and alienating any not from the clan is over. If you cannot remember that, perhaps you do not need to be here."

Surprisingly, the large, armored man bowed his head, conceding, and the hive mother turned back to us. "My apologies, strangers," she said. "You are the first set of outsiders to visit the Scarab Clan—well, in my lifetime, anyway—and we are still learning how to be diplomatic. Allow me to properly introduce us. I am Hive Mother Myrrka Nas'Senna. This is War Chief Vorkyth Rol'k, and Lore Keeper Adynna Na'Devyss. The three of us make up the council of the Scarab Clan. Many important decisions are debated at this table, but we must all be in agreement before any can come to pass."

"Like an outsider being granted the ritual tattoos of a warrior," said a soft, new voice that made me glance up. The third figure had come forward, walking slowly around the table to stand before us. Reaching up, she stripped away her shawl to reveal a smooth face covered in elegant swirls of ink. They decorated her cheeks and brow and trailed a path down her neck until they vanished into the folds of her tunic. Her arms were also covered in ink runes all the way to her fingertips. Like the rest of her clan, she wore sturdy boots, but I suspected the markings continued to the tops of her feet and beyond.

"I am Lore Keeper Adynna," the woman said. Her dark gaze eyed each of us in turn, sharp and assessing. "Human, Fatechaser, kahjai," she murmured. "An interesting combination. Tell me, which of these is the Fateless?"

"The girl," Kysa replied, glancing in my direction. "They call her Sparrow."

"I thought so." The figure beckoned to me with long fingers, and I stepped forward warily. "Young," she muttered, looking me up and down. "Very young for an outsider. Our warriors begin training from the time they can hold a stick, but that is not the case for those who live the soft life of the cities." She gave me a scrutinizing look, then glanced at Kysa, standing beside me. "And this is the outsider whom you wish to receive the markings of the warrior?"

"No," War Chief Vorkyth said immediately. "Absolutely not. The ancient markings are granted only to the strongest, to those worthy of riding the rock beetles. It is a sacred rite of passage for Scarab Clan warriors. An outsider has never been allowed such a privilege."

My stomach twisted, but neither the lore keeper nor the hive mother seemed to react, so maybe this wasn't going as terribly as I thought. "What is your calling, girl?" the lore keeper asked me. "What is your place in Maederyss's tale?"

I bit my lip. For a brief moment, I wondered if I should lie, but decided that might sabotage any chance we had to convince them.

Besides, Raithe, Halek, and Kysa were right there; they would all know I was lying, and I couldn't face that. The thought of their disappointment was even harder to bear than Vorkyth's disdain.

I took a deep breath and answered with the truth. "I was a member of the Thieves Guild in Kovass."

"A thief." Vorkyth made a noise of contempt. "An honorless parasite," he went on, waving a dismissive hand. "This is a waste of time. I don't even know why we are having this conversation when the answer should be clear."

"Council." Raithe moved up behind me, his quiet presence giving me the courage not to flee the room. "If I may." He did not continue immediately, but waited until both the hive mother and the lore keeper nodded for him to go on. "I was sent to Kovass to end the threat the ma'jhet represented," he began. "I failed, and the ma'jhet were able to bring the Deathless King back into the world. Sparrow and I fled the city as it was falling, and we have been traveling to Irrikah ever since.

"When I first met her," Raithe continued, "I thought she was just a thief. I regret that assumption. Sparrow has proven her bravery and her resourcefulness time and time again. I understand now, why she is the Fateless."

"Yeah," Halek echoed, nodding his head. "I'm a Fatechaser. I'm pretty sure I was supposed to die twice since I met her." He glanced at me with a grin. "If anyone can change what Fate or destiny has decided, it's Sparrow."

"She is still an outsider," Vorkyth insisted. "Granting her the tattoos means that she becomes part of the clan. That has never been done before."

"Times are different, War Chief," Kysa replied softly. "The clan no longer hides from the rest of the world. And a Deathless King has risen across the Dust Sea to begin the conquest of all the kingdoms." She nodded at me. "His foul blood mages have relentlessly targeted this girl. She has already been the victim of several magic attacks. Why would a Deathless King want one single human girl dead? Because she is Fateless. Because she can change the course of what is to come."

"The Deathless King." The hive mother let out a long sigh. "Then it is true. I was hoping it would not come to this." Her jaw tightened, and she glanced at the doorway behind us. "If a Deathless King has truly returned, we will have to leave this place," she said. "It is not very defensible. We must venture into the steppes, rally the rest of the clans, and hope that they will listen to us. But first . . ." She sighed again and turned back to me. "The legends of the Fateless are scattered and inconsistent," she murmured. "But if you truly are Fateless, then you might be the only one who can stand against the Deathless King. My choice is that we grant her the protection she needs to make that possible."

War Chief Vorkyth made another sound of disgust. The lore keeper continued to watch me, searching for something I couldn't place. "If I am to grant her the markings," she said at last, "she first must understand where they come from. She must know the history of the Scarab Clan and the Deathless Kings."

The hive mother gave a solemn nod. "Yes," she said. "Agreed. That is the way of the Scarab Clan. We must all know the history of how we came to be, lest we return to it."

The lore keeper, apparently, was not waiting for any approval or objection from the war chief. "Long ago," she began, "before we became insect riders and masters of the Barren Steppes, we served a Deathless King. His name has been lost to time, but the king created our ancestors for one purpose—to hunt down and kill the servants of rival kings. We were not warriors, we were not protectors . . . we were assassins." Her gaze went, very briefly, to Raithe, before turning back to me. Her arms lifted, wrists turned up, displaying the swirls of ink down her skin. "These markings were given by the Deathless King's own ma'jhet, to hide us from the magical sight of the other courts, and over the years, we learned how to craft them ourselves.

"When the War of Kings began," the lore keeper continued, "instead of fighting for our land and ruler, our ancestors abandoned their Deathless and fled into the wastes. For centuries, we hid ourselves not only from the eyes of the king, but from everyone. We knew that should the Deathless King find us again, his wrath would be terrible. We relied on the markings, on the tattoos we took from the ma'jhet themselves, to remain hidden and safe. For eons, our people were invisible, alienated from the rest of the world. We learned to survive the steppes, and we learned to harness the giant beetles, who for millennia were our only company. We did not want to return to an existence of slaughter, where our only purpose was to kill.

"Eras passed," the lore keeper went on. "Gradually, the age of the Deathless Kings was mostly forgotten, and when we emerged once more, we had changed. We had become the Scarab Clan, famous for our relationship with the giant beetles of the Barren Steppes. We no longer needed to hide. The tattoos that once protected us from the eyes of the Deathless King's servants have become a rite of passage for our warriors, marking them as part of the elite. Those worthy to be partnered with the rock beetles. But . . ." She raised her arms again, wrists turned out, to show the full effect of the markings down her skin. "We lore keepers do not forget. We inscribe the history of the clan into our skin and hearts, so that we may always remember where we come from. And what we could return to, should the worst come to pass.

"Now you know the history of the Scarab Clan." The lore keeper looked me straight in the eye. "And the true nature of the runes. They are not simply markings of water and ink. They carry the weight and the legacy of the entire clan. If you are willing to bear that burden, I will inscribe them onto you, and you will become one of us."

"And this will hide her from the magic of the ma'jhet," Raithe said, even as I had to catch my breath with the weight of the decision.

The lore keeper nodded. "A Deathless King has risen again," she said. "But with these markings, neither he nor his servants will be able to find you with magic. The marks will not keep you safe from death," she warned, raising a thin finger. "Nor will they shield you from an attack, should the king turn his wrath onto you directly. But he will have to find you first. And the tattoos will make that difficult."

"You speak as if the decision is already made," Vorkyth growled. We all looked at him, and he crossed his arms. "Unless the rules have changed, all three of us must be in agreement," he said stubbornly. "And I'm still not convinced this thief deserves to be part of the Scarab Clan, much less an honored warrior."

"Vorkyth," the hive mother began, but at that moment, a tremor went through the air, and the smell of decay, rot, and death drifted into the room. My insides twisted, writhing in fear, as a voice echoed overhead, droning and terrible, and completely familiar.

"I have come for the Fateless."

TWENTY-FOUR

Something hovered in the skies above the village. Something massive and terrible, blotting out the suns. A reptile of legend, a great dragon, the size of a sand strider and a hundred times more intimidating, peered down with eyes that blazed a sickly green. Its body was rotted and falling apart, pieces of rancid flesh clinging to exposed bone, more skeleton than beast. Its great tattered wings beat the air, part of a nightmare come to life, seemingly defying the laws of gravity as it hovered over us.

Fear clutched my heart with icy fingers, and wind shrieked in my ears. I looked around and saw that the entire village was surrounded in a familiar, choking sandstorm. The winds swirled madly, cutting off all escape, trapping us in the center.

"Give me the Fateless."

I cringed. The voice was Vahn's, multiplied a hundredfold, but it sounded as if the abomination itself was speaking. I looked up to the top of the reptile's bony skull and saw what I'd feared. A figure in familiar robes, a blackened staff clutched in one hand. Somehow, I knew he was staring at me.

"Vahn," I whispered.

"The Deathless King has returned," the voice went on, booming over the sands. *"Gaze upon his infinite power. He has brought the ancient giants back to life, he will remake the world to his*

liking, and all kingdoms will bow before his might. Give us the Fateless and be spared his wrath when he comes to claim your loyalty."

War Chief Vorkyth strode forward, the light gleaming off his armor as he glared defiantly at the huge abomination. For a moment, I wondered if he was going to agree, hand me over to Vahn and be done with the hassle I represented once and for all.

"The Scarab Clan stands defiant!" Vorkyth shouted, though his voice was muffled by the wind and sand. "We will not bend a knee to any king ever again! If the Deathless King comes for our loyalty, he will find an army waiting for him instead."

"*Fools.*" The giant abomination raised its head, eyes blazing. On its skull, Vahn lifted his staff and swept it forward. "*Then I will take the Fateless by force. And you will regret your defiance. When this day is done, nothing will remain of your clan but bones and dust. Your memory will be scattered to the winds, and no one will remember you existed.*"

A terrified scream rose into the air, sending my insides into a wild twirl. At the edge of the village, figures hurled themselves out of the sands and into the camp. Only a few at first, then dozens. Withered, rotting corpses with the heads of slavering jackals, they bounded into the village, tearing into everything with fangs and swords and ripping claws, and the camp erupted into chaos.

War Chief Vorkyth gave a shout of rage and turned, his eyes wide and furious, toward the hive mother.

The hive mother gave a sharp nod. "Go, Vorkyth," she said. "Do not worry about us. Protect the people."

The war chief nodded and spun back, his face tight. "Guard the hive mother, warrior!" he snapped at Kysa, and shot a glare at the rest of us. "Outsiders, if you wish to fight, you will have earned my respect; otherwise, stay out of the way. I must rally the warriors and drive the abominations back. Fight well!"

He sprinted to an enormous beetle tethered outside the gate and leaped onto its back with a shout. The beetle instantly rose into the air, joining the handful of warriors already in flight, the drone of their wings blending into the cacophony of wind, screams, and howling undead. Beetles and riders descended upon the rampaging horde, and pandemonium erupted through the village.

Kysa blew out a piercing whistle that made me jump, and a heartbeat later, Rhyne lumbered to her side, snorting and tossing his head as if he knew battle was nigh. Swinging astride the rock beetle, she raised her spear, her eyes on the approaching chaos. "Stay together," she called, as Rhyne moved his huge body in front of the gates, huffing and raking the air with his horn. "Don't let the creatures get past us to the hut."

"Sparrow." Raithe hesitated, seeming torn between joining Kysa and staying with me. His gaze flicked from the gate to the interior of the warrior hut and the two women standing in the doorway. "Stay with the hive mother and the lore keeper," he told me. "We'll protect you both."

My heart pounded. I remembered the group of warrior children, who would probably be standing at the ready, spears raised to take on the monsters. My hands shook, but I reached down and drew both daggers, gripping them tightly as I pulled them free. "No," I said. "I'm not running this time."

Halek grinned fiercely. "Our Fateless stands her ground," he said, tossing one of his strange black spheres in one hand. "Let's see if we can cheat destiny one more time."

With his empty hand, Raithe reached out and cupped the back of my head. "Stay close, then," he murmured, the look on his face making my heart stutter. "We're almost to Irrikah. I can't lose you to the Deathless King now."

With ringing snarls, a horde of creatures spilled into the center of the village, leaping at us with swords and talons and gaping jaws. Rhyne let out a trumpeting bugle as he lunged to meet them, sending several flying with one sweep of his massive horn. Atop his back, Kysa twirled her spear, stabbing the monsters that clawed at her before Rhyne spun and knocked them aside.

We rushed to help as a trio of snarling undead came at us, reeking of dust and rotten flesh. Halek hurled his black ball into their midst, and it exploded in a cloud of fire and smoke. Shrieking, two reeled away, flames crackling over their withered flesh, but the third sprang at him with a howl. I lunged to meet it, remembering all my knife lessons with Vahn and what he'd said about fighting.

Brawling is for toughs and fools. But if you must fight, don't waste time with superficial cuts. Strike fast, strike hard, and aim for the vitals: throat, heart, kidneys, the arteries in their legs. If you can't kill them quickly, blind them, hamstring them, cripple them. They can't fight if they can't see or stand.

The blade of my dagger hit the side of the creature's neck, ripping a deep gash through the throat and out the other side. It pitched forward with a strangled snarl and collapsed, its head nearly severed, black tongue lolling between its jaws. My stomach heaved, and I backed away.

"Oh, nice shot, Sparrow!" Halek crowed, leaping up and flinging another sphere into a group of undead harassing Rhyne. The explosion caused several of them to stagger back, withered flesh burning, before Rhyne swept them aside like empty bottles. Halek grinned fiercely and turned to me. "I always thought you could fight better than you claimed," he said. "Someone's been holding out on us."

"Halek, behind you," Raithe snapped, cutting through the arm of a monster slashing at him. Halek spun as an undead leaped at him, fangs bared, and threw another sphere into its gaping jaws. There was a flash of flame and heat, and the creature reeled back with half its face blackened and missing. Halek winced as he took a few steps back. "Right, I should probably focus on the battle. I am fast running out of fire globes, though."

More undead bounded forward, swarming the gate. Kysa and Rhyne stood in front of the entrance, taking the brunt of the attacks. Halek hurled his fire spheres into the mob, to devastating effect, while Raithe and I picked off the creatures that got too close to the gate. I leaped back as the blade of a rusty sword swiped at my head, then darted forward and stabbed the creature below its jaw. It gave a garbled snarl and lunged, snapping at my face, only to meet Raithe's weapon cutting across its muzzle and splitting it in half. I ducked beneath Raithe's arm and stabbed a creature leaping at his back, driving my blade through its chest. It lurched back with a dying howl and Raithe spun, cutting off its head.

Panting, I looked around as the monster's headless body shuddered and collapsed. The warriors of the Scarab Clan were fighting the horde, riders and individual soldiers locked in battle with Vahn's undead army. The jackal monsters were vicious and brutal, but the warriors seemed to be holding their own. Bodies lay scattered throughout the camp, the smell of rot and blood lacing the air, but there seemed to be more undead than Scarab warriors. War Chief Vorkyth's rock beetle flew through the air, plowing into a group of undead tearing apart a hut, and a ragged cheer went up from the rest of the clan.

And then, a cold chill crept up my spine. I looked up at Vahn, standing tall atop his undead abomination. He raised an arm, and I thought I could see something red and lumpy clutched in his hand, before he crushed whatever it was in his fist. Red streamed between his fingers and down his arm, and wisps of green energy rose around him. His lips moved, chanting words I couldn't hear, and I felt the hairs on neck my rise.

A few paces away, the jackal creature Raithe and I had killed twitched, stirred, and climbed back to its feet.

Horror filled me. I looked around and saw all the bodies of the undead rising across the field. Headless, armless, covered in horrific wounds, they still clawed themselves upright and lurched toward the nearest living creature. Their eyes now burned with soulless green fire, bathing everything in a sickly glow. With vicious howls, they threw themselves at the clan with wild abandon, their hate-filled snarls rising into the air.

I leaped back as a monster lunged at me, its claws raking at my face. One side of its body was blackened, and the smell of charred flesh clung to it as it came at me, ruined jaws snapping. I slashed at its chest, cutting a gash straight to the bone, but the corpse didn't pause or slow down. I stabbed it in the leg, but the injury had no effect. It kept pursuing me, snapping and clawing, until Raithe's sword came slashing down to cut off its head. Only then did it finally collapse.

"This is endless." Halek hurled one of his fire spheres into a trio of reanimated corpses, sending a burst of flame into the air. Thankfully, fire still affected the undead, burning their withered flesh and turning it to ash. "How are we supposed to keep fighting things that won't stay dead?"

"We have to stop Vahn."

The words were out of my mouth before I could think about them. Craning my neck, I peered up at the monstrous abomination, at the blood mage perched atop its skull, and clenched my fists. "Vahn is the one controlling everything," I said. "If we stop him, we stop the army."

"We have to bring down that abomination first," Raithe muttered, also gazing up at the blood mage and the monstrous winged creature overhead. His jaw tightened, and he glanced at Kysa, still scything through groups of undead with Rhyne. "Kysa!" he called. "Does your clan have anything that can deal with a creature that large?"

"Perhaps!" Kysa's voice sounded strained as Rhyne swept his head around and battered aside a cluster of undead. "But I cannot leave the lore keeper and the hive mother unprotected."

"Go, Kysa Tal'Rahhe." The hive mother appeared, the lore keeper and a pair of warriors at her side. "The Fateless girl is right. We cannot fight an army that will not die. The blood mage must be stopped, before our entire clan is destroyed."

"We are not defenseless," the lore keeper went on, "and the clan must come first. Take the strangers and stop the blood mage. Put an end to this foul magic, and send the Deathless King the message that the Scarab Clan will never submit!"

"As you wish, Lore Keeper, Hive Mother." Kysa did not sound pleased with that decision, but she would not disobey, either. Glancing at us, she gave a short nod. "Follow me, then. The ballistae are on the other side of camp. Rhyne . . ." Whirling him around, she raised her spear and swept it forward. "Clear a path!"

Rhyne bellowed and charged forward. Howling corpses flung themselves at him, only to bounce off his carapace or be knocked aside. Halek, Raithe, and I followed as the rock beetle plowed his way through the camp, chaos raging around us. I looked back once and saw a horde of undead swarming the central hut, leaping atop the roof and tearing at the walls. I couldn't see the lore keeper or the hive mother, and I hoped we hadn't just abandoned them to die.

We fought our way through pandemonium, cutting down the undead that lunged into our path. Screams and howls echoed around us as Scarab Clan warriors fought back the rising hordes. But there were fewer of them now, and the undead seemed endless. I saw a trio tearing at the dirt beside one of the huts, ripping through clay and earth with their claws as if trying to unearth whatever was buried beneath. Suddenly, there was a crack, and a gout of yellow fluid arced into the air. The undead kept digging frantically at the hole, and the ground beneath them shuddered.

With a rumble, the earth rose up and fell away as a monstrous beetle lurched up out of the dirt, carrying a pair of huts on its back like they weighed nothing at all. Dark and shiny, it dwarfed even Rhyne. My mouth dropped open, a ripple of awe going through me as the huge beetle emerged from the ground. Shaking its head, which looked comically small against its bulk, the giant insect lurched away from the monsters that still clung to it, barely missing another hut as it lumbered past.

I dodged a corpse that pounced at me from the side, avoiding the raking claws by a hair's breadth. Beside me, Halek gave a defiant shout as he sent a pair of monsters reeling back, their bodies entirely on fire. "That's it, I've got one left!" he called, ducking a sword blow aimed at his skull. "Figured I should save it for that big important moment. No, no, monster, stay back. Iylvahn, help!"

Raithe whirled and beheaded the monster as Halek scrambled around him. But the Fatechaser didn't see the pair of undead charging him from behind. Even as I shouted a warning, the massive curved horn of a rock beetle slammed into the monsters, impaling and lifting both into the air, before flinging them away. Rhyne loomed above us, his rider spearing a monster through the skull before kicking it aside.

"Do you require a weapon?" Kysa asked, glaring down at Halek. Her voice hovered on the edge of exasperation. "How does one go into battle so ill-prepared? Had I known you were unarmed, I would have suggested you stay behind with the hive mother."

"I'm not *that* ill-prepared." Halek shook his head, reached into his jacket, and pulled a blade I hadn't known he had into the open. Like the rest of his gear, it was something I hadn't seen before; a short, straight weapon that was bladed on both sides, not curved at all. Grimacing, the Fatechaser gave it a couple of swings. "I can fight the traditional way if I have to—aagh!" He jerked back as an undead lunged at his face, jaws snapping. "I just don't like being that close. No, get away, monster!" He slashed wildly as the thing attacked again, and managed to strike it in the neck through seeming blind luck. "Let's get this over with, so I don't have to be this close to these things ever again."

"Quickly, then." Kysa whirled Rhyne around, taking out another undead as she did. "We are almost there."

We fought our way through the outskirts of the village as the battle continued to rage around us. Rock beetles droned through the air or plowed into combat, though the numbers of the horde were starting to wear them down. I saw a warrior dragged off his mount by a horde of undead and buried under stabbing blades and ripping claws. Several more were tearing into yet another house beetle, digging at the ground until they found the insect buried beneath the earth. With a cascade of rock and dirt, the huge beetle surged upward, crushing bodies underfoot as it fled. I looked up and saw Vahn still standing astride the abomination, watching everything play out with flat, emotionless eyes.

"Here." Kysa led us behind a rise, out of sight of the battle raging in the village. Two large, bulky structures stood covered with sheets of canvas. Kysa leaped down from Rhyne, grabbed the cloth, and tore it free, uncovering what lay beneath.

I blinked. It looked like a monstrous crossbow, twice as long as a man, attached to the shell of a beetle half buried in the earth. The iron bolts lying next to it were about ten feet long, barbed, and tipped with a lethal point.

"What in the Void are those?" Halek wondered, gaping at the massive spikes. "What were you all hunting, thunder titans?"

"In the past, these have been used for war with the other clans," Kysa explained as the rest of us stared at the huge weapon in awe. "But we've been at peace since the treaty was put into place. Now we use them to hunt the giant scorpions that sometimes threaten our territories." She thumped the wood of the ballista with a grim smile. "They can punch through the carapace of a scorpion at five hundred paces. Hopefully, they can do the same to a flying abomination. Stand back a moment," she ordered, and raised her spear. "I need to wake them up."

She brought the butt of the spear down, striking part of the exposed shell and sending a hollow thump reverberating through the ground. With the first two thumps, nothing happened, but on the third, the earth under our feet shifted. An enormous black-and-red beetle crawled up from the ground, short antennae waving sleepily as it stared at us.

"All right, it's up." Kysa took a step back and gestured to the trio of enormous bolts on the ground. "Help me load it, quickly!"

Together, we hefted one of the huge iron shafts and slotted it into the weapon. Halek and Raithe turned the winch at the rear of the weapon, drawing the cable back with a heavy grinding sound. The beetle stood placidly through the whole process, even with the screams and howls of battle echoing over the rise. It made me wonder if the beetles were trained well enough that they could ignore the battle around them, or if they simply couldn't hear it.

"All right." Kysa nodded as Halek gave the winch a final crank, locking it in place. "It's ready." She stared up at the huge abomination, still beating its wings in a slow, rhythmic pattern overhead as Vahn watched the chaos below. "Let's kill that thing."

Using her spear, Kysa poked and prodded the insect in the shell until it turned, slowly and laboriously, to face the abomination. Once she got it into position, she raced around to the back, aiming the shaft up at the target.

"I don't know if it has the height, but we'll try. Raithe," she said, and pointed at the lever. The iylvahn immediately grabbed it in both hands. "Hold," Kysa muttered, one eye closed as she watched the abomination. "Come on, turn, you monster. Turn. Look at us."

As if it heard her, the abomination's head turned, its body lazily shifting in the air. For just a moment, I felt Vahn's gaze, finding me through the chaos, and a flash of rage as he realized what was happening.

"Now!" called Kysa, and Raithe pulled the lever. There was a deafening snap as the ballista hurled the iron bolt into the air toward the abomination. It flew straight and true, but instead of striking the abomination in the chest, it pierced the monster's thigh and stuck there, glinting in the light of the suns. The abomination roared, its voice shaking the air, but it was obviously more angry than hurt.

Kysa blew out a breath. "No good," she muttered. "It's too far up. We don't have the height to hit that thing effectively."

Heart in my throat, I looked up and saw Vahn staring down at us, his glare colder than ice.

"*I grow weary of this defiance, Sparrow.*" My stomach twisted as my name rang out over the battlefield. "*And I find your obstinance trying. You wish me to come to you? Very well. Let me oblige.*"

With an almost lazy flap of its tattered wings, the abomination rose, then came swooping down toward the village. Its bony jaws opened, and a gout of sickly green flame seared forth, carving a fiery path through the center of the battle. Screams rose into the air as huts, beetles, and flesh ignited, and the ghastly flames consumed both humans and undead alike.

As the abomination soared over us, I dove behind a boulder with Raithe, feeling the heat of the fire as it roared across the path. The column of flame caught the ballista dead-on; I heard shrieks coming from the poor beetle as it was cooked alive, and I pressed my face into Raithe's arm.

Memories flooded me, the screams and wails as Kovass crumbled around us. It was happening again. I was watching the destruction of yet another civilization, and I couldn't do anything to stop it.

The abomination whirled lazily away, circling the village, as Vahn's voice rang out overhead. "*I warned you,*" he droned. "*I showed you what would happen to those who defied the one true king. This is on your head, Sparrow. You could have stopped this. You can still stop this. Return with me, and I will spare what is left.*"

I clutched Raithe's sleeve in my fist. There *was* something I could do. I had told myself I wouldn't run away any longer, but I needed to do more. To save Kysa's people, and everyone here, I had to take that final step.

"I have to go back with him," I whispered.

"What?" Raithe pulled back, a look of alarm crossing his face.

"I can stop this," I said. "I can't watch more people die because of me, Raithe. I couldn't do anything for Kovass. I couldn't . . ." My voice faltered as memories flooded in once more, bright and painful. "I couldn't do anything for Jeran, or Rala, or Dahveen, or anyone in the guild. This . . . this is something I can stop."

"No." Raithe gripped my shoulders, his eyes intense. "Sparrow, listen to me. If you die, the Deathless King will slaughter everyone here anyway. We can't give up. There's more at stake than you know."

"People are already dying." I shuddered as the abomination cast its huge shadow over us. "What is more important than saving this village and those who are left? Why shouldn't I go with Vahn if I can stop this?"

"Because without the Fateless, there is no future, for anyone."

I blinked at him. "What do you mean?"

Raithe paused, closing his eyes as if struggling with himself. Finally, he gave a heavy sigh and bowed his head. "The queen of my people is a seer," he murmured. "Someone who can glimpse the future. Recently, she had a vision," he went on in a near whisper. "In this vision, she saw the Deathless rise up to the heavens, to the place where Maederyss sat weaving the Tapestry of the World. And she watched as the Deathless slew the goddess of Fate."

The bottom dropped out of my stomach. I stared at Raithe, a numb horror creeping over me. Suddenly, nothing was sacred, and nowhere in the world was safe. If the Deathless King could kill even a goddess...

"The Weaver perished," Raithe went on grimly, "and the Deathless claimed the Tapestry of the World as their own. All the threads within the tapestry became bound to the will of the Deathless. And as the temples of Fate and Maederyss burned, a new god rose up to enslave the world, holding everyone's lives—and their very fates—in their hands.

"That is why the Fateless is so important," Raithe continued, as I stood there trying to catch my breath. "The queen's visions have never been wrong, but the Fateless can defy prophecy. Fate and destiny have no hold on them, even if that destiny is the death of a goddess and the end of all things." He pressed his palm against my cheek, his expression a curious mix of sorrow, regret, and determination. "If there is a chance to save this world from the Deathless King, Sparrow," he whispered, "you are the only one who can."

The breath left my lungs in a rush, and I struggled to draw it back in. Words seemed inadequate for what I was feeling. A world where the Deathless King had killed the Weaver and was now the new god of Fate. And I, somehow, was supposed to stop this?

Raithe pressed his forehead to mine. "I'm sorry," he murmured. "I wasn't supposed to tell you. The queen should have been the one to explain everything." His eyes opened, searingly bright, gazing down at me. "But you can't give yourself to the

Deathless King, Sparrow. If you die, all hope dies with you."

"But everyone here . . ." I cast a look at the battle, where flames and blood and screams filled the air, and felt pulled in a thousand directions at once. "They're going to be killed if I don't go back with Vahn."

"Do not insult my people with thoughts of surrender." Kysa appeared, not mounted on Rhyne, but sweeping around the boulder to glare at me. Her helmet had been torn off, and gore covered one side of her face, but she stood tall and proud with Rhyne at her back. "You came to us for aid—it is against our honor to turn over someone who is under the protection of the clan. The Scarab Clan does not submit. We will not bend to the will of tyrants. We will fight, and we will die, as a choice. Do not let my people's deaths be for nothing."

"Besides, who said anything about dying?" Halek gasped, staggering around to join us. Soot covered him, streaks of black across his face and hands, and his hair had turned gray with ash. He raked a hand over his scalp, sending a dust cloud into the air, and grinned defiantly. "We're still alive. And there's still one more ballista left, right?"

"Yes." Kysa looked up at the abomination circling overhead. "But it's going to be almost impossible to shoot down now," she muttered. "Even if we had the height, it's too fast. We need it to stop moving if we're going to have any chance of hitting it."

I peeked around the rock, though the burning, shriveled remains of the first beetle ballista, and saw the second still standing, its bulk covered with cloth. Glancing up at Vahn and his enormous undead mount, I clenched my fists.

"Get the ballista ready," I told them, and rose, taking a deep breath. "I'll get Vahn's attention. Just be ready to shoot that thing when it stops moving."

"Sparrow..." Raithe stood as well, his expression conflicted.

I put a hand on his chest before he could say anything else. "You can't come with me, Raithe. This is between me and Vahn."

"I know. I just..." With a sigh, he leaned in and kissed me, making my heart seize. I felt his hands on the sides of my head and shivered. "I trust you," he murmured, his eyes intense as he drew away. "Be careful."

"Sparrow." Halek grabbed my arm as I stepped back. "Here," he said, and pressed something round and warm into my palm. I looked down and saw one of his fire globes cradled between my fingers, and my stomach clenched. "My last one. I think you might get more use out of it now." Halek smiled. "Just in case."

The battlefield seemed strangely muted as I sprinted back through the village, though it was far from silent. Flames roared, licking at structures and the blackened corpses scattered along the path, and the shouts and howls of those still locked in battle rang through the air. But everything felt hauntingly tranquil after the pandemonium of the first attack, with the charred, torn bodies of both warriors and undead a gruesome testament to all the deaths that were, technically, on my head. Vahn had come here for me. I had to make this right.

"You cannot run, Sparrow."

I looked up. The abomination glided above me on tattered wings, and I could see the Guildmaster atop its skull, his eyes scanning the battleground. Looking around, I spotted one of the stone spikes, pointing at my target like a finger. Setting my jaw, I hurried toward it, as Vahn's words droned overhead like a chant of doom.

"*There is nowhere to go,*" Vahn continued, as the abomination wheeled lazily around again. *Nowhere to run. Stop hiding from me. For once in your life, stop trying to escape the things you cannot change. We both know how this is going to end.*"

Reaching the spike, I leaped onto the rocky surface and raced up to the very point. Glaring up at my former Guildmaster, I took a deep breath.

"I'm not hiding!"

The abomination jerked in the air, rearing up and pumping its wings. On its skull, Vahn gazed around the battlefield, searching for my voice.

"I'm not hiding, Vahn!" I called again, and lifted my arms from my sides. "You want me? I'm right here."

Both abomination and blood mage turned, their gazes finding me below. Slowly, the monstrous undead creature drifted down until it was hovering before me, the downbeat from its wings blasting my face. My hood was blown back, and my heart pounded, but I stood firm and forced myself not to move, as both the abomination's and Vahn's gazes seemed to pierce right through me.

"No more," I said quietly, knowing, somehow, that my words would reach him. "Enough, Vahn. I'll come with you, if that's what it takes to stop this."

"*Well.*" The corner of his lip turned up in a humorless smile. "*I will say, I am surprised. The Sparrow I knew would have let the* world burn before she decided to stick her neck out."

Though that statement was justified, it stung a lot more than I expected. "Just answer me one question," I went on, glaring up at my former Guildmaster. "What does the Deathless King want with me? Why put in all this effort? I was no one. I had no intention of getting in his way. We came here, to the Scarab Clan, because you kept trying to kill me with magic. If you had just left me alone, I would have fled to the other side of the kingdom and not looked back."

"*Because you are a force of chaos.*" The Guildmaster's voice was ruthlessly flat. "*It doesn't matter where you go or what you intend, Sparrow. You are the uncertainty in the story, the thorn in the Deathless King's perfect world. Rather than kill you, he will break this curse and turn you into a servant of order.*"

"And you're all right with that?" I had to force the quaver from my voice. Even now, after everything I'd been through, the thought that Vahn would let that happen left a sick feeling in my stomach. "You raised me, Vahn. *You* taught me how to break the rules, how to steal and evade notice, how to defy the laws and challenge order. Everything I know, I learned from you."

"*I did what was required,*" Vahn said. "*To prepare you for the world. To make sure you survived. But a new era has begun, one of law and purpose, and we must evolve. As of now, Sparrow, you have no place in the Deathless King's empire. Look around you.*" He gestured to the devastation surrounding us. "*This is your doing. All this death and violence and suffering is because you decided to come here, and chaos followed you. You insist upon defiance, and like a pebble dropped into a pond, you cause waves of unrest in your wake. The king will fix that. The king will bring about an era where there are no waves, where there is no war or unrest or fighting between kingdoms. There will be only one kingdom, one rule, and everyone will know their place."*

I clenched my fists. "You know what, Vahn? You're right." Wary surprise flickered across his face, but I set my jaw and went on. "I *am* an agent of chaos. Because I refuse to lie down and let someone dictate my fate. Before any of this happened, I just cared about myself. I wasn't willing to stand up and take a chance on anything other than me. But now, thanks to you . . ." I faltered, remembering all the little moments on our journey. Halek, whirling back to fight the abomination on the strider. Kysa, refusing to leave us when the swarm attacked. And Raithe, snatching me back from the edge of the Dust Sea. Shielding me from the two merchant princes. Seeing the look in his eyes when Vahn told him to kill himself.

Kissing him beneath the shade of the tent and realizing just what he meant to me.

"It's not just about me anymore," I finished softly. "I have people I want to protect. And there are things in this world that are worth risking my neck for. If this is what it means to be Fateless, then so be it. I will be the agent of chaos the Deathless King fears. I will stand up and defy him for as long as I am able." I raised my head, looking him right in the eye. "So, congratulations, Vahn," I shouted at him. "You wanted the Fateless—here I am. If I can change the story of everyone around me, I will do everything I can to make certain that happens. And I will make sure the Deathless King never sees his perfect world come to pass."

Vahn's face twisted in anger and resignation. "*Defiant to the end.*" He sighed. "*Your insolence will break when you stand before the king.*" Raising his staff, he made a sharp gesture with the wood. I felt eyes on the back of my neck and turned to see a pair of large undead spring onto the base of the spike. "*But now, Sparrow, the game is over. If you would be so kind as to let these minions bring you to me,*" Vahn went on, "*we can leave this place and return to Kovass. I will warn you, it is a bit different than when you saw it last. But it is still home, and soon, you will realize this new world is far better than the one that stood before.*"

The pair of undead stalked toward me, rotting muzzles pulled back in ghastly snarls, and my heart twisted with fear.

Something bright flashed in the sun. I turned my head and saw the ballista beetle crawling up another spike, driven by Kysa and Halek. Vahn spotted it as well, and his face crinkled in a snarl of anger.

"*Futile.*" He swept his staff around. The abomination's head turned, nostrils flaring as it opened its jaws. I saw what was happening and reached into my belt, my fingers brushing the smooth, round edges of Halek's fire globe. "*I would have spared you now that I have the Fateless,*" Vahn said. "*But you can burn with the rest of them!*"

Vahn pointed. The abomination's jaws gaped. I yanked the globe free, drew my arm back, and threw it as hard as I could at my former Guildmaster.

The little sphere struck the side of the abomination's head just as the creature was breathing fire, and the explosion erupted in a massive cloud of flame and smoke, causing it to reel back with a scream. I saw Raithe spring forward, grab the ballista's lever with both hands, and yank it back. There was a snap that seemed to ring out over the battlefield, and the barbed ten-foot length of iron flew through the air and slammed directly into the abomination's chest, punching halfway out the other side.

The abomination wailed. Its wings jerked and faltered in the air as it tried desperately to keep itself afloat. On its skull, Vahn fell to his knees, bracing himself to keep his balance and not be thrown off.

A snarl rang in my ears. I glanced up just in time to see the claws of an undead scything down at me. There was nowhere to go on the edge of the spike except backward into empty air, and I could only brace myself. The slashing talons missed my face by a hair, but fire raced up my shoulder as it ripped a gash through my tunic ... and I fell.

Instinctively, I turned and rolled with the impact, though the ground still sent a jolt and a flare of pain through my body as I hit the unforgiving earth. Gasping, I clawed myself to my feet and gazed at the turmoil surrounding me.

With a final shriek, the abomination collapsed. I saw the wall of meat, bones, and rotting flesh descending from above, and threw myself beneath the spike, pressing back against the stone. The impact from the huge abomination made the ground tremble, and dirt rained down on me from above.

And then, things got eerily silent. I peeked up, and saw the abomination lying sprawled against the outcropping, only the bottom half of its body visible, the huge, tattered wings motionless in the dirt. The stench of decay was overpowering.

Cautiously, I picked my way forward, leaving the safety of the outcropping to better see what had happened. The monster lay sprawled over the spike, its skull hanging off the side of the rock, huge jaws gaping and silent. Vahn was nowhere to be seen.

"Enough!"

The voice came a split second before a blow to my head sent me reeling to the ground. Gasping, I tried to get up, but Vahn stepped forward, twisted staff raised, and struck me in the chest. Pain exploded, my breath left my lungs in a rush, and I gasped helplessly as Vahn dropped down, driving his knee into my stomach with all his weight behind it.

"Defiant child." His face was cold, his eyes terrifying, as he circled one hand around my neck and pressed backward. I scrabbled weakly at his arm, but I had no air, and my strength was already gone. "I have reached my limit with your insolence, Fateless. Everything I have done has been for a better future, one where we are not thieves or peasants or wretched nobodies. One where we can be kings of lesser men. But you refuse to see that."

Desperately, I tried to pry his fingers from my neck, but he only squeezed harder, sending pain stabbing through my head.

"No matter." Vahn's voice seemed to come from very far away now. "I will bring you back to the king by force if I must, and he will open your stubborn eyes himself."

Darkness swam at the edges of my vision, but through the haze, I saw Raithe's face appear behind Vahn's shoulder, pale eyes furious as he leaped forward. Raithe's sword came slashing down, but Vahn, somehow sensing the danger, whirled around and threw up a hand. Sickly green fire bloomed from his palm and hurtled toward Raithe, who leaped aside. Vahn bared his teeth, the eerie green light making him look like a demon.

I reached down, and my fingers closed around the hilt of my dagger. As Vahn turned back, still smiling that demonic grin, his eyes glowing with a terrible light, I sat up and plunged the blade of the knife into his chest, sinking it into his heart.

He froze. The anger faded from his face as he looked down, fingers touching the hilt of the dagger in his breast. Panting, I scrambled back, away from him, as his gaze rose to mine, stunned and disbelieving.

"You . . ." He fell forward, catching himself with one arm, the stunned look turning to rage. "Ungrateful child," he whispered, glaring at me. "You were . . . nothing. A nobody. The king would have made you . . . so much . . . more."

Then the terrible light in his eyes dimmed, his face went slack, and he collapsed to the dirt.

I stared at the body of the Guildmaster—the man who had raised me, taught me everything I knew, all with the intent of betraying me to the Deathless King—and felt a yawning pit open deep inside me. In that moment, I couldn't feel anything.

"Sparrow!"

And then Raithe was there, dropping to his knees beside me and pulling me close. At his touch, some invisible barrier within me shattered. My eyes blurred, my throat closed up, and the horror of everything that had happened flooded me all at once. I turned my face against Raithe's chest and sobbed, feeling his arms tighten around me as I gasped and cried and soaked his shirt with tears.

Raithe gently placed his hand on the back of my head. "You did what you had to do," he murmured. "He wouldn't have stopped, Sparrow. He would have killed everyone here, and you would be in the hands of the Deathless King now."

"I know," I whispered. "I knew he wouldn't stop. I just . . ." My breath hitched. Gently, I pulled back, wiping at my eyes. I didn't dare look behind me at the body on the ground. "I wish it didn't have to come to this."

With the crunch of boots over the ground, Halek and Kysa appeared, ducking beneath the outcropping to join us. They took in the scene, their gazes lingering on the body sprawled in the dust.

Halek blew out a breath, his expression sympathetic as he glanced at me. "Damn," he said, shaking his head. "You okay, Sparrow?"

I sniffled. "No, I'm not," I admitted in a shaky voice. "But I'm here."

Raithe took my hand and gently drew us both upright. Kysa watched us with solemn eyes. "The undead army has fallen," she told us. "I'm not sure if they were tied to the abomination or the blood mage himself, but a few seconds ago, they turned into lifeless corpses and collapsed where they stood."

A ripple of relief went through me. At least we had put an end to the horde of monsters, though I knew the price was already high. Not just for me, but for everyone here. Their lives would never be the same.

And neither would mine.

"The camp is in chaos," Kysa said, then paused, her perfect

composure cracking just a bit as her face tightened. "We lost a great many, including War Chief Vorkyth, but the hive mother and the lore keeper are all right. When you are ready, they will want to see you."

I nodded. Whatever had happened, we had survived. Vahn would never again torment me through blood magic, though I was sure I would see him in my dreams for a long time after this. The Circle might want retribution, but with their leader gone, perhaps we would have enough time to figure out what we were going to do.

Because dealing with Vahn—one singular blood mage—had been difficult enough. I didn't even want to think about the greatest threat still out there. *He* would be coming for me, too. After Vahn's failure, he couldn't ignore us much longer. Eventually, I was going to have to face the Deathless King himself.

But not today. Today, I was a thief named Sparrow who was overwhelmed, hurt, grieving, and heartsick. Today, I wanted to curl up in a corner and forget the world existed for a little while. Or spend some time in the company of friends, listening to Halek's stories and Kysa's triumphs, and basking in the affection of a kahjai who had once tried to kill me. Today was for mourning those we had lost and celebrating those who still lived. The tale of the Fateless girl who would eventually defy a Deathless King and either save or doom the world was a story for another time.

Tomorrow.

EPILOGUE

"There." The lore keeper sat back, sharp black eyes gazing critically at my arm. "I believe we are done. You can breathe easy now."

I gazed at my arm, resting on the table, where it had lain for the past two hours. At the swirls of green starting from my palm and running up the length of my forearm. Slowly, my jaw unclenched, and I let out a breath of relief; the whole process, where a needle had been stabbed into my skin, over and over again, had not been pleasant, but the marks were finally in place.

"Thank you," I breathed, my voice coming out a bit stiff, as my body was just starting to relax.

The lore keeper gave a sniff and turned away, but the hive mother stepped forward. "These marks proclaim you a warrior of the Scarab Clan," she told me. "You are one of us now, and any Scarab Clan member who sees the marks will treat you as such. Remember," she added, raising a thin finger, "this only conceals you—it does not protect you from direct attacks. But you should now be hidden from the magic of the Deathless King and his servants. I hope this will help you on your journey."

"It's more than I could hope for, Hive Mother," I said, rising from the chair. The markings on my skin throbbed, but I was now a member of the Scarab Clan, something I wasn't certain I deserved but would try my best to be worthy of. "Thank you. For everything."

She gave a brisk nod. "Your friends lurking outside the door can come in now," she said in a louder voice. "The kahjai makes no sound, but I have heard the Fatechaser pacing through the dirt since the ritual started."

"I can't help it. I pace when I'm nervous." The curtains rustled as Halek pushed his way inside, followed by Raithe. The Fatechaser was grinning as he came forward, but Raithe paused long enough to give the two women a respectful bow.

"Forgive the lurking, Hive Mother," he said solemnly. "Not that we doubted the lore keeper, or the sacredness of the ritual. But we wish to get underway as soon as possible and leave your people to grieve their losses in peace."

"Do not worry about the Scarab Clan, iylvahn," the lore keeper said, rising from her stool. "We are no strangers to conflict or survival. We chose to help because aiding the Fateless means defying the Deathless King. May our markings protect both her and those around her from the wrath of the Deathless and his servants."

"Let's see these tattoos, Sparrow," Halek said as he gestured to my hand. I raised my arm and drew back my sleeve, revealing the elegant swirls of green ink on my skin, and Halek whistled in admiration. "Nice. I've seen a fair number of tattoos, but these are some of the best."

Raithe walked up and gently curled his fingers around my wrist as he gazed at the markings. My skin tingled at the contact, the pain forgotten. "Good," he murmured. "I'll rest easier knowing they can't touch you, at least not in your dreams."

There was a rustling at the door, and Kysa appeared, nodding respectfully to the lore keeper and hive mother. "Rhyne and the other mounts have been saddled," she told us. "There are a couple hours of travel left before Demon Hour. If you're prepared, we are ready to go."

"Are you certain this is what you wish, Kysa Tal'Rahhe?" the hive mother asked. "Your pilgrimage is over. You do not need to wander the world anymore. Should you wish to stay, there are others of the clan who can escort the Fateless the rest of the way across the steppes."

"This is my choice," Kysa said, stepping into the room. "For good or ill, I feel as though my thread is woven with theirs. Whatever Fate has in store for us, even if it is no fate at all, their path is now mine to walk as well. Protecting the Fateless is the best thing I can do to protect my clan. I will have it no other way."

"Thank you, Kysa," I said, and gazed around—at Halek, at the hive mother, and finally at Raithe, standing beside me. "Everyone. I don't know what I'm supposed to do, but I swear, I'll try my hardest. I promise I'm not running from this. Not anymore."

Raithe brushed my cheek, a brief, light touch that sent shivers up my spine. "That's all we can ask for," he said softly.

"Well, that, and eventually beating the Deathless King," Halek added, making me wince. "Uh," he went on, as everyone glared at him, "but not for a while, at least."

We left the lore keeper's hut and walked back through the village, which was considerably smaller than it had been before the attack by the undead horde. Two of the house beetles had been killed, and one had fled into the sandstorm and disappeared. I hoped the Scarab Clan would be able to rebuild, to find other beetles, and to continue living their lives as they had always done. Somehow, I didn't think it would be that easy.

We reached the edge of the village, where Rhyne waited patiently. To my surprise, another rock beetle was tethered nearby, saddled and ready to go, though there were no other riders around.

"Is someone else coming with us?" I wondered, looking at Kysa. "Whose mount is that?"

The insect rider gave me a strange smile and glanced at my arm. "Yours, warrior of the Scarab Clan," she said, to my complete amazement. "He belonged to one of our clansmen who died fighting the blood mage's monstrosities, and he needs a new rider. His name is Ratuk."

"But . . ." I stared at the huge insect, heart pounding. "I don't know anything about riding a rock beetle. You make it look so easy, but . . . I've never done this before. What if he doesn't like me?"

"Don't worry." Kysa gave me a genuinely affectionate smile. "I'll teach you. It's not difficult . . . once he accepts you as his new rider, of course. Go ahead and mount up. Be firm with him. Rock beetles respect strength."

A few minutes later, I sat in Ratuk's saddle, trying to remember everything Kysa had just told me about handling and steering rock beetles. We'd had to double up; rock beetles were only granted to proven warriors of the Scarab Clan, so Halek was riding with Kysa and Raithe sat behind me. I could feel him against my back—his breath in my hair, his arm curled around my waist—and tried not to let myself be too distracted.

"Are we ready?" Kysa asked, looking at me. I took a deep, steadying breath and nodded, hoping I wouldn't annoy the rock beetle enough to make him pitch me out of the saddle. Kysa observed me a moment longer, then shook her head. "We'll let you get used to riding on the ground before we attempt to fly."

"Don't worry," Raithe whispered, leaning in. His arms tightened around my waist. "Even if he takes off with us, I won't let you fall."

I put my hand over his and squeezed. Without any prompting, Ratuk began a clicking, steady walk, following Rhyne, carrying us away from the Scarab Clan village and into the looming expanse of the Barren Steppes. Somewhere beyond the desert lay the city of the iylvahn, Raithe's home. And the queen who would determine, once and for all, if I was truly Fateless.

"Your heart is pounding," Raithe murmured, his voice low in my ear as he bent forward. "What's wrong?"

"Just thinking," I whispered back. Gazing at the distant horizon, I swallowed. "It's hard to believe that not even a month ago, I was a thief in Kovass," I said. "Working for the guild, not realizing what was under my feet the entire time. And now . . ."

I shivered. Raithe leaned in, holding me closer, and I closed my eyes. "The world has gone crazy, Raithe. Vahn is dead. The Deathless King is coming, and I . . . am only one person. Even if I am Fateless, what can I really accomplish? I don't know what Fate has in store for any of us."

"None of us do," Raithe murmured back. "But with you here, *nobody* knows what the future holds, not even the goddess of fate."

"That's not exactly comforting, you know."

He chuckled. "I can tell you one thing for certain," he said, running a gentle hand up my arm. "Whether you've changed my story at all, unraveled my thread, undone my fate, it doesn't matter. I'll be with you until my story comes to an end or my thread is cut entirely. And when you stand against the Deathless King, whatever that entails, you won't be alone. That's a promise."

Turning in the saddle, I leaned back and kissed him. Ratuk continued on, plodding across the barren earth toward the mountains silhouetted in the hazy distance. Solasti peered down on us, waiting for her sister to join her in the skies, as the Hourglass of Time turned and we marched on toward whatever fate waited for us at the end of the road.

H|Q

ONE PLACE. MANY STORIES

Bold, innovative and
empowering publishing.

FOLLOW US ON:

@HQStories